...ord College, Oxford, Martin O'Brien joined Condé Nast and was British *Vogue's* travel editor for a number of years. As well as writing for *Vogue*, he has contributed to a wide range of international publications. He was editor of *Sixty Years of Travel in Vogue* and is the author of *All the Girls*. His novels *Jacquot and the Waterman* and *Jacquot and the Angel* are also available from Headline.

Praise for Martin O'Brien:

'Well-drawn, strongly flavoured setting . . . rich, spicy and served with unmistakeable relish' *Literary Review*

'A strikingly different detective, Jacquot walks off the pages effortlessly. And O'Brien seems to bend the plot at will, each time leading readers up an alley only to dart away into the shimmering heat. Roll on Jacquot's next case' *Good Book Guide*

'Murder, mayhem and the seedy side of Marseilles make for a mesmerising mix' *Northern Echo*

'Lovers of thrillers will welcome this new voice' *Irish Examiner*

'Atmospheric and enthralling debut' *Lancashire Evening Post*

'Jacquot is an excellent character, no doubt set for a long and entertaining career, and the scenery of corruption in the South of France is very well painted indeed' *Birmingham Post*

'Exotic and different, exceedingly well-written and entertaining' *Huddersfield Daily Examiner*

JACQUOT AND THE MASTER

Martin O'Brien

headline

Copyright © 2007 Martin O'Brien

The right of Martin O'Brien to be identified as the Author of
the Work has been asserted by him in accordance with the
Copyright, Designs and Patents Act 1988.

First published in 2007 by
HEADLINE PUBLISHING GROUP

First published in paperback in 2007 by
HEADLINE PUBLISHING GROUP

1

Cataloguing in Publication Data is available from the British Library

ISBN 978 0 7553 3505 3

Typeset in New Caledonia by Palimpsest Book Production, Limited,
Grangemouth, Stirlingshire

Printed and bound in Great Britain by
Mackays of Chatham plc, Chatham, Kent

Headline's policy is to use papers that are natural, renewable and recyclable
products and made from wood grown in sustainable forests. The logging
and manufacturing processes are expected to conform to the environmental
regulations of the country of origin.

HEADLINE PUBLISHING GROUP
A division of Hachette Livre UK Ltd
338 Euston Road
London NW1 3BH

www.headline.co.uk
www.hodderheadline.com

For Pa,
with love

Luissac, Provence

*T*he knife struck at the shoulder, a little below the left collar-
bone. If her head hadn't been turned away, a spill of auburn
hair falling across her face, she would have seen it coming;
a flash of lamplight and steel slicing through the air. Her
outstretched arm and raised hand could do nothing to fend off
her attacker's savagery. In less than a second, the blade ripped
through the tight bodice of her dress and tore downwards in
a slanting pitch. Left shoulder to right hip.

The force of the blow bowed him over at the waist, made
him stagger to regain his balance, and sent her spinning to the
floor. And there she lay, silent at last.

For seventeen months she'd been in his life. And for seventeen months he'd painted her, trying to make her real, trying to
capture her elusive, beguiling spirit in form and line, the devious

1

capriciousness of her. Sketch after torn-up sketch. A dozen a day. Chalk, pastel, oil, acrylic. He'd tried them all. Canvas, paper, a panelling of wood. Once, like Matisse, he'd even taken scissors to paper. But nothing he tried ever came close.

She had stood there, in the window, with the mountains behind her, framed by the sky; and there, sitting on the stairs, urchin-like, knees drawn to her chin; below the cracked mirror, on the chaise longue he sometimes used as a day bed; and in his own chair, swinging to and fro, crossing and uncrossing her legs, refusing to keep still, to hold a pose, to take him seriously. A single look from her and he could lose it, whatever it was that drove him on.

Often she was naked. Not that he asked. It seemed she just knew that that was what he wanted; teasing him at first, coy, trying to hide herself behind her thin young arms. As though she felt shy, or somehow vulnerable.

Which only made it all the more . . . powerful.

The way she'd stroll past the easel with hardly a glance at the work he'd done; the way she'd pull distractedly at the buttons of her blouse until the front was open; the way she let the straps from her chemise fall from her shoulders . . . the way she'd touch herself as though no one was there in the room with her, as though she was alone and dreaming through all those stifling, dusty afternoons.

And for fourteen of the seventeen months they spent together, he'd made love to her. Artist and model – the way it is. There on the studio floor, on the chaise longue, on the barber's chair, on the stairs, anywhere but the bedroom above. Always there, in the studio, surrounded by the hanging sheets he used to wipe away the paint from his knives, among the pots and the boxes and the piles of newspapers and stacks of magazines, squirming away from his grasp when the deed was done, shrugging her clothes back on after wiping dry the sweaty residue from the tops of her thighs, counting out the money he paid her as though she'd done no more than deliver groceries.

He wondered sometimes why she did it. That cool, cursory giving. There was no need. He didn't insist. But really, he knew why. Because it gave her a power over him. And she liked that.

It was difficult to say when he knew for certain it was going to end, when the days she came to him were numbered. The last few months she'd keep him waiting – an hour, two hours, later than she'd said – as though there were more important matters for her to attend to. He'd known it was going to happen. It had simply been a question of when . . .

And, from his point of view, of how much more he could take of her. The doubts she drilled into him, the fears she nurtured, all the small weaknesses she played upon. Always there, ready to find him at fault. Un-man him.

He reached for his chair and sat down heavily, breathing hard. For more than a minute he looked at her, waiting to see what would happen next. Waiting for her to push herself up, reach for the torn material and the ragged edges of the wound, drag them together with those slim, beautiful fingers of hers before turning those terrible, taunting eyes upon him, a curl of her lip, that brutal, mocking voice of hers, the way her hand would wave him away as if the coil of air spinning from her fingertips would be enough to send him reeling.

But nothing happened. She didn't move. She lay there among the tubes of paint and the blunt palette knives sent spilling on to the floor as though that single blow had torn out her heart. Not a twitch, not a flicker of movement, the head still turned away, the front of her opened up by the knife.

Martin O'Brien

A breeze slipped through the window, shifted through the drapes, and sent shadows spinning round the room. And he felt the tears come, hot and fast, streaming down his cheeks and into his matted beard.

She was gone; it was over.

And still she'd eluded him, still she was unattainable.

Part One

1

Monday

There are certain streets in the Marais, in Paris's elegantly quartered fourth arrondissement, that come to life each morning slowly, quietly, if at all. The allée des Fauves, between rue St-Gilles and avenue Rochecarle, is one of these. There is no patisserie here, no *tabac*, no corner café, just a cobbled *impasse* running roughly north to south with an arched entrance at one end and a section of the buttressed backside of Eglise Sainte-Roche-du-Feu at the other. Between church and archway, facing each other across the cobbles, stand a dozen townhouses that make up one of the smartest, yet least known addresses not only in the Marais, but in the capital itself.

The first and oldest of these townhouses was built in 1609 by a silk merchant from Lyons who had made his fortune attending to the families that had taken up residence in the recently completed Place Royale, better-known today as the Place des Vosges. His house was four storeys high with four shuttered windows on each floor and a strongly planked carriage gate set with a Judas door.

It was here, in front of this gate, at a little before seven o'clock on a bright, spring Monday in early June, after negotiating a snarl of early morning traffic between rue de Turenne and rue du Parc Royal, that a black Citroën DS21 Prestige drew to a halt. The driver's name was Emile Dutronc and his instructions had come through the evening before, short and precise, the voice soft but certain, left on the ansaphone in the hallway of Dutronc's apartment in Montmartre. 7 a.m.. Pack a bag. That was all he needed to know. A trip out of town. The second in as many months.

Leaving the Citroën's engine running, Dutronc checked his watch and heaved his wide-shouldered bulk from the car. As the bell of Sainte-Roche-du-Feu tolled the hour, he pressed the brass button on a speaker grille set into the stonework beside the gate and waited for his call to be answered. When he heard the tell-tale click he leaned forward and spoke just four words:

'Je vous attends, monsieur.'

Back in the car, he drove to the turning circle in the shadow of the church, swung the Citroën round, and came back down des Fauves. Getting out of the car once more, he opened the boot and the back passenger door, checked the coolbox in the footwell behind the front seat, fanned out the selection of papers and periodicals he'd bought at a metro kiosk on Beaumarchais, and adjusted the air-conditioning vents. When he was satisfied that everything was as it should be, Emile Dutronc stood beside the car and waited. He knew it wouldn't be long.

It wasn't. A minute later, the narrow Judas door swung open and Paul Ginoux stepped out on to des Fauves' black cobbles. A small, wiry man, he was dressed in a blue, open-necked shirt, pale suede blouson, and black cotton chinos. He wore tasselled black loafers and carried a zippered attaché case and a small weekender case. In the seconds before he shut and secured the door, Dutronc caught a tantalising glimpse of a fountained courtyard and an ivy-covered loggia. In the ten years he'd worked for Ginoux, he'd never set foot in the man's house.

Stepping forward with a muted '*M'sieur*', Dutronc reached for the overnight bag and stood aside as Ginoux slid into the back seat. While he made himself comfortable, Dutronc deposited the bag in the boot, closed the lid, and walked round to the driver's door. A minute later, the Citroën slid beneath the archway at the northern end of allée des Fauves and nosed its way into a line of traffic on avenue Rochecarle.

'Where to, monsieur?' asked Dutronc, glancing at his passenger in the rear-view mirror.

'South,' replied Ginoux. 'Luissac.'

2

Nearly eight hundred kilometres south of Paris, the same Monday morning sun that had warmed the cobbles of the allée des Fauves glittered like chips of mirror over the dark water of Marseilles' Vieux Port. Dropping down past the Bassin de Carénage and on to the Quai de Rive Neuve, Roland Bressans squinted against the glare and snapped down the sunshield. The morning sun had yet to chase away shadows on the lawns of the Bressans' family home in Roucas Blanc, but here it winked across the waters of the Vieux Port, blazed across the white hulls and metal masts of the hundreds of yachts moored there, and flashed back like a thousand silver semaphore messages from the shop and hotel windows across the harbour.

Such a marvellous way to start the day, Bressans always thought. That view. That blunt blade of yacht-framed water plunged into the city's guts, the slope of Le Panier rising away to his left and, ahead of him, the wide boulevard of La Canebière running right to the water's edge. Nowhere like it anywhere else in the world.

And, Marseilles-born-and-bred, it was his. All his.

Or would be soon enough.

Rather than accelerate to make a green light, Bressans slowed the BMW and came to a halt on the corner of Quai des Belges. This Monday morning he was in no hurry. Nothing more than an hour's worth of phone calls at the office, lunch with his father, and then the rest of the afternoon on site, conferring with the architect who was tearing out the interior of an old customs house on the Lazaret waterfront, dealing with any problems that might have arisen since his last visit.

Another two months and the place would be finished, the gallery ready to open. Already he had enough works to cover at least the walls of the ground-floor salons: loans from friends, business acquaintances, a few judicious acquisitions of his own from new talent, and family stuff – some of it rather good – which his grandfather had collected over the years.

All he had to do now was acquire the fabled Vilotte collection – and he'd have it all. And that Monday it was all so close. He'd know by the end of the week. One way or the other.

But no, he shook his head . . . that wasn't the way to think. It *would* be his. He'd do it. He'd planned it all meticulously, laid all the groundwork. It was his, that collection, almost a right. He deserved it.

Of course his father had thought him quite mad. But then Bressans had explained about the income, the reprint rights, doing all the publishing themselves through the family firm. Profit – that was the language the old man understood.

The Musée Cantini near the Opéra might be bigger, richer, better-known, but the collection on the second floor of the Musée Bressans (named after his father, of course) would be the one they all came to see. The Salon Vilotte. None of the Master's own work, regrettably – unless he could negotiate a private loan or two – but the great man's private collection. All the bits and pieces it was rumoured he'd picked up along the way, all the great names he'd mixed with. As Bressans swept away from the lights and headed across to the dockland offices of Bressans-Fils off La Joliette, he thought of the treasures he might find: Dufy, Léger, Dubuffet, Chagall, Dérain, Matisse. The Master had known them all, spent time with them, learned from them.

And those other names, too, the ones Roland Bressans occasionally allowed himself to dream of finding: Picasso, Dali, Braque.

Bressans had done his research, read the newspaper stories and ploughed his way through enough biographies and art history books to know what he was talking about. The great Vilotte, the man who'd helped pack up Raoul Dufy's last studio in Fourcalquier; who'd shown Dérain where to buy the finest paintbrushes in Nice; who'd taught Marthe Bonnard how to bake *pain au lait* for her husband Pierre; who'd played harmonica to Braque's penny whistle; got drunk with Picasso and been in Dali's studio the day he first laid brush to canvas for *Christ of St John of the Cross*.

According to one biographer – who'd presumably got the story from Vilotte himself – the two artists had breakfasted together on oysters and champagne before repairing to Dali's studio where the great man selected a finely tipped brush and climbed on to a stack of orange boxes he'd decided to use as a ladder. Reaching forward, Vilotte recalled, Dali had taken a touch of grey on to the brush and, in the top right-hand corner, had started work on the blank canvas.

'It looks like a thumb, Sal,' Vilotte had said.

'The shadow of a thumb,' the great man had replied, dubbing for more paint from his palette and starting work on what looked like a branch, horizontal, the thumb like a stub sticking out of it. 'And this, my friend, this will be an arm. The shadow of an arm. Christ's arm.' Then he had reached for more paint and Vilotte recalled the creak of the orange boxes beneath him, a dangerous, hazardous creak.

But Dali seemed not to be aware of it. Instead he'd continued with his brushwork. 'It will be, I tell you, the greatest crucifixion anyone has ever seen,' the artist had said. 'God's view of his Son on the Cross. Not ours. His Father's. No one has ever done it before. Go and look at the books. Mantegna did it, from the feet. But I, Salvador, will do it from the head. From Heaven.'

It was then, according to Vilotte, that the orange boxes had finally splintered under Dali's weight and he'd come crashing to the floor, leaving a long vertical stripe of paint down the centre of the canvas. Jumping to his feet, he had looked at the mark, turned to Vilotte and declared: 'There, you see. That's where the body will go.'

Of course, Bressans knew where that particular painting had ended up – a gallery in Glasgow, of all places. Out of reach. But maybe there'd been some sketches done before Dali started work on the canvas? Maybe Vilotte had got hold of some early studies? Bressans could only hope and pray. And, at moments like this, let his imagination run riot.

Nor was it just their work that Vilotte was said to have

acquired. There was also all the odds and sods, the bits and pieces, the off-duty ephemera of those great men's lives: the striped Picasso T-shirt signed in wine that Vilotte's biographer had also mentioned; Braque's little penny whistle; Dali's mother-of-pearl moustache clippers; a set of monogrammed napkins from Henri Matisse's place up in Cimiez; and Jean Cocteau's little *cahiers* with their spiral bindings, one of which Picasso had apparently ripped from the book and fashioned into a charging bull. Maybe even that was there, hidden away somewhere in Vilotte's old watchtower.

As he dropped down the ramp into the car park beneath his father's office building, Roland Bressans, chief executive officer of Bressans-Fils, felt a warming flutter of anticipation.

On Wednesday he would leave for Luissac, with his companion, and the game he had planned and constructed would begin. A game he was increasingly certain he would win.

He switched off the engine and sat for a moment in the ticking shadowy silence of the underground car park.

Another week and it would be in the bag. He would have what he wanted.

Treasures beyond imagining.

3

Paul Ginoux knew nothing about cars. As long as they possessed comfortable seats, an automatic transmission and an engine as close to silent as possible so as not to interfere with the Bach and the Handel that he enjoyed listening to, Ginoux was a happy man.

But what Paul Ginoux did know about was beauty. And the moment he saw the 1972 Citroën DS21 Prestige under wraps in a corner of the gallery garage of that fool Lestine, he'd made it his aim to acquire it. Six months later, some six years ago now, Lestine had come a cropper, needed money, and Ginoux had played his hand. Reluctantly, the cash-strapped gallery-owner had given in and the Citroën was Ginoux's.

Of course it wasn't in the best condition. That first glance under the tarpaulin had been enough for Ginoux to see the rust and the dents, the bubbled chrome and blistered paint. But as he raised the cover higher and the car revealed herself,

Ginoux had seen something else. The lines of her! The elegance! Just a fabulous-looking beast. And French, too – though Ginoux possessed not a single patriotic bone in his body.

It had taken a year to renovate and refurbish the Prestige to its original showroom condition: the two-litre engine re-bored and reconfigured, the hydro-pneumatic suspension restored, and the bodywork and interior given a stylish Henri Chapron make-over. But the investment in time and money had been worth it. The car was a jewel, drawing admiring looks wherever it went, the secret aluminium compartments used to carry the canvases Ginoux either delivered or picked up on his travels cunningly concealed in the chassis, welded into place by the man who'd overseen the restoration, the man in front of him, his trusted driver, Emile Dutronc.

As they crossed the Rhône and started the long climb south out of Lyons, after a late lunch on rue Kléber with an old friend from the city's Musée des Beaux Arts, Paul Ginoux's eyes settled on the three bulging rings of flesh that constituted the Belgian's neck, the creases darkened by the shaved black crop that he called a haircut.

Too long in the Legion, thought Ginoux. Old habits . . . But, like the Citroën he drove, a treasured find nonetheless.

The two men had met ten years earlier in Trieste, although 'met' was hardly the word to describe their first encounter.

Ginoux had just delivered the missing third panel of the Silvestro triptych – poplar, Florentine, sixteenth-century – to an apartment in the old town. After only the most cursory examination, the unknown client's lawyer had handed over a banker's draft and then, almost grudgingly, had suggested a drink to celebrate the acquisition. But the lawyer needn't have worried. With the money in his possession, Ginoux was keen to conclude their meeting and had declined the drink. Time enough for celebrations when he got back to his hotel with the cheque locked away in his room safe. It was late, he'd explained, slipping the envelope into his breast pocket; it was a long drive home and he would have to start early the following morning. The lawyer had seen him to the door, shaken his hand and thanked him for the delivery.

A pleasure to do business, Ginoux had replied – two million francs' worth of pleasure, to be precise. It had been Ginoux's first big score. And only three days' work, he seemed to remember, not including the drive from Paris to Trieste and the drive home, returning through Switzerland to bank the cheque.

Or rather, that had been the plan.

It was winter when Ginoux made the delivery, and a thin drizzle had started up, sweeping in from the Gulf of Trieste, shawling around the city's streetlights. Out on the pavement, the door closed behind him, Ginoux headed back to where he'd parked his car, an old Mercedes estate in those days, diesel and manual.

It was only a short walk, the streets pleasingly empty at that time of night. But then, passing the closed and shuttered Museo di Mare on the Grand Canal, just a block from the car, he'd heard two shots. The sounds were unmistakeable – short, sharp cracks – and sounded so close that he'd ducked into the shadows as though he had been the target. Turning in his crouch, in the doorway of the Museo, he'd looked up the quay where the sounds had come from. Another shot – he actually saw the muzzle flash – followed seconds later by a large splash. Something, or someone, had fallen into the canal. Eyes and ears straining, Ginoux made out some shadows and muffled voices. Then footsteps hurrying away, up a side street, car doors slamming, the sound of an engine coughing into life and a wrench of gears.

When the sound of the car had been swallowed up into the night, Ginoux got to his feet, crossed the road to the edge of the quay and looked down. Nothing but an oily skin of water puckered by the drizzle. And then, on the landing steps below him, he'd seen the shape in the water, a body on its back, fingers clawing out for something to hold on to.

As with patriotism, it was not in Ginoux's nature to lend a helping hand. Never had been, and never would be again. But that night in Trieste, for the first and the last time in his life, Ginoux had thought of someone other than himself. As he scuttled down the slippery steps, he'd pushed up the sleeves of his jacket, knelt down and reached out for those fingers.

Somehow he'd managed to pull the man from the water, dragged him up on to the stepped landing, lapping with water, slick and wet. Even in the darkness he could see the torn holes in the man's jacket, the blood spreading across his shirt.

It was the blood that made him go and fetch the car, come back to the landing where he'd left the man. Ten minutes later, he'd found a hospital. It was a friend, he told the nurse on duty. He had fallen in the canal, there was something wrong with his arm. Then he'd jumped back in his car and driven off into the night.

It was only later, in his hotel room, that Ginoux realised that the top pocket of his jacket was empty. The envelope containing a banker's draft for two million francs had vanished.

He'd driven to the hospital first, but the man he'd dragged from the canal had already disappeared, the same nurse told him, looking at him suspiciously, reaching for the phone to call someone. Security? The police? The man had been shot after all. It was clear Ginoux would be unwise to hang around while she made the call. The last thing he wanted was a conversation with the police.

After the hospital, Ginoux had gone to the landing steps where he'd helped the fellow from the canal. The same drizzle, the same lapping suck of water against stone, streetlights from the far side flickering like long flames across its surface. But no envelope. No banker's draft. Nothing. Just a smear of seaweed where he'd pulled the man from the water.

The following morning, feeling foolish, Ginoux had presented himself at the buyer's apartment to request another draft, to cover the one he had lost. He'd practised the story: on his way back to his hotel, he'd slipped and fallen into the canal. When he clambered out, his wallet had gone.

But the concierge at the apartment block, who had not been there the night before, seemed bewildered when Ginoux asked to see the gentleman in 2a.

'But the apartment is empty, *signore*. The family are on holiday. I show you, if you like?'

The lawyer, and the Silvestro panel, were gone.

Two months later, as Ginoux contemplated the sale of his home on allée des Fauves to cover the loan he'd taken out to cover the purchase of the missing triptych panel, the money turned up on his doorstep. And the man who delivered it was the man he'd pulled from the Grand Canal, the man now driving him south, Emile Dutronc, his shoulders wider than the seat, his gun in a hidden section of the glove compartment and, somewhere about his person, his Legion knife.

Ginoux had never asked Dutronc about Trieste, or the men who shot him, and Dutronc never told him. 'If I can be of further assistance . . .' was all he said as he handed over the envelope.

The Legion again, a debt owed and repaid. Loyalty. Not that Dutronc said anything about the Legion either. But Ginoux had eyes – indeed, made his fortune from them – and had seen the tattoo. Faded blue lines covered by a pelt of hair on the man's forearm. The open canopy of a parachute, with 2 *eme* inked below it.

It was enough.

As for being Belgian . . . well, Ginoux had seen the man's passport. Crossing borders the way they did, it would have been hard not to notice. Always in the Citroën, of course, with its hidden compartments and priceless cargoes. Better driving than trust to airports and security checks and clumsy baggage handlers.

Ahead through the windscreen, Ginoux saw the exit sign for Valence. It had been a long drive, but they were nearly there. Another hour for the Cavaillon turn. A few days' business, and then back to Paris. Reaching for the coolbox behind Dutronc's seat, Ginoux pulled out a glass and a quarter-bottle of the widow Clicquot's finest, eased off the wire, and gently popped the cork.

To artists everywhere, he thought, sipping the champagne. And reliable drivers.

4

Tuesday

'I thought you told me you hadn't been here before?' said Meredith Branigan, toying with her white-only omelette. Her order had caused something of a stir at the small brasserie in St Maximin-la-Sainte-Baume where her companion had brought her for lunch. In Cannes they wouldn't have blinked.

'I haven't,' her companion replied, hunched over his plate, cutting away a thick border of yellowing fat from his *entrecôte*. A puddle of bloody *jus* had gathered at the edge of the plate, soaked into his *frites* and turned them a soggy pink. He glanced up at her. 'Why do you ask?'

Meredith shrugged, pushed at her omelette. 'You just seem to know your way around. Where to park, where to eat.'

'It's not difficult, my love. In France every town has a brasserie like this.' He carved out a wedge of meat, speared it

21

with his fork, and popped it into his mouth. 'You just find the centre of town and there you are,' he continued in gruff, heavily accented English, waving around them with his fork, not bothering to look: the plane trees along the edge of the road, the parasols shading them from the midday sun, pigeons strutting beneath the tables, and waiters in long black aprons delivering plates, bottles and bills to other customers. He swallowed the meat and reached for his napkin, wiped his mouth, smiled at her.

She smiled back, left her omelette and picked at her salad. For a moment she wondered if he was lying, if he had been here before. With someone else. But she couldn't be sure. She hadn't known him long enough to catch him out.

Five days, that's all it had been. Five days since she had first set eyes on him. Friday night at the Palais des Festivals in Cannes, the awards ceremonies, when they'd announced the winner for Best Foreign Documentary. *Remains*. Erdâg Kónar. Behind the presenters, a savaged landscape cut with equally savaged peasant faces filled the screen. She'd turned in her seat and seen him jump to his feet, embrace the woman beside him then push his way to the aisle, reaching to shake hands, acknowledging the applause, then leaping up the steps to the stage. Lithe, athletic, a lanky frame that looked uncomfortable in an unfamiliar black tuxedo. Taking the silk-lined box with its golden *Palme*, he'd spoken a few words of thanks in English, Italian and French, then lifted the prize and said something in a language she now knew as Croatian. It had been loud and rousing, a call to arms. The row of seats where he'd been sitting erupted, the men raising their clapping hands over their heads, bravo-ing, fingers to lips, whistling, the woman he'd kissed with tears on her cheeks.

That night, at the reception following the awards, Meredith Branigan had made her move, seen off the competition and taken Erdâg Kónar to her bed. As simply and as easily as that. A single word – congratulations – and that special look of hers. That was all she'd needed to do. Twenty years older than her, she guessed, but still as firm and muscled as a man half his age. The way she liked her men. Fit. Trim. And something else too, something that was new to her. His . . . primitiveness. The rawness of him. His rough, peasant-like ways. She liked that. The way his hands worked her body like a market trader stacking turnips. Big hands, calloused, nails bitten to the quick.

Across the table Erdâg had finished his steak. Now, to Meredith's uncertain fascination, he set about the band of fat he'd earlier removed from the meat, slicing it into bite-sized chunks, spearing them, adding *frites*, a smear of mustard, and popping them into his mouth one after another.

Ugghh! How could he? she thought to herself and glanced away, out to the street, busy when they'd arrived an hour or so earlier, the shops still open, but almost empty now. *Sieste*. The locals closing their shutters, taking to their beds, or maybe a hammock in the garden. How civilised, she thought. But then, such a civilised country.

Meredith Branigan had been out of the States a fortnight now. First time away from home. Two days in Paris (first visit) for a round of interviews and photo-calls in her suite at the Georges V, at the Eiffel Tower, at Notre Dame, on a motor cruiser on the Seine, cheeks and hand kissed till they were sore from bristle-burn. And then the flight south to Nice and the Côte d'Azur (just the cutest little Studio jet), another sumptuous suite of her own at the Majestic Hotel overlooking the Croisette, and all the trimmings – baskets of fruit, sprays of orchid, her own fully stocked bar and regular visits from the man at Van Cleef & Arpels with the kind of jewellery she'd only ever seen in magazine ads. Hers for a night. This party, that party, the oily weight of gems and precious metals against her skin.

And she'd loved it. Every single minute of it. Not America maybe, but as the days passed all that seemed to the good. The capital's cobbled streets, its pavement cafés, the knots of traffic and endless leaning on car horns to express disapproval, impatience, annoyance – yet no one appearing to pay the slightest heed. In Los Angeles, well they'd be dead . . .

And, when the traffic was moving, the way they drove – like lunatics; weaving in and out. They'd have had to pay her to get behind the wheel of a car. But there was no question of that for Miss Meredith Branigan. No-sirree. The Studio laid on everything. Stretch limo. Driver. Bodyguard. A studio exec to keep her company, open doors, deal with the tips – everything. She hadn't had to raise a finger.

It had been the same down south. A week in the sun. Lunch at those cutesy little beach clubs for more photo-calls, cocktail parties thrown by the Studio, dinners in fancy restaurants up in the hills and her suite at the Majestic bigger than her parents' apartment back home in Brooklyn.

And everywhere those crazy accents, those gorgeous waiters, barmen, hotel porters. Every time you wanted something, there was some guy speaking all funny-sounding, seductive English, slipping her their private smiles, the ones no one else saw. The French didn't just look good, they sounded good too. Good enough to eat.

French men, she decided, watching Erdâg wipe up the last of the *jus* with the last *frite* and final chunk of fat, were all just so . . . hot. Meredith reached for her napkin and fanned her cheeks. And not a queen in sight! If there was ever such a thing, she decided, this was a country for girls. You kinda felt special here. It was the way French men made a woman feel.

But what had she gone and done? With all these French guys just chafing at the bit to get their fingers inside her panties? Why, just gone and pulled herself a Croat, that's what. It sounded like a disease, or a coin, or something. But she didn't care because he was gorgeous too, just amazing-looking. And so, so talented.

As Erdâg sat back from the table, a waiter appeared to clear away the plates.

'*Un café, monsieur . . . ?*' he asked, and then, turning to her, lips curling into a smile, '*et pour vous, aussi, mademoiselle?*'

Meredith gave it some thought, looked him straight in the eye, and tried out the little French she'd picked up: '*Oui. Parfait. Merci.*'

5

It had been his idea, the trip. He'd rented a car, he told her; wanted to see something of the country. Why didn't she come too? Away from Cannes, and all the festival hoopla. They could explore together. Just the two of them.

And she'd tipped her sunglasses and given him that trademark look of hers, coy but rebellious. Hey, why not? And here they were, after lunch in St Maximin, heading north to Rians and the Durance.

Erdâg Kónar knew he was taking a risk, knew he needed to concentrate, needed to keep his wits about him. But he couldn't help himself. Four nights in her suite overlooking the Cannes' Croisette was not enough. He wanted more, he wanted . . . time alone.

That last week in Cannes, the girl in the seat beside him had hit the big-time – twelve-foot promo boards running the length of the Croisette, that still from her first scene when she raised her head off the pillow, hunched up on to an elbow and asked for a cigarette. A head and shoulders shot, a dirty sheet draped across her, tousled hair and bruised lips, somewhere between Lolita and Monroe. From the moment her film premiered at the Palais, and the punters got a look at her, the phone never stopped. People always at her door. People from the Studio, the production company, publicity, dressers, stylists. By six in the morning, she was bustling him out into the corridor. Later, later, later, she'd tell him. After lunch, *sieste*. Two knocks and a double. She'd be waiting for him. But just an hour, no more than that. Then he'd be bustled out into the corridor once more.

It was maddening. He hated it. He was the one who'd won the fucking prize. And he was the one who had to skulk around. Best Foreign Documentary? Pah! Just a bauble. This girl was Hollywood, and that counted.

He'd seen her film the fourth day of the festival, a gentle high-sky, rolling-plains Texan domestic called *Tune* – mother and father falling out of love, a marriage disintegrating, and their only child, Meredith, half-girl, half-woman, back from college, quietly observing their distance, humming to herself to fill taut silences. It was powerful stuff, all right. And Meredith Branigan was a natural. Her first big-screen role and she was a wonder. When she found her mother hanging in the barn, the way she crumpled to the straw-covered floor, just her mother's ankles showing, the silent tears . . . and then that humming.

Oh, Meredith Branigan was hot, all right. And as the credits rolled and the house lights went up, the audience stood on their seats and cheered, whistled, bravo'ed, leaving Erdâg in no doubt that she was going to get hotter; Hollywood's next big thing.

But time was tight. A few more days and then she'd be gone.

Back to Los Angeles, the next film, a bigger role, the cover of *Vanity Fair*. She was on her way and he'd be left behind. The side of the road.

It was this, Erdâg decided, that made the risk worthwhile. What he lost in focus, in concentration, he might easily make up for with backing. Hollywood backing. With the *Palme* in his pocket, and Meredith in the seat beside him, he might just be able to make it happen. Finance for the film he'd been planning since *Remains* had wrapped three months earlier. A bauble was good, but big bucks were better. And Meredith Branigan was going to be big bucks very, very soon. It was time to move on, move up, and Erdâg Kónar knew that Meredith was his ticket.

This time next year *Meeting the Master* was going to win him another *Palme*.

As they passed through Ollières, the shadows from a line of cypresses flicking across the dusty windshield, the taste of beef fat still slick in his mouth, Erdâg glanced across at her, legs curled up on the edge of her seat, no shoes, the toes moving to some song in her head, the fingers of her left hand tracing circles round her bare ankle. She was wearing a cotton print dress like the one in the film – the hem lifting and shifting in the draft from the window. Its cream background was splattered with tiny blotches of red. Flowers? Climbing roses? It was hard to tell. They looked like the tiny pricks of blood that small shrapnel caused. He'd seen that. In his time. Filmed the bodies. It was how he had started.

But this body beside him, an elbow at the open window of the rented Peugeot, eyes narrowed against the wind, silver-blonde hair shivering, was alive. Long legs, long arms. Coltish. The collarbones in the open neck of her dress curved and hollowed and a golden brown. All of her golden brown, not an inch of her body unseen by the sun.

And bare. Tiny silvery hairs that looked like a sheen on her belly and lower back, but everything else bare. Clean. It had shocked him that first night in her suite at the Majestic. Where she'd taken him. Watching the crowds from her balcony, the lights on the terrace below, the floodlit pool and the boulevard beyond, snaking lines of headlights and tail-lights. The growl of a sports car revving up, the toot-toot-toot of a horn. Coming up behind her on the balcony, lifting the hem of her dress, sliding his hand down across her belly. And finding – what? Nothing. All so smooth. Smooth as Braç marble.

'So what do you think?' he asked as they drove towards the hills looming ahead of them.

She stretched back in her seat, combed her fingers through her hair, then sighed, almost whispered. 'It's all just so . . . beautiful. I had no idea. Thank you for bringing me . . . showing me.'

Then, unfurling her legs, she reached for the guide he'd brought along, flicked through its pages.

'So where are we headed? What's your plan?' she asked, laying the book across her lap, leaning across to trace a fingernail across his jaw.

He nodded to the book. 'Look in there. The guide. A place called Monastère. It's got a great write-up. I think we will like it there. Take a look.'

'Monastère . . . Monastère . . . Monastère,' she repeated, taking up the book again, riffling through the index at the back.

'I mean . . . Not Monastère. That's the name of the hotel. Luissac. Look up Luissac.'

And so she did.

6

As Erdâg Kónar and Meredith Branigan crossed the Durance after their lunch in St Maximin, KLM flight 641 from Amsterdam's Schiphol airport touched down at Marseilles' Marignane airport. It was the last of three incoming jets and when Lens van der Haage climbed down from the transit bus and entered the terminal, his heart sank at the crowd of people ahead of him. He quickly saw the reason: the usual four Immigration desks were now reduced to two. Joining the queue, only a few feet inside the terminal building, van der Haage gritted his teeth and cursed.

He cursed again nearly an hour later when he pulled his case from the carousel and discovered the damage done to the wheels, bent away from the frame by some slapdash baggage handler. But if he'd thought that was the last straw, Lens van der Haage was mistaken. With passengers from two incoming flights ahead of him, not a single trolley remained in the rank and he was forced to hump the case the length of the concourse, clamping hold of the rolled plans he'd carried as cabin baggage under his arm, heading towards the car rental desks.

As he stumbled along he was aware of two things: four other passengers from his flight headed in the same direction as him, and one of the plan containers gradually shifting loose under his arm. Before he could do anything about it, all four tubes slid from his grip and rolled across the concourse floor. By the time he'd retrieved them, three of the four new arrivals had joined the queue at the rental desk he'd been heading for.

In the old days, mused van der Haage as he waited in yet another line, his name would have been up in lights on the Hertz Gold Club members board, his path fast-tracked to the car park and waiting rental, any delay measured in seconds. But his Hertz gold card was no more, his Amex Platinum assuring him upgrades, and the Priority Pass allowing him use of airport VIP lounges, long since withdrawn.

As he waited his turn, Lens van der Haage suddenly felt grubby, poor and put-upon, bitterly acknowledging that in the last eighteen months his life had certainly taken a downturn.

Business was not good. The practice was going to the dogs. They'd already relocated to Vondel in search of smaller and cheaper premises outside Amsterdam's central ring, and two weeks earlier his partner, Georg, had told him he was looking to move on. It had been a fun ride, he'd said, but Agelkopf Partners had made him an offer he couldn't refuse. His wife would have had his balls . . .

And so Lens van der Haage was alone, the only partner left, the only one with any faith in the Monastère project. But if he was to stand any chance of being shortlisted for this year's Mietzerhager Prize and reviving his dwindling fortunes, the whole thing would have to be a done deal. Completion – full and final. Nothing else mattered.

Which was why he'd flown south.

Moving forward just a few steps at a time, Lens van der Haage knew that there was nothing like the Monastère project. Sure there was competition: Jérome Albert had done a good job on the Frankfurt wharves project; his fellow Amsterdammer, De Linkje, was looking strong with the Kaisergracht warehouse conversions; and the Englishman – Draper – had earned himself some stunning reviews in *Design* and *Build-Plus* for his glass-domed shopping complex in Bayonne.

But Monastère was something else. Sure, it had brought him down – the delays, the budget restrictions, those weasly sub-contractors – but it would raise him up, too. He was certain of it. An entire hill-top monastery rebuilt, renovated and refurbished, all but one small corner of the second cloister – the tower with the finest views, the Monastère's *pièce de résistance* – still to finish. Three months' work, maybe. Four at the outside. And if they could get to work by the end of June and persuade the builders to stay on through August, this year's Mietzerhager would surely be his.

At last van der Haage made the desk and gave the girl his booking reference and driver's licence. As she tapped in the details on her computer, he wondered what the next few days held in store. Three days earlier the Monastère's owner, Claude Bouvet, had phoned to say that the Master had finally given in, told them he was ready to move, had agreed the compensation. After all the delays, they could finally get to work, and finish the job.

As the girl at the hire desk handed back his driving licence, rental agreement and keys, van der Haage decided that the day would come, and come soon if he had anything to do with it, when young Georg would regret his move to Agelkopf Partners.

'Do you need a map, monsieur?' asked the girl reaching for a drawer.

Van der Haage took the keys, slipped them into his pocket and shook his head.

Nee, bedankt.

He knew the way to Luissac.

7

Wednesday

Ghislaine Ladouze slipped off her shoe and raised her foot. Concealed by the heavy folds of their tablecloth, her stockinged toes felt for the edge of his chair then slid forward.

Across the table Roland Bressans smoothed a crust of bread with creamy Daphinoise, popped it into his mouth and smiled – at the taste, or what her toes had begun beneath the table, Ghislaine couldn't be sure. He was a cool one, that was certain.

He'd picked her up that morning at her apartment, two blocks back from the Marseilles Opéra. She'd been watching for him from her fourth-floor balcony, going out every few minutes and looking up the one-way street. Exactly on time, she saw a blue BMW with shaded windows turn into her street and come to a stop across from her building. The driver had double parked and left only the narrowest gap for other traffic to pass. It could only be him.

Closing the shutters, securing the balcony windows, Ghislaine rolled her trolley case out into the hallway. She knew there'd be no ring of the bell. He'd stay in the car, just as Madame had said. All she had to do was lock up the apartment, bid '*adieu*' to the concierge – 'A long weekend in the country? *Quelle bonne chance*,' the old lady had said when Ghislaine had told her that the apartment would be empty for a few days – and cross the cobbled street, stepping from mid-morning sunshine into shade. She couldn't see the driver but, halfway across the road, she heard a click and saw the boot rise a couple of inches. Hoisting her case into it, she closed the lid and came round to the passenger side. As she reached for the handle, a shadow inside leaned across and opened the door for her. Sliding in beside him, she'd wished him '*bonjour*' as though taking a lift to work with a colleague, and reached for her belt. As she settled herself in her seat, the car pulled away and they were off.

It didn't take her more than a moment to take him in. It was what she did, after all – gauging the client, judging the character, a swift personal appraisal to add to the information already provided by Madame. Apart from his teeth, which seemed too large and numerous for such a small mouth and gave his voice a strangely menacing sibilance, he was a good-looking man. The profile was strong and determined – a large but straight nose, chin purposefully raised, and jaw-line well-defined. His skin was smooth and tanned, and his lips looked as though he used salve. He had grey eyes and a full head of wiry grey hair, falling away from an off-centre parting and carefully curled around his ears. And not an ounce of fat to him – she could easily see his belt buckle, and his shirt front, though tailored, was not stretched. He clearly worked out, kept himself in trim and, Ghislaine suspected, probably enjoyed the pleasure it gave him.

According to Madame he was a regular customer, fifty-seven years old, married with three children, and something big in publishing. Or was it printing? Whatever, he was wealthy, well-connected and had never caused any trouble. He paid in advance and some of Madame's other girls had reported that there were no special requirements, beyond an expectation that they did what they were told. Ghislaine had also discovered that he didn't like to kiss, preferred *la pipe* to penetrative sex, and had a penchant for pretty underwear which, occasionally, he seemed to enjoy tearing.

He also knew his way around town. Nimbly negotiating the traffic on the Vieux Port, he'd whisked her through Le Panier and, before she knew it, they were past the wharves and ware-houses of La Joliette and swooping up on to the A7.

Twenty minutes later, sailing along the fast lane past Cabriès, introductions and small-talk dealt with, he'd taken a hand from the steering wheel and slid it softly between her knees, easing them apart, pushing at the hem of her skirt, lifting his chin to indicate that he wanted her to accommodate him, making her move more accessibly in her seat so that another, further intro-duction could be made.

From the moment they'd left town, Ghislaine had been expecting it, and was relieved by it. Madame had said he didn't like to waste time, and that was just fine by her. She preferred those clients who knew the ropes. Down to business, and no messing. So she did as he wanted, slid round in her seat and by the time they passed La Pioline interchange, her cheeks had reddened, her breath was quick and short and she was feeling surprisingly slick and ready. Another minute, another couple of kilometres, and it would have been done. But he seemed to know how far he could take her, removing his fingers as the autoroute busied on its approach to Aix, changing lanes and following the signs for Lambesc with a tight little smile playing about his lips.

Bastard.

Straightening herself up, and snapping down the visor to check her make-up, Ghislaine decided she was going to enjoy the weekend – as much for the money as the company.

'So where are you taking me?' she asked, make-up refreshed, glancing through her window, trying to work out where they were headed.

'Restaurant Lacoste,' he replied as they swung off the Lambesc road and cut right towards Rognes. 'The old Château Desfours. Do you know it?'

She did, and the prospect of a fine lunch warmed her as much as his fingers. But she didn't admit it, telling him only that she'd heard about it, read a review, had always wanted to go. In fact, she'd been there a couple of times, not enough to be known by the staff, but she knew that if she'd told him 'yes', he'd have immediately assumed she'd been there with another man. And clients didn't like to know things like that, especially clients like Roland Bressans.

Of course she'd known from the start that this was no ordinary assignment. Madame had called to brief her. A special request, she'd explained. When Ghislaine had confirmed she'd be available, she was told to expect a package in the mail. In fact it arrived by courier, a cassette tape with a note attached. The note – not in Madame's handwriting – was brief. Watch the tape and practise the movements. Style and dye the hair to match, and find similar clothes. Just that.

She'd called Madame to ask a little more about the assignment.

'You always wanted to be an actress,' the older woman had said, 'now's your chance.'

Across the table, her companion swallowed the last of his cheese, reached for his wine and finished it off; a quick rinse through the teeth to rid himself of breadcrumbs and cheese.

A waiter appeared at the table. Without taking the dessert card offered, Bressans ordered a pineapple and kirsch carpaccio. He looked across at her, a gentle lowering of the eyelids the only indication that he was aware of what her toes were doing. 'And for you, *chérie*?'

'Sounds just the thing,' she replied and smiled sweetly, working the stiffness against her toes. Another minute and she'd take her foot away. Leave him high and dry, just as he had done to her.

Twenty minutes later, the carpaccios and two small espressos dispatched, the empty plates whisked away, Bressans signed the tab and pushed away from the table, taking up his napkin as he did so and slipping it into his trouser pocket.

'Shall we?' he asked, coming round to pull out her chair.

Ghislaine felt his hand on the small of her back and she let him steer her into Reception where he asked her to wait a moment. She watched him approach the concierge at the front desk, heard the words 'some calls to make' and 'business', and saw Bressans reach across, press something into the man's hand.

The concierge tipped his head, stole a glance at her, nodded. '*Bien sûr, monsieur.*' He tapped out something on the computer, then turned and reached for a key. It had a long braided tassel which Bressans swung to and fro as they walked to the lift, occasionally letting it tap against her leg. On the second floor, he led the way down a wide hallway, found the room, unlocked the door and stood aside to usher her in.

Ghislaine Ladouze walked into the room and heard the door close softly behind them. She had little doubt what 'calls' her companion needed to make, what 'business' he needed to attend to.

And she was not mistaken.

'Don't turn round,' she heard him say, his voice a wet, excited whisper. 'Just stand there like that, and close your eyes.'

A moment later, she smelt a mixture of sweet kirsch and pineapple as he reached around to place the napkin over her eyes.

So that's why he'd taken it.

As he tied it behind her head, a loose, stray wisp of hair caught in the knot and she flinched.

She heard his breath catch at that, and she smiled to herself.

When the blindfold was secure, she heard him step back and kick off his shoes, unzip his trousers and then slip past her and settle on the bed in front of her.

'Take off your skirt and your blouse,' he told her. 'Nothing else. I'm here on the bed, right in front of you.'

She did as she was told, reaching round for the zip, letting the skirt slip down her legs, stepping out of it, casting it aside. Then, slowly, she unbuttoned her blouse, pulled it back from her shoulders, feeling his eyes on her breasts.

Then she reached out, felt for his knees and lowered herself between his legs.

Playtime, she thought, and licked her lips.

❋　❋　❋

Two hours later, they crossed the stony bed of the Durance at St Christophe and followed the signs for Cadenet.

'It's not far now,' Bressans said, glancing across at his companion. 'How are you feeling?'

Ghislaine thought for a moment. 'It's exciting,' she said. 'Scary, too.'

'You'll be fine,' he said. 'Just remember what I've told you.'

In Cadenet, they were delayed by a tourist bus, hazard lights flashing as it dropped off a crowd of visitors into Place du Tambour. Bressans tapped his fingers on the steering wheel, glanced at his watch, then leaned forward to switch on the radio for the news. Ten minutes later, they were out of Cadenet and bound for the Lourmarin cut separating the Grands and Petits Lubérons. It was the final part of their journey and Roland Bressans felt a pleasurable sense of certainty course through him. He licked his lips, tasted the pineapple and kirsch and savoured the image of the girl beside him stepping out of her skirt, unbuttoning her blouse. With a body like that – young, pert, proud – she'd have the old man round her little finger in the time it took to split a fig.

'So who was she?' his companion asked, as the road curved up out of Lourmarin and the hills closed in around them. 'The girl in the film, I mean? Do you mind me asking?'

'Not at all,' he replied. 'Her name was Céleste Maroc. She was a country girl. Born in Apt just before the War, died in a car crash sometime in the sixties. She was a wild one by all accounts.'

'Like me?' teased Ghislaine, reaching a hand to his leg.

'Just like you. Exactly like you.'

'And her lover?'

'Much older. She can't have been more than sixteen, seventeen.'

'Dirty old man.'
'Very dirty indeed.'
'Yeah?'
'Oh yes. And he's going to love you.'
Ghislaine chuckled lightly. 'You think so?'
'My dear, I know so.'

8

Thursday

Paul Ginoux was feeling queasy. He always did on the steep, winding hairpins that led down from Luissac to the valley, the Citroën's airy suspension adding an extra softening sway to every corner. It wasn't until they reached the turning on to the Cavaillon road that Ginoux opened his eyes and started to feel a little more settled.

It was his own fault, of course. He should have thought of it in Paris, or picked them up in Lyons with the wine. Cigars. That's what he was after. A box of good cigars. If there was one thing the Master liked it was a good cigar.

The idea had come to him over breakfast in the Monastère's Salle du Matin. He'd gone straight to Reception where Didier, the concierge, about to go off duty, told him all he needed to know.

'We have our own supply, of course, monsieur. Some fine Havanas. But if you are looking for something special, then you must go to Cavaillon. Tabac Rafiné. Just off Cours Léon Gambetta, in the old town. The best tabac this side of Delorme's in Marseilles. The same family have run it for three generations. *C'est sans pareil. Incomparable.*'

Back in his room, Ginoux had put a call through to Dutronc in Monastère's annexe. Ten minutes later, the Citroën purred to a stop in Monastère's forecourt and they were off.

Of course he could have sent Dutronc to fetch the cigars for him, but he'd decided to go himself. Make that extra effort for the Master. He only hoped that his efforts would pay off.

For two days now, he'd been getting nowhere with the old man, no closer to the canvases he'd come for, no nearer to closing a deal. Stonewalled at every turn. It was becoming intolerable.

But at least now he knew why.

Roland Bressans.

The Master was playing him off against Bressans. Of all people. Had to be. Why else would the man be there?

Ginoux and Bressans had never met, but Ginoux knew exactly who he was, what he did and how he did it. He'd recognised the man the moment he saw him, at dinner the night before, gliding into Monastère's dining room, Réfectoire, with a woman young enough to be his daughter. And Ginoux had seen enough pictures of Monsieur and Madame Bressans and read the attendant editorial chronicling their presence at gallery openings and first-night exhibitions around the country to know that the woman coiled around his arm wasn't Bressans' wife, and definitely not his daughter.

Ginoux had known immediately that the man was up to

something. There could be no other explanation. It surely couldn't just be chance that Bressans was staying at Monastère, not with the Master within easy walking distance? And certainly not with that new gallery of Bressans' scheduled to open in Marseilles by the end of the year. The art press had been full of it for months now, pictures of the derelict nineteenth-century Customs House that Bressans was in the process of transforming to hold what *Art France* had suggested in a glowing editorial might just turn out to be one of the country's foremost modernist collections.

The man was up to no good, *c'était certain*, and in Ginoux's book, 'up to no good' meant only two things. Competition. And trouble. And it hadn't taken him more than a moment to guess what it was that Bressans was up to. The man was making a play for the Master. He was after some Vilottes to launch his new gallery.

Over my dead body, thought Ginoux, as they approached the outskirts of Cavaillon. Over my dead, bleeding and battered body, he decided as, minutes later, they turned off Cours Leon Gambetta and drew up outside Tabac Rafine.

'Wait here a moment,' said Ginoux and let himself out of the car.

After the Citroën's air-conditioning, the June heat hit like a blacksmith's hammer and by the time Ginoux pushed open the door to Tabac Rafine he could feel a drop of sweat trickling down his back. Closing the door behind him, he rounded his shoulders so that his shirt absorbed the sweat, and breathed in the sweet, warm scent of tobacco.

Tabac Rafine was just as Didier had described it. *Sans pareil*. None of the usual litter of magazines, newspapers and lottery tickets, the racked banks of chewing gum, *bonbons* and novelty bric-a-brac. Here, Ginoux decided, was a *tabac* that clearly took its smoking, and its customers, seriously. The shelves behind the counter were stacked with a hundred different brands of cigarette, the leather-topped counter furnished with a collection of antique tobacco jars (not a bad collection either, noted Ginoux), and the panelled walls either side of him set with glass-fronted humidors packed with cigar boxes and the paraphernalia of smoking – lighters, cigar-cutters, tapers.

'*Monsieur, bonjour*,' the tobacconist greeted him, smiling, leaning forward over the counter. 'And how can I be of help?'

Ginoux let his eyes range over the cigars on display. Not seeing what he wanted, he turned back to the tobacconist.

'I'm looking for Montechristo *Claros* – a *cabinet* of fifty, if you have such a thing?' Behind him he heard Tabac Rafine's door open and close. Another customer.

'*Claros*? Montechristo? *Un moment, monsieur*.' The tobacconist squatted down behind the counter.

'A fine cigar, the Montechristo,' came a voice behind him.

Ginoux turned. A tall man dressed in jeans and a flamboyant Hawaiian shirt towered above him. A linen jacket was tossed over his shoulder, the loop held in a crooked finger. His eyes were penetrating, a level green gaze, and his hair was pulled back into a ponytail.

'They are indeed,' replied Ginoux, not certain how to continue, slightly flustered by the unexpected comment.

'*Eh voilà*,' interrupted the tobacconist, struggling to his feet and placing a wooden box on the counter. '*Claros*. Montechristo.'

Reaching for his wallet, Ginoux presented his credit card.

'And your car, monsieur,' continued the stranger. 'I couldn't help but notice. A classic.'

'Why, yes indeed. A Prestige. A wonderful motorcar. It

belonged to an old friend,' replied Ginoux, bending down to sign the credit card slip, anxious now to be gone.

'*Merci bien, monsieur*. Would you like me to wrap them for you?'

Ginoux told the tobacconist it wouldn't be necessary. They were fine as they were.

'I hope you enjoy them, monsieur,' he said, returning Ginoux's card and receipt and pushing the box across the counter. '*Et bonne journée.*'

Ducking past the customer behind him, Ginoux headed for the door. As he pulled it open and stepped out on to the pavement, he heard the tobacconist greet the man with the green eyes and the ponytail.

'Monsieur Jacquot. *Quel plaisir*. And how are you today?'

Forty minutes later, with the Montechristos on the seat beside him and everything to play for, Ginoux closed his eyes as Dutronc spun the wheel into the first of the curves leading up to Luissac and Le Grand Monastère.

9

Gilles Gavan was driving too fast, the June sunshine spilling into his rental minibus, a warm breeze battering through its open windows and sunroof. Either side of him the fields swept past, a blood-drop carpet of *pointilliste* poppies bordered by pencil-straight cypress and a blue-grey shading of distant hills, the sky above a bright brush of clear cobalt. Twenty minutes out of Cavaillon, five minutes past Roquefure, he indicated for the left but misjudged the corner, the van's pedals set at an unfamilar angle, the turning sharper than he remembered. In an instant his back wheels skittered across the gravel that had accumulated in a drift at the edge of the road, lost their grip and the minibus, with a bump and a jolt, ended up broadside to the lane. The engine juddered and stalled, and a cloud of Lubéron dust swirled through the open windows. In the ticking silence that followed, Gilles let out his breath, whistled and then laughed like a child on a fairground carousel.

Thank God he was alone, he thought to himself; no one to witness his carelessness.

Doucement, doucement, he reprimanded himself, heart hammering at the closeness of it all. Restarting the engine, he straightened up the van and drove on, more slowly this time, playing the steering wheel carefully now as he followed the curves to Claudine Eddé's house. There was no rush, he told himself. There'd be time for a drink when he got there, maybe lunch on her terrace.

So far everything had gone perfectly. The flights from London and Paris had arrived at Marignane within minutes of each other and, waiting outside the baggage hall, peering into the crowd of arrivals waiting at the carousels whenever the glazed doors slid open, Gilles had identified his charges in no time at all. The easels and paintboxes they carried, or took from the carousel, singled them out.

The fat man with the panama hat, aquamarine trousers and blue shirt would be Philip Gould, the lone American male, an antiques dealer from Albany, fussing around a middle-aged woman in a T-shirt, shorts and espadrilles. A Paisley scarf was shawled around her shoulders and a collection of bulbous turquoise stones were strung from her neck. Gilles recognised the features – long and drawn with a necklace-matching arc of turquoise eye-shadow – from the photo in the catalogue he'd received from her, along with her registration form and cheque. Her name was Naomi West, looking older than the date of birth in her catalogue suggested, the catalogue featuring some half-dozen photos of her work – rather thin, abstract daubs, Gilles had thought with a sniff – which probably looked good on the front of greetings cards or the walls of certain hotels. According to this same catalogue – printed for an

exhibition of her paintings at a gallery in Phoenix, Arizona –
Madame West had had three other shows in places Gilles had
never heard of.

Then there was the English lady, Joanne Nicholls.
Unmistakeable. She had to be English – the pressed slacks,
draped cardigan, sensible shoes and single line of pearls –
waiting at the edge of the carousel, peering at the passing
labels as though she didn't know what her bags looked like,
her paintbox already safely stowed on her trolley.

Waiting for them, at the edge of the crowd, were three older
women standing in a group. It was clear who Hilaire Becque
was, the widow from Vernon. Looking chic and cool in her
button-down safari shirt and pocketed beige skirt, she was a
marked contrast to her companions – the two other Americans
in the group: Mrs Marcie Hughes in a sweat shirt, baggy combat
trousers and trainers, and Mrs Grace Tilley in a creased sleeve-
less shift and plimsolls, her straying brown hair tucked up under
a baseball cap. The art teacher and the librarian. They looked
the part, thought Gilles as, suddenly, they all seemed to be in
possession of their luggage, pushing their trolleys towards him
in a chattering, excited group.

Introductions dealt with on the concourse, Gilles had
escorted them to the minibus that he'd parked as close to the
terminal as he could manage and had set about stowing their
luggage. The minibus seated eight, comfortably, with room
enough behind the back seat for easels and paintboxes, but
it proved a tight squeeze with their baggage too. With some
assistance from Monsieur Gould, everything was finally packed
in and, pressing their shoulders against the hatchback, the
lock was secured.

Thank God that's done, thought Gilles, jumping into the

driving seat as his painting group made themselves comfortable – Philip, Marcie and Gracie in the back seat; Hilaire Becque and Joanne Nicholls in the middle and, commandeering the passenger seat beside him, Naomi West. With a stalling lurch, starting the engine while it was still in gear, Gilles finally got the van moving and they were on their way.

Only one of the Americans, Naomi, of course, and the English lady had been south before and, as Gilles drove from the airport and up through the limestone bluffs and rough garrigue of the country route to Aix, all had exclaimed at the landscape, rattling off the familiar names – Cézanne, Seurat, Braque and others – exchanged as a kind of currency of appreciation, an establishing of tastes and credentials. Everything a picture, they enthused, chattering on excitedly, pointing out this and then that, first one side of the van and then the other: a burst of mimosa, the flicking rows of still-to-bloom lavender, the creamy cliffs crumbling in the heat, dusty paths leading off into the garrigue, sentinel cypresses standing straight as a guard, just their tips trembling in the sunshine, the tiny houses, red rooftops.

But how to do it justice? wondered the librarian Gracie from the back seat. How to capture it? With dots? With cubes? With wild bold sweeps? With oils, acrylics, watercolours, pen and ink maybe, chalk or crayon?

And the light, they all agreed. Oh that light! Even at midday! The sunsets must be magical! And the dawns, too. They'd have to be up early. What time was dawn, by the way?

As they by-passed Aix and headed for Venelles – Naomi shushing everyone to point out the stony slopes of Montagne Sainte-Victoire to the right, as though it were her own private mountain – Gilles waited for the chatter to die down then told them what he had planned: 'After your long journey, I am sure you are all looking forward to getting to your hotel.'

There was a chorus of affirmatives from the group.

'And hungry, too.'

More enthusiastic agreement.

'So, after lunch, I suggest you have the afternoon to yourselves, to unpack, have a rest – whatever you wish. If any of you want to start painting straightaway, I can recommend Luissac. It is a very pretty little village and only a short walk from the hotel. We pass through it on the way to Le Grand Monastère. Otherwise, our first group session will be tomorrow morning. Say nine o'clock?'

The party agreed that nine o'clock would be fine.

'Also, I have arranged a club table in the hotel restaurant. I thought it would be nice for us to dine together, but if any of you would prefer to have your own table, just ask the Maître d'. His name is Yves Lenoir. He will make sure you have everything you need.'

'Is it true Le Monastère is haunted?' asked Naomi beside him, fingering one of her turquoise stones.

'That's what they say, Naomi. But, for myself, I have never seen anything.'

'Haunted? Is that what she said?' asked Gracie in the back. She turned fearfully to Marcie. 'You didn't say it was haunted,' she said accusingly.

'It's news to me,' replied Marcie. 'But I guess with a thousand years of history under its belt, it'd be a surprise if it wasn't.'

'According to the guidebooks,' said Joanne Nicholls helpfully, turning round to the back seat, 'Le Monastère started life as a fortress, or *castrum*, to defend the region from Saracen invaders. Plenty of action back then, I'd imagine . . .'

And as the countryside flew past, Gilles let them talk on, keeping an eye on the road but listening in to the chatter as the blue slopes of the Grand Lubéron rose up ahead of them, hoping his English would see him through.

Now, an hour later, his guests dropped off at the hotel, their rooms allocated, baggage delivered, Gilles felt pleased with the way the pick-up and transfer had gone.

There was just the one tiny problem, he thought, as he reached the top of the lane where Claudine Eddé lived and spotted an angle of terracotta tiling through the pine and holm oak. Just one tiny problem. The weather. According to the forecasts, the first three days of his painting course would be fine – fabulous weather for the rest of the day, the whole of Friday and Saturday. But on Sunday afternoon it was set to break. A massive belt of rain expected from the north and picking up some punch en route. If he was lucky, they might get a few hours' painting on Sunday morning but, by the sound of it, Monday was out. And maybe Tuesday as well. He'd have to think up something to keep his party happy.

With a beep of his horn, he put it out of mind and turned into Claudine's driveway.

10

S inatra. Claudine Eddé loved Frank Sinatra – that voice, that timing, that . . . and 'Summer Wind' just had to be her favourite favourite. The keyboard, the saxophones, those soft cymbals. 'Lady and the Tramp'; 'That Ole Black Magic'; 'Come, Fly with Me'. She loved them all. But 'Summer Wind' . . . It had to be the one. Nothing else came close.

But there was just one problem, she thought, singing along as she rinsed her brushes. Her English was not quite good enough to accompany with any conviction:

> *'Ze zummer win'* . . .
> *'kem blowin' in* . . .
> *'from acrows ze zea* . . .'

If only Sinatra had been French, she thought. But then maybe he wouldn't have sounded so good in French. That was the trouble. The music, the lyrics, that honeyed delivery – they were American. Could only be American. So she'd just have to persevere.

> *'Two sweet'arts an' ze summer wind.*
> *'Lahk pain'ed kites.*
> *'sose days and nights,*
> *'zey went flyin' by . . .'*

She was slotting her brushes into a drying rack above the sink, humming now because she couldn't quite remember the words, the still studio air shot with the sharp, resinous scent of turpentine, when she heard the toot of a horn and a car pull into her drive. Gilles.

She glanced at her watch and wondered how it had gone – the meeting and the greeting, the drive up from Marignane with his first painting group. Gilles, she knew, would be either brimming with exuberant delight or his face creased with anxiety. Switching off the tape, closing the studio door, she went through to the kitchen, opened the fridge and was pulling out a bottle of rosé when the front door opened and slammed shut.

'Claudine? Claudine?' he called out.

'Down here,' she answered, levering the cork from the bottle with a satisfying 'plop'. 'I'm in the kitchen.' She could tell by his voice that Gilles was in good humour, which could only mean that everything had gone according to plan.

By the time he bustled into the kitchen, she had the wine in a jug, two glasses on a tray and was heading for the terrace door. 'Olives there,' she said, pointing her elbow back to a bowl on the table. 'There's bread, some *saucisson*, the cheese.

You must be starved. Come and have some lunch. Tell me all about it.'

Out on the terrace, in the cool, shifting shade of an ancient olive tree whose topmost branches reached as high as her bedroom windows, Claudine listened as Gilles ran her through his morning.

'Such nice people. You wouldn't believe. I've left them at the Monastère to unwind after their journey. I told them that we'd join them there this evening for our welcome dinner. They're dying to meet you. You are still coming, aren't you?'

For the last few weeks Claudine had thought up a dozen different ways to back out of her promise to Gilles, the promise to help him with his painting group. But nothing had worked, one idea after another sadly discarded. She just couldn't do it to him, not now, not at the last minute. Gilles would have been devastated. He needed her, he'd told her. He just couldn't do it without her. He'd pay of course, for her time, for helping out; share the fees . . .

And reluctantly she'd given in. Not for the fees, not for a share in the spoils. But out of friendship, and gratitude. When she had needed someone, Gilles Gavan had been there for her – the gallery owner in Aix who'd offered to show her work, who'd encouraged her, who'd come out here at a moment's notice to hold her hand and hug her and wipe away the tears in those terrible months after her husband's betrayal. What would she have done without Gilles Gavan? And now, she realised, it was payback time. Whether she liked it or not.

Gilles had told her about his plan one morning, over breakfast. He'd fallen asleep on the sofa while she sat at his feet, looking into the fire and recalling, for the hundredth time, the moment she'd come home and found her husband in bed with her best friend. The reason for her tears, the reason she lived alone, the reason she'd dropped her husband's name and retaken her own.

A painting course, he'd said. Half-a-dozen people maximum. He'd placed an advertisement in *Art France* the previous month and had taken a small box in the *Herald Tribune*.

'But where will you put them up?' she'd asked.

'Why, at the Hôtel Grand Monastère des Évêques,' Gilles had replied, taking a bite of his croissant, eyes twinkling mischievously above a ballooning cheek. 'In Luissac.'

'The Monastère? They're going to stay at the Monastère? But it will cost a fortune.'

'Madame Bouvet owes me a favour,' he'd told her. 'Don't ask, it was a long time ago. She's promised six rooms for five days at a very reasonable discount. And there's something else.'

'There's more?'

'Vilotte.'

'Vilotte. Auguste Vilotte? I thought he was dead.'

'Far from it. Well maybe not so far from it. He lives in a part of the monastery, the old tower. He's lived there since the War, moved back when his father died. And he's agreed to a visit. A few words, shake their hands, that sort of thing. I saw him myself, explained what I was doing. The Master! Can you believe it?'

And now it was here, the day she'd been dreading. Having to face the world again after eighteen lost, lonely months.

'Of course I'm coming,' she said and reached for his hand across the table. 'What time do you want me there?'

11

Over an early lunch of Bouzigues oysters and a *premier cru* Chablis taken on the Monastère terrace, Roland Bressans went over the plan once more, everything his companion needed to know. What to say, what to do. The names she needed to remember. The people. The places. She'd be on her own.

Seven o'clock, he told her as they left the terrace, his hand on the small of her back, guiding her through Reception and up the stairs to their rooms, just as he'd done at Lacoste's. At her door, he stood aside as she turned the key in the lock. She went in, then stopped and turned. He was still standing in the passage, the sabre-like leaves of the three palms in the courtyard shuffling lightly in the breeze behind his shoulder. She'd expected him to follow her. She was wearing a silky chemise, the one with the spaghetti straps and border of lace, a border of lace she'd deliberately left showing through the deeply unbuttoned front of her blouse, the taut swell of her beneath its soft

57

satin sheen. She was certain he'd have gone for it. But he hadn't.

'Rest now, but be ready when I knock,' he said, glancing at his watch. 'Four hours. No more.'

And with that he turned and walked back to the stairs at the end of the loggia, the soles of his tennis shoes squeaking on the stone steps and fading away.

With a contented sigh, and a small squeeze of excitement, Ghislaine closed the door and went through the salon to her bedroom. Closing the shutters, but leaving the windows open, she peeled off her clothes and slid into bed. Beside her, on the bedside table was the TV remote. She wondered if she should run the cassette just one more time, the tape that Bressans had sent her. It played like an old home movie, filmed before she was born if the swimsuits and the cars were anything to go by, the action jerky and uncertain, the colours primitive and gaudy. She'd watched it so many times now that she knew every single, scratchy frame of it – the way she walked, the way she smiled, the sway of her hips, that taunting glance back over her shoulder, the way she caught her curling auburn hair and clasped it behind her head. Like one of her exercise videos, Ghislaine had played that tape at least an hour a day, every day. Practising every move, repeating every nuance until she had it down pat.

But there was such a thing as too much preparation, she decided, and she left the remote where it was, puffing up her pillows and making herself comfortable. In a moment she was asleep.

Later, Ghislaine opened her eyes and saw that the shuttered streaks of sunlight on the floor had moved to the side of her bed. She looked at her watch. She'd slept longer than she'd intended – the Chablis, she decided. Time to get moving.

It had taken her a little over an hour to prepare – a long hot soak that left her dizzy, and then a bracing cold shower that made her skin sing. Coddled in one of Monastère's towelling robes, she'd sat in front of her dressing-table mirror and set about removing the scarlet varnish from her toenails and finger-nails, working on her eyebrows with a pair of tweezers, and trying to make her face as good as it could get without make-up – not a trace of lipstick or blusher or eye-shadow, Bressans had told her. 'She was a country girl, remember?'

When she'd finished she turned her head from left to right, kept her eyes on the mirror, checked herself over. Satisfied, she walked to the armoire and laid out the costume she'd wear, the clothes from the video. She'd found them herself, according to instructions. A white layered gypsy dress with a panelled waist and an open scalloped neck. On her own initiative, she'd added a length of blue silk that she bound round her waist like a cummerbund, a matching blue band that she tied bandanna-style through her hair, and a thin, pale blue cardigan that she draped over her shoulders.

Lacing up a pair of cream rope-soled espadrilles, she crossed to the mirror behind the door and twirled around, lifting the frilled layers of her skirt, long brown legs dancing beneath her. The material felt rough, but loose and light and cool. And with no underwear, the breeze of her skirt between her thighs and the texture of the tight cotton across her breasts made her feel . . . made her feel . . .

She stopped spinning, thought of Bressans' hand in the car and felt herself flush, a great rising warmth streaming up from between her legs to flare at her cheeks. She gave a breathless little laugh, just like the girl in the video, and spun round one final time. A country girl, he'd said. A gypsy. Well, that's what she was. Nothing less.

Au revoir, Ghislaine.

Et bonjour . . . Céleste.

It was then that she heard a soft knocking at the door to her salon, and, taking one last look in the mirror, she went to open it.

12

In his time Erdâg Kónar had seen many dead bodies – in snowy woods and on smoking plains, in grimy scorched basements and blood-soaked gymnasia, sprawled singly and heaped in numbers, old and young, civilians and soldiers alike. But he'd never seen a ghost. If asked he would have said he didn't believe in something that he couldn't see with his own two eyes, or through his camera's lens. If it couldn't be filmed, it wasn't there – the camera as all-seeing, documenting eye. Such was his belief.

So he'd found it difficult to explain the icy shiver that ran through his limbs the moment he stepped from the rental car and looked up at the Grand Monastère's battlemented façade when he and Meredith arrived at the hotel after their lunch in St Maximin. It certainly wasn't the weather that accounted for the chill that shook through him, an unseasonably warm June evening. And nor was it the gentle breath of air-conditioning that greeted them in the hotel's reception hall – its stone-block walls and flagged floors always a cool escape from summer's hottest days. There was something else at work, and he looked around as though searching for some explanation.

'You OK, honey?' Meredith had asked, noticing his frown as they were shown to their room.

'Sure, of course,' he replied, tipping the porter and seeing him to the door. 'Just a chill. Coming out of the heat maybe – all this stone. My mother would have said that the devil was passing over my grave. Maybe I've been here before in another life,' he said.

'Maybe it's the Monastère's ghost?' said Meredith. 'Says in your guidebook the place is haunted. Certainly is spooky enough,' she added, peering into the bathroom, then squealing with a mixture of fright and delight as Erdâg came up behind her, hoisted her off her feet and carried her back to the bed.

'You Americans,' he chuckled throatily, reaching down between her knees. 'If it's older than a decade, it's just got to be haunted. Believe me, little princess, there are no such things as ghosts. Only believe in things you can see and touch . . . like this.'

But if Erdâg Kónar didn't believe in ghosts, he found it increasingly difficult over the next couple of days to shift the feeling that he wasn't alone, that somehow he was being followed, being watched. Perhaps, he decided, it had something to do with the request he had made, his request for a meeting with the Master. Maybe they were keeping an eye on him, vetting him, to see if he was suitable, acceptable.

He'd made this request the evening he and Meredith checked in, leaning close to the concierge, Didier, ready with a wad of francs to facilitate what he wanted.

'Madame Champeau,' Didier had told him, without raising his eyes from the registration form that Erdâg had just completed and handed over along with his passport. It seemed as though the concierge was used to issuing these instructions, as though Erdâg was asking for nothing more complicated than a taxi to take him into town. 'Monastère's housekeeper. Speak to her if you wish to see the Master. She is the only person who can arrange it for you. Champeau here, Madame's son, will take you to her.'

Erdâg had turned to the son – impossible to tell his age – taking in the slightly humped shoulder, the wide, accommodating smile and stubby hair pointing like the sharp prow of a boat over a narrow furrowed brow.

'Tomorrow, after breakfast, stay here and I will find you,' said Champeau. And that was that.

On Wednesday morning, just as he said he would, Champeau had sidled up to Erdâg as he waited in Reception and escorted him through a concealed service entrance by the Salle du Matin down to his mother's office, located off the laundry and house-keeping departments one floor beneath the Monastère's lobby.

Ushered into her den, Erdâg had explained what he wanted and the housekeeper, a tall hawk-faced woman who must once have been a beauty but whose looks had been soured and scoured by the ravages of time and a hard life, had taken his money – a thousand francs slipped into her cardigan pocket – and told him she would be in touch. Her son, Champeau, would find him when the Master was ready. Until then, she regretted, he must wait. The Master was a busy man, there were many calls upon his time. She hoped he understood.

He'd thanked Madame Champeau, told her he did indeed understand and that he was happy to await the Master's summons. But two days later Erdâg's patience was wearing thin, two days stalking the ancient monastery with his camera, putting together a series of establishing shots of its grand hall, the main staircase with its carved stone balustrade, the terrace, the cloisters, the restaurant, even hiking down into the spikey scrub below the monastery to capture its towering façade against a blue Provençal sky. Two long days and still he'd heard nothing.

That Thursday evening he'd left Meredith in their bed, as tousled and flushed as she'd appeared in her film, had showered, dressed and then taken up his camera to while away the time it would take her to get ready for dinner.

'I'll meet you in the bar,' he'd told her.

'Mmmmhhh,' she'd replied, pulling the sheet around her.

From a filming point of view, evening had always been Erdâg's favourite time of day, and at the Monastère it had been no different. The worn limestone walls seemed to glow with warmth and light, as though the stone had been brought to life, was somehow breathing, pulsing, in the setting sun. Even in Erdâg's preferred medium of black and white, he had no doubt that this extraordinary glow would somehow shine through, giving the greys a certain depth, a certain texture.

After checking out some of his favourite locations, he'd finally settled down in a corner of the lower cloister and was filming the first bats darting around the cloister garden when he saw a shadow flick across his view-finder, on the first–floor level directly opposite. He pulled away from the eyepiece and looked up to where he had seen it, and the next moment heard footsteps on the stone staircase that led down to the courtyard.

He saw their legs first. Rope-soled espadrilles and tennis shoes. And then they stepped into view – the grey-haired Frenchman and, Erdâg was certain, his mistress. The gypsy look suited her, he thought and he smiled when he caught her eye, wished them both a good evening. It was only when they'd crossed the lawn and disappeared through the door marked *Privé* (which, he'd already discovered, led to the second cloister and the Master's watchtower) that he realised where they were headed. A meeting with the Master. It could be nothing else. And he felt a flush of annoyance that it should be them and not him.

He was wondering if he shouldn't have a word with Madame Champeau's boy, see if he could hurry his mother along a little, when Erdâg caught a glimpse, at the very edge of his vision, of another shadow. He spun round but there was nothing to see, the cloistered garden silent and empty, the only movement in the fading light the darting flicker of bats. He tried to persuade himself that it must have been one of these that had caught his eye. But somehow he wasn't convinced.

Time for dinner, he thought to himself. Time to put away the camera for the day.

13

'I'm telling you, Marcie. It's her. Bethany. Bethany Close. *The Ramblers*. That NBC Special last fall. She was the one who got pregnant, had to leave town.'

'So you keep saying,' replied Marcie, who loved Grace as much as any soul could love another but who could never quite comprehend her companion's fixation with television soap operas. *Dallas. Dynasty. Dawson's Creek.* If a show looked like it might make a second series, Grace became its biggest fan, their downstairs cloakroom packed with old TV guides and celebrity-interview magazines.

What surprised Marcie was that such an otherwise talented, inspired woman could become so hooked on . . . well, trash. In every other way Gracie was what a retired librarian should be – quietly knowledgeable, quietly opinionated, and quietly fastidious. And so it was, until something brought soaps to the fore.

Both women were dog-tired, keen to catch up on some sleep before the painting group set out the following morning for its first session. Determined to beat their jet-lag they'd gone for a walk that afternoon rather than take a rest, exploring Luissac's web of stepped *ruelles*, exclaiming at the blooming terracotta pots and baskets of flowers that seemed to decorate every doorway and window sill in the village, and cooing over the hand-crocheted curtains drawn across every ground-floor window. It was their first time in Europe and they couldn't get enough of the tiny hamlet, teetering on the edge of the Calavon Valley. Everything was so strange, so different and, well, so French.

Back at Monastère, they'd taken tea on the terrace, and while writing their first round of postcards had quietly discussed the other members of the group: Gilles, 'so polite, so enthusiastic'; and Philip, 'such a darling,' said Gracie; 'for a New Yorker,' added Marcie; Hilaire, 'so elegant'; Joanna 'such a gentle soul'; though neither of them could quite seem to agree on Naomi – 'a tad pushy, don't you think?' ventured Gracie, kindly; 'snappy as a yard dog, if you ask me,' was Marcie's less charitable opinion.

That evening they'd been first to the club table in Réfectoire and had been through the menu a couple of times, without really understanding a word of it, before Hilaire had joined them and explained the various dishes, followed by a sleepy-looking Philip and rosy-cheeked Joanne. When Gilles arrived with Claudine, he'd introduced her to everyone ('So beautiful,' whispered Marcie to Gracie; 'but so sad-looking,' whispered Gracie back) and then suggested that, rather than wait any longer for Naomi, they should go ahead and order; he was sure she'd be along in a while. But it was another hour before the lady made an appearance.

'It took me a while,' continued Grace, getting up from the dressing table and pulling off her gown. Tightening the ties of her pyjama bottoms, she came round to her side of the bed, nearest the window, and slid in beside Marcie. 'But I knew I knew her. Just knew I'd seen her someplace. On TV, I mean . . .'

You mean a soap, thought Marcie, but said nothing, lowering the biography of Cézanne that Gracie had bought her for the trip and shifting to make room for her lover.

'And then, when she reached across the table to that man she's with, the way she held her hand, just so, close to his cheek. That's when I knew. Just exactly the same thing she did in *Ramblers*. Her leaning out of the train when she leaves town – pregnant and all – and that boy, what in heavens . . . ? That's it, Scott . . . when Scott runs to the station to say goodbye. And the train's pulling away . . . And it's getting dark . . . And the lights in the carriage . . .'

There was a catch in Gracie's voice as she recalled the scene and Marcie saw her eyes work away the tears that were starting to brim.

Dear Gracie, thought Marcie, so full of heart. So emotional. It had always been so, the one thing that Marcie loved in Gracie.

She'd seen the same tears brimming when they first met, in front of a Correggio *Magdalene* at the New York Metropolitan. Marcie had offered a handkerchief, Gracie had taken it, and they'd started talking, didn't stop, both agreeing that the paintings selected for the *We Are Woman* show were magnificent, some of the really great, great names: a staggering Klimt *Judith*, Millais' *Blind Girl*, a Modigliani head and shoulders, and Bastien-Lepage's *Haymaker* ('Can't you just feel her exhaustion?' – from Gracie, of course), not to mention a host of Eves, Madonnas and blessed saints, corridor after corridor, chamber by chamber.

That's how it had started. Three years and five years out of their respective marriages.

Somewhere along the corridor outside a door slammed shut and Gracie started, eyes wide, gripping their summer quilt to her throat.

'Did you hear that?' she asked.

'It's nothing,' replied Marcie, turning down a corner of the page to mark her place. As she put the book on her bedside table and switched off her light, she listened out for footsteps but could hear nothing. She knew, however, what Gracie was thinking, thanks to Naomi's remark about the Monastère being haunted.

'So what's she called? This actress of yours?' asked Marcie, thinking to distract her. 'The one at dinner. Her real name.'

'Well now,' admitted Grace, falling for the subterfuge, lowering the quilt and giving it some more thought. 'There you have me at a disadvantage. Bethany of course, in *Ramblers*. Like I said, Bethany Close. But in real life . . . Well, there you have me.'

Marcie reached for Gracie's hand. 'Be a honey and switch out that light.'

And, with a sigh and a 'Sure, why not?', Grace did as she was told and switched out her light.

14

It was Naomi West – of course – who kept the painting group waiting that first morning.

Typical, thought Gilles, determined to make the best of the good weather while it lasted. As the rest of the group stowed their gear and took their seats, he wondered what could be taking her so long.

He should have known, he thought, finally securing the hatchback. Of all the group, Naomi West was the one who was going to be difficult. And, glancing anxiously at his watch, he acknowledged that he might as well get used to it sooner rather than later.

It had started the night before, at dinner at the group's club table, where Naomi had behaved as if she was the only one present who knew what to do with a paintbrush. If Le Réfectoire's napkins hadn't been the finest linen, she'd have whipped out a pen and started sketching at the table. Preposterous woman.

The others had noticed too – Philip gently joshing Naomi at her more extreme ideas ('Cézanne would walk naked on the slopes of Mont Sainte Victoire to more closely associate with the mood of that sacred hill' was only one of her more absurd – and increasingly wine-fuelled – declarations); the Englishwoman, Joanne, looking embarrassed and murmuring meekly when Naomi turned to her for support and agreement; Hilaire Becque raising a weary eyebrow as she worked on her lobster *quenelles*; Marcie Hughes and Grace Tilley keeping their thoughts to themselves. Only Claudine had had the nerve to deal with her more fanciful notions, trying repeatedly to redirect the conversation, her English, Gilles had been pleased to note, more fluent and confident than his. Thank God, thank God for Claudine, he thought.

And now, not twelve hours later, here he was, wondering what to do next, when he saw Naomi sally across the forecourt, twenty minutes late, with Champeau hurrying after her with an easel and paintbox under his arm.

'But I did that yesterday,' she declared, a petulant schoolgirl edge to her voice, when Gilles explained that he was taking the group into Luissac to try their hand at some Provençal street scenes. 'I walked down there yesterday afternoon and found the most wonderful spot.' She leaned past him, into the open door of the van where the rest of the party were waiting patiently but starting to sweat gently. 'You'll love it,' she said. 'Such a wonderful little village. *Très typique*, if you know what I mean.' And then, turning back to Gilles, 'Tell you what, I'm going to stay put right here. Steal a march on the rest of you. Those perspectives in the cloister are just asking to be rendered. You've got my packed lunch, haven't you? Why don't I join you later? Say midday? See how you're all doing. How's that?' And without waiting for an answer, she spun round, waved Champeau towards the cloister and left Gilles in a fog of patchouli and exasperation.

'There's always one,' muttered Marcie, as Gilles swung across the Monastère's bridge and set off for Luissac.

15

Meredith Branigan was alone in bed when a discreet tap-tap at her door brought her awake.

'*Oui*,' she called out, stretching under the quilt then gathering it around her. The salon door opened and quick footsteps sounded across the stone floor. There was another tap at the bedroom door and a maid appeared, her little round face lit up with smiles over a basket of towels.

'*Serviettes, mademoiselle*,' she said and, dropping a curtsey, hurried towards the bathroom.

'Thank you, just leave them there by the door, that'll be fine.'

'*Bien sûr, mademoiselle. Et bonne journée.*' With another bob and beaming smile, the maid retreated and a moment later the salon door clicked closed.

Slipping from the bed Meredith picked up the towels – thicker and fluffier than the ones in Cannes – and took them through into the bathroom. Dropping them on to the *chaise longue* where Erdâg liked to sit while she bathed, she went to the tub, levered down the plug and turned on the big brass taps. When she was happy with the temperature, she went to the window, unlatched the shutters and opened them to a view of the Calavon Valley, the distant fields ribbed with tidy lines of budding lavender and straggling vines, their borders spikey with dark pencil-straight cypresses. The view was like every travel poster she'd ever seen, and for a moment she leaned there on the sill, taking it all in, a warm breeze sliding across her shoulders and whispering at her neck.

Pushing away from the window, Meredith turned off the taps, selected a jasmine-scented *bain moussant* from the collection beside the tub, and poured it into the steaming water. In an instant the room was suffused with a rich, sensual perfume and as she slid into the foam she thought of Erdâg, his hands, his lips, roaming over her warm sleepy body . . .

It was the first morning she had woken alone and, as she stirred her hands through the warm soapy water, Meredith acknowledged a small pique of irritation that he had let her sleep without waking her, that he had been able to leave their bed without . . . attending to her, and she let her thoughts stray to the rough and ready way he always initiated their love-making. Which rather excited her, even if it did frighten her a little. The way he manhandled her body, the way his thick, hairy-knuckled fingers sought her out and the way his mouth closed over hers until she was almost fighting for breath.

She knew the reason, of course. The reason for his absence. His other mistress. That damned camera of his. In the short time that they'd been together, he'd never gone anywhere without it. Right now, she guessed, he'd be wandering around the hotel, filming this and that, waiting for his assignation with the Master.

He'd told her all about it, of course – pretty much his only topic of conversation since they'd arrived; this great artist who lived in a part of the Monastère, the man he wanted to film, his next award-winning documentary. He'd even suggested she do the voice-over when he'd written the script. And though she'd expressed delight at the prospect of working with him, she knew in her heart that it would never happen. Not now, not after *Tune*. These few days were just a tantalising delay, nothing more. An adventure, a brief interlude, maybe the last she'd have for a long time to come. She might have been young, but she was a realist, too, and knew the machine that would be waiting for her when she returned to Los Angeles.

This was her chance. This was her time. And she wasn't going to let the moment slip through her fingers. Not even for the man who shared her bed and her body.

16

At exactly ten that morning, in the far corner of the Monastère's cloister, just as Champeau had said, Erdâg Kónar spotted the black-suited figure of Madame Champeau.

Her boy had cornered him on his way to the Salle du Matin after an early morning spent filming in the village.

'The Master will see you at ten,' Champeau had told him. 'Just go to the door marked *Privé* on the far side of the cloister and *Maman* will be waiting for you.'

And there she was, just as the boy had said.

'Monsieur, if you'd follow me,' the housekeeper had said and, without further ado, she'd led him through the passage and across the second courtyard to the watchtower. At the bottom of a flight of steps, she'd knocked once on a studded door greyed and splintered with age, then reached for the latch. '*Voilà, monsieur*,' she said, and pushed it open. '*Une demi-heure*, and I will be back.'

Erdâg felt a jolt of disappointment. After all the effort, and expense, that he'd gone to he'd been expecting something a little longer, a little more luxurious than thirty minutes. But thirty minutes was thirty minutes, he thought as he stepped past the housekeeper, his to play with as he chose. And thirty minutes, he reckoned, as the door closed behind him, might just be enough. Thirty minutes of real, raw footage. Cut to twenty-five, mix with archive, then edit-in the establishing shots he'd already put together. If the gods were on his side, then thirty minutes with the Master might just do it.

And thirty minutes later Erdâg knew he'd been right. That spare, lean half-an-hour had given him all he needed: the *grande salle* with its rounded, plum-coloured stone walls; the forest of sheets hanging like silken stalactites from its closely beamed ceiling, their pointed ends heavy with dried scabs of paint. And there, at the far end of the room, in what looked like an old barber's chair, an arm reaching behind him for one of the sheets, pulling himself round to greet his visitor, a spread of distant sun-drenched hills across the valley filling the window behind him . . . the man himself.

The last of them. Auguste Vilotte. The genius. The monster. *Le Maître*. And alive – just.

And a gift to the camera: the long grey hair of an Old Testament prophet; a straggling beard slashed with purple lips; bloodhound eyes the milky colour of meltwater; arthritic hands and curving yellowed fingernails rimmed with dirt; and a monk's white surplice smeared with paint.

Keeping his camera by his side, cupped in the palm of his hand, Erdâg had stepped forward and introduced himself.

'You look like Pablo,' the old man said to him. 'You know that? Pablo, Pablo, Pablo – damn him. The same nose, the same black eyes. Are you Spanish? You don't sound Spanish. Kónar? What sort of name is that?'

'Croatian. From a place called—'

'Cro-what? Cro-magnon? Speak up. *Un peu plus fort*. You're not in church, goddammit!'

And so it had gone. The two of them. There in the Master's studio. Shouting at each other for thirty minutes. Erdâg circling the barber's chair, keeping on the move, trying to film as much as he could in the short time available. And there, the focus of his attention, the old man, fists clamping the arms of the barber's chair, turning his head, his bloodshot eyes unwavering, watching every move.

'A what?' he'd bellowed.

'A film. About you.'

'Haven't seen it. And for the love of every merciful God, stand still, man.'

'It's a film I want to make.'

'So how could I possibly have seen it? If you haven't even made it yet. And what's that you've got there? In your hand there. A camera? Is that what it is? You're taking pictures? Of me?'

And then, finally, pulling himself out of the chair, head down like a bull, shoulders squared as though he intended to attack, the old man had roared, 'Enough! *Ça suffit*. Out with you. Out you go!'

It was exactly then, at that very moment, pushing back through the hanging sheets with Vilotte shouting after him – 'Enough! Out!' – that Madame Champeau tapped at the door as though she'd been waiting there the whole time, listening out for something like this, the door-latch clicking up and down. Exactly thirty minutes after she'd left him there. No more, no less. With Vilotte chasing after him down the length of the *grande salle*, brushing aside the hanging cloths like a crazed silverback charging through undergrowth, the door slammed shut behind him, hard enough to have dust leap from the planking.

'A good meeting, monsieur?' Madame Champeau had asked, raising an eyebrow. And as she ushered him up the steps and into the sunlight, he'd heard laughter. A bellowing cackle of laughter that spluttered into a distant, fading cough.

Laughter was good, Erdâg decided as he parted company with Madame Champeau and climbed the stairs to the room he shared with Meredith. Maybe, without realising it, he'd managed to win the man over? Maybe he'd be able to set up another appointment?

And then, letting himself into their room, Erdâg was suddenly aware of a warm, coiling scent of jasmine and the sound of splashing. He stowed away his camera in its case and, pulling the T-shirt over his head, he made his way silently to the bathroom.

17

Claude and Régine Bouvet, owners of Le Grand Monastère, and Lens van der Haage had taken their lunch in the Bouvets' apartment at the top of a narrow flight of steps inside the Monastère's gatehouse. The apartment, designed by van der Haage, was cool and spacious, the walls lime-washed stone, the floors a rich burnished teak and the furnishings low and modern. Claude, a balding, anxious-looking man in his early fifties, and his wife Régine, flame-haired, just the slightest padding on her hips and wrinkles round the eyes to hint at their closeness in age, could easily have called up Room Service, but they'd chosen to prepare their own lunch – melon, omelettes, a frisée salad and cheese. After Régine had cleared away the plates, she and her husband watched as van der Haage unrolled the drawings and sketches that he had brought from Amsterdam. The plans for the watchtower.

'Two large suites,' Lens explained, pointing to the vertical elevations of the tower from the north, 'reached from the corridors here, and here,' he added, indicating the cloisters of the second courtyard. 'The top suite will have the roof space, and the best views, of course; the lower suite will have the large studio window and, if we can secure the relevant permissions, an encircling balcony and small garden here, reached from the tower salon, currently Monsieur Vilotte's studio.'

'And your estimate of the cost?' asked Régine, clipping a fall of copper-coloured hair behind her ear.

Van der Haage smiled. 'As you know I have not had the chance to properly examine the existing interior fabric of the property. Monsieur Vilotte did not take kindly to my "poking about" as he called it the last time I was here, but maybe now he might be more amenable to closer inspection. From outside, I'd say the structure looks stable, though we'll need to replace some of the lower stonework on the west exterior.'

'Well, let's assume it's more likely that we will find the interior in not the very best of condition,' replied Régine with a short smile. 'We must think of it as a shell, something to be stripped out. New flooring, new staircases, new power supplies. And then the furnishings and fittings.'

'In which case,' said van der Haage, 'I estimate we won't complete for less than three million francs. A million for any exterior requirements and a million each for the two suites.'

Claude whistled.

'It's an estimate, of course,' added van der Haage. 'It could easily be less . . .'

'And it could just as easily be more,' added Régine.

'Yes, it could,' van der Haage conceded, 'but—'

'But it must be done,' said Régine, 'one way or the other. Until the watchtower is complete we cannot sensibly start operating the twelve new suites in courtyard two – so much space going to waste, *n'est-ce pas?*'

'How long will the work take, do you suppose?' asked Claude, adding more wine to their glasses.

'Well, as Régine has pointed out, the other rooms are finished and await only final fittings. So if we started work, say tomorrow, I would expect to complete within three months. Four at the outside. You will miss your main season, of course, but be ready for Noël – if you're planning to stay open over the Christmas holiday, that is.'

'To cover such costs, I regret we will have no option,' replied Claude.

'But it will be worth it, *chéri*. Two years, maybe three, and we'll be clear,' said Régine, her eyes glittering. 'It is the way forward. It has to be.'

There was silence around the table. Claude pursed his lips, nodded. His wife, as usual, was right. Sitting there at their kitchen table, he wished he had a fraction of her resolve.

Van der Haage broke the silence. 'So, then. What is the score with Vilotte? Please don't tell me he's changed his mind again?'

'Absolutely not,' said Régine. 'Claude saw him yesterday and he repeated that he's prepared to go ahead. As you know, we've looked at several likely places for him in St Mas, Auribeau, Castellet, Sivergues. And we've also offered him a substantial part of the annexe in Luissac. He went down to see it last week, said he liked the light, the lay-out – all on one level, with a terrace facing north, altogether much easier and more convenient for him.'

'What about Madame Champeau?' asked van der Haage. 'How does she feel about the move?'

As the three of them at the table well knew, Madame Champeau wielded considerable influence with Vilotte. Back in her twenties, she'd been his muse and model, a five-year reign that came to an end when a new girl took her place. She'd taken her dismissal well, left Luissac with the savings she'd put aside during her time with Vilotte and returned to Cavaillon where she'd married a *pompier*. No one was really sure if the child she bore some six months later was Vilotte's or the fireman's, but the moment the fireman found out that the boy had a problem with his spine, he was up and off from Cavaillon, taking her savings with him.

When Régine's father heard about her straitened circumstances, he'd promptly brought her back to Luissac and offered her work at Monastère. He'd also persuaded Vilotte to take her on as his housekeeper, part-time duties that she could easily manage alongside her work in the hotel. Thirty years later Madame Champeau was still there.

'She's quite happy about it,' said Régine. 'In fact, she's played a quite crucial role in steering Vilotte in our direction. She has, however, made it clear that if we want her to stay on as housekeeper – which we do – then the house in Luissac would be her preferred option for the old man.'

Van der Haage felt his spirits lift. If Madame Champeau was agreeable, then things really were looking good. All three of them at the table knew the tricks that Madame Champeau got up to, the way she played Vilotte, profited from him. So long as she remained on side, van der Haage was certain they'd have no trouble with the Master.

'So what's the next move?' asked van der Haage. 'I take it you approve of the plans . . . the budgeting?'

Claude and Régine looked at each other, then turned to him and nodded.

'Well, then,' said the Dutchman, reaching for his glass. 'Here's to the new Tower suites, and a Christmas opening at Hôtel Grand Monastère des Évêques.'

18

Roland Bressans couldn't have been more pleased with the way things had worked out. It was evening and he was dining alone in Réfectoire. Earlier that afternoon, while he and Ghislaine lay in the sun by the Monastère's terrace pool, a note had been brought out to her from Reception. Monsieur Vilotte was asking for Mademoiselle. Would she care to make a visit?

It was the invitation Bressans had been waiting for. Later, dressed once again in her gypsy costume, hair bound in a flower-print bandanna, the ties of her espadrilles laced around her slim brown ankles, Ghislaine had gone back to the watch-tower. And, judging by her absence at dinner, she was still there.

Of course, Bressans had not been surprised to receive the summons. Relieved, yes, but not surprised. Ghislaine's first meeting with Vilotte the day before had been a *tour de force*, the old man's eyes latching on to her like a barnacle to a rock.

After introducing herself – '*Céleste, monsieur, et comme toujours un plaisir de vous revoir*' – she had timed it to the second, putting a finger to her lip exactly as Céleste had done in the video, recalling the last time they'd met, when Pablo called by, or was it Henri from Cimiez? she'd asked lightly. And the picnic at Céret. Remember? And that dear old fellow they'd met on the Promenade des Anglais in Nice, Raoul Something . . . such a gentleman!

Bressans had seen the old boy frown, trying to get some kind of grip on what the girl was saying – those names, those places – and knew what would be going through his head. How could this be, Vilotte would be thinking? Pablo? Cimiez? But that was years ago . . . Yet, here she is . . . Close enough to touch . . . Real again . . . Exactly as she was.

And then, just as Bressans had hoped, Vilotte had finally lost himself, surrendered to her, memories seeping back, his mind starting to wander, the old fellow seduced by the past and the girl in front of him. The girl who looked so like Céleste . . . was Céleste. Even recalling how old Raoul had invited them to stay for lunch that time – 'You remember, *chérie*?' – and how she'd spilt the ice cream down the front of her dress . . . 'The very one you're wearing, I'd swear it.' And that picnic, he continued, in the hills above Céret, when Pablo fashioned those long stalks of grass into a necklace set with spring flowers. '*Mais oui, mais oui. Je me souviens.*'

And Ghislaine picking up on it – the change in him – and playing it like a pro, luring him on.

And then, something Bressans hadn't expected. Sitting there at the Master's feet, on the paint trunk in front of the barber's chair, she'd suddenly stood and gone to the window, reached for the shutter, half closed it – posed.

Theatre – pure, bewitching theatre. And Vilotte, leaning forward in his chair, had been transfixed.

And now, thought Bressans, signing the dinner bill to his room and getting up from the table, she was there again, summoned by the Master, no further booking fee required, right there in Vilotte's studio, playing the old fish for all she was worth.

Or rather, all he was worth.

As he climbed the stairs to his room, Bressans had a fair idea what Ghislaine would be doing. She'd be posing for him. Just like Céleste all those years ago, bringing his past to life, weaving her spell. The way she'd stood at that window? Vilotte wouldn't have been able to resist. Either he'd have suggested it himself, or she would have.

The more Bressans thought about it, the more certain he was that the bait had been taken.

19

Philip Gould closed his bedroom door and leaned back against it. Without raising his arm, he tilted his left wrist and looked at his watch. A little after eleven . . . And. He. Was. Pooped. P.O.O.P.E.D., as his old mother used to say.

But then it had been a long day. The walkabout in Luissac, looking for a likely spot to set up his easel and finally deciding on that corner where the old bakery had stood. It had been in shadow till about three, but then the sun had reached him. It couldn't have been on him for more than an hour but it had been enough – a hot, red tightness across the small circle of exposed scalp on the top of his head where the hair refused to grow. He didn't need to look in the bathroom mirror to know that that tiny island of white skin would now be a bright and burning pink disc. He should have taken his hat; how stupid.

Pushing himself away from the door, Philip started to

88

undress, folding his clothes and laying them on to the ottoman at the end of his bed. When he was down to his striped shorts, he stepped behind the Murano glass panel that concealed bathroom from bedroom, pulled on a dressing gown and set to work with the aloe vera, small circular movements with his fingertips, clockwise and then anti-clockwise, bending over the basin, smoothing the cream into his exposed scalp. When he had finished, he set to on his cheeks and neck, cleaned and flossed his teeth, then stepped back into the bedroom.

He looked at his watch again. Nearly midnight. It was time for bed, but before he pulled back the quilt and lowered the lights, Philip went over to the armoire, pushed aside the clothes hanging there and opened the room safe. He bent down to look inside. It was still there. The small rectangular package he'd brought from the States, a piece of thin board wrapped in tissue that fitted exactly the dimensions of his guidebook. Unable to resist, he reached for it, slid it from its tissue wrap, turned it to the light. A woman's face, in half-profile, the colours maybe a little faded but the better for it in Philip's opinion. It gave the portrait a softer, gentler texture. Almost dream-like.

He'd found it six months earlier at an auction house in New England, part of a job lot of prints and postcards and assorted watercolours stacked in a box in a far corner of the room. He'd spotted the painting immediately. It wasn't signed but he knew, just knew what it was. And so he'd waited there, in that chilly auction hall, until the lot finally came under the hammer and the box was his for twenty dollars. Twenty dollars. For a Vilotte.

He'd had it looked at, of course, and the expert he'd consulted had agreed it seemed highly likely the work could have been done by the Master. Those strokes there, that slash of colour for the lips. Absolutely typical.

But without a signature, sir . . .

The shrug. The smile. The portrait handed back.

And then, not a month after that auction in New England, he'd spotted the advertisement in the *Herald Tribune*. A painting course in Provence, a small select group, experienced artists only – each of his companions, Philip had no doubt, persuaded to apply as he had been by the possibility of meeting one of the great masters. How many of the courses advertised in the travel supplements and classified pages offered anything like that? None. And he'd been on enough of them to know.

When he saw that *Tribune* ad, it was like a sign. A voice calling to him. And he hadn't delayed. Cheque in the post and flight booked. The second course in a year, but so what? He enjoyed them. They were fun – the painting, the meeting new friends, another trip to Europe. And he was definitely getting the hang of it, he'd decided, the pastel sketch he'd finished that afternoon a very fine effort indeed.

All he had to do in the next few days was to try and get a moment alone with the man, show him the work, judge his reaction.

And if all went well – please God, please God – get it signed.

With a sigh, Philip folded the tissue over the portrait, put it back in the safe and locked it away.

20

Régine Bouvet watched her husband cross Monastère's courtyard heading for their private quarters. He'd had a long day and it was late, stars glittering in a warm, velvet sky, ivy rustling in the breeze, a few bats flitting through the arches of the first cloister. Dinner in Le Réfectoire was long over, most of the staff had gone back to their lodgings and the bar would soon close. Somewhere from the cloister came the sound of a door slamming.

Out in the lobby Didier was tidying up the reception desk as the end of his shift approached. Any minute now he'd follow Claude across the courtyard and close the main gate. Turning back to her keyboard, Régine scrolled through the guest list.

Of the seven rooms on the cloister level, Gilles Gavan's painting party accounted for the six facing north with valley views – the four Americans, Madame Becque, the *Anglaise* and Gilles himself – while Lens was accommodated in the smaller guest room with the more limited views of the approach road and Luissac.

Up on the loggia Monsieur Ginoux had his usual suite, the largest of the four on that level, his driver accommodated in the hotel annexe down in Luissac. Next to Ginoux, in the 'double' suite, was Roland Bressans, his third visit so far that year but the first time he'd had company. Régine blew out her cheeks as she read the name, and let out a soft, dismissive *pouff*! What Mademoiselle Ghislaine Ladouze knew about taking a letter or keeping an appointments book, Régine could write on the tip of the perfectly manicured nail of her little finger. She wondered why Bressans should have bothered with the two suites. Why not just the one?

Then, at the far end of the loggia, there was that swarthy-looking Monsieur Kónar, always skulking around with that camera of his. According to his registration form, the man lived in Rome. He also carried a well-stamped Italian passport, the sullen, unshaven features in the accompanying photo giving him the shifty look of a Corsican bandit. *Arabe*, for sure, thought Régine; she'd put money on it. As for his companion, Mademoiselle Branigan, she'd written 'actress' on her form and 'BeeJay Productions' in Los Angeles for her address. Régine had thought she looked familiar when the two of them checked in but she still hadn't managed to place her. A pretty little thing, no doubt about that, but just a little . . . vacant. *Un peu vide*.

With a contented sigh Régine clicked out of the page and sat back in her chair.

Tout complet.

Her favourite words. The comforting ring of them. Their simple, three-syllable . . . completeness. And such a powerful meaning, so warming, so invigorating. Not even the prospect of the late shift on Reception – covering for Marcel who'd called in sick – could quite dilute the wonder of those words.

Across the courtyard, Régine saw the lights switch off in their gatehouse bedroom, to be replaced by the glow of a television. Claude would fall asleep in front of it for sure, thought Régine, which meant she'd have to leave the desk in an hour or so to turn it off.

Outside her office she heard Champeau tunelessly whistling his way across the lobby. She glanced at the clock on her desk and smiled. Midnight exactly. Champeau was never late. Never had been, never would be. The ever-reliable Champeau with those brown soulful eyes and that wide innocent face – a prankster, a joker, always up to no good. But you couldn't be cross with him . . . that big mischievous smile of his. And the small hump, of course. The curvature of the spine that hadn't been corrected when it should have been. The reason that, behind his misshapen back, there were some amongst the staff who dropped the 'p' and called him 'Chameau'. Camel. Of course they never dared say it to his face, or if his mother was within earshot. In matters pertaining to the running of the hotel and her son, Madame Champeau was not a woman to cross.

Some people could be very cruel, Régine reflected. But not Didier. Out in Reception she heard the old concierge briefing Champeau, running him through everything that had to be done – collecting and returning shoes left outside rooms for cleaning, tidying the salons, lowering lights, emptying ashtrays, watering plants. Champeau would have heard the same night-shift briefing a thousand times, but dear Champeau always needed reminding.

A moment later, Didier poked his head round the office door.

'*Bonsoir, madame, à demain.*'

'*Oui, à demain, Didier, et merci.*'

'Full house again, madame. Seven weekends in a row. It's good, no?'

'Very good, Didier. Very good indeed.'

21

Emile Dutronc did what he did best, keeping to the shadows, watching, listening. After coming up from Luissac he'd checked the perimeter walls, then slipped through the Monastère's main gates just moments before the concierge crossed the courtyard to close them. He didn't think the man had spotted him. Just a shadow. Just as it should be.

Skirting the far wall of the gravelled courtyard, he'd ducked through the passage that led to the cloisters and climbed the outside stairs to the first level where his boss, Ginoux, had his room.

Once Ginoux's lights were out, Dutronc padded around the loggia and settled himself across the cloister, hunkering down by the small chapel where he had the best view of the gardens, the upper and lower guest levels and, beyond, through the pillared cloisters, the Monastère's courtyard. Pulling a cigarette from his pocket he lit up and listened to the gentle shuffle and rattle of the palm fronds. Except for the cigarette it was like any other night op he'd ever done. Staying low, keeping his eyes and ears open. With no moon showing yet, the only light came from a ceiling of stars. It reminded him of the desert – dark, empty, eerily comforting – where he'd been trained, and fought. In Montparnasse you were lucky to see a full moon, let alone stars.

Which was one of the reasons Dutronc so liked these little outings, their trips out of town. Taking care of the man, keeping him safe, watching out for any threat. It was like the old days.

Dutronc pulled back his cuff and glanced at his watch. Closing on two o'clock. Another ten minutes and he'd call it a night. He was about to light up another cigarette when he suddenly tensed. Glanced to his left. Down there, in the far corner of the cloister, he was sure of it. A shadow, the softest whisper of a shoe on stone.

He scanned the line of columns forming the cloistered arcade below him but could see nothing.

It was just when he thought he'd been imagining things that he heard another shuffle of feet and what sounded like a grunt. It could have been a dog but he'd seen none on the property, and his instincts told him differently. Instead of leaving the cloister, heading back to Luissac, he stayed on. Another thirty minutes. An hour. He was used to it.

Later, Emile Dutronc made his way back to the courtyard, opened the small Judas door and slipped back the way he had come.

Part Two

Part Two

22

Saturday

Daniel Jacquot reached for his cigarettes, tapped one on the table-top and lit up. A deep, long pull. He sat back in his chair and let out his breath with an appreciative 'Aaaahhh', though no sound could be heard. It was in his head only, that 'Aaaahhh'. The pleasure of it, at last. He'd held off right through the meal – as much to enjoy the moment when it finally arrived, as to placate old Madame Hublé who did not approve of her guests smoking, even less of them smoking between courses. Even if, like Jacquot, they were taking their Saturday lunch in Le Tilleul's gravelled garden, a warm summer breeze shuffling over the auberge's ivy skin, shifting lazily through the acacias in the parking lot and in the branches of the lime tree that spread a dancing shade over his table.

Dressed in stifling widow's weeds, winter or summer, Madame

Hublé always sat in the same place, in a wicker chair outside the kitchen door in the shade of a trellis bound with jasmine, stout shoes set apart like black bookends in the gravel, eyes darting from one table to the next. Occasionally she would stir herself to secure the corner of a tablecloth flapping in the breeze. Or she'd call out for her granddaughter – '*Laure! Laure! Viens ici. Vite! Vite!*' when she saw a bottle of wine emptied, or the last crust of bread taken from a basket, or a piece of cutlery fall from a table. The only thing Madame Hublé didn't bother with was a full ashtray. Fill it as much as you like, her disapproving look seemed to say, but you'll never get a clean one from me.

The first time he caught that look, Jacquot had tried to soften her displeasure.

'I smoke between courses, *chère* madame, because I could be called away at any moment,' he'd told her gently, with a smile, waving the cigarette between his fingers.

'It makes no difference,' she'd replied sternly. 'It's bad for you. It's dangerous. You know it and I know it.'

'And so is police work, madame,' Jacquot had continued, hardening just a little. 'And driving a car. Or taking a train, or an aeroplane . . .'

She hadn't replied, just looked at him. A dark disapproving look. He wasn't sure whether he had just won, or lost, his argument.

It was familiar, that disapproving look. It reminded Jacquot of another widow he knew, the equally formidable Madame Foraque, his landlady back in Marseilles, her grey woollen leggings pulled up over thick stockings, her black beret perched on its bed of wiry terracotta hair, her cheeks rouged and her narrow eyes thickly, globbily mascara'ed. Except, of course, that the Widow Foraque smoked – ferociously – those evil little cheroots from Tabac Delorme that she loved so much, puffing away as she sat at her window with her chattering budgerigars, Mittie and Chirrie, watching the world go by. And watching for him too – usually with that same disapproving eye: his comings and goings, his late nights and early mornings, his occasional companions, his ponytail, his boots.

He'd sent her postcards, of course – always liked a postcard, did Madame Foraque. Every couple of weeks, a scribbled message saying how he missed her rabbit stew, or that Cavaillon wasn't Marseilles. Of course, she never wrote back.

Inevitably, thinking of Madame Foraque – *Gran'maman*, he called her – was usually the sad prelude to other memories. Marseilles, the city he'd grown up in, the city he loved: his sunlit apartment high on the hill of Le Panier; the bustle and energy of La Canebière and République and Paradis and St-Ferréol; the markets of Quai des Belges and Capucins; the shifting glare of the sun off the sea and the snapping of the wind through the forest of masts on the Vieux Port.

And then there were the friends he'd left behind: Sydné and César and their roof-terrace parties overlooking the Vieux Port; the Harbour Master, Salette, and that little sloop of his, the two of them setting sail for an evening's drinking in some deserted *calanque* down the coast; Rully, his partner on Homicide and those endless games of backgammon they'd play at Bar de la Marine on Quai de Rive Neuve, or Café Parisien on Place Sadi Carnot.

And the rest of the squad – the team he played with, all of them working homicide with the Marseilles *Judiciaire*: Claude Peluze, the ex-Legionnaire who always looked like he needed a shave five minutes after putting down the razor; Al Grenier, the oldest man on the team and the only one who didn't call Jacquot 'boss'; the stutterer Chevin (single) and the surfer Dutoit (divorced) who shared a flat together overlooking Prado Plage; Laganne, always chewing a toothpick and the smoker Charlie Serre (Madame Hublé would have loved him); Bernie Muzon with his signature black jeans and scuffed trainers; and Isabelle Cassier, the only woman on the homicide squad back then.

Isabelle, with the urchin haircut and sinuous, willing little body, the one who'd helped him move to Cavaillon after Yves Guimpier, the section chief, suspended him, gave him the choice between early retirement or a dead-end posting in the Vaucluse. Isabelle, who'd helped him find the cramped *atelier* where he now lived in the rafters above Cavaillon's Cours Bournissac, helped him furnish it, brought a feminine touch, turned it into a kind of home away from home.

Isabelle.

Four months they'd been together, his first months in the new posting, the odd overnight here and there when their jobs allowed and most weekends when she could get away from Marseilles, driving up to Cavaillon to be with him. Having her had made the move easier to bear, something to look forward to as he worked his way through a week of odds and sods that, in the Vaucluse, never seemed to amount to anything.

And then she'd called one evening, from Marseilles, to say that she wouldn't be coming to visit any more, that she'd decided to call it a day. Said she knew his heart wasn't in it. Said she didn't blame him, but it wasn't doing her any good, felt that their little *liaison* wasn't going anywhere.

Jacquot suspected that she was right. And that was that.

Later, he learned from Bernie Muzon that she'd requested a transfer to Paris, to be close to an ailing mother.

Jacquot leaned forward and stubbed out his cigarette, reached for the last of his wine. He caught Madame Hublé's eye and raised the glass to her. She lifted her chin and nodded, acknowledging the toast – and the fact that he wasn't smoking any more. Jacquot wondered how long it would be, that glorious Saturday afternoon, sitting in the garden at Le Tilleul, before he reached for another cigarette and set the cat among the pigeons once more.

They knew him here, of course. He'd eaten at Le Tilleul a dozen times or more since his transfer from Marseilles. Rochet, his new station chief, who also liked his food, had recommended the place, an old coaching inn off the Apt-Cavaillon road. The Mathieux, he'd said, the family that run it, they do a good table. Jacquot, of course, had followed up the recommendation. And Rochet was right. They did, indeed, do a good table. Along with Gaillard's Brasserie in Cavaillon, Le Tilleul had quickly become a favourite.

The first time Jacquot had visited – driving back from Apt after confronting a farmer who'd killed a neighbour's truffle hound – a late lunch had meant time for a main course only: a fillet of sea-trout poached in anise and served with samphire, and a *demi* of Pradeaux Rosé. The following weekend he was back again, dinner this time, with Isabelle, their pavé steaks grilled *au feu du bois*, the vine trimmings spitting and crackling beneath the meat giving it a sweet, smoky taste that made them both fall silent from the first mouthful. Not a word till they finished. That good. And since then . . . well, any excuse would do. And a twenty, even a thirty kilometre detour . . . *pouff!* Just a small inconvenience when measured against the certain pleasures of a Tilleul table.

But it wasn't simply because he'd become a regular customer that the Mathieux family knew him. That was down to Jacquot's past.

Patric, the Tilleul's *chef-patron* and Madame Hublé's long-suffering son-in-law, had been the first to recognise him. Coming out of the kitchen that first lunchtime, wiping his hands on his apron and seeing who was still there, his eyes had settled on Jacquot in the far corner of the garden.

Glancing up from his newspaper – open at the Sports section: Béziers back in the rankings; the French squad looking for a new manager and trainer; Bidulphes off the pitch with a cruciate ligament injury – Jacquot had caught Patric's eye, a nod of greeting from the *patron*, a returned nod of thanks for a fine lunch. And then, as Patric turned back to the house, a frown had settled across the owner's brow. A second look back. Something familiar. But where? When? An old customer returned?

Jacquot knew what was going through Patric's head, and knew that Patric had him placed by the time he reached the bar to check the lunchtime's take. A pause, another glance back through the door just to be sure, a whisper to his wife Viviane. It was the ponytail that always gave Jacquot away, that and the broken nose and the bulk of him.

Jacquot could imagine the words. 'It's him, I'm telling you, Viv. Number six. The try. You know the one. Ran the length of the pitch. In London. One of the great tries, *hein*?'

And Madame, not altogether sure, but prepared to take it from her husband, nodding. 'If you say so . . .'

And then, a few minutes later, Patric had come to his table, two glasses of white wine in his hands – big, strong hands that dwarfed the glasses, the kind of hands that could hold down a squealing piglet, the nails short, fingers thick, red and scored with nicks.

'Bandol's all well and good down by the coast,' he'd begun by way of introduction, 'but there's nothing wrong with what we've got out there,' he continued, nodding to the vines beyond the garden wall. He placed one of the glasses in front of Jacquot. '*Voilà*, Château La Verrerie, down near Cadenet.' With a flick of his wrist he swirled the wine in his glass, sniffed, took a sip. 'A '93. Still fresh but building well.' And then, with a twinkle in his eye. 'A player, you might say. *N'est-ce pas*, monsieur . . . Jacquot? *Le numéro six*, eh?'

And so it had begun. Patric had sat himself down at Jacquot's table and for the next two hours, to Madame Hublé's considerable displeasure, the two of them had talked rugby and wine and smoked like bushfires fanned by an evil wind. And in the months that followed, with regular instruction from Patric Mathieu and Laurent Gaillard in Cavaillon, Jacquot ditched the Bandols and, under their direction, made his way through most of the Lubéron's finest names: Val-Joanis, Grand Callamand, de Mille and de l'Isolette from Apt, Saint-Pierre de Méjans from Puyvert and Canorgue in its signature blue bottle.

Watching the shadows of the lime tree playing gently across his table – thinking back over Patric's *rillette du Lapereau*, the *tranche* of sea bass, its silvery skin grilled to a blistered coat, and last year's plums soaked in Armagnac and served with *biscotti* – Jacquot decided that this was how all Saturdays should be spent. How every day should be.

It was moments like these, he thought, when life was good. A fine lunch, cool shade, the company of friends and the swirling tinkle of ice in the wine bucket.

And that first cigarette . . .

The rest of the time, well, you got through it. Somehow. Work was OK; it passed the time – phones ringing, people to see, truffle-hound killers to put the fear of God into. It was afterwards, when the sun slipped past the chapel on the hill of St Jacques back in Cavaillon, and shadows pooled into twilight, that things deteriorated. Evenings alone on Cours Bournissac – after maybe a couple of calvas at Fin de Siècle. Watching TV, hiring a video if there was nothing on, catching up with his laundry, cooking something for supper that he never seemed able to finish.

And then, worst of all, *le weekend*. That long haul from Friday night – whatever time he got home – until Monday morning. A couple of times, he had met up with Rully and Peluze, a drink together, dinner somewhere, hearing how Yves Guimpier, their station chief, was trying to sort things, get him back to Marseilles.

Until then, it was Cavaillon. Whether Jacquot liked it or not.

But it wasn't all bad. As time passed and the seasons changed, Jacquot had decided that while Cavaillon would never be Marseilles, the melons were the best he'd ever tasted, the countryside as glorious as any he knew and, with summer settling around him, the Lubéron was far from a hardship posting.

Especially when you'd just enjoyed a long, leisurely lunch at Le Tilleul, albeit under the watchful eye of old Madame Hublé.

Somewhere inside the house a telephone started to bleat. Jacquot glanced at his watch. A little after three. He was reaching for his cigarettes and wondering if he should have another glass of wine, or maybe something stronger, when Patric's daughter, Laure, leaned out of the back door with the phone cradled against her shoulder. She wore a soft angora cardigan, just like her mother's, but pink, not blue.

'*Monsieur Daniel, c'est pour vous. Vous êtes ici? Ou non?*'

23

The phone smelled of Laure, a sweet, fresh, flowery scent. Leaning up against the door jamb, Jacquot watched her cross the dining room and start clearing one of the tables, a thin cotton print dress lifting and flicking around the backs of her suntanned legs, heels lifting out of her flat-backed espadrilles.

He gave a sigh. What was she? Eighteen? Nineteen? Maybe twenty?

'Daniel? *Tu es là?*'

Jacquot had seen her in Cavaillon only the week before – laced espadrilles this time, a pair of blue short-shorts, a tight T-shirt and what looked like an old man's waistcoat – swinging through the old town arm in arm with the son of the owner of the Loge d'Épines. She'd seen Jacquot and waved, but he'd recognised the smile that went with it: 'Look,' the smile said. 'It's a beautiful day and I'm in love and isn't he gorgeous?'

Jacquot had waved back, smiled and flicked his hand at the wrist. He was pleased for her. But sad too. For the rest of the day he'd felt as old as Methuselah. And twice as lonely.

'Daniel? Daniel, is that you?' said the voice again.

Jacquot came to with a start. He recognised the caller immediately, but the christian name took him by surprise. As far as he could remember, it was the first time that Rochet, his new station chief at Cavaillon, had used it.

'Oui. Oui. C'est moi,' said Jacquot.

'A good choice, Le Tilleul,' continued Rochet. 'Did you have Madame's *figues*?'

'The plums in Armagnac,' replied Jacquot. 'With Monsieur's rillettes to start, and the sea bass.' He could almost see Rochet nodding, that slim smile of approval, but Jacquot knew that Rochet wasn't calling to ask about lunch or to compare notes on the Mathieux's table. Also, clearly, Rochet had been determined to find him. So far as Jacquot could recall he had told no one he was going to Le Tilleul for lunch that Saturday, and the station chief would have had to call round to track him down. There was also, as well as his use of Jacquot's christian name, an unfamiliar softness to his boss's voice, a hesitancy, a sense of . . . embarrassment.

'I tried Pascal at Scaramouche and then Gaillard's,' continued Rochet, confirming Jacquot's suspicions, 'but then I thought, a day like this, I'd want to be in the countryside. In a garden.'

So Rochet had been looking for him, and clearly determined to find him. He wondered what Rochet was after.

'They still have goldfish in their carafes?'

Jacquot glanced at the nearest table. A pair of angel-winged goldfish stared out through the glass. It was Viviane, Patric's wife, who'd explained why they did it. One summer, she told

Jacquot, Henri Toulouse-Lautrec had stayed at the house on one of his many excursions from Paris. During his stay the painter had been an extravagant host, entertaining a number of local friends, but since he disapproved of people drinking water he'd put goldfish into the carafes to deter them. *Voilà!*

'Still the goldfish,' Jacquot replied.

For a moment or two there was silence down the line. Across the room, Laure snapped out a clean linen cloth and laid it across the table she'd just cleared, there was a clatter of pans from the kitchen and Madame Hublé hobbled in from the courtyard. She gave Jacquot a nod and headed for the bar, as much for the shade as the opportunity to listen into his conversation.

And then, softly, down the line: 'Of course, I know it's your weekend off, Daniel, but there's something I need you to do . . . A favour . . . In Luissac . . . It's not that far from Le Tilleul . . . I'd be most grateful . . .'

24

The Hôtel Grand Monastère des Évêques stood on a point of gold, grey limestone rearing up over the Gaudins Cut on the northern slopes of the Grand Lubéron.

Jacquot saw it first as he took the right-hand fork out of St-Mas-des-Tombes, a glimpse of stone ramparts still some distance above him, flickering between the holm oak and cypress trees that bordered the road. It looked like the prow of some mighty ship thrusting out into thin air, breaking over the calm sea of the Calavon Valley.

He'd heard about it, of course; it was widely regarded as one of the finest hotels in the Lubéron, in Vaucluse too, and way up there with the very best in the whole of Provence. That's what they all said, when the name Grand Monastère was mentioned, or Le Réfectoire, the Monastère's equally celebrated dining room.

'*Sensationnel.*'

'*Sans pareil.*'

'Next year, for certain, a Michelin star. Or two.' That was what the reviewers declared. But Jacquot had never visited it.

On the telephone at Le Tilleul, Rochet had given little away and, with old Madame Hublé standing so close, Jacquot had taken care in his responses; and catching the old woman's eye as she leafed through the spiked lunch receipts, been even more guarded with his questions. All he could really say, as he settled *l'addition* with Viviane and bid '*adieu*' to Laure, Patric and, of course, Madame Hublé, was that he'd been asked to check out a problem at the Hôtel Grand Monastère; that he should speak to the Monastère's owner, a Claude Bouvet, who'd bring him up to speed; and that whatever the 'problem' turned out to be it would, Rochet had stressed, require a certain tact, a certain . . . softening of focus, that the 'problem', whatever it was, should be dealt with quietly . . . *sans bruit*.

Rochet's instructions had been as vague, but as pointed as that. Instructions, Jacquot suspected, that Rochet had received himself, probably word for word, from someone higher up the chain of command. A little job that needed doing. A blind eye. That was what all this was about. Jacquot also suspected that, even if he'd been able to ask more probing questions, out of Madame Hublé's earshot, his boss would have been unable to supply any more concrete information. Maybe, thought Jacquot, he didn't know the details himself.

As he climbed away from the valley, light-headed from lunch, the swollen rows of lavender flicking past, the scent of pine and wild fennel growing stronger the higher the road climbed, Jacquot speculated on the likely reason for this Saturday afternoon call-out. A fight maybe, between two of Monastère's often celebrated and certainly wealthy guests? Or a lover's tiff gone wrong – a bleeding nose or broken furniture? Some problem with staff? A theft? Whatever it was, he'd find out soon enough.

On the cassette player, the Steely Dan tape he'd been playing on the drive to Le Tilleul came to an end. As he negotiated the turns out of St-Mas he flipped it out, flung it on the passenger seat and reached for a new tape from the door pocket. He didn't bother to look at who or what it was. César, his old friend in Marseilles, knew and shared his musical tastes and every month or so sent a compilation to Cours Bournissac. Every song that César selected either was, or rapidly became, a favourite. In fact, it was always something of a treat to hear those first few bars and realise what his friend had selected. Lucky dip. This time it began with an old Rolling Stones' number, and as Jagger growled his way through 'Midnight Mile', Jacquot played the wheel with one hand and tapped the fingers of the other on the outside door panel.

Saturday afternoon, a good lunch honourably despatched, fine music and gorgeous sun-warmed countryside. It didn't get much better than this, he decided. And whatever lay in store, Jacquot had to admit he was glad for this unexpected diversion. Before the call, sitting in Le Tilleul's garden, he'd been wondering how to spend the rest of the day. Now, tracked down by his station chief, he had something to do.

When Jagger reached the end of his moonlit mile, a brief silence from the tape was followed by a tripping piano intro. Then came the high-hat cymbals and that gentle dum-dum boom of the double bass that reached down, deep inside. Jacquot smiled. No doubt about it. The King. Not Elvis – Nat. Nat 'King' Cole. One of Jacquot's all-time favourites. No matter how many times he heard it, he never tired of it – those trickly sweet, schoolyard lyrics and that magnificent piano.

As the road narrowed and rose, Jacquot started to hum and then sing along – the words rushing back:

> *. . . Someone to bless me,*
> *Whenever I sneeze . . .*
> *Let there be cuckoos,*
> *A lark and a dove.*
> *But first of all, pleeeease . . . let there be love.*
> *Mmm-mmh, love. Ah-ooh love.*
> *Let there be lo-ve.'*

Then that piano again, that trickling, tripping finale.
And the voice. *'Oh yea . . . hhhhh!'*
The sign for Luissac, half-buried in a high bank of clambering rose, took Jacquot by surprise, and he swung to the right as indicated, up an even steeper, narrower road than the one out of St-Mas-des-Tombes, the Peugeot's transmission groaning for a moment at the unexpected incline, then settling into the correct gear.

It wasn't until he reached the outskirts of Luissac and passed two more signs that Jacquot realised the journey wasn't yet over. The first sign, with white letters on a brown ground, bore the legend *'Monument Historique'*, and a few metres further on there was another board with an arrow pointing upwards, and the words: 'Hôtel Grand Monastère des Évêques. *Toute droite, à trois kilometres'*.

The distance surprised Jacquot. From the road, twisting up through the woods, it had looked as though the Grand Monastère was actually in Luissac, its battlements rising up from the village's rooftops, rather than three kilometres beyond it. Slowing his speed as he entered the settlement, Jacquot drove along Luissac's main street and across the tiny *place*, tyres drubbing over the cobbles, noting as he passed that every window appeared to be shuttered, as though the people who lived there were inside sleeping off lunch. Indeed, some of the dwellings looked so silent, so empty, that Jacquot guessed they must be holiday homes, opened up for the weekend, or summer rentals, but otherwise deserted.

On the other side of Luissac, past a road-sign indicating *Sans Issue*, the road narrowed again though the surface, thankfully, remained good. The only difference here was that the rising battlements and buttresses of the Grand Monastère had now vanished, hidden by the steeply wooded slopes and garrigue-covered ledges that loomed above him, the road ahead curving round to the right, and then the left, cutting into a wall of limestone on one side and flirting with a sheer drop on the other, just the tips of cypress trees growing somewhere down below showing above the low wall that edged the road.

The tape came to an end but Jacquot didn't replace it, playing the wheel with both hands as he negotiated the increasingly sharper twists of the road, passing in and out of the sunshine with every turn.

And then he was there, the final turn, tyres swishing through a watery run-off from the heights above. And, he had to admit, he did draw in his breath. The road ahead, now curving away from the limestone bluffs, crossed an arched bridge spanning the Gaudins Cut, the only possible access to the Grand Monastère, its lofty stone walls rising up against a blue Provençal sky. A minute or two later, coming off the bridge, Jacquot swung the Peugeot into a wide cobbled turning circle, and parked in the shade beside a half-dozen other cars.

So this was it, thought Jacquot. The great Monastère. Leaning forward he looked up through the windscreen at the stone-blocked walls towering above him. Big, bold and implacable – more a fortress than a monastery – its single entrance a large arched gate of chevroned timbers, the two halves swung open to reveal a gravelled courtyard beyond.

As he got out of the car and walked to the gate, Jacquot wondered what was in store.

It didn't take him long to find out.

25

Crossing the gravelled courtyard, now cast into late-afternoon shadow, Jacquot stepped between a pair of chipped romanesque columns, laid artfully either side of an arched panel of glass, and entered the main reception hall of the Grand Monastère.

As the door whispered shut behind him, Jacquot paused to take in the view – a stone-flagged floor some twenty square metres in size set with a half-dozen fluted stone columns that fanned out to support a barrel-vaulted ceiling patched here and there with pale fragments of fresco. The space was cool, clean and lean, just two nests of sofas and scroll-winged armchairs in the centre of the room, each of the room's four corners set with a copper cauldron planted with flowering cacti.

From where he stood Jacquot could also see, on his left, the wide sweep of a stone staircase and, beyond it, three separate arches of glass, each with its own glass door, that led, he assumed, to dining room, bar and terrace. As at Le Tilleul, lunch was long over and the hall deserted, silent save for a muted Pachelbel adagio rising from unseen speakers. Monastère's guests were either out by the pool, up in their rooms rousing themselves from their *siestes*, or still not returned from their afternoon outings.

On his right, facing the stairs and stretching at least half the length of the hall, was a single length of solid dressed stone resting on a subtly lit but shorter wood pedestal. With candles and cloth and Eucharist it would have served as an extravagant altar, but nothing save a pair of small copper cauldrons filled with lilies and set at either end decorated its surface. The only thing that Jacquot could make out was what appeared to be a suitably tonsured head midway between the lilies, peeping over the ledge of stone.

As Jacquot made for the head – and presumably the reception desk – a phone sounded somewhere behind it and the head promptly disappeared. When Jacquot was only a few steps away, the head reappeared and a man, somewhere in his fifties, turned towards him, smiled, then pointed at the phone, held up his hand. He would only be a minute, he mimed.

'*Bonjour, Grand Monastère,*' he began, the greeting automatic, the voice silkily welcoming and helpful.

'A reservation for two for dinner? This evening? I'm afraid we're fully booked, monsieur.' This apology was accompanied by a hand stroked over his bald pate, a hitch to his open shirt collar and then, out of sight below the stone ledge, a loosening tug at his belt.

'A table for six? Lunch tomorrow? *Je suis désolé, monsieur.* We are fully booked for tomorrow lunch as well. *Tout complet. Je regrette . . . de rien, monsieur.*'

Putting down the phone, the man behind the desk placed both hands on the stone counter and leaned towards Jacquot.

'Monsieur, welcome to Hôtel Grand Monastère des Évêques. I'm so sorry . . .' he continued, nodding at the phone. 'How may I be of help?'

And then Jacquot saw the man suddenly stiffen, work his shoulders, the smile fade. He had suddenly realised who Jacquot was and what he was going to say.

Jacquot didn't disappoint him.

'*Bonjour, monsieur*. I'm looking for a Claude Bouvet?'

'*Oui. C'est moi. C'est moi*,' replied Bouvet, keen to get the introductions over with, anxiously casting around the hall in case a guest should appear.

'My name is Chief Inspector Jacquot, from Cavaillon. I believe you were expecting me? That I may be of help in some way?'

'Of course, yes.' For a second he seemed not to know what else to say, then he reached below the stone, opened a drawer and held up a large iron key. 'Let me take you straight up.'

A moment later Bouvet bustled around the end of the stone slab and, after the two men had shaken hands, he indicated that Jacquot should follow him.

'You got here much sooner than I imagined,' said Bouvet, heading towards the staircase.

'I was in the neighbourhood, monsieur. It was no trouble,' replied Jacquot.

The two men trotted up the stairs.

'A beautiful place,' said Jacquot when they reached the first landing, as grandly vaulted as the hall below.

'Thank you,' replied Bouvet, pointing to a stone passage on their left and letting Jacquot go ahead. 'It is very special, isn't it? Sixteenth- and seventeenth-century mostly, but one or two parts are even older.' Enclosed by the stone, his voice took on a dull, hollow sound. 'So you haven't been here before, then?'

'First time,' replied Jacquot, stepping out of the passage into a stone-flagged loggia that overlooked an expanse of cloistered garden. They were high enough now for the setting sun to show above the Monastère's walls and both men instinctively held up a hand to shade their eyes.

'And you are the owner, I believe?' Jacquot continued. So far as he could see, the two levels of cloister ran round all four sides of the garden below, a darting flash of swallows swooping around the three palm trees that rose up from its centre, the air filled with their twittering and the fast brush of their flight.

'My wife and I,' said Bouvet, leading Jacquot along the gallery. 'The place has been in her family for close to a hundred years now . . .' And then, 'It's here,' he said, stopping at a door with a *Pas Dérangez* sign hanging from its handle. Bending down, Bouvet fitted the key into the lock. He turned it with a suitably ancient clunk, swung open the door, then stood aside.

'*Voilà, monsieur*. After you.'

26

Jacquot stood in the doorway and looked into the room. It was in shadow, the closed shutters of its four open windows slicing slatted lines of warm gold sunlight across the stone floor. A breeze had started up and the muslin drops each side of the windows stirred gently. It was not, as Jacquot had suspected, a bedroom, but a comfortably appointed salon, its ceiling closely beamed and its walls an ancient pitted stone decorated in certain areas by ragged patches of the palest frescoes.

Like good hotels the world over, the room was furnished for its purpose – a chair and a desk between two of the windows, a roll-top sofa and two elegantly winged armchairs placed around a stone fireplace, and a pair of armoire doors set into the far wall. One of the doors was open and Jacquot could see three shelves set with a hi-fi unit, a selection of CDs and books. There was a rug in the middle of the stone floor, pictures on the wall, and a phone and notepad on the desk, a small rubbish bin beneath.

But that's where all similarity with other hotels ended. This was a salon with a difference. As clean and lean in style as the Monastère's reception hall, this room had had a designer make-over: the armchairs and sofa upholstered in vibrant yellow dots the size of a side plate scattered across a blue background, the pictures on the walls opaque glass panels etched with the kind of extravagant plants that one might see in the borders of some ancient bestiary, the rug a sisal mat dyed the same yellow as the dots on the furniture, with blue spots this time. A coat of arms – a pyramid of cardinals' hats linked by their tasselled ties – and the year 1647 had been cut into the stone mantle above the hearth, the incisions highlighted with gold. Where once logs had burned, a tall glass vase held a spray of purple and yellow irises, a half-dozen smaller glass bowls set around it holding church candles.

Jacquot took a breath and smelled perfume – expensive perfume – and noted the fashion magazines in an armchair by the stone fireplace, a pair of cream open-toed stilettos and a woman's jacket over the back of the desk chair. As far as Jacquot could see, standing in the doorway, there was nothing out of order.

'Quite a place,' said Jacquot, stepping at last into the room.

'It used to be the Abbot's study,' offered Bouvet, following behind, closing the door after them. 'Before that, who knows?'

'And the problem, exactly?' asked Jacquot, glancing back at Bouvet.

The man looked suddenly nervous. His hands clasped, and his breath came short and sharp.

'Through there. In the bedroom,' replied Bouvet, pointing to a frescoed stone panel on the left of the fireplace.

Jacquot crossed to the panel, as solid-looking as any of the walls, a long fluted panel of stone running from floor to ceiling.

Only it wasn't stone. It was painted wood, with no giveaway edges that Jacquot could see, and no handle save a smudge about halfway up on one side.

'You just push it, like this,' said Bouvet, reaching forward. And, with the tiniest click, the entire panel swung back to reveal the bedroom beyond.

'Ingenious, don't you think? Such convincing *trompe l'oeil*. The designer, Monsieur van der Haage, is staying with us at the moment. It is he who has . . .' Bouvet waved his hand at the panel, at the other changes that had clearly been wrought.

Standing in the doorway, Jacquot looked around the room. A chest of drawers, a dainty dressing table and chair, another armoire set into the walls, and a king-sized bed with bevelled posts at each corner that supported a pelmet of scarlet muslin and loosely clasped scarlet drapes. Immediately behind the bed was a floor-to-ceiling panel of scarlet glass. The richness of the colour against the bare stone walls and floor was extraordinary.

Once again, as far as Jacquot could determine, everything appeared to be in order: the bed made, the scarlet drapes shifting in the breeze from the open windows, the bedside tables tidily arranged.

Jacquot turned to Bouvet. 'Exactly what is it I'm supposed to be looking at here?'

'Why, the bed, monsieur. Just look at the bed.'

Jacquot went to the bed, raised on a small skirt of stone with a step around it. Again, nothing seemed to be amiss. The bed and its dressings were exactly as he would expect them to be – the scarlet drapes, the scarlet cover, the polished and bevelled corner posts. He went to the side of the bed and stepped up, looking down at it from another angle. But still he could see nothing.

'Pull back the bedding, monsieur. You will see.'

Jacquot did as he was told, reaching forward for the scarlet cover and peeling it back.

The pillows were as he would expect them, crisply ironed, prettily edged and embossed with 'GMdE' in the corner, resting on a bolster that ran the width of the bed. The quilt and bottom sheet were also white and still precisely creased down the middle. The bed had not been slept in.

'Further, monsieur. At the bottom of the bed,' said Bouvet from the door.

Jacquot did as he was told, feeling a certain resistance as he raised the quilt higher and drew it back. A sudden heaviness, as though the bedding was somehow wet.

Which it was.

Sodden and drenched.

With what looked like blood.

27

Jacquot dropped the quilt and reached out a hand to the scarlet cover. Though it was impossible to make out any blood on its surface, the material was damp to the touch. He looked at his fingers and saw faint smears of red on their tips, as though dye had come from the cover. He lifted the fingers to his nose, sniffed once. Nothing. Then touched the fingertips together. A definite stickiness. He leaned forward for the corner of the cover and wiped his fingers on it, then looked more carefully at the bed.

The bedclothes, he could see now, were soaked through, as though someone had emptied a bucket of blood on to the end of the bed. Animal or human, he wondered?

Stepping away he knelt down to examine the floor. No drop of blood could be seen. He returned to the foot of the bed and did the same, this time running his finger down the groove between the stone slabs. He examined his finger again. There was a scrawl of dirt on it, but also, unmistakeably, a damp brown smear that might once have been red. If it was blood, Jacquot decided, it had been spilt many hours earlier.

Jacquot got to his feet and walked around the room.

'Was the "Do Not Disturb" sign on the door when you found this?' asked Jacquot.

'It was, monsieur.'

'So Housekeeping won't have been in today to clean the room?'

'Absolutely not, monsieur. Our guests' privacy is strictly respected.'

Jacquot took this in, nodded. At one of the windows, he pushed open the shutters and leaned out. A twenty-metre drop ended in a bank of cactus and sabre-leaved aloe that sloped away at a steep angle towards the stony bed of the Gaudins Cut. Turning back to the room, he moved to the scarlet glass panel at the head of the bed, and looked around it. The panel concealed a bathroom in the middle of which stood an ancient roll-top tub.

'Tell me, how many towels are provided for each guest?'

'Two large bath wraps and four smaller hand towels,' replied Bouvet.

'And towelling robes?'

'Of course, monsieur. A pair. Large and small.'

Jacquot nodded. As far as he could see there was not a single towel to be seen. And no sign of the robes either. Not even a bath mat.

Back in the bedroom he crossed to the dressing table, its surface covered with combs, brushes, pins, make-up and scent bottles, then opened the armoire doors and trailed his fingers through a rack of skirts, dresses, jeans and jackets – enough clothes for a long stay. Closing its doors, he moved to the chest of drawers and pulled open the top drawer. As it slid open, the same perfume he could smell in the room rose from an extravagant tangle of silk and satin underwear – garters, suspender belts, a corset and basque, chemises, and sheer silk stockings, some still in their wrapping.

Jacquot was suddenly aware that Bouvet was watching him intently.

'And the guest, Monsieur Bouvet?' asked Jacquot, trawling his fingers through the contents of the drawer, pulling it right out so that he could see to the back panel. 'The lady to whom this room belongs?'

'Mademoiselle Ladouze. Ghislaine Ladouze.'

It was not Bouvet's voice.

Someone else had answered.

28

Jacquot turned to the voice, a rather garbled voice as though its owner was speaking through a mouthful of frappé ice. The man who had spoken was standing in the doorway beside Monsieur Bouvet. Taller and a little older than the hotelier, he was somewhere in his late fifties, Jacquot judged, but in good trim for his age; a striking-looking man with a canny sharpness to the face, a tight crop of wavy grey hair, and chill grey eyes that a smile did nothing to warm. The collar on his polo shirt was turned up, the tennis shorts were neatly creased and his white socks drawn to just below the knee. Stepping past Bouvet, he strode across the bedroom and, as he closed on Jacquot, he held out his hand. Jacquot had no option but to take it.

'Chief Inspector, this is—' Bouvet began, but the man held up a hand to silence him. He clearly made his own introductions.

'Bressans,' he said. 'Roland Bressans. And you are?'

'Jacquot, monsieur. Chief Inspector Jacquot. From Cavaillon.'

Bressans let go of Jacquot's hand and stepped back, looked him up and down. Jacquot suspected it was the kind of thing Bressans did when he met someone for the first time – a cool, calculating appraisal. But it rather annoyed him. He didn't really appreciate being measured up in such a brazen manner.

'It's kind of you to come out at such short notice, Chief Inspector. I'm sure it's nothing . . . a joke or something. She'll probably walk through the door any moment.' Bressans gave a light laugh.

'So, monsieur,' Jacquot began, taking back the initiative, 'you know this . . . this Mademoiselle Ladouze?'

'We are travelling together, the two of us. We arrived here on Wednesday evening. Up from Marseilles. I have the room next door.'

'And you were the one who found this?' Jacquot turned to the bed, gestured to the scarlet cover.

'That's correct, Chief Inspector.'

'And when was that?'

'Just before lunch. I'd reserved a table for the two of us on the terrace . . . such a lovely day . . . but when I came to collect her, there was a "Do Not Disturb" sign on her door.'

'This sign. Do you know how long it had been there?'

Bressans gave it some thought. 'I really can't say.'

'You didn't notice it earlier? When you went down to breakfast, perhaps?'

'I had Room Service bring me breakfast. I had some work to attend to.'

'But you knocked on the door anyway? Despite the sign.'

Bressans shook his head. 'Not immediately, no. I assumed that Ghislaine was resting, or having a bath. That she would join me for lunch when she was ready. So I went down ahead of her.'

'And then?'

'I had a drink at the bar, half-an-hour or so, then, when she still hadn't appeared, I came back. It was getting late. Lunch was in full swing and I was hungry. So this time I knocked, but there was still no answer. I tried the door handle but it was locked. So I went to my own room and came in through the connecting door.'

'These two suites are connected?'

'That's right. In the salon there is a panel which—'

'Perhaps you would show me, monsieur.'

'Why, of course,' replied Bressans, waving at Bouvet to make space for them as he turned to leave the bedroom, and indicating that Jacquot should follow him. 'It's here. Beside the desk.' Bressans touched the wall and it split apart, two *trompe l'oeil* doors opening on to another salon, decorated and furnished in the same designer style. Jacquot noted a packed suitcase standing by the sofa.

Jacquot turned to Bouvet. 'Are all the suites on this level connected in this way?'

'Just these two, monsieur. The others have frescoes on the party walls and, well, there was no way the Bureau des Rénovations was going to let us—'

'This panel, can it be locked? Both sides?'

'Of course, monsieur,' said Bouvet. 'But for families, and for travelling companions like Monsieur Bressans and Mademoiselle Ladouze, it can be unlocked, *comme ça*. Opened up. For work, for entertaining. It makes a grand set of rooms. As you can see.'

Jacquot turned back to Bressans.

'So, when you returned from the bar, and received no answer from your knocking, you went to your own room and came through here?'

'That's correct,' replied Bressans.

'. . . called out her name, and then went into the bedroom?'

'Correct, Chief Inspector.'

'But you didn't think to use this way in, when it was time to go down for lunch? Rather than go to the other door, outside, on the loggia?'

Bressans shook his head, as though the idea had never occurred to him. 'Of course, I could have done so. But . . . I simply didn't think of it.'

'So these doors were closed when you left your room?'

'That's right.'

'And locked?'

'No, just closed.'

'So they have been open during your stay?'

'Of course, when it was convenient. Work and things.'

'And when you came through into the salon, was the door to her bedroom open or closed?'

'Closed, I think. Yes, it was closed. I remember knocking.'

'But there was no answer. So you went in?'

'That's right, Chief Inspector. Which is when I noticed the bed. The blood . . .'

'If that's what it is, monsieur,' said Jacquot, wondering at Bressans' keen eyesight. It had taken Bouvet's instructions for him to find it. 'And that was when you called Monsieur Bouvet, here?'

'That's right.'

'Why particularly Monsieur Bouvet?'

Bressans frowned. 'I thought he, or someone on his staff,

might have seen her. Or that maybe she had left a note, saying where she was.'

'But no one had seen her? There was no note?'

'Correct, Chief Inspector.'

'And did you phone anyone else, monsieur?' asked Jacquot.

'No, not immediately.'

'But you did make other calls?'

'Yes, I did.'

'To do with your companion's disappearance?'

'That's correct.'

'Because of the blood?'

'Well, it did all seem rather mysterious. Her not being here, and neither Monsieur Bouvet nor any of his staff having seen her around . . .'

'So who did you call, monsieur?'

'My uncle. It seemed to me we should have someone investigate. Someone to find out what was happening.'

And someone, thought Jacquot, to be discreet if things turned ugly.

'And for that you had to call your uncle?' asked Jacquot lightly. He couldn't resist it. 'Could you not have called the police yourself, if you were concerned about Mademoiselle Ladouze's whereabouts? Possibly, her safety?'

Bressans looked uncomfortable 'Of course, but it seemed wiser.'

'So when did you last see Mademoiselle Ladouze?'

'Late yesterday afternoon.'

'Which was when you agreed to meet for lunch?'

'Correct.'

'But not since then?'

Bressans shook his head.

'Tell me, monsieur, what exactly is your relationship with Mademoiselle Ladouze? If you wouldn't mind. You said you were travelling together? Work?'

'That's correct, yes,' began Bressans. 'She is . . . I suppose you would call her a researcher. Though she is much more than that, of course. Quite *formidable*. There is a project we are working on . . .' Bressans spread his hand as though he didn't want to bother Jacquot with the details.

Jacquot wasn't surprised. There weren't too many researchers he knew who packed the kind of underwear that Mademoiselle Ladouze had selected for her 'working' weekend.

It was then, for the first time since being in her room, that Jacquot wondered what she looked like. If this had been her apartment, her home, there would have been photos to look at, an image to conjure with. But here, in an anonymous hotel suite, there was nothing to give her any form or feature. Just her clothes – and the scent of her.

'And this project, monsieur,' continued Jacquot, 'where exactly did the two of you work? There appears to be no indication . . .' He cast around the salon – the tidy desk top, the absence of attachés or briefcases.

Bressans' easy manner seemed to tighten. He glanced at Bouvet, still hovering, and then gave a wet, throaty cough. 'Maybe, Chief Inspector, it would be better – aah, more convenient, if we continue this conversation in my room. I'm sure Monsieur Bouvet, here, has . . .' He turned to the man, switched on a smile.

It was immediately clear to Bouvet, and Jacquot, what Bressans was after – a little privacy.

'Of course, of course, messieurs,' said Bouvet, catching on quickly and making for the door. 'So. I will leave you to it. And if there is anything you need, anything you want, please . . . I will be at Reception. Or in the office behind.'

He was almost at the door when Jacquot called after him. 'Ah, Monsieur Bouvet. A moment please.'

Bouvet turned. 'Monsieur?'

'Exactly who knows about this?'

'I have told no one, Chief Inspector. Monsieur Bressans suggested that that would be the correct course. At this stage. And I saw no reason to – to spread alarm . . . I thought . . .'

'Well for now, Monsieur Bouvet, let's keep it that way. And please make sure that no one comes into this room,' continued Jacquot. 'In fact, perhaps you would be so kind as to lock it, from the outside?'

Bouvet made a small bow and, with a volley of *bien sûrs* and *certainements*, he backed out of the room, closed the door behind him, and locked it from the loggia side.

29

There had been no need for Roland Bressans to introduce himself. The moment Jacquot saw Bressans standing beside Monsieur Bouvet, he'd known immediately who the man was. And known, too, exactly who it was who'd initiated the call to Rochet's superiors, to make sure that the matter of Ghislaine Ladouze's 'disappearance' would be handled . . . diplomatically. If something untoward had happened, it would need covering up and, more important, Bressans' possible involvement kept out of any story that might subsequently appear in the press.

Not that Bressans was unused to the attentions of the press. As Jacquot knew only too well. There'd even been a story about him in that morning's paper, the one Jacquot had left on the table at Le Tilleul. The coming man, the headline had said. One of Marseilles' most generous benefactors and, it was being whispered, a potential political appointee.

And it wasn't just newspapers. The last time Jacquot had visited Marseilles, a couple of months' earlier, Bressans' face had been plastered on billboards all over town.

'Old family from out L'Estaque way. *Ancien*, you get my drift,' Jacquot's friend, Salette, had told him when Jacquot asked about the billboards. 'His grandfather started up a print works way back and the family's gone on from there. Made a bomb, they have – newspapers, magazines, greetings cards, postcards – you name it. The old man's got the money, but it's the uncle that's got the clout. The *piston*. Political clout, that is. And if you ask me, that's what Bressans is after. A political appointment. A seat on the board. And he's pulled off some pretty major stunts to get it, that's for sure. Real eye-catchers, if you get my meaning. A veterans' stand for L'Olympique – ticket price subsidised half by the State and half by some charity he set up; licence concessions for all the city's street-traders; and then his latest prank – that museum he's opening down Lazaret. You'd think it was another Louvre, the fuss everyone's making.'

And now here was the man himself, ushering Jacquot through into his own salon and closing the connecting doors between the two suites. Crossing to his armoire Bressans reached for a glass, threw in some ice and poured himself a whisky.

'Chief Inspector?' he turned and waved the decanter.

'Thank you, yes. *Mais pas de glace.*'

Bressans found another glass, poured out a measure and handed it to Jacquot. Taking a sip of his drink, he waved Jacquot to the sofa and took one of the two armchairs beside the fire.

'So, monsieur,' began Bressans. 'Where were we?'

'I was asking about your relationship with Mademoiselle Ladouze,' replied Jacquot, making himself comfortable on the sofa, tasting his whisky, amused that Bressans should pretend he was not vividly aware of where their conversation had been headed a few minutes earlier. He decided he was rather looking forward to the coming exchange.

'Ah, yes. So you were.'

A silence settled between them, long enough for Jacquot to wonder whether Bressans had any intention of replying.

'And, monsieur?'

Bressans stirred, crossed his legs, took another, longer sip of his drink.

'Monsieur Bressans, I should remind you that I have come here at your invitation, to find out what has happened to Mademoiselle Ladouze. In order to do that, I need to have as much information at my disposal as possible. It is the way that these things are done. It is what I do, monsieur. I am sure you understand.'

'As I said, she's a researcher. We're working . . .'

Jacquot sighed, thinking again of the underwear in the drawer. 'Please, monsieur. Let us waste no more time. The truth, *s'il vous plaît.*'

Even behind the tan, Jacquot could see the man's cheeks flush with annoyance. This was clearly not how Bressans liked to be spoken to. Or was used to being treated.

'OK, OK,' said Bressans, holding up his hands as if in surrender. 'She's a . . . not a lover, exactly . . . let's just say a friend.' He gave a small, trickling chuckle, as though it might somehow lighten the mood.

'And how long have you known Mademoiselle Ladouze?'

'Since Wednesday morning.'

Jacquot nodded. Just as he'd suspected. 'And where is she from?'

'Marseilles.'

'How did you . . . meet?'

'I . . . I have a contact. Such things can be arranged, as I'm sure you know.'

Jacquot recognised when he was being drawn into something, made complicit. He didn't much like it.

'And, of course, everything very discreet,' Bressans continued, laying suitable emphasis on the word.

Jacquot nodded, smiled. 'You are married, is that correct, monsieur?'

'Yes, I am,' replied Bressans, suddenly uncertain about this new direction.

'Does your wife know where you are?'

'A briefing in Lyons. That's what I told her. My wife has no interest in my business activities. I'm sure she is very happy having the house to herself for a few days.' Bressans tried another laugh, tossed back a mouthful of his drink.

'So would I be correct in saying there is no "project" that the two of you are working on. Mademoiselle Ladouze and yourself. Just a . . . weekend away?'

'Well, there is something she's helping me with. But I'm afraid it's confidential,' he added with another conspiratorial smile.

'Monsieur, I should remind you that, however informal it may appear at this stage, this is still a police investigation, and that "confidential" is not a word we in the *Judiciaire* take kindly to. So, if you please, what exactly is Ghislaine Ladouze "helping" you with?'

Bressans gave Jacquot a sharp look.

'If you must know,' he began, after a slight pause, 'I am currently in talks with Monsieur Auguste Vilotte. He is a painter who lives here, in a part of the Monastère. I have been trying to secure some of his estate for a new museum in Marseilles. His own private things, his own collection, a legacy, you understand. To celebrate his extraordinary talent and his equally extraordinary services to Art. He is an old man, after all . . . And he seems most enthusiastic about it.'

Jacquot took this in.

'And Mademoiselle Ladouze, how exactly does she fit in with these "talks"?'

Bressans sighed. 'Like many painters, Auguste Vilotte enjoys a certain reputation. I thought if I visited him with someone young, someone pretty, then he might look more favourably on my endeavours.'

'These negotiations have been going on for some time?'

'A few months, yes. It is not something you can rush, you understand. It all takes time. Setting up something like this. A most delicate touch is needed in negotiation with the artistic . . . the, ah . . . the creative temperament.'

'So you have been here before, monsieur? With Mademoiselle Ladouze?'

'No, this is the first time with Ghislaine.'

'But you have been before? To the Monastère? To visit Monsieur Vilotte?'

'Correct.'

'And how many times would that be, monsieur?'

'Twice, three times maybe.'

'But this, you say, is the first time with Mademoiselle Ladouze?'

'Yes it is. And it appears Monsieur Vilotte was quite taken by her. Which was what I had hoped would happen. So persuasive. The feminine presence, you understand . . .'

'So would I be correct in thinking that Mademoiselle Ladouze was with Monsieur Vilotte after you last saw her? Yesterday afternoon?'

'Yes she was. He asked to see her. A message was sent, requesting the pleasure of her company. She went to his studio late yesterday afternoon, early evening,' said Bressans, starting to relax a little. 'He lives in the old watchtower.'

'And has anyone checked with this Monsieur Vilotte? To find out if she is still with him? Or where she might have gone after she left him?'

'Meetings with Monsieur Vilotte are arranged through the hotel's housekeeper, Madame Champeau. According to her, Ghislaine left his studio late last night.'

'She was seen leaving the studio?'

Bressans spread his hands. 'Apparently Madame Champeau checked with Monsieur Vilotte this morning and that is what he told her. That Ghislaine left him around midnight last night.'

'And you did not see her then? Or hear her return to her room? She did not report back to you, to say how things had gone?'

'No, she did not.'

'So the sign on her door that you saw this morning was the first indication you had that she had returned from his studio?'

'That is correct.'

'So what do you suppose might be the reason for her disappearance? The blood – if that is what it is – on the end of the bed?'

Bressans gave him a look. 'I have no idea. I am as mystified as . . .'

'I mean, you'll agree there must be some explanation for her disappearance? And the blood?'

'Of course, of course. But I cannot imagine—'

'Is it possible, monsieur, that the two of you had an argument? Maybe you asked her to do something she was not comfortable with?'

'*Pas de tout, inspecteur*. We were having a wonderful – and constructive – stay. The only reason I got in touch with my uncle . . . well, it was the blood. Rather unsettling, I'm sure you'll agree.'

'As I said, if it is blood, monsieur. Human blood. Maybe she got something from the kitchens? Maybe she is making some kind of statement? Maybe, you never know, she is setting you up for something? I'm sure, like me, that she knows exactly who you are.'

For a brief moment Bressans looked pleased that he had been recognised. And then suddenly perturbed by what Jacquot was suggesting. 'I hadn't thought . . . But no, it's not possible.'

'Who can say, monsieur? Who can say? Tell me, has anyone gone looking for her. You? Monsieur Bouvet? The staff? Has anyone searched the hotel, the grounds?'

'Not that I know of. And, as I said, we didn't want to arouse suspicions. A search party, that sort of thing.'

'Quite. Quite,' said Jacquot. He paused for a moment, as though considering something. 'Tell me, monsieur. What was Mademoiselle Ladouze wearing when you last saw her?'

'A white cotton dress, I believe. Like a gypsy kind of thing. The skirt was frilled, layered.'

'A sweater? Cardigan?'

Bressans shook his head. 'I don't think so, but I may be wrong.'

'Jewellery?'

'No, nothing that I can recall.'

'And what was she wearing on her feet, monsieur? Her shoes?'

Bressans puffed out his cheeks, cast around, as though trying to remember something so small, so inconsequential. 'Espadrilles. Cream canvas espadrilles. With laced ties around the ankles.'

Jacquot took this in. 'And do you have a photo of Mademoiselle Ghislaine?'

'No I don't. I'm sorry.'

'Then maybe you could describe her?'

'Tall. Short dark hair, no longer than the shoulders – a kind of browny black. Brown eyes. A very good figure, of course. Beautiful hands, fingers. And tanned.'

'Age?'

'Mid- to late twenties. No more than that.'

Again Jacquot nodded. A silence settled between them.

'So what happens now?' asked Bressans breezily, sensing at last that he was probably through the worst. Getting up from his chair, he crossed to the armoire and poured himself another measure of the whisky. 'Now that you have all the relevant information, I mean?' He held up the decanter, but Jacquot shook his head.

'We wait, Monsieur Bressans. Normally, a person isn't posted as officially missing for forty-eight hours. As you said earlier, Mademoiselle Ladouze could just come walking through that door at any moment.'

Bressans nodded. 'And if she doesn't?'

'Then things will change, monsieur. Staff and guests will be questioned, the grounds and hotel thoroughly searched. It is likely, too, that the newspapers and TV will become involved – the report of a disappearance in the media can often kick-start an investigation. Memories jogged, that sort of thing. People who might have seen her, known her, coming forward.'

Bressans' face fell.

'But right now, monsieur, we cannot yet be certain we even have a missing person. For some reason or another, your friend may just have gone off in a sulk . . . making a point, perhaps. Who knows?'

Jacquot finished his drink, set it on the table and got to his feet.

Bressans accompanied him to the door, then made to hold him back – there was something he needed to say. 'I would just like to . . . thank you, Chief Inspector, for being so . . . reasonable. So understanding. I'm sure you'll appreciate . . .'

Jacquot nodded. 'As I said, monsieur, right now we have no evidence that a crime has been committed. The substance on the bed linen will be tested, of course. To establish if it is human. Or not. And if it is human, we will then endeavour to find out who it belongs to. But it is the weekend. Such things take time.'

'Quite so,' said Bressans, reaching for Jacquot's hand and shaking it. 'Quite so.'

When the handshaking was over, Jacquot nodded over Bressans' shoulder to the packed suitcase by the sofa.

'I trust you're not thinking of leaving us?' he asked, lightly.

Bressans looked stunned. 'Well, yes, I am. Of course. I have things to do . . .'

Jacquot shook his head, smiled. 'And so do I, monsieur. Here. At your invitation.'

'But it's simply not possible . . .'

'How long did you book your rooms for, monsieur?'

'We check out on Monday.'

'Then I'm sure it can't be too . . . inconvenient for you to remain here till then. After all, you're at a briefing in Lyons, *n'est-ce pas?*'

Bressans' eyes turned steely and his voice, when he finally spoke, took on a soft, menacing sibilance: 'I can make things very difficult for you, Chief Inspector. Please remember that.'

'And I for you, Monsieur Bressans,' replied Jacquot.

The two men looked at each other – Jacquot smiling pleasantly, Bressans' face taut and clenched, reddening under the tan.

'I won't stay here . . .' he began.

'Oh I think you will, monsieur. And I think you must.'

30

After leaving Bressans, Jacquot returned to Reception. Monsieur Bouvet looked up from behind the stone desk, his expression midway between helpful and concerned.

'Monsieur, everything is in order, I hope? Is there anything I can help you with?' He glanced at the man beside him; a tall, gaunt individual who was rolling up the sheaf of papers they'd been looking through when Jacquot came down the stairs.

'I thought, maybe, if you weren't too busy,' began Jacquot, 'that perhaps you might show me round the hotel, monsieur. So that I can get my bearings.'

'Why, of course, of course, I should be delighted. But . . .' Bouvet turned to the man with the roll of papers. 'Perhaps you would enjoy it more, learn more, with my colleague here, Monsieur van der Haage. He probably knows the hotel better than anyone. He designed it . . . *en effet*, is still working on it.'

And then, to his companion, Bouvet said: 'I wonder, Lens, would you mind? This is Monsieur Jacquot. He is a—' Bouvet stopped short, a panicked expression settling across his features. 'What I mean, he's . . .'

'A journalist,' said Jacquot helpfully. 'Travel stuff, you know, for *L'Hebdo Marseille*.'

Lens slipped the last of the papers into his briefcase and stowed it under the desk. 'Of course, it would be my pleasure.' He gave Jacquot a look. 'So, do you want the long tour? Or the short one?'

'You have me at a disadvantage, monsieur,' replied Jacquot.

'The long one – structural harmony, spacial perspective, historic integrity – that sort of thing. Or the short one. Walkabout. Bit of history. See a few rooms.' He turned to Bouvet. 'Maybe we could take some keys?'

Bouvet looked alarmed. 'I'm not sure. All the rooms are taken. But perhaps you could show a couple of the painters' rooms. I believe they were calling in at the Musée Granet this afternoon, after their painting session. Or was it Cézanne's studio? How silly of me. I can't seem to recall. Anyway, they're sure to be late back. So please, here . . .' Bouvet took some keys from the drawer and handed them to van der Haage. 'Seven, eight and ten. Such nice people. And I'm sure they won't mind.'

31

'It's good of you to spare the time,' said Jacquot, as Lens van der Haage came out from behind the desk and led him back to the stairs.

'The press is a powerful tool,' replied van der Haage with a wry smile. 'It would be a dereliction – that is the word, yes? – not to take advantage of your interest . . . and of your pages. So, why don't we start at the top and work our way down?'

Five minutes later, the sun not noticeably lower in the sky but somehow bigger, as though it had drawn closer, an oily orange beachball hovering over blue wooded slopes, van der Haage and Jacquot reached the topmost level of the Grand Monastère.

'The original ramparts,' said van der Haage, waving his hand at a stone-paved oblong of crenellated battlements surrounding the Monastère's cloistered gardens far below. The view in all directions was simply staggering: to the south, east and west, the slanting flanks of the Lubéron hills, the clustered, rose-coloured rooftops of Luissac and, between the trees, various string-thin sections of the coiling road that Jacquot had negotiated not two hours earlier.

But it was the view to the north that took the breath away. Far below the battlements, the Gaudins Cut sliced a steep-sided gash through the lower foothills before opening up on to the wide sweep of the Calavon plain. From the ramparts of the Grand Monastère it was as if the whole of the Lubéron had been laid out at their feet.

'It may only be a few hundred metres above the valley floor,' said van der Haage, 'but it seems so much higher, does it not?'

'It certainly does,' replied Jacquot, who was not at his best when it came to heights.

'After Les Baux,' continued the Dutchman, tamping down his wind-flicked hair, 'it is maybe the most important fortified hilltop in the whole of Provence. Probably one of the most complete Saracen fortresses in the south.'

'So when did it become a monastery?' asked Jacquot, peering cautiously over a low retaining wall into the cloistered gardens below.

'Sometime in the seventeenth century,' replied van der Haage, pointing Jacquot to a small tower in the western corner of the ramparts. Leading the way down a head-spinning spiral of worn stone steps he brought them out on to the first-floor loggia, no more than a few metres from Ghislaine Ladouze's room.

'So far as we know, the property was given by the ruling Comte de Vessaillon to a soldier of fortune called Lampert de Roq; sometime after the end of the Italian Wars, we think. But with no male heir, and maybe to atone for his many sins on the field of battle, Monsieur de Roq left the property to the Brothers of Saint Sulpice at Apt, a small teaching order attached to the Benedictines.'

Descending another flight of stone steps, they reached the garden and van der Haage started to sort through his keys. 'At the height of its fame, there were more than thirty monks in residence, teaching maybe double that number of postulants,' he explained, opening the first of the guest rooms and showing Jacquot in. The room was much smaller than the suites above, Jacquot noticed, but no less comfortably appointed. A pair of gaudy aquamarine trousers were neatly folded over the back of a chair. A man's room, Jacquot decided.

'This would have been one of the original cells,' continued van der Haage. 'Six novices to each cell on this level. But only five hours' sleep allowed. Lights out at nine. Matins at three. It must have been a rigorous apprenticeship,' he said, ushering Jacquot out and locking the door after them. 'But all the better for that, it would seem. In three hundred years this monastery supplied more bishops than any other religious foundation in the country. Which is how it earned its name: Monastère des Évêques. So far as we can ascertain, more than sixty of its students were awarded their own bishoprics – in Cavaillon, Aix, Carpentras, and as far afield as Trêche in Brittany and Lornheim in Alsace.'

'Was there much work to do in terms of actual renovation?' asked Jacquot. 'It all seems . . .'

'Natural? Original? Is that what you mean?'

Jacquot nodded uncertainly, hoping he hadn't said anything wrong, hoping he hadn't offended the man.

'Then of course you are absolutely correct.' Van der Haage beamed, as though this was exactly what he had wanted to hear. 'It is precisely what I – what we, Claude and Régine – wanted to achieve. From an aesthetic point of view, we agreed it was essential we keep things simple. To preserve and utilise the original fabric of the property wherever possible. The dining room, for example – once the monks' refectory – the lobby, the small *Chapelle des Pénitents* over there in the corner, or the *libraria* which serves now as a small reading room for our guests. No frills, no – how do you say? Gimmicks? Just the real thing, true to heritage, but with all the comforts.'

As van der Haage spoke, he opened up the two remaining guest rooms for which he had keys and waited while Jacquot prowled around, trying to build up a picture – from the personal things they'd innocently left lying round – of the absent occupants, who even then might be driving up that twisting road to Luissac.

Closing and locking the last door, and clearly encouraged by Jacquot's interest, van der Haage was positively chattering away. His French, which up until then had been passably good, was now delivered with a busy southern twang, with the kind of rough constructions and odd abbreviations he must have picked up on the building site. It was, reflected Jacquot, a little like talking to a local roofer, or bricklayer. But language apart, Lens van der Haage was clearly a man of immense enthusiasm, his work the most important thing in his life. As they walked around the garden cloister, Jacquot wondered if he was married. If he was, any wife would have a lot to compete with.

'So how did the Bouvets find you?' asked Jacquot.

'So typical,' said van der Haage. 'I had been working on a place in Avignon. The Hôtel Grex, you may have heard of it? When the job was completed, it was featured in a number of magazines – *Suites Décoratives*, *Côte Sud* . . . Anyway, Régine saw the piece in *Côte Sud* and called me in. I visited, I looked, and, well, it seemed to me a most exciting project.'

'And how long has it all taken – the renovations, I mean?' It struck Jacquot that he was sounding just like a journalist should. And van der Haage was responding accordingly, imagining the story that would surely result in *L'Hebdo Marseille*.

'Four years now. Since the death of Régine's father. The real problem, of course, was access – the stone from Quercy, the marble from Sarragon, the new ovens for the kitchen, in excess of two tons each; and getting it all up here. Such a road! Just dreadful. At one point it looked like the bridge would not be strong enough to support the weight of the lorries. But it all happened, everything worked out in the end. Electrics first, then kitchen, and finally the rooms.'

'They're beautifully done,' said Jacquot. 'You must be very pleased.'

In the centre of the courtyard the palm fronds stirred and rattled and the swallows swooped through the colonnades to their spittle nests.

'You should have seen them before we got to work. The old man had stone-patterned linoleum on the floors. Can you imagine? And plaster board covering the walls. And, like many French hoteliers, he was keen to have as many different patterns of wallpaper in one room as possible. But you musn't quote me on that,' he said, waving it away with a nervous little laugh.

'But now it's finished?'

'Not quite,' van der Haage corrected him. 'We still have to complete the second cloister. Here, I will show you,' he said and, pushing through a door marked *Privé*, he led Jacquot down another covered corridor and into a smaller cloistered courtyard.

More a builders' yard than a cloister, the place was a mess – littered with construction debris, overgrown with weeds and patched here and there with scabs of crusty grey cement. In the middle of the yard was what looked like a stone well and set around its edge three colonnaded arcades, similar to the cloisters of the first courtyard but at ground level only. Through the stone arches Jacquot counted a dozen doors.

'Just a little tidying up and you'll be ready for business,' said Jacquot.

Van der Haage shook his head. 'Not until work is finished on the tower. Still more waiting,' he sighed. 'But soon . . . Soon we will begin.'

'Is that where the painter lives? In the watchtower? Vilotte something?'

'Auguste Vilotte. That's right,' said van der Haage. 'And his tower is the oldest part of the property, dating back to the Saracens. Maybe as far back as the ninth century. The first thing they built.'

'So how come he owns it?' asked Jacquot, taking in the rounded stone walls, the rusting hinges on the shuttered windows and the drab front door almost hidden down a flight of worn stone steps.

'It's a long story, monsieur. When Madame Bouvet's grand-father bought the property from the State back in 1902, he had to take out a loan to make up the purchase price. He borrowed that money from Auguste Vilotte's father, granting Vilotte *père* a lease on a part of this second courtyard and the watchtower. While the *famille* Vilotte worked their vines in the valley below, Régine's *gran'père* turned his part into a small hotel. And that's how it stands today. Auguste Vilotte was born here, in the tower, and when his father died after the War, he came back to take up residence, and the lease. Forty years on he's still here.'

'Won't that cause problems?'

Van der Haage shook his head, smiled. 'For a while, there were problems. But not now. He has agreed to exchange the lease for other accommodation in the village.'

'What's he like? Have you met him?'

'Oh yes, I have met him. Many times. And none of them pleasant. A quite remarkable artist, truly gifted, but a monster. Just as old men can be. Arrogant. Stubborn, you know. Take the tower. For two years he has prevaricated. One moment he wants to move, the next he says he doesn't know what we're talking about. He plays with us. He plays with everyone. It is . . . infuriating. But now, I believe, the end is in sight.'

'So,' said Jacquot, 'good news . . .'

Van de Haage nodded. 'This time I think so. As I said, he is old now. The time is right, and I think he knows it.'

32

Back at the front desk, Jacquot thanked van der Haage for the tour. The Dutchman said that it had been his pleasure, if there was anything more he could do . . . then he retrieved his briefcase and hurried off.

Turning to the concierge, Jacquot asked if he could use a phone. He pulled it towards him and called Rochet's home number. When the older man answered, Jacquot could hear a Mozart opera playing softly in the background. He tried to picture the scene. Old Rochet in his slippers, listening to his favourite arias. His wife had died a couple of years before and he kept himself sane with opera and birdwatching.

'So what seems to be the problem?' asked Rochet casually, as if he didn't already know.

Jacquot brought his boss up to speed: Ghislaine Ladouze, a call-girl from Marseilles, currently missing; her companion, a Monsieur Roland Bressans, also from Marseilles, looking as guilty and shifty as hell, probably knew more than he was letting on.

And the blood, of course.

'At the moment,' continued Jacquot, 'it seems to be nothing more than a missing person, but—'

There was a sigh at the end of the line. 'Please don't tell me it's going to turn messy?'

'That's my bet. Sooner or later our friend is going to reappear, but my guess is she won't be in the best of health.'

'Let's hope your guess is wrong.'

'If it's not, we can't be doing any favours, Chief. It'll have to be by the book.'

'Of course, of course,' Rochet assured him. 'It could be no other way. But I'd like to keep a lid on this until we know for sure what's going on.'

'I'll need to have the blood tested,' Jacquot continued. 'And there's the possibility we'll have to get Fournier and the boys in. If the bedroom's a crime scene, he'll need to see it.'

But Rochet, as Jacquot had suspected, was not happy about Forensics being called in, making the point that it was, after all, nothing more than a missing person at this stage.

'Early days still, don't you think?' Rochet continued. 'But by all means bring in the bedding. We can have it tested here. No reason to bother Fournier just yet.'

It was clear from Rochet's tone that Bressans' uncle had pulled some important strings.

Jacquot listened for a moment more, said that he understood, then replaced the receiver.

At that moment Monsieur Bouvet came out of the office behind Reception.

'A word, monsieur,' said Jacquot.

'*Mais oui. Bien sûr*. Of course,' Bouvet replied, coming out from behind the desk and steering Jacquot out of the concierge's hearing. 'You enjoyed your excursion, I trust? Lens has done some wonderful work, don't you think? An inspired designer. At the Grex he—'

But Jacquot held up a hand. It was as if Bouvet imagined that rattling on about the little things would somehow negate the bigger things.

Jacquot got straight to the point: 'If you please, monsieur. First I would like to have a print-out of your staff. And their resumés – any details you may have of previous employment. And guests. Anyone who's checked in since Monday. Home address, telephone numbers. And any extra information you may have – repeat visitors? Jobs? Anything you might know, or have heard.'

Bouvet nodded. He would see to it.

'Also, has anyone checked out since, say, Thursday?'

'The last departure we had was Wednesday morning. An Italian couple who stay with us every year. They used to come with their children, now they come alone.'

'And non-residents, coming in for lunch or dinner, also, since Thursday.'

'I'll see what I can do, monsieur. But with non-residents it is more difficult. All we will have is a name, a contact number and credit card details . . .'

'That will be fine,' said Jacquot. 'But not a word to anyone, if you please.' No chance of that, thought Jacquot. 'And a map, if you have one? A brochure . . . the lay-out of the hotel?'

'Of course, monsieur. Not a problem. And I am most grateful. Is there anything else I can do?'

'As a matter of fact there is,' replied Jacquot, the idea forming that very instant in his mind. If Rochet was being coy – down-grading whatever had been going on at Grand Monastère – and if strings were being pulled, then he'd pull a few himself. If liberties were being taken, then he would take some too. 'There is indeed. Yes. I'd like a room.'

It seemed to take a moment for Bouvet to comprehend what it was that Jacquot had asked for. And then: 'But we are full, monsieur. We have no rooms available. We are *complet. Tout complet.*' Claude Bouvet cast around, helplessly, as though Jacquot had asked him for a million francs.

Jacquot smiled. 'As of this morning, you're not.'

Bouvet frowned, still not understanding. And then, 'But that is Mademoiselle Ladouze's room. She could return at any moment . . .'

Jacquot gave Bouvet a long appraising look. 'I don't think that's very likely, do you, monsieur?'

Bouvet looked stricken at the thought, but finally he nodded. 'Of course, monsieur. As you wish.'

'Oh, one more thing. I will need a bin liner.'

33

Jacquot made the journey back to Cavaillon in less than an hour, the bin liner that Bouvet had given him swaying to and fro on the back seat of his Peugeot as he swung the car through the turns down to St-Mas. The bin liner was filled with the bedding Jacquot had removed from Ghislaine Ladouze's bed – scarlet cover, quilt, sheet and under-blanket. Even sealed, the perfumed contents of the sack gave off a heady scent that quickly covered the more usual aromas of warm plastic, petrol and tobacco in Jacquot's car.

Once back in Cavaillon, Jacquot's first stop was Police Headquarters where he left a copy of the guest and staff lists that Bouvet had printed off for him, along with the bin liner containing Mademoiselle Ladouze's bed linen with instructions for someone to take it down to the labs for testing.

'But it's the weekend,' complained the Duty Sergeant, Mougeon. 'Everyone's gone home.'

'Then get someone in. It's just a blood sample. Animal or human. An hour at most. Tell them Rochet requested it. Oh, and get that lanyard properly fixed to your gun, sergeant. One of these days . . .'

'Sure, boss. Sorry,' said Mougeon, reaching for the lanyard, clipping it to the butt of his gun. It was something of a running joke that Mougeon was one of the untidiest cops in the shop. In Marseilles, he would have been on report for the oversight; in Cavaillon, they just shrugged.

Back at his apartment on Cours Bournissac, Jacquot took a shower, packed some things and left a message with Jean Brunet. His assistant had been on a timed cycle trial that afternoon (Jacquot had passed him that morning on the drive to Le Tilleul, hunched over his handlebars in skin-tight yellow racing kit) and Jacquot knew that he'd be out somewhere with his cronies, going over the route or refining tactics for the next race. 'I've given Mougeon a list of names,' he said, when the beep sounded on the ansaphone. 'I know it's the weekend, but I'd be grateful if you could check them out as soon as you can. If you need me, I'm at the Hôtel Monastère in Luissac. Work, you understand. I'll give you a call tomorrow.' And then, as a friendly sign-off, 'How was the race? You look good in yellow!'

Twenty minutes later, Jacquot was back in the Peugeot and heading out of Cavaillon, the setting sun a burnished gold in his rear-view mirror. This time he played no music, using the journey back to Luissac to review what he'd learned so far in the case of the missing Ghislaine Ladouze.

As far as he could see, the main players most likely to be involved in her disappearance were, obviously, Bressans and the painter, Auguste Vilotte. According to the housekeeper, Madame Champeau, the girl had left Vilotte's studio the night before. But, so far as Jacquot knew, no one had actually seen her leave the tower, or return to her room. All they had was Vilotte's word for that. As for Bressans, well, the man was a devious, greedy little *crapaud* who looked like he'd do anything to get his own way.

As Cavaillon slipped behind him and the road to Apt opened up ahead, flanked on the right by the rising slopes of the Petit Lubéron and on the left by the foothills of the Monts de Vaucluse, Jacquot was also increasingly certain that this was not so much a missing person as a missing body, and that the blood on the bed linen would turn out to be human. And hers. It was this blood that gave the lie to Mademoiselle Ladouze going for a walk that morning and getting into some kind of trouble – and anyway, the landscape around Monastère was hardly conducive to a nature stroll, especially in espadrilles. It also gave the lie to the possibility of suicide. If she had committed suicide by, say, opening a vein, then where was the body now? And who had moved it? And why? What she hadn't done – Jacquot was certain on this point – was to leave the hotel without telling anyone and return home to Marseilles. He'd have someone look into it, of course – Bouvet could check with local cab firms and he'd have someone call at her address in Marseilles – but he wasn't going to hold his breath. Her trolley-bag still stood beside the chest of drawers and no woman Jacquot had ever known would willingly or accidentally leave behind her clothes and make-up.

As he indicated for the cut off the Apt road and headed towards St Mas and Luissac through darkening twilight lanes, he was in little doubt that someone had killed the call-girl from Marseilles and that he had a murder inquiry on his hands.

And Bouvet? What of Bouvet, thought Jacquot as he slid

quietly into Luissac, following the main street and crossing the square (the place still hauntingly quiet – where were the evening boules players, the old ladies, the open doors and shutters?). He might look the hand-wringing hotelier – attentive, helpful, disingenuous – but Jacquot had come across enough 'who-me?' types in his time not to discount Monsieur Bouvet quite yet.

It was almost dark by the time Jacquot reached the Monastère, its ancient stonework discreetly flood-lit against the night sky, a few pale stars blinking bravely to the east. It was cooler, too, he noticed, though the walls still radiated a gentle early-summer warmth.

As on his first visit, Bouvet was there to greet him, this time with Ghislaine Ladouze's room key and a detailed ground plan of the hotel – room numbers, stairs, dining rooms, pool and tennis court – that looked as though it might have been put together by Lens van der Haage.

Bouvet gave the smallest of bows, more a tip of the head. 'Should I come with you, monsieur?'

Jacquot told him he'd be fine by himself. He knew the way, after all.

'And do you want me to set up any interviews?' asked Bouvet, in a conspiratorial whisper. 'With the staff, you know; with—'

'Not just yet, monsieur. Let's just see how things develop.'

Bouvet looked relieved.

'In fact,' continued Jacquot, 'I really don't see any need for either your guests or your staff to know who I am. So, for now, I'll just be another guest. Or maybe . . . how did I do as a journalist? Maybe that's what I'll be.'

Jacquot might not have liked the subterfuge, but since only Bressans and Bouvet knew who he was, it did give him a certain edge.

'Quite so Chief In— monsieur. I would be most grateful. Although I should also say that, ah, I have had to tell my wife about all this. I trust you understand . . .' Bouvet gave Jacquot what was almost a pleading look.

'That's not a problem,' Jacquot assured him. 'But thank you for telling me.' And then, 'So . . . do you suppose a famous travel writer needs to book a table for dinner?'

'A table for dinner, monsieur? *Mais c'est pas une problème.*' Bouvet beamed. '*Un plaisir, en effet.*'

'And maybe,' added Jacquot, 'if you have a moment, maybe you could join me? For a drink. Some questions, perhaps. Some background?'

'Of course, of course. *Toujours à votre servis*, monsieur.'

And then, turning away, Jacquot paused, noticed something, turned back. 'The music's not playing.'

Bouvet looked perplexed. 'The music, monsieur?'

'The Pachelbel. Or was it Albinoni? In the lobby here?'

'But there is no music here, monsieur, I assure you. Not at Le Grand Monastère.'

34

Despite Bouvet's robust denial Jacquot was certain, as he climbed to the first floor and turned towards Mademoiselle Ladouze's room, that he'd heard music that afternoon, when he had first arrived. A low, doleful adagio. It had rather suited its surroundings, Jacquot had thought. Classy, too. Just the kind of thing that Monastère's guests might expect, the kind of music they'd feel comfortable with. No tinny top-ten instrumentals or old favourite covers for them.

And yet, apparently, there had been nothing. That's what Bouvet had said. No Pachelbel. No Albinoni. Jacquot shook his head. It couldn't be. He was certain he'd heard it. But then, he admitted to himself, maybe it wasn't exactly Muzak. Maybe that was what Bouvet had suspected he was suggesting, and was so keen to deny. Maybe it was a radio somewhere, or someone actually playing? Maybe Grand Monastère had an organ that residents could use? It had been a monastery, after all. And monasteries surely had organs? Didn't they?

As he turned into the loggia, the first thing Jacquot saw was a covered wicker-work basket outside Mademoiselle Ladouze's room. When he reached it he lifted the lid – a pile of neatly folded linen and towels. Either Bouvet, or someone from Housekeeping, had delivered it in his absence and, more importantly, left it at the door rather than place it inside. He'd asked that the room not be disturbed and it appeared that Bouvet had done as he'd been told.

Switching on the lights – no overheads here, just low-wattage wall lights behind their etched-glass panels and a couple of sidelights by the desk and chairs – Jacquot dropped his shoulder bag on a chair in the salon and carried the linen basket through to the bedroom. Five minutes later the bed was made, the towels and robes were in the bathroom and Jacquot was flicking through the clothes in the armoire, looking for a white, layered gypsy dress. He could find no sign of it nor, for that matter, a pair of lace-tie espadrilles. Remembering something, he went back to the bathroom and checked the dirty-linen basket just inside the door. Again, nothing bar a tangle of white T-shirts, some knotted knickers, and a pale blue blouse.

As expected, he thought to himself. With a last look around the bedroom and salon, he stepped out into the loggia and locked the door behind him.

Down in the reception hall, Bouvet was nowhere to be seen. Listening out for Pachelbel or Albinoni, Jacquot went to the stone slab of a desk and asked the concierge where he might be found.

'He's in the bar, Monsieur Jacquot,' the concierge replied, smiling helpfully. He was a narrowly built man in his early sixties, the cross keys on his jacket lapels glinting in the light, a tiny gold plate pinned to his breast pocket identifying him as 'Didier'. 'It's across the hall and through the first glass doors, monsieur. You can't miss it.'

Jacquot thanked him and followed the directions, noting that his name – if not profession – was already known to at least one member of staff. But then, reflected Jacquot, in a hotel like Grand Monastère that shouldn't have been too surprising. This was the kind of lodging where members of staff as high up the pecking order as Concierge would know the names of every guest. It was expected. The personal touch.

Passing through the glass doors, as instructed, Jacquot stepped into the bar, a long room vaulted and floored in herring-boned brick that, at its far end, opened on to an outside terrace. Like the reception desk, the bar itself was another length of stone, another altar of sorts, softly uplit from its base, its polished surface set with tall church candles that stood in pools of hardened wax, cast shifting shadows on the vaulted ceiling, and filled the air with a sweet vanilla scent.

Sitting on a stool halfway down its length, chatting to the barman, was Claude Bouvet. He was the only customer there and looked less the hotel owner than he had earlier. In the twenty or so minutes since Jacquot had last seen him, he'd changed into a freshly pressed collarless shirt and cream cotton Chinos. When Bouvet spotted Jacquot he swung off his stool and waved him over.

'You've missed the rush,' he said, explaining away the empty bar. 'Fifteen minutes ago, Jean-Luc here was mixing Martinis and Bloody Marys by the dozen and now he's polishing glasses. If I wasn't here, he'd have mixed one for himself and nipped out back for a cigarette.'

'*Non, non, monsieur*. Absolutely not,' Jean-Luc began, then, turning to Jacquot, asked him what he would like to drink.

'A pastis,' replied Jacquot.

'Monsieur has a preference? Ricard? Bardouin? Granier, Casanis?'

For a moment Jacquot was taken aback. At Fin de Siècle in Cavaillon, an order for pastis automatically brought a measure of Suze or Cinquante et Un poured over ice and set down with a jug of water. Being offered a choice of brands was something of a luxury. But then, this was Le Grand Monastère.

'Make it Granier, Jean-Luc,' said Bouvet. 'A good local brew. For two.' And, turning to Jacquot, he suggested they move to a table. A moment later, as they settled themselves by the terrace door, Jean-Luc came over with their drinks on a tray. He laid out the glasses, a bowl of ice, a jug of water and a small silver dish crowded with skin-puckered Luques olives.

'*Eh, voilà, messieurs. À vot' santé*,' said Jean-Luc and, sliding the tray under his arm, he retreated to the bar.

'You must be very proud of Grand Monastère,' began Jacquot, as Bouvet added ice to their glasses and splashed in the water, the clear pastis turning a dark, smoking cream. Jacquot raised his glass, tipped it to Bouvet and took a sip. The Granier had a stronger aniseed flavour than he'd expected.

'Very proud indeed,' replied Bouvet, clearly savouring both his drink and his achievement. 'It has been hard work, all these years, but now we are nearly there.'

The two men settled back in their chairs.

'So how did you start in the business, monsieur?'

'In a kitchen. As a *plongeur*. A lowly dishwasher. *En effet*, like many in my profession.'

'And this was where?'

'Geneva. Restaurant Gallini.'

'You are Swiss?'

'Swiss-French. My father was French, my mother Swiss. They had their own business – a chain of *depôts ventes* – you know, discount shops. Mainly fashion. Last year's styles at knock-down prices today. They were very successful.'

'Your parents are still alive?'

Bouvet shook his head. 'My father died first. My mother just a year later.'

'And this was?'

'Eight years ago. They had sold the business by then. Retired.'

'You didn't think of taking it over?'

Bouvet shook his head, swirled the ice in his glass. 'For me, that kind of life was . . . not what I wanted. They were disappointed, of course. But I think they understood, finally, that I was happiest in a kitchen.'

'As a *plongeur*?'

Bouvet gave a short bark of a laugh. 'Not as a *plongeur*, maybe. But then I moved on. Into the main kitchen – out of my steamy little room.'

'At the Gallini.'

'In the beginning, yes.'

'But you didn't stay?'

Bouvet shook his head. 'It is important for chefs to work in many kitchens, monsieur. To learn the trade, to hone their skills. So I moved around. Six, seven years. A year here, a year there. From kitchen to kitchen. A Commis chef, to start, prepping, helping, sometimes cooking; then Chef de Partie; then Sous-chef – Paris, Biarritz, Mougins, then, finally, to Avignon. Hiély-Lucullus on rue de la République. One of the truly great kitchens. It was a privilege, you understand.'

Jacquot nodded, smiled; an invitation for Bouvet to continue.

'And then I came here, to Grand Monastère. Monsieur Ravet, Régine's father, had suffered a stroke and they were looking for a Head Chef. It was a position I wanted, the next in line, if you like. The move you are waiting for when you're a sous-chef. At Hiély-Lucullus it would never have happened – I would never have been considered good enough. But at Monastère they liked me, offered me the job, and I took it. And after they gave me the job, I took the daughter too, eh!' Bouvet chuckled and sipped his pastis. 'Life – such a wonder, *n'est-ce pas*?'

'You have children?'

'*Mais oui*. A son, Alain. He is at hotel school now, in the States. Then, I guess, he will do what I did. Kitchen to kitchen.'

'Do you miss it?'

'Sometimes, yes. But most times, now, no. It is a young man's game, you know? The kitchen can be a terrible place.' He held up his hands, turned them. Even in the low light Jacquot could make out the old scars and shiny burn-marks. 'War wounds, monsieur. It is a battlefield in there,' he said, nodding to the gentle murmur of voices from the dining room and, presumably, the kitchens beyond. 'But it doesn't put us off. Me. Our son. Régine, her father, his father before him. The whole family. My wife's cousin, too. Viviane Mathieu. She has her own place just a few miles from here. Le Tilleul. Maybe you know it?'

Jacquot was taken by surprise. 'Well, of course I know it. Just lunchtime, today. The rillette du Lapereau, the sea bass, the plums in Armagnac.'

'Ah-hah,' cried Bouvet. 'The famous Ravet rillettes. Régine's grandmother's recipe. Old Madame Ravet. The first cook at Monastère. We both have it on our menus, Patric and I, but we always argue. His version or mine. Like Régine's *gran'maman*, he favours more fat. Me . . .' Bouvet waved his hand, index finger up as though he was spinning a pizza base. 'Me, I go for more lean. But I also add a teaspoon of goose fat right at the end. Which is maybe cheating, I know, but it works.'

And then Bouvet stopped short and the smile faded from his lips.

Jacquot knew the reason. For a moment there, reminiscing, Bouvet had forgotten who Jacquot was, what he was doing there. And then he'd remembered. Blood on a bed. A Monastère guest unaccountably missing. And not just a guest, but the companion of Monsieur Roland Bressans, a most important person. And the man sitting across the table from him, the man he was chatting to so enthusiastically, was a police officer from Cavaillon.

'But enough of me, monsieur,' continued Bouvet, glancing over Jacquot's shoulder. 'It is getting late and it would appear that your table is ready.'

Jacquot turned. A tall, good-looking young man in a simple black suit and opened-necked white shirt had entered the bar and was heading in their direction.

Bouvet finished his drink and got to his feet. Jacquot did the same.

'Monsieur Jacquot, allow me to introduce our Maître d'Hôtel, Yves Lenoir.'

Lenoir tipped his head, bowing from the shoulder. 'Monsieur Jacquot. A pleasure. If you are ready? *Le Réfectoire vous attend.*'

35

If ever Jacquot regretted a meal it was now. Not the meal he was about to take, but the one he had already eaten. If he'd known he was going to be dining at Le Réfectoire that night he'd almost certainly have held off at Le Tilleul, making do with one of Viviane's omelettes.

'A beautiful room,' said Jacquot, as he followed Lenoir into the Monastère's celebrated restaurant, taking in the lofty, hammer-beamed ceiling, a pair of Gothic windows set high above a massive stone hearth at the far end of the room, and a wall of glass to his right that opened on to a terrace and the distant Calavon Valley.

'Indeed it is, monsieur. The original dining hall. Late sixteenth-century,' replied Lenoir, steering Jacquot to a corner table, his chair already being drawn out by a waiter dressed in a white waistcoat and black apron. 'If it was a warmer evening, I would have recommended the terrace,' continued Lenoir.

'But it is getting late now and, even for June, there is a little too much chill, I think.'

Taking his seat, and the menu and Cartes des Vins that Lenoir handed him, Jacquot made himself comfortable.

'Is there anything I can get you, Monsieur Jacquot? While you take a look at the Carte? An apéritif, perhaps?'

'No, no, everything is fine, thank you,' replied Jacquot, noting that Lenoir hadn't used the word 'another' in front of 'apéritif', referring to the pastis he'd already had with Bouvet – very slick.

'Then perhaps some wine with your meal,' continued Lenoir. 'I will send over our sommelier when you have made your order. So, please, enjoy your dinner with us.' And, with a spread of his hands, the minutest little bow, Lenoir faded away.

Opening the menu that Lenoir had given him, bound between the kind of cream waxed-parchment covers that looked as though they might once have held some religious tract, Jacquot settled down to the serious business of choosing what to order from the two handwritten pages inside.

Across the top of each sheet – *à la carte* on the left and the *table d'hôte* on the right – were the words: '*Maître Cancale, Chef-de-Cuisine, vous presente* . . .'

Well . . . Just about the most tempting dishes that Jacquot could imagine. Even when he dragged his eyes from the longer left-hand page and concentrated only on the *plats du jour*, the task seemed no easier: there, the little squid called *soupions* that he hadn't tasted since leaving Marseilles; there, a *Carbonnade Nîmoise*; there, a *ris de veau* with freshly picked sorrel; and there, last but one on the list of *entrées*, a *Bœuf à la Gardiane* that he'd first eaten at his grandmother's table. It was all too much. Jacquot closed the menu with a hungry sigh. He would order what he could remember – the first things that came into his head – when Lenoir returned.

He didn't have long to wait. Jacquot was casually observing his fellow diners – every table taken, impossible to tell who was resident and who was non-resident, save perhaps the party of painters that Bouvet had mentioned, sitting at the long table in the middle of the room, and a man dining by himself who looked vaguely familiar – when suddenly Lenoir was at his side, hands clasped behind his back. It was as though he had appeared from nowhere.

'*Vous avez choisi, monsieur?*'

'I have indeed,' replied Jacquot and, damning the consequences, he ordered the panaché of foie gras, the *ris de veau* with sorrel and the cherry clafoutis.

No note of Jacquot's order was taken – simply a nod, a '*très bien*, Monsieur Jacquot' – and, in the time it must have taken Lenoir to pass on Jacquot's selection, it was the sommelier's turn to approach, Hervé Dutalle, according to his name plate, suggesting an iced Alsatian Riesling rather than the more familiar Sauternes to accompany the panaché, a young Rhône with the sweetbreads and, perhaps, a Muscat with the clafoutis?

Jacquot agreed that the recommendations sounded fine. With a Carte des Vins that looked easily sixty pages long, he was happy to have someone else make the decisions for him.

There was another '*très bien, monsieur*,' accompanied by an approving nod, as though it was Jacquot who had made the selection, and Hervé Dutalle, like Lenoir before him, was gone.

It was at that moment – pulling from his inside pocket the list of guests that Bouvet had provided, and noting that Monsieur

Bressans was not among the diners – that Jacquot's eye was drawn to a woman at the far end of the room, moving from table to table, a word here, a word there. Putting aside the list he watched her work the room – a hand on a shoulder, a laugh, a handshake, a bow, a whispered aside to a waiter – until, finally, she turned towards his table. Pushing back his chair, Jacquot rose to his feet. He knew who she was.

'Monsieur Jacquot? Régine Bouvet. A pleasure.'

'Madame Bouvet. *Enchanté. Un plaisir aussi*. Please, won't you join me.'

'Thank you,' she said, and a waiter swooped forward from nowhere to draw back a chair for her. 'And how is the *Hebdo Marseille* these days?' she added, shooting him a conspiratorial smile as she made herself comfortable. 'I'm so sorry I was not here to greet you myself. I was covering for one of our staff – the night shift. I lasted until lunchtime, then . . . I was just asleep on my feet.' She raised her hands, let them drop lightly to the table. 'It was time to retire . . . So, Monsieur Jacquot, is this your first visit to Grand Monastère?'

Jacquot said that it was, noting both Madame Bouvet's steely self-assurance – it was easy to see who held the power in the Bouvet household – as well as her still considerable good looks. She was, Jacquot guessed, in her late forties, an inch or two taller than her husband, and admirably well put together. She was dressed in lightweight beige trousers and frock coat and, beyond the opening orchid bud in her buttonhole, was discreetly but effectively jewelled – a wedding ring, emerald studs, a thin gold bracelet and a single strand of pearls resting above a tanned centimetre of freckled cleavage. Her rust-red hair was cut to the shoulder and only a little make-up – or make-up expertly applied – showed on her lightly freckled skin. Her deep brown eyes were gently lined at the corners, her nails unvarnished and her fingers, as she wove them together on the table–top, were long and slender.

'I'm just so sorry', she continued, 'that your visit has to be under these rather strange circumstances.'

Jacquot nodded at this. 'Strange indeed, madame.' And then, coming straight to the point: 'Tell me, you met Mademoiselle Ladouze?'

'Of course, monsieur. We meet and talk to *all* our guests. As you can see,' she said, indicating her own presence at his table.

'And what were your impressions, madame?'

Régine Bouvet gave Jacquot an arched look, accompanied by a thin, almost disapproving smile. 'If you had seen her, monsieur, I'm sure you would have drawn a similar conclusion . . .'

'That she was of a nervous disposition?' suggested Jacquot innocently. 'Given to making a scene, perhaps? The kind who might just decide to up and off with no explanation, no thought to the consequences?'

Madame Bouvet caught the intended smile. 'Maybe those things too, monsieur. I hope so . . . What I meant was—'

'That she was not the researcher Monsieur Bressans would have had you believe?'

Régine Bouvet unlaced her fingers, spread her hands. 'As I said, if you had seen her, you would have drawn the same conclusions.'

'So what do you imagine might have happened to Mademoiselle Ladouze?'

'I wish I knew, Monsieur Jacquot. My husband tells me she

has left a full wardrobe, so I doubt she has gone home early. Wherever home happens to be.'

'Marseilles, madame.'

'*Ça signifie*,' replied Madame Bouvet, letting her fingertips brush against the orchid bud.

'Has she ever been here before, that you can remember?'

Madame Bouvet shook her head. 'Never. To my knowledge.'

'And Monsieur Bressans?'

'*Mais oui*. Twice, three times now.'

'In how long?'

'Since last November. Thereabouts.'

'And always with researchers?'

'This was the first time.'

'So he came alone, the other times. No party, or delegation, or anything official?'

'Not that I recall.'

'So, what? Just a kind of short holiday?'

'I believe so. I remember he plays tennis, swims. He keeps himself in good condition, *n'est-ce pas*?'

Jacquot nodded. 'Anything else? Did he meet, or spend time with, any of his fellow guests?'

Madame Bouvet gave the question some thought, then shook her head. 'I don't believe so. Although I believe he visits our resident master – Auguste Vilotte. I'm sure Claude will have told you all about him.'

'*En effet*, it was your architect, Monsieur van der Haage. But coming back to Monsieur Bressans . . . Do you happen to know why he would want to see Monsieur Vilotte?'

Madame Bouvet took a moment before she answered, as though weighing her words carefully, the discreet hotelier, unused to discussing the character or business of one of her guests. 'Monsieur Bressans is a well-known businessman, is he not? With political ambitions, *sans doute*? I expect he thought that an association with the Master might be . . . helpful in some way. And didn't I read somewhere that he is opening a museum in Marseilles? Perhaps he hoped that something of the Master's work might find its way on to its walls?'

'Indeed, madame. That is certainly a possibility.' And then, 'I wonder, would it be possible to meet with Monsieur Vilotte? There are certain questions I would like to ask him.'

'I'm sure that would be possible. In the circumstances. But you will have to speak to Madame Champeau, our housekeeper. She has a closer relationship with him than anyone else.'

'How so, madame?'

'She . . . looks after his interests.'

Jacquot raised an eyebrow.

Madame Bouvet sighed, as though she found these continued disclosures a strain on her professional discretion. 'There is a story that a long time ago . . . I believe she was a model for him. For only a short time, but it was enough. She is most protective of the man, and his art. Ah,' she exclaimed, looking up. 'It's you, Yves.'

'Monsieur Jacquot, Madame Bouvet . . .' Lenoir was back. There was a waiter beside him, the panaché of foie gras held in a gloved right hand, offered for inspection on a crisply jacketed left sleeve. Jacquot noted the man wore no watch, no bracelet, just bare wrists showing from his cuffs.

'Monsieur Jacquot,' said Madame Bouvet, getting to her feet and straightening her coat. 'Let me leave you to your panaché. It has been a pleasure talking with you. And, again, welcome to Grand Monastère. I trust you will enjoy your stay with us. If you need anything, please don't hesitate to let me know.'

And with a nod and a smile, Madame Bouvet retreated the way she had come, leaving Jacquot to the tender mercies of Maître Cancale, Yves Lenoir, Hervé Dutalle and an army of waiters.

36

It was close to midnight when Jacquot returned to his room, closing the door behind him and leaning back against it with a groan. His mother, Marie-Anne, would have been cross with him. Always leave the table hungry, she'd say. Easy enough when he was growing up in Le Panier, but there'd been little chance of that this evening, the panaché, *ris de veau* and clafoutis presented with a full supporting cast of unordered 'tasting notes', as Lenoir called them: a melon and ginger sorbet, a velouté of creamed artichoke hearts, a crisped fish-skin 'pizza' piled with caviar, a pair of guinea-fowl olives poached in an anchovy sauce – on and on, one after another, just a mouthful each, a simple scoop and swallow but, by the time he pushed away from his table, Jacquot had been undone. As had the top button of his trousers.

With a soft moan, he made his way to Ghislaine Ladouze's bedroom, thankful that he'd had the forethought to make the bed before dinner, rather than now – all that stooping and tucking would have undone him even further. Clinging to one of the bed's four corner posts – courtesy of the Riesling, Rhône and Muscat – he pulled off his clothes, dropped them where he stood and went behind the screen to fill the bath. The taps were brass, set to one side of the tub and laced with a coil of bronze-coloured shower hose. Reaching for the plug lever set between the taps, Jacquot pushed it to *fermé*, but the plug refused to engage. Wincing with the effort, he stooped down to do it by hand then noticed something lodged beneath it. He pulled up the plug from its gearing.

Blue. Something blue. He pulled it out and looked at it. A plaster. A blue sticky plaster with a rectangle of gauze. A brown stain on the gauze the size of an old sou.

Jacquot felt a squeeze of excitement. With no visit from housekeeping, thanks to the *Pas Dérangez* sign, Ghislaine's bathroom had to be exactly as she'd left it the night before – the bath not cleaned since the previous day.

So the plaster belonged to whom?

Ghislaine?

Or her killer? If, indeed, she had been murdered.

Jacquot tried to picture the scene. Whoever it is, kills her on the bed then comes in here to wash his or her hands? The blade of the knife? And the plaster comes off, wedged into the plug hole by the flow of water?

Naked, Jacquot took the plaster through to the salon and found an envelope in the desk drawer, dropped it in and sealed it.

Something for Fournier if the Forensic boys had to be called in.

But that wasn't all.

Martin O'Brien

Deciding he'd take his bath in the morning, Jacquot switched out the bathroom lights and slid gratefully, bloatedly, beneath the quilt. For a moment or two he lay there, thinking about the plaster, then pulled off the band that held his ponytail in place and reached for the TV remote.

With a blink, the late-night movie came on; made in the fifties, judging by its lurid colours. It was a little jerky, the focus uncertain – one of those experimental 'auteur'-type, cinéma vérité films by the look of it. A young woman walking along a beach, the wind off the sea (or maybe it was a lake?) tugging at her skirts.

Jacquot watched for a moment, then remembered that he still had the remains of the joint he'd smoked on the way to Le Tilleul that morning. In a jacket pocket, if he wasn't mistaken. He hoped he wasn't. Dragging himself from the bed, he went to the chair where he'd hung his jacket, hunkered down and felt through its pockets. He found what he was looking for, then his lighter, and crept back into bed. Across the room, the girl on the beach was now sitting outside a café in what looked like Paris. Smoking a cigarette, laughing at the camera.

Jacquot lit up his joint, taking care that no tiny burning embers fell on to the cover, sheet or pillowcase. He took a drag and blew out the smoke. It had a hot, bitter taste – just the one toke, then. Sadly, he mashed it out in the ashtray and reached again for the TV remote, searching for the volume control so that he could hear what the girl in the movie was saying. But it didn't seem to be working. He pressed the 'mute' button a couple of times but there was no response, then he turned up the volume until the graph on the screen showed a 'twenty'. But still there was no sound, not even the hiss of static.

180

Without thinking, Jacquot changed channels. The voice of a newscaster blared out and Jacquot jumped, scrabbling at the remote to reduce the sound. Puzzled, he turned back to the girl in the café. Still no soundtrack, though he could see her lips moving. As he watched, a man moved into frame, adjusted the hat the girl was wearing, then stepped back behind the camera. She righted the hat and laughed again, then took it off, flung it at the camera. There was a blur of static and the next instant the same girl was walking along a crowded street, looking over her shoulder, waving goodbye.

Pushing back the quilt, Jacquot got out of bed and crossed to the TV. A small video player that he hadn't noticed before was recessed beneath the screen and a green 'on' light wavered slightly. As he reached out a hand to it, there was a clunk, a flash of static on the screen, and the whine of a 'rewind' engaging. When the winding ceased, he pushed the 'eject' button and a cassette tape slid out of its panel. Jacquot pulled it clear, turned it in his hands. A sticky label was attached to one side. Written in a careless, sloping hand were the words: *Céleste M.*

Beneath the video player was a rack of videos for the use of guests. Jacquot checked the rack – a half-dozen spaces, all of them filled. He checked the covers – none of them empty. He turned the video in his hand. Did this belong to Ghislaine Ladouze, Jacquot wondered? Had she brought it with her? Some old home movie? Had she been watching this? The answer, he was certain, was 'yes'.

He pushed the tape back into the machine, pressed the 'play' button and returned to the bed. He ran the tape from beginning to end.

Twice.

Martin O'Brien

It took Jacquot that long to notice that the girl sitting at the café and walking down the street was wearing espadrilles.

And a white cotton dress, its full skirt layered in frilled panels. A gypsy dress.

37

He waited till the sliver of moon slipped behind the slopes above Grand Monastère before he made his move.

Softly, stopping every few steps, keeping to the shadows and the smooth flagstones that bordered the courtyard, he reached the passage to the lower cloister suites. At its far end he paused, peeped into the cloister and waited. No door light showed on either level. It was late, all the guests asleep, the only sound an occasional rattle of palm fronds as the night air stirred through them. But still he kept to the shadows, listening for the slightest sound, eyes scouring for movement. But there was nothing. He took a breath and stepped out into the cloister.

At the far end he turned to the right and felt his way along the Bishops' Wall, its stone surface coated with a score of scrolled plaques, the marble shields polished with time, incised with a blackened, shorthand Latin – dates, prayers and earnest benedictions. And the names: Blessed Pierre-Louis, Bishop of Sarlat; Blessed Augustine, papal legate to the Court of the Sun King; Blessed Jean-Louis, the scheming Bishop of Amiens; the great Arnaud of Auch, whose portrait hung in the Curia itself; and the builder bishop Hubert of Valence who'd transformed the Cathédrale St-Apollinaire and added the second cloister at Luissac. All those remembered on these memorial plaques had taught at Grand Monastère, or been taught here, and all had achieved high office, called upon to leave their cells and the order to work for a greater good. He knew the names by heart.

Out of the shadows, a bat flittered past, the tiniest squeak making him freeze for a moment. Back against the wall, feeling the corner of Hubert's plaque pressing against his shoulder, he looked back through the cloister's arches, following the line of the courtyard from left to right and, where visible, the level above; listening again, watching for movement. Nothing.

Reaching out with the toes of his shoes, he felt his way forward and pushed open the planked door with its copperplate sign, *Privé*. Two days before he'd oiled the old hinges which turned now without a sound, just the lightest grating of metal on metal, something felt rather than heard. But he didn't push his luck, opening the old door only wide enough for him to slip through like a draught of air.

On the other side, he waited again, then remembered that he'd need more room on the way back, easing the door open a few more centimetres rather than closing it behind him. Across the courtyard, a flickering light shone from the topmost window in the watchtower, giving a sense of space and form to the shadows around him, the ceiling of stars above his head providing just enough light for him to find what he had come for.

Pulling back the cover he squatted down, worked at the ground and hoisted the bundle into his arms. As he tried to stand, however, he felt a slight resistance followed by a short, sharp tearing sound that made him freeze. He lowered the bundle again, teasing it free from whatever held it, the muscles in his legs burning with the effort.

Slowly, slowly, he straightened up and, now free of the snag, he jerked the load to his chin, then tipped it over his shoulder. As he did so he sensed something fall away from the bundle. Metal or wood? he thought in the split-second before it hit the ground. What was it made of? And what would it hit, bounce off? What was below him? What would the sound be?

A hollow, deadened tap. Then silence.

Wood. Wood hitting wood. He breathed a sigh of relief. If anyone had been watching – waiting, as he had, for sound and movement – he'd have given the game away. Twice. With the sounds of tearing and that hollow tap. And when it came to games, he never liked to lose.

Careful where he put his feet, he turned back the way he had come and, step by cautious step, made for the narrow rectangle of light that marked out the door he had left ajar. This time it was a tighter squeeze and he had to twist himself sideways to get through the space, the load he carried brushing against the stone. Just a whisper, but enough to have him pause again. But this time he had the wall to lean against, and to ease the weight from his shoulder as he reached out a hand and closed the door behind him.

His breath was coming fast now – as much from the exertion as from a fluttering of excitement. Now was the difficult part, crossing the first cloister again, back into the gravelled courtyard and back where he had come from, everything ready, everything prepared.

Thirty minutes later, he sank into his bed and slept.

Part Three

Part Three

38

Sunday

Lens van der Haage opened his eyes and shifted his head on the pillow. In an instant he regretted both movements, the first accompanied by a squint and the second with a wince. Somewhere at the top of his neck, a giant with a sledgehammer had set up residence and was pounding away at the base of his skull.

The night before Lens had drunk too much wine, too much cognac. Not to celebrate – as he'd expected – but to drown his sorrows. Now, as he struggled from his bed and made for the bathroom, he acknowledged that his trip south to Luissac had been just another waste of time and money. And Lens van der Haage could ill afford to waste either.

The hangover was an additional burden. Lens usually had a stiff, protestant approach to drinking – a little and not too often. But he'd needed something more when the Bouvets had broken the news over a late supper the night before. Something to soften the shock, something to block the disappointment, to settle the frustration. Four days he'd been there, four days at Grand Monastère, his hopes and his dreams raised to the heights, then dashed down.

So close, and now . . . ?

As he clutched the sink, peering painfully into the mirror to examine the bloodshot whites of his eyes, he still couldn't quite believe it.

He'd known from the moment he sat at the Bouvets' table that something was wrong. His companions appeared ill-at-ease and their conversation was forced and over-friendly, so unlike their lunch the day before. And then, as Régine finished ladling the *blanquette de lotte* into their bowls, he'd found out just how bad it really was.

The deal with Vilotte was off, Régine had finally announced, returning the casserole to the centre of the table and taking her seat. She and Claude were so sorry, she added, catching her breath, bringing him all that way for nothing. But what could they do? A few days earlier it had all seemed so certain. Yet now . . .

When Régine finally fell silent, as confounded as he was by this unexpected turn of events, her husband Claude had taken over. As Lens already knew, Claude began, Vilotte had told them that he'd finally made up his mind. It was time for him to go. Time to sell. If the Bouvets paid what he wanted – a higher price than they'd anticipated – and made their house in Luissac available, then the tower was theirs.

And they'd gone along with it, agreed to all his terms and conditions. But now, Claude told him, just half an hour earlier,

Vilotte had called to say the sale was off. Said he didn't think he'd got long to live, and didn't want to waste time moving, upsetting everything. Said he'd decided to live out the rest of his days in the tower, simply couldn't leave it, too many memories. And anyway, they'd get the lease back when he died, so what was the hurry?

And according to Claude there was nothing they'd been able to say or do to change his mind.

Which was when Lens had reached for the bottle beside the casserole and filled his glass.

Stepping into the shower stall, Lens set the controls for *froid* and prepared himself for the shock. In an instant the breath was snatched from his body and he gasped as the water splashed over him. But the icy pummelling soon had the desired effect, as he knew it would. After only a few moments the sledgehammer blows in his head began to subside and the tension in his shoulders eased. Finally, increasing the temperature, he decided that things might not, after all, seem as bleak as they had the night before. He would find a way round this latest problem. Just as he'd found his way round all the other problems that had beset him since he'd started work on the Monastère project: securing the relevant *permis* from the planning authorities, or negotiating with the quarry boss down at Sarragon, or the kitchen suppliers in Aix, or the electrical merchants in St Étienne – even managing the Bouvets themselves, constantly refining his plans and schedules to accommodate their ever-more fanciful whims and demands for economies.

Of course Lens had known from the start that the Bouvets didn't own the whole Monastère site, that the property wasn't all theirs. They'd told him that when he first arrived, brought in after the Bouvets had seen the photo-spread in *Côte-Sud* of his renovations to the old Hôtel Grex off Cours Mirabeau in Avignon.

They'd shown him round the property, explained what they wanted to do and he'd accepted the commission without a second thought. A difficult, daunting proposition – it made the Grex project look like a walk in the park – there had been no doubt in Lens's mind that the renovation and redesign of Grand Monastère would make his name, secure his future. The possibility there might be problems at some future date with a sitting tenant had simply failed to dilute his enthusiasm.

And the old boy's days were surely numbered, they'd both assured him. Well into his eighties and increasingly unsteady in both mind and body. And after meeting the Master, Lens had had no good reason to disbelieve them. The man was a wreck. He might have been a celebrated artist, with a gilded reputation, but he was drinking far too much, smoking far too much – he surely wouldn't last.

But of course he had, constantly complaining about the noise of the renovations as Lens and his team set to work on the new courtyard suites – the dirt and the dust, the inconvenience of it all. He'd been a nightmare from day one and, over Réfectoire's *blanquette de lotte* the night before, it had become clear that Auguste Vilotte was being a nightmare still.

39

Jacquot was doing what he assumed all good journalists would do – leafing through a newspaper to see what stories had made the first edition, while keeping a weather eye on the comings and goings of the Monastère's staff and guests. From where he sat, in a glass-warmed slant of sunshine by the front entrance, Jacquot had an almost uninterrupted view of the whole reception area – from the stone slab desk on his right to the doors of the Salle du Matin at the end of the lobby and the stone stairs leading to the upper loggia suites.

Jacquot had taken up this position nearly an hour earlier, after waking at a little before six, feeling surprisingly fit and clear-headed considering his shameful over-indulgence the night before. A pot of strong black coffee ordered from Room Service and a plate of sugar-dusted pastries had further restored him and, after a long hot soak in the tub, he had left Ghislaine

Ladouze's room with the *Pas Dérangez* sign still on the handle and come down to Reception.

At that hour of the morning, the lobby had been quiet. A couple of staff manned the Monastère's reception desk and a porter with a slight but noticeable hump in his shoulder was working his way round the copper cauldrons with a watering can. Apart from that there was little other activity until Bouvet crossed the courtyard and came into the hotel. They exchanged greetings but Bouvet, it seemed to Jacquot, appeared preoccupied and after a brief chat – how was the room? did he sleep well? – Bouvet had excused himself and disappeared into his office behind Reception.

Some twenty minutes later, riffling through the last of his newspaper, the tap-tap of leather soles on stone alerted Jacquot that someone was coming down the stairs from the upper suites. Glancing to his left, Jacquot saw the man who'd been dining alone in Le Réfectoire the evening before. The one who'd seemed vaguely familiar. He wore tasselled loafers, an open-necked shirt, a suede blouson and black cotton trousers and, when he reached the main hall, he crossed to the reception desk and helped himself, as Jacquot had done, to the newspapers left out for guests. Turning smartly on his heel, as though he knew his way around, he headed off towards the Salle du Matin where, Jacquot knew from the map that Bouvet had given him, breakfast was served to those guests who, unlike him, chose to forego Room Service.

As the man passed between the pillars, Jacquot tried to place him. Where had they met? Where had Jacquot seen him? In Marseilles? In Cavaillon? Or was it someone he'd seen on TV, or in the papers? This was Grand Monastère, after all. And then, as the door to the Salle du Matin closed behind him, Jacquot had it. The suede blouson, soft as a *chamois* pelt, and those turned, casually unbuttoned cuffs. Tabac Rafine in Cavaillon. The man in front of him. The cigars. The Montechristos. The Citroën. Small world, thought Jacquot, wondering whether he was Monsieur Erdâg Kónar or Monsieur Paul Ginoux, the only other male guests on his list who were staying at the Monastère but who were not members of the painting group. He didn't look like a Kónar, Jacquot decided, so he was probably Monsieur Ginoux, the art dealer from Paris. According to the list Bouvet had given him, which Jacquot had studied in the bath that morning, Monsieur Ginoux had a driver, a man called Dutronc, who'd been billeted in a guest annexe down in Luissac.

After Monsieur Ginoux, other guests appeared and Jacquot recognised five of the people he'd seen dining at the painters' club table the evening before: the two American ladies, Hughes and Tilley (though which was which he couldn't yet say), arm in arm, stepping from the passageway that led to the garden rooms, their sneakers squeaking over the stone floor; the other American lady, Madame West, in a swirling rainbow-coloured kaftan cinched at the waist by a wide brown belt; and then the English lady. She had to be English, thought Jacquot – the cardigan, the slacks, the pearls.

The last of the group was their tour leader, hurrying across the hall to speak to Bouvet. He wore loose linen trousers pleated at the waist, a crisply collared white shirt and a pale blue jumper shawled round his shoulders. He also carried a small brown bag, looped around his wrist. His name, Jacquot remembered, was Gavan – Gilles Gavan, or was it Guy Gavan? – and, though he hated speculating, Jacquot guessed that Gilles (he was certain now it was Gilles) was probably gay. The way he stood at the desk, leaning against it with open palms, standing on tiptoe, the way he rescued his jumper as it slid from his shoulder, the way he reached out for Bouvet's hands to thank him for something, clasping them in his own and, most significant, how uncomfortable Bouvet suddenly looked, unsure how to withdraw his hands without causing offence. He managed it by extricating one of them from Gavan's grasp and pointing towards the Salle du Matin.

It was then, moments after Gavan disappeared into the breakfast room, that Roland Bressans made his appearance, coming down the stairs and crossing to the front desk, the collar of a pink sports shirt turned jauntily up, his sockless feet shod in immaculately polished moccasins.

Putting down his paper, Jacquot pushed out of his chair and headed in his direction.

Just the man he wanted to see.

Even if, as Bressans turned from the desk with his newspaper, Jacquot could see that the feeling was not reciprocated. A wince of annoyance flashed across Bressans' features, followed by a swift, almost involuntary glance to left and right as though seeking a way to avoid a meeting. But it was not to be. The two men met in the centre of the vaulted hall.

'Monsieur, *bonjour*,' began Jacquot.

'Ah, Jacquot. Good to see you,' replied Bressans, attempting a certain friendly familiarity which Jacquot knew he certainly didn't feel. 'And here so early.'

'I stayed overnight, monsieur, in Mademoiselle Ladouze's room.'

Bressans' eyes widened. 'In her room? But she might have returned.'

'In which case, everything would have been neatly resolved,

n'est-ce pas? But I regret to say that she did not return. Last night, or this morning. And since it is now more than thirty hours since she was last seen, her failure to return must now, I fear, be treated a little more seriously. I'm sure you'll agree?'

Jacquot waited for Bressans to say something, but the man remained silent. Just the merest clenching of his jaw suggested that he had heard what Jacquot had said and understood that the investigation into his companion's disappearance might soon have to move up a gear. A prospect, Jacquot knew, that Bressans would hardly find pleasing.

On the other side of the hall, Gilles Gavan reappeared, herding his painters from the Salle du Matin. 'So sorry to rush you,' he was saying, 'but we really must be going. Packed lunches are in the van. It's just packed painters we're missing.'

There was laughter at this, as the party swept past Jacquot and Bressans and headed for the front entrance.

'It is for this reason, monsieur,' continued Jacquot with a friendly smile, 'that I must now ask you for the contact details in Marseilles that you used to, ah . . . locate Mademoiselle Ladouze. I'm sure you understand.'

Jacquot knew he should have asked for the details the previous afternoon when Bressans told him about it, but guessed, when he remembered it in the bath that morning, that his usually sharp faculties had probably been dulled by his lunch at Le Tilleul. But those faculties weren't dulled now. Once Jacquot had those contact details, he could get one of his chums in Marseilles to check things out. Peluze or Laganne. One of the old squad on rue de L'Évêché. They'd know how to handle it. A discreet call, or maybe even a visit, to the lady who managed Mademoiselle Ladouze – her dealings with Monsieur Bressans (if that was the name he'd given), and all she knew of Mademoiselle Ladouze: how long they'd been working together, other clients and, more important, where she lived. Ten minutes in her apartment and the boys would get Jacquot all he needed – an address book, a diary perhaps, photographs – enough to build up some kind of profile without raising too much attention. Rochet would have approved.

But not Bressans. Bressans wasn't at all happy about it. He frowned, shook his head. 'The contact, you say? I don't think . . . I'm not sure . . .' he blustered.

But Jacquot said nothing, kept his smile pinned on the man. He'd have the information off Bressans if they had to stand there in the lobby all day.

And Bressans knew it.

Finally he gave up the bluster, let out an irritated hiss and reached into his back pocket for his wallet. He flipped it open, found a card and handed it to Jacquot. One side was a dusty pink and blank, the other side white. On the white side, in a dusty pink copperplate, was a name – Jacqueline de Ternay – and, in the bottom right-hand corner, a telephone number.

'And the address, monsieur?'

'The address? I really don't . . .'

Jacquot levelled a look at him.

Another hiss of irritation. 'Place du Maréchal. Number 17. It's in Castellane,' replied Bressans curtly, hardly able to hold back his temper.

'Thank you, monsieur,' said Jacquot, flicking the card lightly against his knuckles. 'As I had hoped, you continue to be most helpful. And please be assured that any inquiries we make will, at this early stage, be handled most . . . carefully.'

Bressans slipped the wallet back into his pocket and gave

Jacquot a glare. 'If that is all, monsieur?' he said, and, without waiting for an answer, he strode off towards the Salle du Matin.

Pompous, pampered little *perle*, thought Jacquot with a grin, watching him cross the lobby, slap-slapping the newspaper against his thigh. What a delight it was to wind the man up, and watch him spin.

Irresistible.

But disappointing, too.

So far as Jacquot had been able to see, there was not a single cut or abrasion anywhere on the man's hands. However much he might have wished it, the plaster he'd found the previous night did not, it seemed, belong to Bressans.

40

The first thing that Claudine Eddé saw as she turned on to the Monastère bridge was Gilles' white minibus parked in front of the gates. She breathed out a sigh of relief. Thanks to a queue at the only petrol pump within twenty kilometres of her home, she was running badly late. All the way up to Luissac, tearing through the hairpins, she'd worried that she'd be holding the group up, that Gilles would be in a tizz. He had told her the previous afternoon that he was taking them all to a secret destination, that she should come to Monastère first thing and follow them, that she'd never find it on her own. As she pulled up behind the van she counted four heads and realised she was in the clear. Someone else in the party was holding them up.

'He's gone to look for Philip and Hilaire,' Joanne explained in passable French when Claudine came round to the sliding side door, left open for a snatch of cool breeze. 'He said we should stay here. That he wouldn't be long.'

'*Tu parle très bien en français, Joanne. Bravo,*' replied Claudine, noting the immediate glow of pleasure that raced up Joanne's neck and into her cheeks. 'I'll go and see if I can help,' she continued and, with a smile at the others and a 'Good morning, ladies' in English, she turned from the van and walked through Monastère's gate.

Joanne. Such a sweet lady, Claudine thought as she stepped into the courtyard. So helpful, so sincere. And how she loved to paint. It was as though painting brought something out in her, the real Joanne – passionate, committed, determined. The absorption with which she worked, her determination to get it right – colours, texture, approach. If she had a problem, Claudine and Gilles had decided, it was that Joanne hadn't yet learned to paint for herself. Everything she did, she still did for the approval of others. Maybe, thought Claudine, they'd hammer that out of her by the end of the trip.

That was what Claudine was thinking, striding across the courtyard, headed for the arched entrance to the lower cloister gardens, when she looked up and saw him.

Recognised him instantly.

The policeman from Marseilles.

It was the ponytail that did it, that curl of lustrous black hair caught in what looked like a thick red rubber band. The size of him, too – a big man, but trim and fit with an easy, idling grace. Even the clothes were familiar – the linen jacket, open-necked shirt, cotton trousers, espadrilles. Standing right there, not ten metres away, talking to one of the guests in the lobby.

Just as she remembered him.

Which was when it struck Claudine that if she could see him, and recognise him, then he had only to make a half-turn, glance in her direction and, possibly, he might also recognise her. It was what policemen did, after all – file away faces, information. She'd seen the movies, read the books. She knew. Which was why, in mid-stride, Claudine spun round and, breath catching, hurried back to her car.

Safely in the Citroën, squirming down in her seat, it all came tumbling back. Not quite a year ago. The Gallery Ton-Ton a few blocks from Marseilles' Vieux Port. Her sister, Delphie, had set it up. Said she'd met this man at a party, a policeman, invited him to Claudine's first-ever show. As it turned out he hadn't shown up and Claudine had been relieved. Her first First Night and still raw from her husband's betrayal, the last thing she'd wanted was a blind date set up by her sister.

But then, the following day, the man standing there in the Monastère's lobby – she'd swear it was him – had just turned up at the gallery, out of the blue. And even bought a painting. The plate of lemons. She remembered his chequebook, but couldn't for the life of her recall the name printed on it. Just the ponytail, and the clothes. And though she couldn't see from this distance, chancing another look through the driver's window, she remembered his eyes. They were green, astonishingly, stirringly green, and caught in a net of laugh lines.

But what had she gone and done, that long-ago Sunday afternoon, just the two of them alone in the gallery? Just pretended she was the sales assistant, that's what. Lied to him. Too shy, too . . . silly, to admit that she was the artist. Which was all well and good until he said how he'd come back and pick up the picture at the end of the week, when the exhibition was over, so that he could meet the artist, apologise for missing the First-Night party. If Delphie hadn't slipped off that kerb on Quai des Belges and twisted her ankle, necessitating a trip to the hospital, Claudine would have had to endure untold embarrassment.

And now, nearly a year later, here he was at the Monastère. And the horrible prospect of embarrassment had returned.

But was he staying, she wondered? Or was he there on police business?

Hunkered down in the Citroën, she was wondering if she dared start up the car and reverse out of his line of sight – her Citroën could be temperamental in matters relating to reverse gear – when Gilles' voice brought her to with a start.

'Claudine, Claudine. You made it. *Superbe.*'

She looked up and saw him hurrying through the gate, herding Gould and Madame Becque ahead of him, Madame's paintbox, stool and easel shared between the two men. 'Maybe you could take Philip and Hilaire? Give us a little more space in the van,' he said, steering them towards her.

'Of course, of course,' she replied, relieved that at last they could be on their way, leaning across to open the passenger door for Hilaire while Gould dumped their things on to the back seat and clambered in after them.

'So, ladies,' he said, making himself comfortable then drumming his fingers on the paintbox next to him, 'let's go paint us some masterpieces, huh?'

Still keeping low, not daring to look back at the hotel, Claudine started the car and, as quietly and as smoothly as possible, she swung the Citroën round and followed after Gilles in the van. Only when she reached the bridge did she dare a glance in the rear-view mirror.

There, over Gould's shoulder, she could see the policeman coming out from the shadow of the gate where, just a minute or two earlier, she'd been parked. Looking back to the road, she felt a wave of relief that she'd got away in time. But then, unexpectedly, surprisingly, as she followed Gilles down the road to Luissac, she felt the smallest flutter of excitement and, like Joanne, a flush of warmth reached up into her cheeks.

41

Standing in the Monastère gateway, watching the painters turn off the bridge and start down the road to Luissac, Jacquot decided that life could hardly be more agreeable. After savouring the pleasure of seeing Monsieur Roland Bressans squirm, all he had to do now was address himself to the prospect of a lazy day stretching enticingly ahead of him. A Sunday in early June, in the foothills of the Grand Lubéron, with a strengthening sun warming the gravel at his feet and soaking into the night-chilled stone walls of one of the finest hotels in Provence. A hotel that, for the time being, was to be his home. Better still, it was something he'd been asked to do. A favour. Low profile – maybe something, maybe nothing. And on the house.

Going to his car, retrieving a fresh pack of cigarettes from the glove compartment, Jacquot considered the day ahead. A gentle stroll down to Luissac when the dust from the painters' convoy had subsided, some phone calls on his return to Brunet in Cavaillon and the boys in Marseilles, a leisurely lunch on the terrace (something small; he had a feeling he might well be availing himself of another dinner in Le Réfectoire) and, finally, a meeting with the Master. Monsieur Auguste Vilotte. After Bressans had stalked off to his breakfast, Jacquot had asked Bouvet to set up a meeting. Bouvet had put a call through to the housekeeper, confirmed two-thirty as a suitable time, and that, barring unforeseen circumstances (like the reappearance, in one form or another, of Mademoiselle Ladouze), seemed to be the limit of his duties.

Having had the tour of the hotel on the inside, courtesy of Lens van der Haage the previous day, Jacquot had decided that it was maybe time to familiarise himself with the hotel's exterior. Not that there was much to explore. Sitting on its limestone plinth the Monastère might have had a majestic spread of land around it, but not much of it was easily accessible. From Mademoiselle Ladouze's windows and from the battlements he'd visited with van der Haage, Jacquot knew that there was nothing but precipitous, cactus-strewn slopes on the northern side of Monastère. It wasn't a great deal different here, on the southern side, where guests parked their cars, the low retaining wall that enclosed the cobbled turning circle reaching from one corner of Monastère's looming windowless façade to the other.

Pulling off his jacket in the already thunderous heat and swinging it over his shoulder, Jacquot walked the length of this wall, leaning over here and there to scan the slopes beneath – the rocky skirts of Monastère lethally cloaked in sabre-leaved aloe and spiky cactus – and the hillside opposite, a stony scrub of gorse and olive and pine reaching less steeply but no less inhospitably to a distant skyline. So far as he could see, any approach to or departure from Monastère by any means other than the bridge looked a questionable proposition. It appeared, in short, to be utterly impregnable – ideally situated to serve as both strategic position and spiritual hideaway – and he wondered how on earth they'd ever managed to supply the place before the bridge was built.

Leaving the forecourt and starting out across the bridge, a different perspective provided the answer. Looking down, Jacquot could see what remained of a narrow pathway through the blades of aloe and cactus spike, a stony track dropping down from the Luissac slope, weaving between the three arches of the bridge before rising up to a ledge set below a ten-metre wall of stone. And there, at the top of that rocky face, was what looked like the mouth of a chute built out from Monastère's lower wall. So far as Jacquot could estimate the top of this chute would have been in the furthest corner of the second courtyard, somewhere close to the watchtower. With a block and tackle and a length of sturdy rope, it was suddenly clear how the fortress and monastery had been supplied.

Pleased with his detective work, Jacquot reached the end of the bridge and set off for Luissac. Keeping to the outside verge, just a line of stone posts to mark its plunging edge, unseen crickets chirruped his progress, lizards flitted across what looked like a storm run-off, and his nostrils filled with the hot, dusty-sharp scents of wild fennel, lemon verbena and pine. Every few metres he looked back at Monastère, seeming to rise out of thin air, and he marvelled at it until, without realising it, the road curved into the hillside. The next time he turned, Hôtel Grand Monastère des Évêques had vanished.

42

Suppressing the urge to laugh out loud, for he would still be heard, Champeau made do with a deep glow of satisfaction as he lay back near the storm run-off and stretched out his legs. The top of his thighs were burning and his ankles were stiff as wood. But he didn't mind that. It was the price you paid. For being invisible.

Champeau knew how to hide, all right. Still as stone. Not a blink of an eyelash. Even when that cricket landed on his shoulder, rubbed its back legs and clambered across his cheek. Nothing. That *flic* had passed by no more than ten metres distant, had even looked him in the eye. And he hadn't seen a thing.

Champeau knew he was a policeman. He'd sat in the man's car the night before, opened the glovebox and seen the blue light, the kind they put out of the window when they were chasing baddies. He'd seen them do it on TV. And what about that bin liner filled with bedding? What kind of journalist took someone else's bedding away in a black bin liner? Because that was what everyone else at Monastère seemed to think he was. A journalist. There to write a story about the hotel.

But why anyone would want to write about, or even read about, Monastère, when it was right there, staring them in the face, was a question that eluded Champeau. It was just one of life's many imponderables, and for that reason best left to the grown-ups to figure out. If they were happy, Champeau was happy.

And right now Champeau was happier than he'd been in a long time. He liked a joke, did Champeau, but this was a cracker. That *flic*. So close. And nothing. At night it was easy. Daylight was different.

Champeau had been on the desk again the night before and after sorting the newspapers and watering the plants, he'd knocked off for the day. But instead of seeking out his bed, he'd run to his room, grabbed a towel and headed off for a swim. Not to the terrace, of course – that was reserved for guests – but up to Bassin Vert, a natural rockpool hidden away on the slopes above Monastère. He'd just struck off the road, clambering up the storm-drain and into the scrub, the painters roaring past beneath, when he'd spotted him, the *flic*, leaning over the side of the bridge and looking into the cut like he'd lost something.

It was then that Champeau decided to hide, to stay where he was and make himself invisible, just a few metres from the road. If the *flic* decided on a stroll, this was the way he would come, the only way he could come.

And he'd done just that, coat over his shoulder, whistling

to himself, strolling down the road. Right past him. Not quite close enough to touch, but close enough.

With a jubilant hoot of delight – at his cleverness, and the closeness of it – Champeau struggled to his feet and continued on his climb to Bassin Vert.

43

Walking down the main street that he had driven along the previous day, the same feeling of absence and emptiness hit Jacquot. It was the curse of the south, he thought. So many owners who used their luxury boltholes for a month in the summer and a couple of weeks at Christmas. Nothing more. The rest of the time their properties stayed shuttered and closed, or loudly rented out to a dozen different families throughout the year. It was no way to secure the spirit of a village like Luissac. And it showed. At other villages like this – with maybe not such a wonderful view or such celebrated neighbours – Sunday morning would have had the *gran'mamans* out in their finest, the old boys at a table in the shade, the tinkle of pastis ice and the smell of Sunday lunch filling the street. But there was none of that here in Luissac, and Jacquot felt the poorer for it.

Damn all tourists, he was thinking to himself when he heard shouting up one of the alleys that led off the main street. He followed it up a slope between silent, shuttered houses until he stepped out into a courtyard with open doors and open windows. Half a dozen young men, and two women, were playing netball, the hoop secured to a length of scaffolding above the front door of an old village house currently being transformed into another luxury bolthole.

No one noticed his appearance so he stood a moment in the shadows, recognising the players one after another from Le Réfectoire the night before: Lenoir, the Maître d'; Hervé, the sommelier; the waitress who'd brushed the crumbs from his table and removed his empty plates with a whispered '*Je m'excuse*'. All of them staff from Monastère, the men in sweats and the two girls in cut-off jeans.

Taller than the rest, Lenoir was clearly a master of the game. He swooped and feinted across the sloping cobbles and rose like a ballerina to slot the ball into the hoop. Lenoir. Yves Lenoir. Thirty-two. Third year at Réfectoire. From La Mirande in Avignon according to the staff list that Bouvet had given him. He tried to recall the details on the sommelier, Hervé . . . ? Hervé . . . ? Dutalle. From . . . Talloires? Auberge du Père Bise? Or was it Moulin de Mougins? One of them, anyway.

Coming back from another successful hoop, Lenoir caught Jacquot's eye and, telling his friends he was taking five, he trotted over.

'Monsieur, good to see you. I hope you enjoyed your meal with us last night.' He pushed back a mop of hair off his forehead, the sweat from his game slicking through it, sticking it to his scalp.

'Difficult not to, wouldn't you say?'

Lenoir beamed.

'So who's looking after the shop while you're down here playing ball?'

'No one,' he replied. 'But you'll find me there in exactly . . .' – Lenoir checked his watch – 'in exactly one hour and twenty minutes.'

Jacquot nodded, took it in.

'I see you've cut yourself,' he said, gesturing at Lenoir's right hand. The plaster wasn't blue but it was clearly visible; a strip of pink around his index finger.

Lenoir frowned, held up his hand. 'A broken nail. Not good in my line of work.'

'I guess that's true,' said Jacquot. 'So,' he asked, 'you live down here?' Over Lenoir's shoulder the other players had called it quits and were filing into one of the houses on the small square.

'That's right. Across the *place*, the two houses there on the right.' He gestured over his shoulder without looking round. 'It works well. Nothing worse than living above the shop.'

'There's a guest annexe down here, too, isn't there?'

'That's right. Off the main square, right by the church. Kind of an overflow, if you like, when it's busy. Right now, there's just Monsieur Ginoux's driver there. Got the place to himself.'

'And all the staff live down here? In Luissac?'

'Most of us, yes. Or further down in St-Mas. The locals, with their families.'

'And the rest?'

'Our chef, Le Maître Cancale, the Bouvets, Madame Champeau and her son . . . they all have apartments in the hotel. Then there're a couple of rooms for the junior staff – waiters, waitresses. That's it, really. The rest of us, we live here.'

'It must be a bit of a hike, back and forth, every day?'

Lenoir shrugged. 'Not really, monsieur. The hotel lays on bicycles for those who want them. It's not that steep a journey, and coming back you don't have to pedal once you've crossed the bridge.'

'And you, you cycle?'

'Ducati. The only way to travel. Although Hervé, the sommelier, will try to tell you that a Suzuki is better,' said Lenoir with a chuckle. 'So what brings you down here, monsieur? Most Monastère guests never leave the pool.'

'Taking a look around, really. A breath of fresh air before it gets too hot.'

Lenoir glanced at the sky. 'It's going to be a hot one, all right. But there's rain forecast. A lot of it.'

Jacquot nodded. 'Tell me,' he began. 'I had hoped to meet up with a friend while I was here. A guest, at Monastère . . .'

'One of the painters?'

'No, she came with another friend. Monsieur Bressans.'

A fence of frown lines settled across Lenoir's brow, then he smiled a small, knowing smile. 'Ah yes, La Mademoiselle.'

'You know who I mean?'

'She would be hard to miss, monsieur. Oufff.'

'She certainly would, but we were supposed to meet up yesterday. Only she didn't show.'

Lenoir shrugged, glanced at his watch.

'Have you seen her around?'

The Maître d' gave it some thought. 'Friday lunchtime. That was the last time I saw her. She and Monsieur Bressans had lunch on the terrace. After that they went to the pool, I think.'

'Not at dinner?'

Lenoir shook his head. 'My night off.'

'Was she wearing white, a white dress, when you saw her? Do you happen to remember?'

Lenoir shook his head. 'A sarong and bikini top. Black, monsieur. As sin.'

44

At about the same time that Jacquot crossed the Monastère bridge bound for Luissac, Paul Ginoux put down his newspaper, pushed back from his breakfast table in the Salle du Matin, and strolled out on to the terrace. Across the valley, settling like a bruise along the ridge-line, he could see a band of dark cloud, but overhead the sky was as blue as it had been all week, a cobalt canvas scored with the chalky contrails of jets.

Pulling out a chair, he sat at one of the terrace tables and looked the sky. Ginoux loved contrails. And, for a man who had never set foot in an aeroplane, he marvelled at them. Three hundred people up there, thousands of metres above him, eating, drinking, sleeping, watching movies, speeding across the sky in temperatures that would freeze the blood. And where were they going, those travellers in the sky? Who were they, and where had they come from? Ginoux pulled a crumpled pack of filterless Gitanes from his blouson pocket, lit one, inhaled deeply and gazed up into the sky in wonder. Surely that one was too high, he thought to himself, to have taken off from Marseilles? Maybe it had come from Rome? Or still further afield? The Middle or Far East? The world was now such a small place.

That Sunday morning was the first time in a week that Ginoux had felt so relaxed, prepared to indulge in such leisurely reflection. After six days at Monastère, three days longer than anticipated, he had finally got what he came for – or as close to it as he could wish. It had been a difficult journey, but the end was in sight.

Since he'd arrived in Luissac, he'd been in to see the old man only three times. The first visit, on Tuesday afternoon, he'd taken the Master's favourite Bordeaux, a dozen bottles, 1961, but the bastard had pretended not to know him, refused to acknowledge him, sitting there in his barber's chair, staring through the window as though there was no one else in the room. After twenty minutes of unanswered questions, Ginoux had taken his leave, hard pressed not to pick up the wine when he departed.

Two days later he'd persuaded Madame Champeau to go in ahead of him, do some groundwork and, sure enough, the old boy had been hospitality itself. Delighted to see him. How long had it been? As if he hadn't been there just forty-eight hours earlier. A drink, Vilotte had insisted, splashing out a tumbler of *vin du pays*, the Pétrus spirited away somewhere. At which Paul Ginoux had made his second offering, the 'cabinet' of fifty Montechristo *claros* which Vilotte had tossed on to his chair only to beg a cigarette from Ginoux.

The cigarette had set the Master off on to a round of

dangerous coughing and spluttering, the old man pulling on it until the tip was glowing red and Ginoux began to fear that the bush of his beard would ignite at any moment. Finally, thankfully, he'd thrown it to the floor and stamped it out, sparks flying to flicker momentarily on the rags and brushes and news-papers that lay there.

And then, much to Ginoux's relief, the old man had come out with it, as though answering a question that had been asked at their previous meeting.

'Certainly I've got some paintings,' he'd said. 'Three complete and one close to dry. Another month,' he'd continued, swigging from his glass. 'No longer than that. End of the summer.'

'Could I see them?' Ginoux had asked, looking around the grande salle. He'd felt a prickle of excitement. He'd expected two maybe, but four!

'I'll find them for you,' the old codger had told him, taunt-ingly. 'Know they're here somewhere. Why don't you come back, say, Saturday? Would you mind? After dinner. Best seen in lamplight.'

So Ginoux had gone back the previous evening as requested, after an early dinner, with Dutronc outside the door so he wouldn't be disturbed.

When Ginoux arrived, pushing his way through those blessed hanging sheets, Vilotte had been in a mellow mood, which had raised Ginoux's hopes. They were raised even more when he spotted the four canvases placed here and there around the room, turned tantalisingly to the wall, a half-dozen hurricane lamps strategically placed to light the works. With a frame, what's more – the plain grey ash that Ginoux supplied which had become something of a Vilotte signature.

So far as Ginoux could see, they were smaller than he had

expected, maybe one-ninety by one-forty centimetres. But still too big for Vilotte to handle. There was no way he could have managed them by himself, getting them down from upstairs where he always kept his finished pieces. He'd have got Champeau to bring them down, set them up for him. Any heavy work needed doing, the old boy always roped in Champeau.

Ginoux had looked around, as he always did, wondering if the boy was concealed somewhere. It was the kind of trick one of them might think to play – Vilotte always at pains to discomfort his guests; the boy Champeau, only too happy to assist in any tomfoolery, always appearing when you least expected, slipping through Monastère like a shadow. It always unnerved him, that little hunchback keeping to the shadows, sliding silently behind the shifting linen that hung from the ceiling.

On this third visit the Pétrus was open but Ginoux had to endure an agonising delay while Vilotte insisted on finding a clean glass. He was doing it deliberately, Ginoux well knew, but he humoured the man. Clean, dirty, it wouldn't have bothered Ginoux one jot. He'd have drunk from the old man's piss-pot if it had meant seeing – and getting his hands on – the paintings five minutes sooner.

And then, finally, the moment came and Vilotte reached for the first canvas, resting a hand against the wall as he twisted it around for Ginoux to see, then going to the next, and the next, and the next ('this is the wet one'), this last slipping from his grip, missing two of the hurricane lamps by a whisker and ending up face-down in a pile of newspapers.

Ginoux had retrieved it for the Master, set it back against the wall, then stepped away into the centre of the room before turning to view them properly.

Vilotte might have been old and foolish, Ginoux thought, but he was never less than the showman. And a canny one to boot. As the Master had said, the effect of lamplight on the paintings was mesmerising, each work fractured into a kind of scattered Cubist jigsaw which a gentle shift of focus brought to staggering life. Look at them for a moment and nothing happened. And then, as though the splinters of colour had a life of their own, they seemed to move into each other, to blend and match and contrast until the subject was plain. In this case, Vilotte himself, the first self-portraits (so far as Ginoux could remember) that the Master had ever done. There, the shards of grey for a beard; there, a ruby spill for the cheeks and what looked like wavering stripes on a flannel nightshirt.

Ginoux had felt an unexpected shiver as he looked at the four paintings. While Vilotte stretched back in his barber's chair to savour his wine – and the effect his work was having on his dealer – Ginoux turned from one picture to the next.

'They're strong, Maître,' Ginoux had said at last, stepping forward to reposition the second painting. 'Very strong indeed. New ground for you, too. And, as you say, so much more powerful in the lamplight.'

And they were. There was no doubt in Ginoux's mind. The real thing. Powerful. Playful. But pained, too. An artist at the height of his game. Confident. Assured. But maybe reaching the end, like a wine about to turn. Ginoux had seen the old man's hands clasp the wine bottle, the glass – fingers gnarled as olive stumps. It wouldn't be long now.

'I want four million,' said Vilotte. 'Each.'

'Two million,' Ginoux replied swiftly, knowing the Master liked a game, especially a game he could win.

'*Absurde! Totalement absurde!* These are good, Paul, and you know it.'

The 'Paul' was deliberate. Vilotte never used either of his names. It was always 'You again' whenever he visited. Or 'You can't stay away, can you?' Now, as Ginoux circled the paintings, he was suddenly 'Paul'.

'The market is not good, Maître.'

'Bollocks! You've already got a buyer. You can't fool me.'

Ginoux had felt the fever on him. He wanted them. He would have them. He could do it. But he had to play the Master right, or the old boy would change his mind. 'I'll go ten for the four.'

'Then you've come a long way from Paris for a weekend break, my friend,' Vilotte replied.

Ginoux had turned from the pictures, reached for the wine and poured himself a glass. He lifted the glass to his nose, swirled the wine in the lamplight, sipped it.

'I don't know, Maître,' he'd sighed.

'Of course you do. And you know it's a bargain, too.'

And then, in a rush. The way it always was.

'I could take three for nine.'

'It's the four, or none. And it's still four each.'

'I'd want them now.'

'When I have the money.'

'Monday morning.'

'At your convenience, monsieur.'

And the deal had been done.

Four million more than he could afford, but he had the weekend to raise the excess.

'A phone call for you, monsieur.'

Ginoux jumped a little in his chair, turned to find a Monastère porter beside him.

'You can take it in the lobby,' the porter continued. 'The caller said it was important.'

It was the money. Did he have it? Or did he not?

'Of course,' said Ginoux, reaching for his cigarettes and lighter, getting to his feet. 'Yes, of course. I'll come straightaway.'

45

'That blood you brought in,' said Brunet. 'It's human.'

Jacquot nodded, as though Brunet was sitting there with him in Ghislaine Ladouze's salon.

'Valentine at the clinic comfirmed it,' his assistant continued. 'Type "O". At least a quart soaked into the material. A big bleed. He says you owe him a drink.'

Jacquot had returned to Monastère a few minutes earlier and come straight to his room, picked up the phone and called Brunet in Cavaillon. The news was just as he had expected.

'Does Rochet know?'

'He dropped by about ten minutes ago. I told him.'

'Has he briefed you? You know what's been happening?'

'"Missing person", was all he said. Now presumed dead, by the look of it. And tied in with someone big, is my guess.'

'Your guess, as ever, is pretty accurate.'

'So, what's going on?' continued Brunet. 'You need me out there?'

He was intrigued, Jacquot could tell. But he also knew that Brunet would be keeping his fingers crossed that Jacquot wouldn't call him in. It was a Sunday after all. And he had his time trials.

'Don't you have another time trial?'

'In an hour. But if it's important . . .'

'Not at the moment, although the blood certainly changes things.'

'So you've got the blood, but you can't find the body?'

'That's about it.'

'Anyone I know? *C'est à dire*, the Monastère's hardly a country *pension*.'

'I'd be surprised if you knew the missing person,' replied Jacquot with a chuckle. 'But you've got the list of names there. Anyone familiar?'

'Just the one. Roland Bressans. Is it *the* Bressans?'

'It is indeed. But he's not the one who's missing.'

'At a guess, then I'd say one of the mesdemoiselles. Nicholls, Tilley, Hughes, Becque, West, Branigan, Ladouze.' There was a moment's silence down the line as Brunet considered the names. And then, 'I'd go for Mademoiselle Ladouze. Sounds sweet.'

'Correct. On both counts.'

'Bressans' companion?'

'In one. You ought to be a detective.'

'How long since she's been gone?'

'Last seen, Friday night.'

'Doesn't sound good.'

'No, it doesn't. Which is why I'm here, playing the diplomat.'

Brunet gave a rich little chuckle. 'You got roped in?'

'Rochet asked nicely. It was the weekend. I didn't have anything planned.'

'And Monastère looked like a good billet.'

'You could say. Anything else on the list that might be of interest?'

'I've done an initial run on the names, guests and staff, but there's nothing so far that's shouting. More form on the staff than the guests, but nothing serious. One of the waitresses was done for shoplifting just before Christmas, a couple of the commis chefs have been picked up for drugs – possession, not dealing. And your head chef there, Monsieur Alexandre Charles Guillaume Cancale, got in some trouble a few years ago for assault . . .'

'Assault? The head chef? Here at Monastère?'

'This was three years back. La Ferme Bertrand in Besançon. He branded one of his juniors with a hot knife. The lad sued and won. Cancale was . . . let go.'

Jacquot whistled. 'I better watch out. Anything else?'

'The Bouvets, not a thing; your Champeaux – mother and son – nothing. And that's about it so far. There's still more to come through on the guests and we're still waiting for information on the Americans. But given it's Sunday, and the time difference . . . Hopefully, there'll be something later today. I'll call it through to you as soon as I have anything.'

'Good. Good. Let me know whenever. Oh, and good luck with the race.'

Breaking the connection but keeping the phone in his hand, Jacquot dialled another number and waited. He recognised the gruff voice immediately.

'*Ça colle*, Claude, you lard of shit. *Ça va bien?*' Claude

Peluze was an old friend from Marseilles days, one of the homicide squad on rue de l'Évêché.

'That you, Jacquot? You got nothing better to do on a Sunday? So how're the melons up there in Cavaillon?'

'Sweet and round, just like you.'

'Yeah, yeah. I heard that.'

After a few more pleasantries, Jacquot got down to business.

'*Écoute*, Claude, I need a favour. Something you might like. First thing tomorrow, maybe you or one of the boys could pay a call on a Jacqueline de Ternay, 17 Place du Maréchal. It's up around Castellane. Seems the lady runs a line of high-class girls so, at a guess, I'd say she'll only be helpful if you apply a little pressure. I need all you can get on one of her girls – Ghislaine Ladouze, if that's her real name. Friends. Family. *Le tout*. Also, find out about her doctor – either through de Ternay, or her family. I need a confirm on type "O". And check out where she lives. Neighbours, concierge, whatever. A photo would be good, too. Oh, and try the name Roland Bressans on Madame; see what you get.'

Jacquot listened for a moment. 'Yup, *the* Bressans. That's right . . . They're guests at the Grand Monastère here in Luissac – a long weekend. As of now, it's a straight MP but I'm not holding my breath . . . That's right. Nice and discreet. But don't let the lady think she can squirm any. And call me back here . . . The Monastère. That's right. As of last night I'm a guest, too . . . I know, I know, but someone's got to do it, right? And you're always telling me I need to get out more . . .'

After the call, Jacquot went through to the bedroom. The bed was still unmade, which meant Housekeeping had kept away.

But there was something that caught his eye. The light on the video player was red.

Crossing the room, Jacquot squatted down in front of the TV and inspected the video. He reached out and pressed the 'eject' button.

The machine whirred. Nothing.

The tape he'd watched the night before was gone.

46

After a light lunch beneath a parasol on the Réfectoire terrace Jacquot presented himself as requested at the far end of the cloister garden of the Grand Monastère, a fold of francs in the back pocket of his trousers. If he wished to keep up his false identity, Bouvet had warned him, then he'd have to pay for the visit, suggesting that a thousand francs would likely cover it. It was the way the Master – and Madame Champeau – worked, Bouvet had explained, following the explanation with an embarrassed little shrug as though to say – *What can one do, monsieur?*

But a thousand francs or not, there appeared to be no sign of Madame Champeau. Just the door marked *Privé* where, Bouvet had told him, she would be waiting. He looked at his watch – exactly on time.

And then, from nowhere, she was there, though no shadow, no movement, no sound had signalled her approach. One minute Jacquot was on his own, the next, she was standing there right beside him. He was startled, as much by the sudden appearance, as by her looks. She was dressed in what Jacquot immediately thought of as housekeeper-black, the collar of her dress buttoned tight and high, its sleeves cut to the elbow, and its front narrowly pleated. Wedged against a hip, she carried a wicker basket filled with clean linen, exactly like the one that had been left for him outside Ghislaine Ladouze's room the evening before.

As tall as Jacquot, with wide shoulders and strong, workman-like forearms, Madame Champeau looked to be in her late fifties or early sixties. But, he conceded, it could easily have been more. The face was long and lined and her hair was grey, parted a little to the left of centre and clasped by tortoiseshell combs above each ear. A pair of frameless spectacles, perched high on a bony nose, made her blue eyes look watery and showed a red rim where the lower lids had started to collapse. She wore no make-up and no jewellery, and a brief, business-like smile of acknowledgement did little to soften an otherwise tight and disapproving expression.

Though her eyes didn't move from his, Jacquot knew she was taking him in – every inch of him. The espadrilles, the cotton jeans, the crumpled linen jacket over his shoulder, and the ponytail. She looked . . . disappointed, Jacquot thought, whether at him or life in general he could not be certain. He guessed, though, that once she must have been beautiful and imagined the grey hair black, the cheeks unlined and the eyes sparkling with youthful exuberance.

And her voice, when she spoke, was surprisingly soft and warm, neither as sharp nor as disapproving as he had expected.

'You are the gentleman who wishes to see the Master?' she asked.

'That's right,' replied Jacquot.

'There is . . . a fee. I'm sure you understand.'

'Monsieur Bouvet explained,' said Jacquot, taking the notes from his pocket and handing them over.

She took the money without a glance and, stepping past him, pushed open the door marked *Privé* with her foot. 'If you'll follow me then,' she said.

'Please, allow me,' said Jacquot, making to take the linen.

'I've managed long enough without help,' she said, shifting the basket away from him. 'I daresay I can do so now, thank you all the same.' And with that, she bustled ahead of him down the passageway, the wicker basket creaking against her hip.

'I believe a friend of mine, Ghislaine Ladouze, visited Monsieur Vilotte,' said Jacquot, coming up beside her as they stepped from the cool shadow of the passage into the sunlit second cloister.

Madame Champeau glanced at him as they crossed the courtyard, skirting the builders' mess. 'The lady who was staying in your room? She was a friend of yours?'

'That's right. From Marseilles. She told me how excited she was at the prospect of visiting Monsieur Vilotte.'

'It can be very special,' was all she said in reply.

'It was very kind of Monsieur Bressans to arrange it.'

'Monsieur Bressans?'

'The gentleman she was with. He is also from Marseilles.'

'Ah, Marseilles. A fine city, *n'est-ce pas*?'

It was clear to Jacquot that he was getting nowhere with Madame Champeau. 'That's right. I believe there is some business he wishes to discuss with the Master.'

'That I cannot say, monsieur,' she replied, as the shadow of the tower fell across them. A moment later, she led the way down the short flight of stone steps that he'd seen the day before and, taking a bunch of keys from her pocket, Madame Champeau selected one and slipped it into the lock.

'You lock him in?' asked Jacquot.

'The Master has his own key, of course,' said Madame Champeau over her shoulder. 'But people find out where he is. Sometimes, they think they can just barge in without an invitation. It can be very upsetting for an old man. This way . . . well, the Master is assured of his privacy.' And then, telling him to wait, she swung the basket ahead of her, stepped through the open door and closed it after her. A minute or so later, she reappeared with a tray in her hands – the remains of the Master's lunch. 'You'll find him by the window,' she said. 'He is feeling a little low today. If he cries, pay no attention. The tears never last long. And remember, thirty minutes only.'

And with that Madame Champeau mounted the steps and set off across the courtyard.

Jacquot pushed open the door and stepped inside. The smell of white spirit and linseed was immediate and almost overpowering, with a dusty, musty odour of age and decay woven into it.

And then there was the voice. Bold and brutal, loud and piqued. It stopped Jacquot in his tracks, bouncing off the plum-coloured stone walls, ringing through the sheets that hung like a forest of shifting stalactites from the beamed ceiling above his head.

'Chagall,' the voice boomed. 'Old Marc, he gets the Grand Cross of the Légion d'Honneur. Matisse – dear old Henri – a Commander, no less. Pablo is offered the same honour but, of course, refuses. Salvi, they make him a count, bless him, and anything else they can think of. But me? Me? Auguste

Vilotte? Nothing. Nothing. Nothing. Now, of course, when time is short, when the years have piled up on me, they come sniffing, you know, like dogs on a bitch's bloom. But that's all it is,' the voice continued. 'Looking for a final fuck, they are. While they still can. Pablo was right. Tell the bastards to swivel. Then piss all over their dancing shoes.' There was a moment's pause, and then: 'Where are you? Who are you? Come forward, into the light, where I can see you!'

Pushing his way through the draped sheets, Jacquot stepped into a wide open space dominated by a massive picture window overlooking the Calavon Valley and the rising slopes of the Monts de Vaucluse. A large canvas had been set on an easel, its surface raked with a scrawl of charcoal lines. Behind and above it, hanging lopsidedly on a length of brass chain, was a gilt-framed mirror as large as a snooker table, its silvered glass foxed and splintered, the fracture lines spanning out like cobwebs from what looked suspiciously like four tiny bullet holes stitched diagonally across the glass. And there, sitting in front of the easel, in a metal-framed barber's chair, his image shattered into a thousand angles by the mirror, was the man that Jacquot had come to see, the floor around him littered with a mess of paintbrushes, bottles, rags and newspapers.

Even sitting, Jacquot could tell, Auguste Vilotte was a giant of a man. His lounging frame dwarfed the chair which he spun round when Jacquot came close, pushing with his slippered feet off a brass-bound travelling trunk splashed with paint. He was dressed in a long striped nightshirt, draped around him like an Arab dish-dash, its collar completely concealed beneath a spread of beard as grey as granite, laced with strands of white and dappled and matted here and there with what looked like smears of paint. His cheeks, what Jacquot could see of them, were red and scattered with the tiny purple worms of broken veins, and a pair of sharp, squinting eyes were set beneath a ledge of wiry, tangled brows almost as thick as his beard. On his head he wore a woollen bobble hat the colour of blood, pulled down tight to his ancient, hair-sprigged ears, and around his wrists were a tangle of bracelets – silver and gold and copper and ivory – that jangled as he moved.

But even in repose, sitting like a king on his throne, the energy poured off the man. He might be old, Jacquot thought, but he was vibrantly, pulsingly alive.

Immediately Jacquot felt the man's eyes taking him in. It was a disconcerting and unexpected examination.

'You look like a fighter,' said Vilotte at last. 'That's good. I like fighters. Here,' he continued, reaching for a plastic cup which he tossed to Jacquot. 'Let's have a drink. Sorry it's plastic but my hands . . .' he held them up, turned them, tried to work the fingers '. . . sometimes they lose their grip. And broken glass . . . Ooooh, Madame would not be happy. No, no, no. Not happy at all. I'd collect a good spanking . . . Oh yes I would,' he chuckled naughtily.

Stepping closer, Jacquot held out his cup and Vilotte splashed in a full measure from a bottle of what Jacquot could clearly see was a Pétrus '61.

Vilotte saw Jacquot's glance at the label.

'1961. One of the very best. From . . . an admirer.' Another sinful chuckle, as though he was gargling with wet grapes. 'Nineteen-sixty-one. What a year. The year Pablo married that Roque woman at Vallauris. Eighty years old, he was. And still up for it. Eh? Eh? Not many that age still have paint in their pot.' And then, filling his own cup, he put down the bottle on the trunk and cast around: 'There's some cheese somewhere,

233

if you like to eat with your wine. Me, I just take it where I can find it, wine and food both, like an old dog on the scrounge.'

Vilotte sank back in his chair, tipped back his cup and took a mouthful, cheeks swelling. Then he swallowed, gasped, smacked his lips – red from the wine, a gash of scarlet in the grey brush of his beard. Once again, his eyes turned and settled on Jacquot. 'Well, well? Cat got your tongue? Who are you? Apart from a fighter. And what do you want?'

Jacquot introduced himself, held out his hand, but Vilotte didn't take it.

'Yes? Yes? Yes? Well?'

'I'm investigating a disappearance, I believe you know . . .'

'You're a *flic*? A cop? You don't look like one.'

'Well, monsieur, I assure you—'

Vilotte's eyes narrowed and he leaned forward. 'I know you, don't I?'

'Again, monsieur, I assure you . . .'

'God's teeth, stop assuring me all the time, dammit.' And then, dropping his voice: 'Not met, exactly. I mean, I know you. Recognise you. From somewhere. Tell me, your nose is broken. How?'

Jacquot took a deep breath. He knew what was coming. 'I was kicked. When I was younger . . .'

'Kicked, you say? Kicked. Now, now, now . . .' He opened his mouth, tapped his teeth together as though about to bite into something. And then: 'Yes! I have it! You were kicked. You were. But kicked . . . in a game of rugby,' Vilotte guessed triumphantly. 'It's you, isn't it? You're him, aren't you? The one who beat those English shits. Pissed on their boots, you did. Ran them off the pitch, you did. My God, what a run! What a run! And here you are. *Mon Dieu, mon Dieu!* So you *are* a fighter. I was right.'

With surprising speed, Vilotte sprang off his chair and grabbed Jacquot by his arms, pinning them to his sides, dragging him into an embrace. Jacquot could feel the Pétrus in his plastic cup slopping through his fingers, could feel the man's beard rasping against his cheek and was overwhelmed by the mixed scents of turpentine and garlic and old sweat.

'*Jésu Christi! Jésu Christi!* You're nearly as big as me,' continued Vilotte, now holding him out at arm's length as though the better to examine him. 'Me, I played, you know. Two seasons. In Toulouse. Number Eight, they put me. You'll know about that. Head between two arses, and your nose up a third. Not a place to be, not a place to be. But I could dance that ball, monsieur. These feet . . .' Vilotte released Jacquot's arms and suddenly stooped down to grab him around the waist, his head locking against Jacquot's hip, his feet tiptoeing behind him, pushing Jacquot backwards into the first line of hanging sheets.

Abruptly Vilotte released him and Jacquot tottered back on his heels as the old man returned to his drink and his chair.

'Come with me. Come,' he called out over his shoulder, beckoning Jacquot forward. 'Another drink. You smoke? You want a cigar? Havana. The best. Here,' he said, tossing a cigar box underarm at Jacquot.

Jacquot reached for it, caught it, noted the name.

Vilotte clapped and shouted out: 'Still got the hands, haven't you? Still got the hands. Go on, help yourself.' Vilotte kicked at the debris around his feet. 'There's a light here somewhere, had it just a while ago. Ah, I remember.' And he went to the easel, snatched up a box of matches from beside the canvas he was working on, and flourished it above his head, rattling the matches inside. 'Haven't got a cutter, you'll just have to bite it off,' Vilotte told him. 'Or here, use this,' he said, fumbling on the paint table beside the canvas and coming up with a knife, its handle grubbily bandaged, its blade black and scabbed with paint. 'Just chop it. Here, like this.' He reached for the cigar that Jacquot had taken from the box, laid it on the mess of the paint table and brought the blade down with a great 'thunk' that sent brushes and tubes of paint tumbling on to the floor and the tip of the cigar spinning into the air.

'So,' he said, fumbling at the drawer of the matchbox, pulling out a match and striking it against the sandpaper strip, holding it to the tip of Jacquot's cigar then tossing it away. 'So. What is it you want? Monsieur . . . Monsieur . . .'

'Jacquot. Daniel Jacquot.'

'That's the one. That's the name. I've got it now. And? And? Did you say you were looking for someone? Here, sit, sit,' he said, waving at the brass-bound trunk.

'A woman,' said Jacquot, perching on the edge of the trunk, as Vilotte collapsed back in his barber's chair. 'She was staying at the hotel.'

'*Framboises!* There are always enough of those, you know, at the Monastère.' He lifted his bent fingers, sniffed them, flung the hand down. 'Spoilt, rich bitches, most of them. But, now and then, a pearl. Name?'

'Ghislaine Ladouze.'

Vilotte shook his head. 'Doesn't mean a thing. What does she look like?'

Jacquot remembered Lenoir's expression.

'Hard to miss.'

'Ahhh! The best kind.'

'She's staying with a gentleman friend. Monsieur Bressans.'

'Aahhhh, the *petit bronze*. Then I do know her. She came here with him.' Vilotte's eyes latched on to Jacquot's. 'You're right. Hard to miss. But she's no Ghislaine whatsit. The name you said.'

And then, as if somehow prompted by Madame Champeau's words, tears suddenly spilled down his cheeks and soaked into his beard.

'She had a different name?' asked Jacquot, taken aback by the tears. 'Not Ghislaine? You're sure?'

'Sure? Course I am sure.' Vilotte sniffed, pitching back another slug of the wine, then pulling up the front of his night-shirt and wiping his cheeks.

'And do you remember the name she used, monsieur?'

Vilotte turned his glistening, bloodshot eyes on Jacquot. 'How could I forget, eh? Tell me that. "Call me Céleste," she said . . . Céleste.'

Jacquot tensed at the name. The name on the cassette? The cassette that had gone missing from his room? It had to be.

'And when was this, monsieur?'

Vilotte scrunched up his brow, looked to the window. 'Thursday. Friday. Two times, I think.'

'Both times with Monsieur Bressans?'

'The first time only. The second time I sent for her. She came alone.'

'On Friday?'

Vilotte rolled his eyes. 'Friday. Wednesday. Who gives a fuck? It was Céleste. That was the thing. Céleste, as I live and breathe. Right there. Right there where you're standing.'

'But you think it was Friday,' Jacquot persisted.

'Friday then. Yes. Friday.'

'And at what time, monsieur?'

'It was late I think. Night-time. I'm an old man; I don't look at the clock.'

'And she stayed how long?'

Vilotte shook his head. 'We talked, you know. An hour? Maybe longer.'

'And what did you talk about, if I might ask?'

Vilotte turned to Jacquot, looked him up and down as though it was no business of his. For a moment Jacquot thought that the old man was going to terminate the meeting.

'We talked of the old days. Old friends. People we'd known.'

'People you'd known? Together? Had you met before?'

Vilotte frowned at this. 'Of course . . . Way back . . . When Céleste . . .'

'When Céleste . . . ?'

Vilotte shook his head, worked his fingers through his beard, looked off towards the window as though reliving his time with her. Then he frowned, as though there was something he couldn't quite put together, something he couldn't quite understand.

'Of course, it's impossible . . .' he began. 'Impossible. I see that now. Trying to explain it to you . . .'

Jacquot said nothing, sensing any interruption would tip Vilotte off target.

'But they were so alike . . . Exactly . . . You wouldn't believe. The way she spoke, the way she moved. The names, the places. Everything. She remembered everything. It was . . .' Vilotte paused. 'But it couldn't be, could it? It's not possible.' He looked at Jacquot as though for some kind of confirmation. 'Céleste,' he whispered. 'Céleste . . . No, of course it couldn't have been her. It's just me . . . an old man, you know. And yet . . . while she was here, while she was with me, it all seemed so real, so possible.' More tears sprang from his eyes, but this time he didn't bother to wipe them away. 'I suppose . . . I suppose I just . . . wanted it to be true . . .'

'Why couldn't it have been true?'

Even with the tears streaming over his cheeks and soaking into his beard Vilotte began to laugh, but it degenerated into a throaty barrage of coughs. 'Because, young man . . . because . . .' The coughing subsided. 'Because . . . Céleste Maroc is dead. Thirty years ago. Too late for anything now. But for a moment . . . for a moment . . .'

Jacquot took it in, sifted through the information as he'd sifted through the underwear in Ghislaine Ladouze's drawers.

'Your friend,' he began, 'Céleste. Did she ever wear a gypsy dress?'

'All the time, all the time,' replied Vilotte, as though the question did not surprise him. 'She had gypsy blood, I'd swear to it. And a temper to match, heh? Like bellows to a flame, she'd explode.'

The words had hardly passed his lips when Jacquot was suddenly aware of someone else in the room. He'd heard nothing but he knew they were no longer alone. He turned. Standing behind him was Madame Champeau.

'Thirty minutes, monsieur. It's time for Monsieur Auguste's nap,' she said.

'Maybe just another few questions, madame,' Jacquot began but, as he turned back to Vilotte, he saw the old man was in another world, his rubied cheeks shiny with tears. Whether he liked it or not there was no continuing now. Putting his empty cup on the trunk, Jacquot stood, thanked Vilotte and bid him adieu.

But there was no response, no reply.

With a nod to Madame Champeau, he followed her from the *grande salle*, waiting while she locked the door behind them.

'Has he family?' asked Jacquot as they climbed the steps into the courtyard.

'None that's known of, monsieur. Just those that are close to him, that care for him.'

Jacquot took this in and followed Madame Champeau across the courtyard, weaving around the builders' mess. He was about to ask how long she herself had been at Monastère when his eye was caught by something amongst the rubble. A flash of white amid the darker background of the site.

'*Un moment, madame, s'il vous plaît,*' he said and stepped between the rubble towards a sheet of corrugated iron.

It was tipped sideways against a mound of freshly turned sand and a stack of wood. It was exactly the sort of rubble that you would expect to see. With one exception. A shred of white cotton hanging from the corner of the corrugated iron.

Not from a dress, Jacquot decided. It was more like the thread from a towelling dressing gown.

47

Meredith Branigan took a deep breath, stretched idly in the sun and looked at her watch. She lowered her arm and sighed. She was bored. She couldn't help herself. Five days and all she'd done was sleep late, blow Erdâg, and spend the day by the pool.

And put on weight. That was the other thing that she'd done. All that food. It had been pretty good in Paris and Cannes – all those fancy joints the Studio took her to. But this place Monastère was just awesome. Just so . . . let me have more, you know? Guiltily she slid her hand to a hip and her fingers felt something between them for the first time in she didn't know how long. Tomorrow, first thing, she'd go to Monastère's gym, wherever it was, and do some circuits, some reps, work those abs.

Beside her, Erdâg's arm fell from the edge of the lounger and he snorted awake, shuffled himself over on to his chest and was snoring again in a heartbeat. Meredith looked at his back – swirling currents of sweaty black hair – and winced. Didn't these guys hear of waxing? I mean, it was a carpet there.

Meredith listened to the snoring for a minute or two longer then sat up and swung her legs off the lounger. Time for a swim, she thought; go right to the far edge of the pool and just float out over the valley. Infinity. Such a great view. So high. Perched on the very edge.

Untying her sarong she stepped down into the water, slid forward and started for the far end of the pool. It was like swimming all the way to the mountains. When she reached as far as she could go, she clung there, water chuckling over the edge, and gazed across the valley to the mountains beyond. Awesome.

Behind her, she heard a gentle splash and a whoosh of breath, and she felt a shot of irritation. Erdâg, awake at last and joining her. She knew what he'd do – come up behind her, grab her round the waist, and just spoil her private moment here.

But he didn't, because it wasn't Erdâg.

Instead, someone else came to the edge of the pool, to rest there, just like her. A man. A big guy. And – she couldn't believe it – a ponytail; she hadn't seen a ponytail since High School rep.

'Ça va verser, c'est sûr,' he said, looking out across the valley.

The words sounded like the water lapping around her; and if she hadn't seen his lips move, she wouldn't have known he was speaking.

'I'm sorry?' she replied, looking across at him, shading her eyes.

'I said to you, it will be raining, for sure.'

'You're kidding me, it's like . . . an oven.'

'Maybe now, but look there. Big cloud. Black cloud.' Ponytail nodded to the distant ridges, whistled lightly and flicked his fingers.

'But that's like, miles away.'

'Maybe miles away, as you say, but it will be coming soon. Tonight for certain.' He turned towards her, just the one elbow resting on the side of the pool, the water playing around his shoulders.

And inside, she just gasped. Those eyes, just the greenest . . . and long eyelashes glittering in the sun, and the cutest laugh lines. She felt that familiar flustered feeling . . . Jeez, she thought, these French guys . . .

But he was talking again. 'You are staying here? At Grand Monastère?'

And if the eyes gave her goose bumps, that voice . . . She could listen to that voice for like . . . a century.

'Five days so far,' she said, her thighs rubbing together gently as she trod water.

'And for how long?'

'I gotta get back to the States this week.'

'New York?'

'California, Los Angeles. You been there?'

'Only in the *cinéma*, you understand. On the screen.'

'And you? You staying here?'

'A couple of nights maybe.'

'You come far? I mean, you being French and all?'

'Cavaillon, mademoiselle. Not far. Just down the road a bit.'

There it was again, that 'Mademoiselle'. Seemed like these French guys just made these words up to make them sound sexy. Meredith just loved being called 'Mademoiselle'. I

243

mean . . . 'Miss'? Forget it. But give her one 'Mademoiselle' and it felt like her panties were being tugged round her knees.

'You with the painting group?' she asked.

'*Non, non*. I am . . . how you say? Journalist. Writing about Grand Monastère.'

'And you get to stay? Hey . . . great job.' She moved closer, held out a hand to him. 'Meredith. Meredith Branigan.'

'Meredith,' he said, taking her hand and giving it a single shake, but holding it just a second or two longer than he needed to. '*Un plaisir*, Meredith.'

May-ray-deeth. May-ray-deeth. She'd never heard it sound like that before. She shaded her eyes again and, behind the ledge of her fingers, she let them drop to his body. A big guy, good tan, late forties and just in great condition. And there, wavering beneath the surface, just a single ribbon of black hair sliding into the top of his shorts.

'And you are?'

'I'm so sorry. Daniel. Daniel Jacquot.'

Crazy name she thought. Dan. Danny. No, she decided. Definitely a Daniel – Dan-yell. Just as he had pronounced it.

'And your friend? He is from America also?'

'He lives in Rome right now, but originally he's like from Croatia someplace.'

'Rome is a nice city.'

'Hey, you been there?'

'*Non*, but, like California, I have seen the pictures.'

That very second there was an enormous splash from the other end of the pool followed by a surge of water that hit the ledge they were clinging to and cascaded over the side. A moment or two later, after much energetic splashing, Erdâg came up behind Meredith and, just as she had known he would, he grabbed her from behind, completely ignoring her companion.

As she was pulled away, Meredith waved a hand over Erdâg's shoulder. '*Au revoir*,' she called out, laughing and bucking as Erdâg tickled her.

'*À la prochaine*,' replied Jacquot.

48

Roland Bressans was on the phone when he opened the door to Jacquot. He was barefoot and dressed in a towelling robe, his hair slicked back from his forehead, a strong citrus smell of aftershave wafting off him.

'That's right,' he was saying. 'You don't have to tell me that.' He glanced at Jacquot, indicated that he should come in, take a seat. 'Of course I will. As soon as I get back.'

Bressans put down the phone. 'Chief Inspector? There is news?'

Jacquot shook his head, settling himself in the sofa. 'Not at this time, monsieur. But there are some more questions I would like to ask.'

Bressans sighed. 'I really think I have told you all I know.'

'Sometimes, monsieur, it is surprising how much one . . . forgets. Things you might not consider important, or imagine

246

have nothing to do with the case. Sometimes, a policeman must jog the memory. I'm sure you understand.'

'Very well,' replied Bressans, taking a seat, crossing his legs, adjusting the folds of his towelling robe. 'So, please, jog my memory.'

'First of all, Monsieur Bressans, I would like to know, exactly, the nature of Mademoiselle Ladouze's participation in your negotiations with Monsieur Vilotte.'

Bressans did not reply immediately, as though giving serious consideration to the form his answer should take.

'As I said,' he began at last. 'I believed that the Master would enjoy her company, that she might possibly bring some pressure to bear . . . might be able to persuade him that a small gift to the museum – works from his studio, something like that – would prove a lasting testament to his considerable talent . . .'

'And what form did you imagine this "pressure" might take? Did you intend that Mademoiselle Ladouze should make herself available to Monsieur Vilotte? That she should offer sexual favours as a kind of payment for these "works"? Were you, *en effect*, pimping Mademoiselle Ladouze to achieve your aims?'

Bressans looked as though he would explode with indignation, but when he spoke his voice was low and quiet.

'That is a quite monstrous suggestion, Chief Inspector.'

'But it would be true to say that on previous visits, when you came to Monastère by yourself, you were unsuccessful in your attempts to persuade Monsieur Vilotte to accede to your requests?'

'It is never easy or straightforward negotiating with an artistic temperament.'

'So you thought that Mademoiselle Ladouze might help in your endeavours?'

'As I said, Monsieur Vilotte has always enjoyed a certain reputation when it comes to the ladies . . .'

'Did you tell Mademoiselle Ladouze that she should make a sexual advance? Or be amenable if Monsieur Vilotte suggested it?'

'I think she understood . . .'

'Given her profession . . .'

Bressans nodded, grudgingly. 'Yes, I suppose . . .'

'And did Madame de Ternay know what was involved? What Mademoiselle Ladouze would be expected to do?' Jacquot could see that Madame de Ternay's name discomforted Bressans. He wondered if Bressans had been in touch with her, after giving Jacquot the card that morning.

'Obviously, she understood . . . what I mean is . . .'

'That hiring out one of her girls meant that sex would probably be involved?'

'Of course.'

'And that's what was being paid for?'

'Yes.'

'And how much exactly did you pay for Mademoiselle Ladouze's services?'

'I don't see . . .'

'How much, monsieur?'

'One hundred thousand.'

Jacquot nodded. Nearly two months' pay for a senior officer on the *Judiciaire*.

'That is a considerable amount of money, monsieur. A substantial *petit cadeau*. Might I ask why such a large amount was involved?'

'I'm afraid I don't quite follow you?'

'I'm sure that your contact, Madame de Ternay, will confirm that that is a very significant payment for what amounts to no more than five days' work. Was there anything else involved that I should know about?'

Bressans shook his head. 'Madame de Ternay, as you or your colleagues will discover, runs a very . . . prestigious, ah . . . exclusive operation. Services like that, monsieur, services of that . . . calibre, do not come cheap.'

'Of course, of course. So there was never any suggestion that Mademoiselle Ladouze should play a part – beyond her ordinary professional services?'

'Play a part? I don't quite follow . . .'

Jacquot could see that Bressans was not enjoying their exchange. He knew what was going through the man's mind. Had Madame de Ternay said something about Ghislaine reprising Céleste Maroc? Had Vilotte? And just how far could he, Bressans, afford to hold back without risking a possible charge of withholding information or obstructing the police in the course of their investigations?

'I'm asking if Mademoiselle Ladouze was expected to do more than just offer sexual favours? Was she, for instance, expected to play the part of someone Monsieur Vilotte might once have known?'

'I really don't see where this is all going, Chief Inspector.'

'Then please allow me to explain, monsieur. I believe that Ghislaine Ladouze was introduced to Monsieur Vilotte under another name. That she assumed, probably at your direction, another character. Not Ladouze, but Maroc. Céleste Maroc.'

Bressans stiffened at the name, a very slight tensing of the shoulders.

'Well, monsieur? Do you think that might be the case? That Mademoiselle Ladouze . . . deceived Monsieur Vilotte in this way? In order to secure the artwork that you were after?'

Bressans gathered himself. 'I wouldn't say there was any more deception in Ghislaine's behaviour than there would be in any of her, ah . . . transactions. It is in the very nature of her work, Chief Inspector, to . . . let us say . . . pamper the male ego . . . say things that aren't necessarily true . . .' Bressans smiled at his nifty footwork.

'Quite so, monsieur. Quite so. But let us move on. Did you at any time give Mademoiselle Ladouze any . . . instructions – what she should say, how she should behave? In short, did you brief her in any way for the role that she played with Monsieur Vilotte?'

'Not really, Chief Inspector. Nothing more than a few pointers, you understand. Monsieur Vilotte likes this, likes that. His tastes, his life, friends . . . that sort of thing. So that she would be properly prepared in her negotiations with him.'

'So that he would look kindly on any requests she might make . . . on your behalf?'

Bressans got to his feet, Jacquot's questions clearly beginning to rattle him.

'If you are trying to suggest that I have done anything illegal here, then you are wrong, Chief Inspector.'

'I'm not suggesting anything, monsieur,' replied Jacquot lightly. 'I simply need to have all the facts if, as looks increasingly likely, the disappearance of Mademoiselle Ladouze should become, well, something more than a disappearance. I'm sure you understand.'

Jacquot got to his feet and moved towards the door. As he reached for the door-handle he paused, turned.

'Just one more thing, monsieur.'

'What now?' snapped Bressans.

'Last night there was a cassette in Ghislaine Ladouze's video-player. A film of a young girl, walking along a beach. This morning it was gone. I would be most grateful for its return.'

'I trust, Chief Inspector, that you're not suggesting—'

'Monsieur Bressans, it is *exactly* what I am suggesting.'

'This is ridiculous. A cassette? In Ghislaine's room? What would I know of any cassette?'

'Because I believe it is a cassette that you gave her. I can think of no other way that it could have come into her possession.'

'But any number of people could have gone into her room, taken this . . . this cassette. Whatever it is. Housekeeping, for instance. A maid tidying up. It might even have belonged to whoever stayed in the room before Ghislaine. These things happen.'

'Of course they do, monsieur. But it would be an extraordinary coincidence if some previous guest in that room had a tape with the name 'Céleste M' written on it. Wouldn't you agree? As for Housekeeping, or a maid tidying the room and removing it, Mademoiselle Ladouze's room has been closed off as a possible scene-of-crime and staff have been forbidden to enter. Also, according to Housekeeping, there was no cassette in the video machine when the room was prepared for Mademoiselle Ladouze. Therefore, I can only assume . . .'

A silence descended. Bressans worked his jaw, Jacquot waited patiently by the door.

'I don't like this one little bit, Chief Inspector,' snarled Bressans, going to his desk. 'Not one little bit.' He snapped open a drawer and brought out the tape, handed it over to Jacquot.

'Neither, monsieur, do I. And so that it doesn't happen again, perhaps you would be kind enough to lock the connecting doors between our rooms and give me the key.'

Snatching up his keys, Bressans slid one off the ring and tossed it to Jacquot. 'I'm sure you can manage that simple task by yourself, Chief Inspector. And now, if you wouldn't mind, I have some business to attend to.'

49

Erdâg pulled away from Meredith, rolled on to his back and waited for his heartbeat to slow, his breathing to settle.

Age. Ten years ago – five years ago, even – he'd have stayed where he'd been, a few moments to recover before starting again, until whoever it was begged him to cease, to have mercy. Ten years on, it was sometimes a relief to reach the end and call it quits.

A relief, but a worry, too. He was forty-seven years old. Still young. Surely his time hadn't passed? He looked at the ceiling, a spider web strung like a hammock across two of the beams. Surely he was still the man he had been?

It had to be her fault, he reasoned. Meredith. Her curved, bare back may still have been turned to him, the rise of her hip still angled in his direction, but there was nothing more from her to indicate any annoyance that he had withdrawn, a desire for him, a wish to continue. If the hip had moved, if the back had arched, if an arm had reached out to search for him, he was certain he would have responded. But there was nothing. Not a flicker of movement or invitation.

It was just . . . she was too young, too inept he decided, didn't understand how to keep a lover interested. Beautiful, yes; sensuous, yes. But not yet experienced in the ways of man.

Beside him, Meredith pushed her legs down the bed and rolled slowly, luxuriously on to her stomach, her head turned away from him. A moment later he heards a soft 'mmmmmh-hhhh' which would have raised his spirits if it hadn't been followed by a correspondingly soft rumble from her chest, a sleepy clearing of her throat and the first, unmistakeable *susurrer* of a snore.

The body was sublime – no question. The face a picture. Exquisite. And soon she'd be the biggest name in Hollywood. With a bank account to match. But that screen sexiness simply didn't translate. She might look a million dollars on-screen, have a million men lusting after her, hold that sheet just so to her spilling breasts and pout wet-lipped like a spoilt, sex-hungry little schoolgirl . . . but in real life, here beside him, in a five-star Monastère bedroom, she was no different from any other of the less memorable lovers that Erdâg had had in his bed. She might flirt with men, like she had with that Frenchman in the pool, but she didn't know how to carry it through beyond showing her body, pressing it against her lover, and waiting for him to execute the most basic of moves.

If it wasn't for the promise . . . for the money . . . for the opportunity she'd soon provide for him to move on up the Hollywood ladder, then he'd have been out of there faster than . . . faster than . . . well, faster than one of her orgasms!

Erdâg turned his head on the pillow. The sun, he could tell

from the wide zebra stripes across the stone floor, was low. The golden hour. The perfect light. He didn't need an excuse to do anything, but this was as good a reason as any to slide from their bed, shower, get dressed and go out on the prowl with his camera.

Forty minutes later, on the top balustrade above the cloistered garden, Erdâg looked north towards the distant Ventoux ridge. A storm was brewing. He could see it in the boiling black clouds massing there, smell it in the dusty, metallic air. An hour, no more, and he'd have to wrap his camera in plastic, just as he'd done on the killing fields of Bosnia, or shoot indoors. This was his last real chance to complete the Provençal exterior he'd plotted for Vilotte so he set to – the topmost edges of the old man's watchtower, the valley spread below, the wooded hillsides rising above him, the distant cluttered rooftops of Luissac.

As he filmed, he wondered about the old man, wondered how long he'd have to wait for his next visit, a last chance to complete the sequence. Close-ups. He wanted more close-ups this time – those ravaged purpling cheeks, that straggling grey beard, those rheumy dog-tired eyes.

He'd already paid for another visit, given Madame Champeau another wedge of notes before they even left the second courtyard. She'd slid them away like a croupier collecting lost chips, and told him she would do what she could. He had no doubt that she would. The old man had liked him. They'd hit it off, Erdâg knew. He only hoped she'd manage something soon. One more visit and he'd get what he came for.

By now he had made his way round the battlements, the Ventoux highlands at his back, across the garden. Below him was the bridge, and, clinging to the distant hillsides, the approach road from Luissac. As he panned the camera across the bridge, a car came into frame. He was about to curse, stop shooting, when he saw through the viewfinder that the car was old, a classic, one of those magnificent Citroëns, the kind de Gaulle used to drive around in. He kept the camera rolling and followed the car, tipping over the wall as it came to a halt in the turning circle below, fortunately well clear of the blue BMW that was also parked there. Somewhere, he knew, the sequence would come in handy. An establishing shot. Another of the great masters arriving to visit Vilotte in his watchtower. It was his film. He could do as he liked. A little sleight of hand . . . Who was to say?

Below him, the driver's door opened and a figure stepped out, a large, broad-shouldered hulk – more minder than driver. Closing the car door he started towards the gate, shoulders swaying with each measured step. And then, through the viewfinder, Erdâg saw the man pause and turn – as though he sensed he was being watched. Turn and look back, and then raise his head to the battlements.

Erdâg jerked back, out of sight.

He'd seen that face before.

But it couldn't be, he thought.

Not possible.

Just not possible.

50

Back in his room, Jacquot locked the connecting doors between his and Bressans' suites, threw the keys on to the sofa and put the video into his desk drawer. As he turned for the bedroom, the phone began to ring.

It was Claude Peluze in Marseilles.

'I didn't expect to hear from you so soon,' said Jacquot, settling down beside his keys.

'It was a quiet day in the big city,' replied Peluze. 'And the sun was shining, and there's this great little Arab restaurant up near Maréchal . . . So I thought, hey, why not?'

'And?'

'Lunch was great. *Formidable*. The best couscous . . .'

Jacquot smiled. Peluze loved his food. 'What I meant . . .'

A dark river of a laugh chuckled down the line. 'I know, I know. Forget the food, tell me about the lady, right? Time was you'd have wanted the name of the restaurant first and then the low-down. Things must be tough up there in the Lubéron. Even if you are staying at Monastère. By the way, is it as good as they say?'

'So-so,' replied Jacquot, thinking of his *ris de veau* the night before. One of the best he'd ever tasted and Peluze's favourite dish. 'No complaints so far.'

'Yeah, I can imagine. Like Michelin isn't going to give the place a dozen stars next year . . .' Peluze gave a grunt.

It was a grunt Jacquot recognised. His way of saying *chit-chat over, down to business*. Jacquot was right.

'So,' Peluze began, 'this lady of yours. Jacqueline de Ternay. Well, nothing showed up on records under that name, so I thought I might as well pay a call. Place du Maréchal, like you said. Third-floor corner apartment with a view of the fountain. Must have cost a bomb. One of those old blocks off Castellane, turn-of-the-century place, but she'd ripped the heart out of it. All glass and chrome and nothing you'd want to sit on, if you get my meaning. Anyway, a maid answers the door, says Madame is busy. I show her the badge and request an audience – pronto. So she closes the door on me and I'm left there in the hallway till I'm beginning to think they've forgotten all about me. I'm just getting ready to hammer down the door when it suddenly opens and there's Madame. Forty max, and a stunner. Tall, dark hair, slinky jeans, silk shirt, some pretty savoury jewels, as well – I'm telling you. Sporty, too, fit-looking. One of those yacht-club types.

'Anyway, she shows me into a small study off the entrance hall, tells me she's having lunch with her parents – her daddy's birthday – and what is it she can do for me? Cool as a cucumber. Until I mention your friend's name. Ghislaine Ladouze. That gets her attention.'

Cradling the phone against his shoulder, Jacquot sat forward on the sofa and reached for the fruit bowl on the table in front of him. The bananas had blackened, the pears were soft to his fingertip, but the apples were still fresh. He picked one out, rubbed a shine on to it and, in the absence of a fruit knife to slice it with, he took a crunching bite.

'Hey, you eating there? You want me to call back when you're not so busy?' said Peluze, his voice larded with sarcasm.

'She didn't deny knowing her, then?' asked Jacquot, ignoring the jibe.

'No way,' replied Peluze. 'It was like I'd mentioned a friend. Was she in trouble, Madame asks? How could she be of help? All concerned, like. So I say I want to know all there is to know about her, like you asked. How long Ladouze has worked for her, where does she live, dah-de-dah.'

'And?'

'I get it all. No hesitation. Like it's a beauty salon she's running and not a top-of-the-line cat house. If you ask me, she's got friends in the *Judiciaire* that are higher up the ladder than we are and she knows it.'

'It wouldn't surprise me,' said Jacquot. 'So what did you get?'

'Ladouze is a new girl, she said. Eighteen months top. Done some magazine work. Local girl. Lives down by the Opéra. Gave an address, phone number. Said she'd find out about the blood group – told me she has all her girls tested weekly; her own doctor – said she'd call with the info the moment she got it. That helpful.'

'And Bressans. Did you mention Bressans?'

'Right at the end. Asked if Ladouze was working this weekend, and if so, who with? Which is when the lady does start to get tricky . . . tries to squirm out of it . . .'

'But you persuade her to cooperate . . .'

'In one. You scratch mine, I'll scratch yours. It will go no further, I tell her. She has my word.'

'I bet that made her feel happier. And?'

'Monsieur Bressans is a friend, she tells me. A close friend. A close friend who occasionally needs a certain kind of companion for business meetings, colleagues, parties, that sort of thing. And Madame is only too happy to help.'

'And how long have the two of them been friends?'

'She says just a year or two but I got the impression it was longer. Said there'd never been any trouble. He'd always been well behaved . . . and a most generous client. No complaints. Not a bad word from the girls.'

'And was this the first time she'd set him up with Ladouze?'

'That's what she said.'

'Did she know what was on the cards? Why he wanted Ladouze particularly?'

'Something about a party, she said. Bressans wanted the girl to play a part . . . like acting. A surprise appearance. And the looks had to be right. Bressans had been quite specific, she said.'

'Did she say anything about a video?'

'Video? Nope, nothing.'

'You had a chance to check out where the girl lives yet?'

'Not yet, I haven't. And I'm gonna leave it for the morning, if that's OK? We got the grandchildren coming round any minute . . .'

'Not a problem,' said Jacquot, swallowing the last of the apple, his fingers sticky from the juice. 'Just give me a call when you've got something. Blood group, anything interesting in the apartment. Tomorrow's fine.'

'It's done,' replied Peluze and he broke the connection.

Jacquot replaced the phone in its cradle and went through to the bathroom to wash the stickiness from his fingers. Now he knew for certain what Bressans had been up to. But had he broken any law? Had he been criminal, or just foolish?

Jacquot sighed. He'd have loved to put Bressans in the frame for something, but it just wasn't hanging together yet. He needed more.

As the water splashed into the sink, a gust of wind slapped at one of the bathroom shutters and sent it crashing into the window frame.

Drying his hands, Jacquot went to the windows and secured the shutters. Across the valley the sky was darkening fast, clouds starting to tumble over the Vaucluse ridge like fat black horses jumping a hedge.

Another twenty minutes, thought Jacquot. Twenty minutes and it would be lashing down.

51

As she folded the rugs and packed up the lunch hampers, Claudine decided that, when it came to landscapes, Gilles Gavan was a genius. And he'd been right. She'd never have found the place on her own, even if she did live just a few kilometres distant.

That morning, leading the way in his van, Gilles had brought them to a field outside La Bégude, a rising slope of land between the Lubéron hills and the Monts de Vaucluse about thirty kilometres from the Monastère and just a few hundred metres north of the road to Céreste. He'd found it the previous week, he told them as they unloaded their easels and paintboxes from the back of the van, and the poppies, he promised them, were '*extraordinaire*' – a raft of soft pinks, blood-reds with a swathe of dusty orange cutting through its heart. And if that was not enough, he'd added, there was even a small *village perché* in the background, with the slopes of the Vaucluse beyond.

'According to the *Météo*,' he'd warned them as he led them along a stone-rutted path through a shadowy stand of holm oak, 'we have until late afternoon before the weather changes and that rarest of Provençal jewels – rain – has us packing away our palettes. Hope you've got your watercolours with you!'

Then, with a flourish, he'd stood aside so they could step past the last of the trees that bordered the field and see what he had seen. What he had found.

There'd been gasps from the group when they saw the field and the poppies and the distant village clinging to a hilltop. Just a perfect Provençal landscape. Joanna simply shook her head and set up her easel where she stood, while the others spread out, keeping to the shade, looking for their perfect spot: Grace and Marcie no more than a couple of metres apart at the edge of the field; Hilaire on her own a little further up; Naomi and Philip heading down the slopes, looking back occasionally to check the view, Naomi first to choose her spot, Philip going on a few more metres until he, too, was satisfied, clearing himself a space in the border of tall grass that surrounded the poppy field and setting up his easel.

In just a few minutes the chatter had died away and the group had started painting in earnest, their brushes dipping and darting at the puddles of colour on their palettes, nothing to distract their attention beyond the dry rattle of cicadas in the long grass, the occasional trill of a song-bird and, just the once, the throaty complaining of a distant donkey.

Not even the delights of a Monastère lunch – a tureen of chilled vichyssoise, a selection of local charcuterie, a cold risotto, hot chicken wings, cheese and fruits – had kept them long from their easels. It was a scene that reminded Claudine of a shady *Déjeuner sur l'Herbe* except there was no pool of water at this picnic site, no rowing boat tethered to the bank and none of the ladies was naked. But it lasted no more than an hour, the painters anxious to finish their work before the weather turned.

Alone in the ticking, dappled shade, everything packed and stowed away in the back of the van, Claudine was tempted to snooze for an hour in the languorous warmth. But there was work to do and, after a contemplative cigarette, she joined Gilles, the two of them moving between the painters, gently discussing their work, making suggestions and offering advice when invited to do so.

Both Gilles and Claudine had their own particular favourites among the group. For Gilles the star turn was Gracie: her man with melons in Cavaillon, her two mongrels curled up together in a shady Luissac doorway, and a still-life of the flowers in her room – a copper vase of roses and vine sprigs drooping over a folded newspaper. The detail, Gilles enthused, you could almost read the newsprint.

But for Claudine there was only the one painter, only one real talent. Not Grace, not Marcie, nor Naomi – though her work had a certain bold narrative to it – nor Philip nor Joanne. No, for Claudine, the painter whose work she adored was Hilaire's. So easy, so gentle, so effortless. Standing a few metres behind her that afternoon, so as not to disturb her, and off at an angle so that she could see what Hilaire was doing, Claudine watched her at work: sitting sideways on her stool, jeans, boots, a simple plaid shirt, her hair twisted up under a sun hat whose brim cast her face in shadow. The field that Hilaire was painting was a landscape that none of the others had seen. Four pale strokes only and she had the slope, a simple cluster of three ochre rectangles, balancing one atop the other, and she had the distant *village perché*, with maybe just a score of poppies spread across her paper, menaced by a looming sky she'd rendered with just a watery smear of grey. The result was simple and striking and, in Claudine's opinion, none of the other painters had come close.

And those colours, those colours Hilaire mixed, the way she worked her palette, looked at the scene, worked the palette again and then, pausing, took the brush-tip to the paper, leaning forward, like a surgeon with a scalpel. A touch. A dab. A stroke. Done.

'You've caught it beautifully,' Claudine said, giving a small cough first to alert Hilaire that she was there.

Hilaire glanced around, smiled. 'The trouble is, *chérie*, not knowing when to stop. Should I leave it here, or carry on? Twenty years I've been painting and still I never know.'

But the decision was made for her, and for all the painters on that slope of land off the Céreste road. The storm that Gilles had warned them about was finally making its presence felt. In just a few moments the light flattened, colours lost their vibrancy and shadows shrank away as though they'd been soaked up by the land.

At least the storm was generous. It gave them all a five-minute warning, a sharp chill breeze brushing over the heads of the poppies towards them, tugging at the paper pinned to their easel boards, even snapping shut Philip Gould's paintbox lid with the crack of a gunshot.

By the time the first raindrops fell, they were under the trees and stacking their equipment into the van.

'It's just biblical,' remarked Philip wonderingly, clamping down his panama with its topaz hat-band as the rain battered through the leaves.

'Jesus,' exclaimed Naomi, bundling herself into the van.

'Quick, quick,' said Marcie, helping Grace in while Gilles swung into the driver's seat. Which left Joanna and Hilaire to take their seats in Claudine's car. Reversing back down the lane, the rain hammered on to the roof of the car and the wipers had no chance of clearing the windscreen. Cautiously, Claudine pulled out on to the Céreste road and headed back the way they'd come, a black bank of cloud swooping down the slopes and chasing after them, squalls of rain lashing the road ahead into a fog of water, Gilles' headlights showing smearingly in the rear-view mirror.

To their right came a rumble of thunder and a sliver of lightning slashed through the grey lowering skies like a jagged pink blade. At a little after four in the afternoon, it felt like night, no chance today of the sun reappearing.

The journey back was a nightmare. In all her years in the Lubéron Claudine had never seen such a downpour, or heard such thunder, the sky shivering with strands of lightning, suspended against black muscly clouds, the cambered road with its deadly drop-off coursing with rain-water, rivers of it cascading down the hillsides, tumbling stones and torn branches lurching across the beam of her headlights. By the time she drew into the Monastère's parking area, her heart was thumping as loudly as the rain on the Citroën's roof. Beside her, Hilaire was as white as a sheet, hands clasped round her paintbox, and in the back seat, Joanna clung white-knuckled to her seat belt.

'Glory be,' she said as Claudine switched off the engine and the rain hammered down even louder than before. 'Now that's what I call a storm.'

Minutes later, dashing through the rain with their paintboxes over their heads, the group tumbled into the Monastère's lobby like a net of wriggling, freshly caught fish tossed on to the quayside.

As they shook themselves off, went to fetch their keys, decided what time they should meet up for dinner, Claudine felt a tap on her shoulder and a man's voice:

'*Bonsoir, mademoiselle*, we meet again.'

52

Jacquot had been idly leafing through his printout of staff and guests in one of the sofas in the centre of the lobby when the painters returned. He watched them stumble in from the courtyard, laughing and exclaiming at the fury of the storm as the rain smashed at the glass panels behind them. Without referring to his list, he went through the names – Naomi West, in the streaming cape; Philip Gould, pulling off his panama hat and shaking it vigorously, Marcie Hughes and Grace Tilley brushing the rain off one another, Hilaire Becque patting a sleeve across her cheeks and forehead, and the English lady, Madame Nicholls, making the best of her rain-slicked hair.

And then, behind them, Jacquot saw her, coming in with the group leader, Gilles Gavan. Soaked to the skin, she was. A white shirt clamped to her shoulders by the rain, long dark hair clinging like a nest of snakes to her shiny cheeks. And laughing at the absurdity of it all, getting so drenched in such a short flight from car to door. Relieved, too, to have made it back without mishap.

And immediately he knew the face, a face he recognised. Something familiar. But not a painter. Not one of the group. He looked back at his list of guests but there was no name for her, no room allocated to her that he could see. Everyone accounted for save her. Jacquot frowned, tried to place her.

And then, dismissive of her own needs, she was moving amongst the painters, helping with coats and paintboxes and easels, and Jacquot realised she must be with Gavan, an assistant of some kind.

An assistant!

Now Jacquot remembered. A gallery in Marseilles. A year earlier. She'd sold him that picture, a plate of lemons, the cheapest in the gallery, the one hanging in the entrance hall of his apartment in Cours Bournissac, the first thing he saw when he came home each evening. It made him think of Marseilles, and sometimes it made him so homesick he felt like taking it off the wall, hanging it somewhere he wouldn't see it so often. But he never had. It stayed where he'd put it.

Only she wasn't a gallery assistant, she was the artist, the one who'd painted the lemons. A month after the show, he'd seen her photo in *Côte Sud*, beside a flattering critique of her work. He reached for the name . . . Claudine . . . Claudine something . . . And then he had it: Eddé. Claudine Eddé.

Of course, he'd called the magazine, asked if they had an address, but they were unable to help him. All they had was an agent's number. When he called it, the agent had moved, no forwarding address.

It had been a disappointment. There had been something about her, as he strolled round that gallery, that had caught him unawares. And he'd suspected she had felt the same. He'd tried to remember what she'd said, what he had said, whether she had given any clues about where he could find her, where she lived. But there had been nothing.

And then, in the weeks that followed, there'd been no time to think of her. The reassignment to Cavaillon and the move from Marseilles and, for those first few months, Isabelle. He knew now that she'd been right to end it. She'd known his heart wasn't in it. Because somewhere in the back of his mind, he'd been thinking of the woman not ten metres from where he sat, here, at Grand Monastère. He was sure it was her.

So certain that he got up from the sofa and strolled across the lobby, approached the group now recovered from their dash through the rain. Before he knew it, his hand was reaching forward, tapping her on the shoulder.

And she was turning . . . looking up . . .

And the moment those eyes settled on him, Jacquot's world suddenly tipped off its axis and his heart lurched.

Just the most beautiful, breathless face he had ever seen, eyes glittering at the excitement of it all. Then that tiny frown, a questioning look on her face until she, too, recognised him, her cheeks suddenly flushing under her tan.

'Oh,' she said. 'It's you.'

53

Sitting alone at Monastère's bar, Paul Ginoux was quietly celebrating with a half-bottle of his favourite Clicquot – a *Grande Réserve* '85. In less than twenty-four hours he had raised the extra four million francs he needed to secure the new Vilottes – maybe the Master's last serious work – and by lunchtime tomorrow, those four self-portraits would be safely stored in the Citroën and he'd be on his way back to Paris, back to his home on the allée des Fauves.

And Bressans would have nothing.

It didn't get any better than that.

Ginoux poured the last of his champagne and turned to watch the rain battering the line of arched windows, the lightning crackling down. He raised his glass. To Monsieur Roland Bressans. And bare walls in that ridiculous Marseilles museum of his.

But as he raised the glass to his lips, Ginoux couldn't help

271

but acknowledge a tiny wash of icy doubt. He wasn't in the clear quite yet. He might have done the deal with Vilotte, he might have raised the money, and sometime tomorrow sixteen million francs would be credited to the Master's account. But the fact remained that Ginoux did not yet have the paintings. Those four extraordinary self-portraits were still in the watchtower. Still in Vilotte's possession.

Still accessible. And, therefore, still on the market.

If there was one thing Ginoux had learned in all the years he'd known the Master, it was to never take anything for granted. When you worked with Vilotte, you left any trust or expectation with the coat-check girl. Like every other artist Ginoux had ever done business with, the man was a schemer and a twister. And greedy and vain. In the few brief meetings Ginoux had had with the Master in the last few days, Vilotte may have said nothing about Bressans, or about the possibility of a counter-bid – God forbid, an auction between the two of them – but that didn't mean there wasn't going to be one.

Ginoux had played his hand, made his offer, and had had it accepted. But what if Vilotte turned to Bressans to see if he could get more? *My dealer's prepared to pay four each*, Ginoux could hear the old man saying, *care to raise him?* And while Bressans was no collector, he was certainly wealthy. With a museum to furnish. Maybe he'd go to five each – what then?

Ginoux was no fool. Collectors were one thing, museum curators quite another. And the difference between those two beasts was tiny but crucial. A collector bought for himself. He hung a painting on a wall and thrilled at its possession, enjoyed showing it off, only seeing a return on investment when the time – if ever – came to sell. But a museum curator, or owner

– or whatever it was that Bressans was calling himself – was different. From the moment that work of art came into his possession, it generated an income. People paid to come and see the painting. They bought drinks in the café, they bought lunch in the caféteria, they bought catalogues and postcards, gift vouchers and guidebooks, souvenirs and spin-offs. And if, like Bressans, you owned the museum, and your fortune was founded on printing and publishing . . .

Ever since he'd seen Bressans and that woman at dinner in Réfectoire, Ginoux had smelled trouble. Bressans, it was obvious, wasn't staying at Monastère for his health, or to pleasure himself with his mistress. He was here for the Master. And, thanks to Dutronc, Ginoux knew it for certain.

Over the years his driver, on Ginoux's instruction, had cultivated a sort of friendship with Madame Champeau. Or as close to it as you could get with such a formidably frosty creature. They were two of a kind, both of them at someone else's beck and call, both – to one degree or another – employed by unscrupulous, uncaring masters to look after their interests. And over the years Dutronc had played this card most successfully. Ginoux now knew, for instance, that this was Bressans' second or third visit so far this year and that he had had access to the Master on two separate occasions in the last week. Once with the girl, once just the girl by herself.

Ginoux allowed himself a brief chuckle as he thought about it. He, Ginoux, brought Pétrus and Montechristos, but Bressans brought live bait.

Of course, Ginoux acknowledged, there was always the possibility that Bressans was after something else altogether. Maybe he didn't even know about the self-portraits? Maybe he hadn't even seen them? Maybe, maybe he was making a play for

Vilotte himself? Something grand and magnificent with which to launch his museum?

Something grand and magnificent like the fabled Vilotte collection.

Everyone in the know had heard of Vilotte's collection. Everyone had heard the stories – and there were many – about Auguste Vilotte and his light-fingered past. And who was to say that Bressans hadn't heard the stories too, and decided to investigate?

Why, just the other day, in Lyons, Ginoux's friend at the Beaux Arts had added another rumour to the pile when Ginoux mentioned that he was on his way to Luissac. To see Vilotte.

Just a rumour, of course, the friend had teased, but . . .

Delacroix. None other.

The great Ferdinand-Victor-Eugène Delacroix! One of his sketchbooks, so it was said. Maybe fifty preliminary studies collected in Algeria. According to Ginoux's friend, who'd heard the story from a researcher who'd heard it from another curator, Delacroix had left the sketchbook on the steamship to Marseilles. The great man had been devastated by its loss, telling friends they were the best, the most inspiring studies he'd ever created.

And that, said the friend in Lyons, had been that. Until Henri Matisse reported a theft from his home in Cimiez – a number of his own sketchbooks and a treasured collection of bound studies by, amongst others, Delacroix.

The thief had never been apprehended, of course, and the haul had never been recovered. But a week before the burglary, so it was said, Auguste Vilotte had been a house guest at Cimiez . . .

Just another Vilotte story, the Beaux Arts friend had concluded, just another rumour. But still . . . Just imagine . . .

Just a rumour, thought Ginoux, savouring the last of his champagne. With Vilotte it was always just a rumour.

Except . . . Except . . .

Ginoux knew different.

Or rather, he suspected that, quite probably, the Vilotte Collection – the Master's private hoard of ill-gotten gains – was not a rumour, a myth, an art world fable.

Years back, early on in their association, Ginoux had arranged for a pair of Vilotte's smaller oils – two Provençal landscapes – to go to auction to sort out two squabbling collectors. Ginoux had made sure that the paintings had appeared as separate lots and furious bidding had followed. The two collectors had pushed the price of each landscape to over a million francs apiece but at the last moment – as they tugged hotly at their collars and glared at each other – both had been roundly outbid on both lots by a Saudi prince.

Vilotte had been in Paris for the sale, standing incognito in the back of the main *salle*, and afterwards he and Ginoux had gone out to celebrate – back when Vilotte was still in charge of his marbles and Ginoux had some influence.

Ginoux remembered the evening well. Vilotte had taken him to La Coupole, bought him dinner and then, after their shared *plateau des fruits de mer*, the Master had handed him a small gift wrapped in torn newspaper pages.

'Don't open it till later,' Vilotte had said, waving away Ginoux's thanks.

And Ginoux hadn't. He had waited until he returned to his home on allée des Fauves. He'd poured himself a drink, pulled on a pair of white gloves and opened the package as carefully as an archaeologist unwinding the bandages from the head of a mummy.

It had been worth the wait.

Folded amongst the newsprint was a small, square linen napkin which, when Ginoux opened it up, showed a smudged pen-and-ink sketch of a hunter aiming a phallus-shaped rifle at a ludicrously cross-eyed man sitting at what looked like a typewriter. It was signed 'Pablo' and dated 'Juillet 1938'.

But that was not all. On the reverse of the napkin were the words: 'Anyone could draw crap like this', and, beneath it, the name 'Ernest Hemingway'.

As commissions went, Ginoux decided, he couldn't really have done better. Which was just as well because it was the last gift Ginoux had ever received from that mean old bastard in the watchtower.

And now, to add to all those other names, Delacroix. Ginoux shivered at the possibility.

The more he thought about it, the more convinced he was that the story was true, that the haul from Cimiez had ended up in Luissac.

Which meant, if Ginoux didn't want Bressans to walk away with the biggest prize of all, that he'd have to do something about it.

A collection like that, in Bressans' possession? It was unthinkable.

Ginoux finished his champagne and signalled to Jean-Luc for the *note*.

Maybe the time had come to have one last look for the old man's treasure and, if he found anything, he would do what Vilotte had done.

Steal it.

54

Turning off the taps, Jacquot slid down into the foamy bath that he'd drawn for himself and marvelled at it.

She'd looked back, glanced over her shoulder at him, as she followed the painters to their rooms.

That's all he could think of.

That last look, just to see if he was still standing there, watching her. And in that moment they'd smiled at each other a little uncertainly, nodded, and then she was gone.

Taking a breath, Jacquot ducked his head under the bath water, held his breath as long as he could and came up spluttering.

Which was, he decided, exactly what he'd done with Mademoiselle Eddé.

Lying there in the bath, Jacquot went over it all again, played their meeting through in his head.

He hadn't been prepared. As simple as that. Not at all. He'd just gone up to her in the lobby and tapped her on the shoulder.

Just like that. Just as he would have done with any old friend he hadn't seen for a while. Someone he knew. Someone he recognised.

And that was it. When she turned and levelled those laughing grey-blue eyes on him, slipped back that rain-slicked hair from her cheeks, he'd lost it, didn't know how to continue, had no idea what to say, like a teenager on his first date.

But if she'd felt the same, she'd hidden it well, behind an enquiring smile which had forced him to stammer out his name and say something stupid.

What had he said? What was it he'd stunned her with?

'So, what brings you here to Monastère?'

The moment the words were out of his mouth, he'd wanted them back, so he could say something a little more arresting, memorable. But it was too late. They'd been spoken.

'I'm with the group,' she'd said, waving her hand to the painters – gathering at the desk to get their keys, arranging a time to meet for dinner.

And then he'd said something equally trite about the gallery in Marseilles, and how he had thought she was the assistant . . .

'. . . It was only later I realised . . . some magazine article . . .'

And she'd lowered her eyes from his, smiled bashfully, apologised prettily for her little deception, and then looked back up at him.

And he was lost again, simply lost, the words drying up somewhere in the back of his throat.

All he'd managed next, so far as he could remember, was a cow-like, cud-chewing silence, the mouth moving but the words not coming.

Dieu . . . *dieu* . . . *dieu* . . . *dieu* . . . What to say? How to say it? Where to find the words and how to speak them?

Until she saved his hide.

'Look,' she'd said. 'I'm soaked, *totalement*,' fingertips brushing at her sodden blouse. 'Why don't we do this at the bar. Catch up. Say in an hour?'

And then she'd turned to the painters, taken a couple of paintboxes to ease the load, and was crossing the lobby with them.

Which was when she'd looked back, smiled.

And Jacquot had been filled with the most extraordinary surge of elation.

Was filled with it still, lying there in Ghislaine Ladouze's bathtub.

So unexpected. So unfamiliar. So . . . exhilarating.

For a brief moment, the name Ladouze and the words 'investigation' and 'missing person' came into his head, the reason he was there at Monastère.

But they didn't stay long.

Suddenly all Jacquot could think about was a woman called Claudine Eddé.

55

At the arched entrance to Le Réfectoire, Yves Lenoir stood at his lectern and ran his finger down the reservations book. Already, thanks to the rain, there had been four cancellations that Sunday evening from non-residents and, within the next hour, he expected the two remaining non-resident tables to call in and cancel as well. The storm was a beauty and would surely put anyone off the hike from St-Mas along a road that, in this kind of weather, could prove exceedingly hazardous.

Which left just thirteen covers. All resident. The first reservation had come from the two American ladies – Lenoir glanced at his watch – due any moment. He'd taken the call himself, shortly after the painters returned from their expedition. Apparently the two ladies had decided to eat early, by themselves, rather than join the rest of the group at the club table which Monsieur Gavan had reserved for eight-thirty. It was the younger of the two American ladies who had called, the one with a little French, enough to wish people *'bonjour'* and *'bonsoir'* and *'merci'* and *'s'il vous plaît'*, but, when pressed, would dry up, stutter, look lost.

But at least she tried, thought Lenoir approvingly. At least she made the effort. Unlike some in her party.

Lenoir had assured her there wouldn't be a problem, and had enquired, in English, if Mesdames would prefer a table by the terrace window to better admire the storm raging outside, or a quieter table against the back wall?

As well as the painters, Messieurs Bressans and Ginoux had also booked tables – the dapper little Parisian with his varnished fingernails and turned cuffs, and the big wheel from Marseilles, puffed up with self-importance, rarely making eye contact with Lenoir or the staff, speaking as though to thin air, as if they weren't even there. And for the second night in a row he'd be dining alone, sadly unaccompanied by his delectable companion.

And then the phone beside the lectern bleated. It was the American girl from Cannes, the actress whose picture they'd all seen in the newspapers, the one who had all the waiters loitering around her table like mother-sick puppies. She was so sorry, she said in that breathless voice of hers, but she and her companion had changed their minds; they'd be ordering room service. She was soooo, soooo sorry . . .

Lenoir told her he quite understood, wished her a pleasant evening and, putting down the phone, leaned forward to cross their names off his list. A pity, he thought; she was such a beauty. No wonder the papers were full of her. Which was more than you could say for the boyfriend, the one who picked his teeth with the point of his knife, cupping a hand over his mouth to conceal the deed. Whatever did she see in a creature like that? A Balkan, by the look of him. Or Turkish. Or Middle Eastern.

Some place like that. Swarthy, stubbly, ill-bred, badly mannered. Never a please or a thank-you, just those hairy-knuckled fingers of his working away at his teeth or flicking in the air to attract the attention of a member of staff.

Women, he thought. Who could fathom them?

Shaking his head, Lenoir closed the reservations book and turned to check his brigade, immaculate in their brasserie-style black aprons and tailored white jackets. Hand-picked, every last one of them. Lured away from Pyramide, Balthazar, Le Meurice, Nice Passédat. Only the best addresses. And it showed; not a man nor a woman idle, working their way through the room, checking every table one last time, picking up wine glasses for a final polish, or a plate, or a piece of cutlery, removing fallen petals from the flower decorations, adjusting a chair or a napkin, going over the specials that Maître Cancale had told them about at staff supper, remembering the couplings of pernod sauce with the trout, harissa with the lamb and the *crème à l'anglaise* with the loin of veal.

Outside a squall of rain battered against the glass panels. Lenoir heard it but didn't move. His first two guests were approaching, arm in arm.

'*Bonsoir, monsieur, nous avons une table pour ce soir,*' said the younger of the two ladies, labouring over her pronunciation.

'*Bien sûr, madame. Un plaisir. Si vous me suiverez . . .*' He saw her smile uncertainly. He had spoken too quickly. He gestured towards the restaurant. 'Please, this way.'

Three hours later, as the last guest left Le Réfectoire, Yves Lenoir closed the reservations book.

Just the one no-show.

56

It was late when Jacquot woke. He was lying on Ghislaine Ladouze's bed, a damp towel knotted round his waist and a wet pillow beneath his head. He looked at his watch and swore.

They'd agreed to meet for a drink. An hour to get ready and they'd see each other in the bar. He'd also decided to ask her to join him for dinner. And he'd gone and fallen asleep.

Merde, merde, merde . . .

It might have been late but Jacquot sprang off the bed and reached into his case for a fresh shirt, pulled on his jeans and slipped bare feet into espadrilles. Maybe she'd still be down there. He'd explain, try to make up for his bad manners. Yet somehow he had a feeling she wouldn't make him pay too dearly for his rudeness. Her blush, when he had tapped her on the shoulder and she had turned, had filled him with an inexplicable sense of . . . a sense that their meeting, their paths crossing, had been meant to happen.

But it wasn't to be. By the time he reached the bottom of the main staircase and started across the lobby, he could see that the lights in Le Réfectoire had been dimmed, the candles extinguished, and the waiting staff long gone, anxious to get back to Luissac before the storm grew any worse.

It was the same in the bar, all the bottles taken down from the shelves behind the stone slab and stowed away. The place seemed deserted.

Back in the lobby, Jacquot crossed to the front desk. Didier was on duty, Champeau concentrating on a house of cards in the office beyond, bottom lip sucking up under his front teeth as he placed another card.

'I wonder,' Jacquot began, 'is it too late for a drink?'

'*Pas de tout, monsieur*. What would you like?'

Jacquot ordered an espresso and calva and wandered back to the bar. He felt suddenly foolish, cross with himself and guilty. How stupid . . . He tried to make himself comfortable on one of the stools but it didn't feel right, sitting there all alone. Instead, he crossed to the black Steinway in the corner of the room, pulled out the seat, sat down and tried the lid. It opened with a tiny creak of hinges, and a soft clunk as wood touched wood. The instrument smelled of wax and steel, wood and varnish, taut wire and soft felt – all its component parts in a single breath. It was a long time since he'd played. He let his fingers brush across the keys, pressed his toes against the pedals.

Didier appeared beside him, snapped out a white cloth on to the top of the piano, and laid out his coffee and calva.

'You play, monsieur?' he asked, stepping back, tray and hands disappearing behind his back.

'Badly but happily. And when no one's listening.'

'Then I will go back to my desk, monsieur, and put my fingers in my ears.'

'A wise precaution,' said Jacquot with a smile.

Didier gave him a brief bow and departed.

If it was a long time since Jacquot had played a piano, it was an even longer time since he'd played on a Steinway. He found 'C', pressed it lightly and the note rose from the body of the instrument like a tender summons. As the note died away he shifted his fingers and reached for the 'F', then the 'A', then the 'A' flat, the keys as smooth as paper. He repeated the three notes a little louder, then again, a little faster. The next phrasing came slower. He thought of Ghislaine Ladouze and wished her well. Wherever she was. But this was no time for such considerations. Somewhere between his body and the machine there was music to be found.

He brought up his left hand and felt for position, eased his wrists, wondered for a moment whether he could remember. And then began.

The top-end, trickling high-wire notes and the tumbling, falling-down doubles, index and middle finger of his left hand reaching for the blacks and whites. Humming the snares in the pauses. The timing just a few beats slower than the real thing, but still not bad, it seemed to him, the phrasing growing a little in confidence. Until a sharp for a flat threw him for a note or two . . . made him momentarily cross. But he turned the mistake into another pause and, softly, he began to hum the lyrics, knowing the words, of course, but not brave enough yet.

And then they came, whispered, under his breath: '*Let there be you . . .*' duuum-dum . . . '*Let there be me . . .*'

And then, from behind him, came another voice. *'Let there be oysters . . . under the sea.'*

Jacquot swung round, hands jerking away from the keys as though they were suddenly hot.

'No, go on. Don't stop,' she said and pointed him back to the keyboard.

It was Claudine. Right there. She could have seen him and walked on, thought Jacquot with a flash of hope, but she'd stayed, come up behind him . . .

Feeling his own face redden this time, Jacquot did as he was told, straightened his back, found the keys and started again. There were more mistakes this time, but he managed to cover them, make them sound not quite as bad as they might have been. He closed his eyes, tried not to think of his audience and let his fingers find the tune.

Suddenly he was aware of something flowery in the air. Something warm and tropical. If his eyes hadn't been closed he'd have seen her come past him, rest her elbows on the Steinway, reach out for and take a sip of his calva. When he opened his eyes hers were closed and he had a moment to take her in. A pair of jeans like him, cinched with a tie, a man's shirt with the collar up and that dark, lustrous fall of black hair.

There was a gentle smile on her lips as though the tune brought back happy memories. He played on, eyes glancing between Claudine and the keys until, with a flourish, he hit the last note, gave it some pedal, and her eyes slowly opened.

She turned and gave him an appraising look. 'You stood me up,' she said. 'I waited, oohh, three, maybe four minutes . . .'

'I'm sorry. I just . . . You wouldn't believe me.'

'You're right, I probably wouldn't.'

'It won't happen again.'

'It had better not.'

'Can I get you something to drink? I'm sure Didier . . .'

'No, no. This will do fine,' she said, swirling the calvados in the glass, lifting it to her nose, breathing it in, then sipping it. 'And play something else. Play something . . . low and smoky.'

He played four more tunes before she let him leave the piano. Some JJ Cale – thank God for the repetition on 'After Midnight'; a double dose of the opening bars of 'As Time Goes By', followed by 'They Can't Take That Away From Me' – all of which he managed without too many slips. Not particularly low or smoky but the only ones he felt confident enough to play with any control.

'You should practise more. You'd be good. Possibly.'

In doleful reply, Jacquot gave her the opening notes of a sombre adagio.

She gave him an odd look. 'You hear it too?'

Jacquot frowned. 'Pachelbel? The muzak?'

'*En effet*, it's mostly Albinoni. And it's not muzak. Some people hear it, others don't.'

'I don't understand.'

'Who does?' she replied. 'It's just there . . . an echo, if you like. I think of them as happenings.'

'I still don't . . . ?'

'The Monastère. It's haunted. Didn't you know? But not ghosts. No shrouded figures. No hooded monks. Just sounds – music, a door closing, sandals on stone. Gilles told me about it. I think it's rather nice. Not everyone hearing it. It makes it special, don't you think?'

She pushed away from the piano and walked over to a sofa, made herself comfortable. 'You don't have a cigarette, do you?'

Jacquot followed her, took a low armchair, reached for his cigarettes and offered her one. She took it and he lit it.

'So tell me, Monsieur Daniel Jacquot, what exactly is a policeman from Marseilles doing in a hotel in the Lubéron?'

57

Jacquot was stunned. How on earth did she know he was a policeman? As far as he knew, only Claude Bouvet, his wife Régine, Vilotte and Roland Bressans knew who he was. And he couldn't imagine any of them telling anyone else.

'Don't worry. I won't give the game away,' said Claudine, tipping the ash off her cigarette and giving him a conspiratorial smile.

'How did you know?' asked Jacquot.

'My sister, Delphie. You met her at a party in Marseilles. This time last year. She invited you to my show, remember? She was the one who told me. And I have a good memory. So? What's a big city *flic* doing in the country. A little off your beat, isn't it?'

Jacquot shrugged, tried to gather his thoughts, took another sip of calva. In an instant he was back on rue de l'Évêché, in Guimpier's office. 'There was some trouble,' he replied. 'Some problems with a case . . .' More precisely with Gastal. Alain Gastal. His partner on the Waterman investigation. For a moment, Gastal's leering face swam into his vision. The last time Jacquot had seen him, Gastal had been sprawled across Guimpier's floor, a broken nose and blood on his shirt. 'My partner . . . my partner and I didn't get on. There was a disagreement. I got transferred. Here, to Cavaillon.'

Claudine gave him a look. 'It must have been some disagreement, Marseilles to Cavaillon,' she said. 'Naughty boy.'

'These things happen . . .'

'I'm sure they do,' she agreed lightly and smiled. 'So what's the story now. Here. At the Monastère?'

'Nothing much,' replied Jacquot, playing it down. 'One of the guests seems to have gone missing. We're trying to find her.'

As soon as he said it, Jacquot realised he'd unthinkingly given away far too much information. There were only two women staying at the hotel who were not members of the painting group. Meredith Branigan and Ghislaine Ladouze.

'Don't tell me. The mistress?'

Jacquot was taken aback. Not just that Claudine had guessed correctly, but that she had also spotted the relationship.

'Well that's what she is, isn't she?' continued Claudine. 'I mean, you have seen her, haven't you?'

'As a matter of fact, I haven't.'

'No picture? No photofit? Isn't that what you call it?'

Jacquot shook his head.

'Well she's quite a package, I can tell you. And now I come to think of it, you're right. I haven't seen her around. Do you suppose her gentleman friend is up to no good?'

'Who knows. We'll see.'

A silence settled between them. And then:

'So how come the ponytail? Hardly regulation, I'd have thought.'

Jacquot chuckled. 'People always tell me to get it cut, but—'

'So why don't you?'

'Because, well, I guess it's me. We've been together a long time.'

'Change is good.'

'Maybe one day . . .'

58

Naomi West sat in front of her mirror and wiped away the arcs of crimson from her eyelids with a ball of creamed cotton wool. Closing one eye after another to see that she'd done the job properly, she tossed the smeared ball into the bin beside the dressing table, reached for another, dabbed it into the cream and set to work on her cheeks, forehead, then her neck – cotton wool, cream and fingertips scouring at the make-up with irritated swipes.

She was cross.

Not a word. Nothing.

A thousand francs the first day she arrived. To the house-keeper of all people, her way in to the Master, apparently. And then, how do you like it, another five hundred the following day? But so far she'd heard nothing. Not a word from Madame Champeau and no indication that the great man would see her. On her own. Her very own private audience, ahead of the other painters. Time was running short – the official group meeting with Vilotte had been tentatively scheduled for Tuesday – and she'd so wanted to be the first.

Pulling the band from her hair, Naomi pushed back her chair and stood, tightening the robe around her.

But maybe, she thought, smoothing her fingertips over the side of her neck, feeling a heat in her cheeks from the angry removal of her make-up, maybe she could skip the following morning's session that Gilles had set up for them? Maybe she could track down the housekeeper and get something sorted out?

After all, she'd paid, hadn't she?

She was considering this, pulling back the quilt from her bed, when she heard a soft knock at her door. Gathering up her robe, she went to the door and opened it an inch.

'*Je vous en prie, madame, mais il est prêt. Si vous voulez?*'

It was Madame Champeau, hovering in the shadows.

For a moment Naomi couldn't understand what was being said.

And then, suddenly, she did, followed just as suddenly by a wave of panic.

'*Un moment, s'il vous plaît,*' she replied and closed the door.

Hurrying back to her dressing table, Naomi West sat herself down in front of the mirror and reached for her make-up bag.

'Of course I damn well *voulez*,' she muttered.

59

Given the downpour, Gilles had insisted that Claudine spend the night at Monastère. There was no way he was going to allow her to drive home in such foul – and dangerous – conditions. She could share his bed, he told her. She'd be quite safe. And when she said she didn't have a thing to wear, he'd found some of his own clothes – the two of them were about the same build, he said, rooting around in his case and pulling out a clean shirt and a pair of jeans and holding them up against her. So that had been that.

Now Gilles was snoring lightly as Claudine crept into their room. She took off her clothes and slipped in beside him. As the storm raged outside, buffeting against walls and windows as though searching for a way in, she realised she was trembling. And that she'd been trembling pretty much from the moment she saw Jacquot at the piano and decided not to let the moment pass.

But how bold she'd been. How challenging. She wondered what had possessed her. How could she have dared? And she felt herself flush. What would he think?

But she knew why she'd been like that.

Because, from the very moment she had seen him there in that gallery in Marseilles – the no-show at her first-night party, the policeman her sister Delphie had told her about – he'd never altogether slipped from her mind. The clothes he wore, the way he'd strolled around the gallery, looking at her paintings, admiring them, saying how much he liked them. And then buying one. The small canvas of the lemons on a plate. Not as ambitious as some of her other work but still one of her favourites, and one of the first that she'd painted, when she still wasn't sure she could do it.

Maybe, too, she remembered him because he hadn't made a pass. Just that easy smile. No suggestion in word or gesture that there was anything else on his mind beyond her paintings. It had pleased her, but perplexed her too.

And now, here he was at Grand Monastère. Just a few rooms away. Looking just as she remembered him.

Such a big man, she thought, bringing up her knees and slipping her fingertips between them – the way she always slept. But gentle, too – slow, measured movements that somehow served to conceal his power and his presence. The way his fingers brushed across the keys, the way his eyes closed for the music, the way his lips pursed and tsked-tsked over an incorrect note. He seemed as far away from her image of a policeman as it was possible to be. He had, she decided, the look of a composer – but then, that was probably because he was sitting there at the piano.

But tough, too, she had no doubt. A real *vrai dur* if he

needed to be. You didn't get to work long for the Marseilles *Judiciaire* unless you knew how to look after yourself. She couldn't imagine too many people with the nerve to confront him.

Beside her, Gilles shifted in the bed and she found herself wondering what it would be like to love a man like Daniel Jacquot . . . but that was ridiculous, she chided herself. She wasn't interested, wasn't able to be interested. Her heart had broken and it still wasn't mended. Now was just not the right time.

Which made her smile. It hadn't been the right time a year ago either, but he'd still made an impression, looking much like he looked this evening – cool, calm, the most alluring green eyes and those big, gentle hands.

She caught herself thinking more about the hands than she felt she ought to, and felt herself blush, then shiver. Something about them, moving over that keyboard, reaching for the notes. But it wasn't right . . . She didn't think things like that. Not any more. There was no room . . .

But there'd been a moment there, when she said it was time for her bed, and he'd seen her to her room . . . there'd been a moment there when she thought she might say something. Or he might. And how she'd respond. Or how he might. And then, that very moment, remembering, insanely, how she hadn't shaved her legs in a month. Which meant . . . She couldn't. She just couldn't. And the moment had passed.

But he was . . . gorgeous. She'd seen the other women take him in, there in the lobby, getting out of their wet things, when he came over and introduced himself: Marcie and Gracie, despite themselves, giving him the once-over; Naomi so obviously dropping her umbrella for him to pick up (and him not noticing); Joanna darting little looks at them as they talked; and then Hilaire giving her a knowing wink as they walked together to their rooms. Gilles and Philip had noticed him too. Which was probably the real reason why Gilles had insisted she spend the night. Without her saying a word, he'd sensed the change in her, and known the reason for it. It wasn't just landscapes he spotted.

And such a lovely, easy twinkling smile. His eyes just disappeared into a web of crinkles, the corners of his mouth slicing into his cheeks.

But it was the voice, Claudine decided, that did it. Warm as an evening breeze. The words just seemed to wrap around you like a furry stole. If he hadn't been a policeman, he'd have made just a great hypnotist. One word and you'd be out – completely in his control. She wished now he'd sung those words a little louder, rather than just whispering them, as an after-thought, to accompany the notes. And she smiled when she recalled the soft murmuring he put in during the pauses, as though keen to provide some accompaniment.

She wondered how old he was. Over forty, that was certain. Midway maybe, or even closing on the fifties. The ponytail dated him, she thought, but suited him too. He had enough planes and angles to his face to make the hair work. The sun-bruised cheekbones, the broad forehead lightly etched with lines, the straight-talking chin and that slightly busted nose that seemed to throw off the eyes a degree or two to make their perfection just a little . . .

But the overriding feeling she'd had in his company was safety. And warmth. She felt . . . protected. And not just because he was a policeman.

Beside her, Gilles moaned lightly and turned around, his

knees coming up behind hers. Which was the moment she realised that she wanted to sleep with Jacquot. And that, given the hour they'd spent together, the way he'd looked at her, the way he'd treated her, he would probably not mind sleeping with her either.

Just so long as he wanted to do it for the right reasons, she decided.

But what were the right reasons?

And then, did they really matter?

Anyway, a man like that, he was certain to be taken. No likelihood of him being left on his own. Someone somewhere was sure to be keeping the bed warm for him . . . and once again Claudine felt herself blush.

Perhaps that was another reason she'd been drawn to him. Perhaps that was why he made her feel so safe. Because he was already taken. Unavailable.

But then, as she closed her eyes and took a deep, deep breath, she remembered, for no apparent reason but with a certain satisfaction – his fingers reaching for the notes, spreading across the keys – that there had been no wedding ring.

60

Claude Bouvet pushed through the service doors into the kitchen and let them swing back behind him. It was not quite midnight and already the place was deserted, work surfaces gleaming with a scoured metallic shine, Cancale's duckboards stacked against the pantry wall, and the concrete floor still shiny from its nightly mopping.

The duckboards had been Cancale's idea.

'Not so dangerous,' he'd said, when he first visited the kitchens, the week after Delabre left in a huff. 'Food or oil on this floor and, poufff, you have a fall and an injury and who knows what kind of legal follow-up. Wooden palettes, plastic, it makes no difference. Get them in and it will be a pleasure to work with you, monsieur.'

Bouvet had noted the 'with you', not 'for you', but promptly ordered up the palettes that Cancale had requested. Two months later the master moved in.

Judging by the state of the kitchen – wiped clean and empty – the evening's dinner service had been a breeze, just the ten covers between seven and ten-thirty and a nine-thirty Room Service order from the couple in Room Four – a bottle of Tequila, champagne, an Eggs Benedict and a lamb with harissa.

With such an easy service, Cancale would probably have let most of the kitchen staff go early, given the rain and the trip down to Luissac, keeping back just one or two commis to finish up, shut down the ovens, grills and hotplates.

Stepping past the service station, its polished surface still warm from the line of coppery-domed heating lamps that hung above it, Bouvet called out Cancale's name. 'Alexandre. You still here?'

His voice echoed in the empty space, just a few of the dozen or so ceiling panels still lit, the smooth concrete floors spilt with shadows from the copper-bottomed saucepans, skillets and sieves hanging from their racks.

Everything neat and tidy, everything put away.

Bouvet looked around, nodded his head. Except . . . to his astonishment, Bouvet's eyes settled on an object at the back of a work station – a knife. He walked over and picked it up, a narrow vegetable paring knife. He turned the blade in the light. Henckels. It was a Henckels. Which would mean it belonged to – Bouvet thought back. Lasalle. Had to be. The new assistant commis from the Brasserie Chez Gaillard in Cavaillon.

The boss there, Laurent Gaillard, had made the call. 'We have a chef here, Claude. We are good but he is better. We have tried to keep him to ourselves but his time has come. He needs more of a challenge. Is there anything at Monastère?'

A nice kid, thought Bouvet, but still on Brasserie time – even if the Brasserie Chez Gaillard was one of the best tables you could hope to find in this neck of the Lubéron. Leaving your knives around was not what real chefs did A chef's knife was his most valued and treasured possession, and no chef worth his toque ever left it lying around for someone else to find, or use. Or keep.

All the young sous like Allie and Guy and Jimi kept their blades in a wrap – the carvers, the cleavers, the saw-edged, the parers. Oyuki Ceramic, Mac, Global, Wüsthof – whatever brand they favoured. In Lasalle's case a set of well-worn Henckels.

Putting down the knife, Bouvet wandered around the kitchen, noting with satisfaction the gleam on the stainless steel fridges, just a small smudge on the glass front of an oven. A professional kitchen. Immaculate. Wonderful to see. Once this had been his world. Even now, sometimes, he missed it.

Bouvet swung open one of the chill cabinets and peered in. A dozen plastic bowls, tightly sealed. In one, the remains of a *sauce antiboise* prepared that evening for the fillets of John Dory; in another, a red puddle of strawberry coulis that had decorated the fondant *chocolat*; and there, in larger containers on a shelf by themselves, the stocks: beef, the colour of burnt bones; chicken, a creamier shade; and the fish, almost grey red with a heavy sediment.

On the bottom shelf, a stack of rectangular boxes had been squeezed in. Bouvet prised one out and, holding it against his chest, peeled back the lid. Inside, laid between layers of wax paper, were a dozen floured squares of that evening's Ravioli des Écrevisses. He closed the lid and drew out another – a dozen of Cancale's celebrated choux pastry balls filled with truffled cream cheese; and, in a third, a half-dozen fillets of beef, the narrowing tail end, but still a good size.

Bouvet knew the story here. The night staff making up more units for the dinner menu to leave for the lunch staff the following day. Anything left over from one service, put in the chill cabinet for the next rota. The only problem, as Bouvet noted, was that the items 'left over' and stowed away were more often than not the more expensive ones. And rather a lot of them. That, he knew, was how profit margins took a shave. Or in this case, a slice. He'd have to have a quiet word with Cancale.

It was as Bouvet closed the chill cabinet, that he heard it, the slamming of a latched freezer door coming from the passageway beyond the main kitchen. If the extractors above the ranges had been working he wouldn't have heard a thing, but the hum of the fridges was too low to cover the sound. He crossed the kitchen and pushed through the heavy plastic doors that led to the cold rooms, aware now of a soft grunting sound.

Turning the first corner he ran straight into his master chef, the stiffened back legs of the pig carcass slung over Cancale's shoulder catching him a glancing blow on the shoulder. If he'd been a couple of centimetres shorter, the pig's toenails would have taken out an eye.

'Jésu, Alex. You nearly blinded me,' said Bouvet, pulling his cardigan back into shape and brushing it down.

'Out of the way, Claude, out of the way before I rupture myself,' cried Cancale, pushing past Bouvet and reaching forward to open one of the cold-room doors.

'But what are you doing? Why didn't you get one of the boys to help?'

'Let 'em go early. Last order by ten and they were out of here, off so quick I forgot about the bloody pig.'

Inside the cool room Cancale reached up to the rack of

hooks, pulled one into place, then positioned himself and the pig under it. With a trumpeter's cheeks, he hoisted the carcass off his shoulder and up over the hook until its point slid between the front leg tendon.

'Oufff, that's a bastard,' said Cancale, putting out a hand to steady the swinging carcass.

'But why do you want it here? Shouldn't it stay in the freezer?'

'Your painter chum. Monsieur Gavan? Came in earlier to see if I could set something up for his group. A still life, he said. So we agreed on the pig, hanging from a hook.' Cancale pulled a knife from a sheath concealed in his apron.

'No, no. That's fine,' said Bouvet. 'Not a problem.'

'Didn't think you'd mind,' said Cancale. 'And they'll be out of the way back here . . .'

Reaching into the pig's belly, Cancale cut out its kidneys.

'Something for breakfast,' he said with a grin, and slipped them into a jacket pocket.

61

Jacquot couldn't sleep. He wasn't surprised. He lay on the bed fully clothed, ankles crossed, fingers laced across his stomach, listening for the thunder, waiting for the lightning. And thinking about Claudine Eddé.

Dieu, but he liked her. Such a woman. Just so easy, so confident in herself. He could have stayed in that bar for hours, jousting gently with her. That clear, unwavering voice, soft and luscious, and those tight, challenging little remarks: how she'd waited two, three minutes before giving up on him and joining the painters for dinner; how she hoped he didn't make a habit of it – which was encouraging; and how, maybe, he'd make a reasonable piano player – maybe . . .

From the moment she came to the piano and picked up his glass of calva she had him banged to rights. And she knew it. Knew just how to punch his buttons, pull his strings. He might have been the one sitting at the keyboard, but there was no

304

doubt she was the better player. Whatever game she chose to play. Not that difficult a trick after his appalling performance in the lobby earlier that evening.

He tried to get a picture of her in his head, but it was difficult. Shoulder-length hair, black, parted a little to one side and curling below the jawline; strong, angled cheekbones, and pearly blue-grey eyes. Like a husky's. Cool, sharp, intelligent.

Tall, too; willowy almost. But not thin. The jeans might have been a fraction too large for her but she still filled them. Gorgeously. Provocatively.

She was, he decided . . . she was . . . very beautiful. And sexy, too.

And married, obviously. Had to be. There was no way a woman like that lived by herself. No chance. If he hadn't known better, Jacquot would have said that Gilles Gavan was the husband. Or at least the man in her life.

Which, if she was married, or otherwise accounted for, made her interest in him surprising. The way she'd engaged him, his attention – almost flirting; those long legs of hers crossing one way and then the other; the cigarettes she smoked held just so, smiling at him through the smoke; the way she teased him . . . tested him, knowing she was more in control than he was.

So why should she bother, if she had someone waiting at home?

And what about children? She looked as though she knew what it was to have a child. Something elevated, knowing, patient. Something warm and loving. But not so young a child that she couldn't stay away for a night. Maybe the father was looking after it?

Or maybe, maybe she was divorced, Jacquot considered? Or a widow, recovering from a loss?

Come to think of it, for all her spirit, her jokiness, her studied cool, there had been something . . . sad about her. Something isolated. A kind of distance.

Jacquot took a breath, tried to clear his head.

If these feelings, these thoughts that he was entertaining, were unexpected, then they were also somehow comforting. Out of the blue he had met someone he liked. Someone he was attracted to. There was no denying it. Even back in Marseilles, in that gallery, he had noticed her. The gallery assistant, sitting behind her counter . . . And now? Now he was even more certain, and blessed the strange congruence of events that had brought them together again. He, Jacquot, investigating a missing person. She, Claudine, hosting a painting group. Both of them there at the Monastère. There was, he decided, a pleasing significance about it all. As though somehow they'd been meant to meet, a year or more after that first, incomplete encounter.

Swinging his legs off the bed, Jacquot sat up, rubbed his hands over his cheeks, then slid them across his scalp. A breath of air, he thought to himself. That's what he needed. Out on the loggia – with a joint if he had one, but a cigarette would do – watching the rain, listening for the thunder, waiting for the lightning. Jacquot loved a storm and this one was turning into a monster.

He was in the salon, pulling on his jacket, when he heard it – a scuffling somewhere outside his room. And what sounded like a muffled cry. He was at the door in an instant, flung it open. But there was nothing to see, the passage lights in their wrought-iron sconces that came on automatically when a guest-room door was opened or the stair sensors triggered were clearly not operating. Instead, a flash of lightning lit up the wild, wind-whipped sheets of rain pouring down into the cloister, cascading over the guttering, pounding on the roof above his head and hammering through the palms. Maybe the storm had blown a circuit somewhere.

Peering into the darkness, Jacquot looked left and right, across to the other side of the loggia, but there was nothing. He wondered for a moment if what he'd heard was one of Claudine's little 'happenings' – one of Monastère's more refined entertainments – like the music in the lobby, like sandals on stone, a door slamming.

But Jacquot wasn't convinced. Whatever it was had sounded so real, so close, as if someone had actually been attacked, was being dragged off against their will, screams of fear and protest muffled under a meaty hand. And so far as he knew, ghosts didn't engage in unseemly scuffles like that.

But then, no one else seemed to have heard it. Bressans next door, or Ginoux at the end. Neither of their doors had opened.

Jacquot stepped away from his door, letting it click closed behind him, and went to the balustrade, leaned over and looked down into the cloister garden. A swirling gust of wind slapped rain into his face – making his heart leap – and another crackling flash of lightning forked down beyond the walls bright enough to show the racing clouds whence it came. And in that instant of light, wiping the rain from his eyes, further away than he'd expected, Jacquot caught a movement, a shadow. In the far corner of the cloister, by the wall of scrolled memorials.

Pushing away from the balustrade Jacquot hurried to the end of the passage and down the spiral of stone stairs that he and van der Haage had taken to the cloister, slowing as he came to the bottom step, but making no effort to keep silent. The rain and thunder and lightning easily covered the sound of his shoes on the stone.

Immediately to his left was the line of guest rooms where the painters were accommodated and to the right the wall of memorials where he'd seen the shadow. But there was nothing there now. Just the marble scrollwork, the stone arches of the cloister and the door marked *Privé* that led to the second court-yard and Vilotte's watchtower.

Stepping away from the stairs he made a circuit of the cloister, found nothing, then returned to the door marked *Privé*. He was about to reach out for the handle when the door sprang open and the beam of a torch lit his face.

His heart leapt and he threw up an arm to block the sudden, blinding light. '*Qui est là?*,' he said, ducking away from the beam and reaching forward with his other hand for the light, catching hold of a thin wrist and twisting the torch upwards.

The beam fell upon the startled, wide-eyed face of Naomi West. A macintosh was pulled round her shoulders but there was nothing on her head. Her short black hair was slicked down by the rain, a trail of mascara weeping over her cheeks.

'Let me go,' she cried. 'Let go, you're hurting my wrist.' Something she was carrying dropped to the ground. A case of some sort.

'*Madame. Je m'excuse*,' said Jacquot, releasing her. 'I am so sorry. I thought you were someone else.'

'Well I'm not. It's just me. And you scared me half to death.'

And you me, thought Jacquot. 'It's the lights,' he said instead. 'A fuse has blown, I think. The storm. I heard something, I came out to see. Here, permit me to help you.' Jacquot leaned down beside her and picked up the bag she had dropped. 'But what are you doing here so late?' he asked. 'And in such a terrible weather?'

'I . . . I was visiting the Master. He wanted to see me,' she replied, taking the portfolio from Jacquot and tucking it under her arm, trying to shuffle past him in the doorway, the beam of light now playing between their feet.

He stepped aside. 'A little late for a visit?'

'I had some things for him.' She indicated the portfolio under her arm. 'My paintings. He had asked to see them.'

Jacquot nodded. 'He is a strange man, the Master. To ask for paintings so late at night, *n'est-ce pas*?'

'Strange indeed,' she replied and, stepping past him, she hurried to her room.

62

Vilotte was tired. God-awful, deadly, bone-weary tired. Weighed down by it. Sometimes he felt he didn't have the strength to lift a brush, squeeze the paint from a tube.

And tonight, too, maybe just a little drunk, a little *hors de combat*. The last bottle but one of Ginoux's fine old wine lying empty on the studio floor. That and the cognac he'd poured himself not ten minutes earlier. And the pastis that Madame C had brought him with his dinner tray. A treat, she'd told him. A small apéritif to calm him. He'd been working too hard.

As he climbed the stairs to his bedroom, slowly, step by cautious step, reaching for the wall to balance himself, Vilotte hoped he'd make his bed before the pain hit him. It was always easier lying down. Not the pain itself – there was no easing that – but the dizziness that came with it. That terrible spinning in his head – like a coin in the air – that snatched the meat from his old legs and had him weaving about like a pavement pisshead looking for a lamp-post to hang on to.

And it was getting worse. Of that he was certain. The more he drank, the worse it became – those sudden, stifling, blinding flares of pain, there, right there, behind his left ear.

At the top of the stairs, Vilotte stopped for a moment to catch his breath.

Tired. Certainly.

Drunk, too. He'd have nodded if he'd dared.

But that wasn't all.

Angry. Head-throbbing, blood-boiling angry.

That woman! That damnable American. Of all the . . .

The nerve, he thought, starting to slide his slippered feet across the floor like a walker on a tightrope, arms reaching out either side of him. A chimpanzee could paint better. She wasn't even pretty, though she clearly thought she was, flirting like that as she laid out her not-so-pretty daubs.

And bold as brass, as he poked through them with a finger, she'd pulled out some tape machine and would he mind answering some questions about the work, what he thought of it – some kind of audio-performance she was planning for her next show?

Show?

She showed those . . . things? People came to see them?

Bloody nerve, he called it.

But he'd sent her packing sharp enough – the only way he knew how.

'*C'est du bidon! C'est une merde! Caca! Tout caca!*' he'd shouted at the machine. 'It's all crap. Crap. Bloody crap . . .' And then he'd reached out a hand and caught hold of one of her itsy little tits, near falling out of her blouse anyway.

And squeezed and leered.

That had sent her scampering off, all right.

Two steps from the bed, Vilotte stopped once more and searched for breath.

Those bloody cigars, he thought. The man was trying to kill him. Shouldn't have bothered. Could have saved himself some money.

He reached for his pills, slipped two on to his tongue and sucked them down with the spit in his mouth. Not that they were doing much good, he thought. But all the same.

With a long weary sigh, he lowered himself on to the bed and laid his head on the pillow.

He'd pull up his legs in a minute, he thought; straighten himself out to sleep.

And then, with a clap of thunder and flash of lightning, everything went black.

Part Four

Part Four

63

Monday

Jacquot woke to an explosive crack of thunder that sounded as though it were directly outside his shutters. The rain was still hammering down and a jagged silver stream of lightning scorched through the slats.

All night, it seemed, the storm had swung backwards and forwards like a wild animal tethered to a post, the thunder and lightning fading away then growling back with a vengeance. But always the rain. Slanting this way and that. Utterly, endlessly relentless.

Jacquot pushed back the cover and hauled himself out of bed, drew a bath and pushed open the shutters to marvel at the storm. Down in the valley, the Calavon plain was puddled with steely stretches of water, and only the lower slopes of the Monts de Vaucluse were visible, its higher reaches and the ridges beyond shrouded in shawls of boiling black cloud.

As he stretched back in the bath, working the taps with his toes, Jacquot decided the storm was there to stay, little chance of any immediate break in the weather. Which, he decided, was good. He'd be able to work the guests, talk to them, ask about Mademoiselle Ladouze as though enquiring after a friend. And, if anything had happened to her, he was certain he would find the answers among Monastère's guests. Or staff. The question that nagged at him was, why would either guest or staff member see fit to harm Ghislaine Ladouze?

As he was dressing, the phone rang. It was Brunet, in Cavaillon.

'Hear you've got some rain up there.'

'You know about it?' replied Jacquot.

'We've made TV. Flooding all over. Roads closed – you name it.'

Jacquot picked up the remote and switched on the TV. He found a news programme and caught footage of torrents pouring down hillsides and a gloomy-looking gendarme wading through a flooded street in Cavaillon.

'Which might prove problematic,' continued Brunet.

'How so?' asked Jacquot, sitting on the bed to pull on his shoes, phone cradled in his shoulder.

'I mean, if you find anything . . . if you need assistance.'

'Nothing to report yet,' replied Jacquot. 'Still looking. Still waiting. And having to do it Rochet's way.'

'Quietly.'

'Correct. So, what's new? What have you got?'

'Nothing that stands out and sings a solo.'

'Anything close?'

'This and that. They got e-mail out there at Monastère? Or you want me to fax everything over to you?'

'Just run me through it – the highlights,' replied Jacquot.

'Not a whole lot,' said Brunet. 'Anyway, here goes . . .'

Down the line, Jacquot could hear the rustle of paper.

'. . . Ginoux. Paul Ginoux. He's an art dealer. Never married. Fancy address in Paris and known to the authorities.'

'Police?'

'Tax. He's been flagged. There are certain questions concerning declared income and, let's say, quality of life. Accounts are always in order, but the tax boys reckon they're only getting a small portion of the whole. There have been a couple of investigations but nothing's ever stuck. It seems, like your friend Bressans, that he has important contacts. Patrons, clients. Presumably the people he sells to.

'. . . then there's the American. Branigan. Mademoiselle Meredith Branigan . . .'

Adjusting the pillow and lying back, Jacquot remembered. The girl in the pool. Criminally pretty, but somehow . . . vacant.

'. . . Hit the headlines a couple of weeks back, in Cannes. The film festival. Seems she's an actress. And according to the press about to hit the big time. The man she's with, the same room, this Kónar character, he's also in films. Won some prize down there for a documentary on Bosnian battlefields. Lives in Rome. Can't say whether the two of them met at the festival or sometime before, but Cannes seems the likely bet. According to Immigration, it's Branigan's first time out of the States.

'Next, Lens Pieter van der Haage – nothing. Married, two children. Small design/architecture practice in Amsterdam, and not doing too well, the shape his credit cards are in . . .

'. . . Gilles Gavan. Single. Runs his own gallery in Aix. On Cours Mirabeau, so he can't be doing that badly . . .

'. . . Emile Dutronc. Lives in Paris, but Belgian, not French. No wife. No children. Military pension . . .'

'Belgian military or Legion?' asked Jacquot.

'. . . Legion. Nothing known about him before he joined up – you know the Legion. Just what he chose to tell them. Name, age, nationality. We don't even know for certain if Dutronc's his original name.

'Then there's your painting group. All of them clean as a whistle. Gould, single, runs an antiques business in Albany, New York; West, divorced, has a gallery in Phoenix, Arizona; Tilley, a retired librarian, and Hughes a teacher – both divorced, both living in Virginia. Same address; Becque, originally Canadian, not French. Runs a *pharmacie* in Vernon, west of Paris.'

'Single? Married?'

'Husband died six years ago. A doctor. But not actually her husband. They lived together but never married. No children.'

'Anything else?'

'Not a thing, but I'll keep looking, if you want me to . . .'

'No point. Leave it there for now. But call me if anything else comes in.'

'*T'as pigé* – you got it.'

64

As soon as Jacquot entered the Salle du Matin that Monday morning, he knew what everyone was talking about.

'Didn't sleep but a wink,' he heard Philip Gould say as he passed the painters' table, nodding *Bonjour* to Madame Becque who happened to catch his eye. She smiled, then looked away, wiping at the corners of her mouth with her napkin.

'And have you seen the news?' exclaimed Marcie Hughes. 'You wouldn't believe the flooding. And in just a few hours.'

'Cavaillon looked like Venice,' said Grace.

'We should hire a gondola and try our hand at Canaletto,' suggested Joanne.

At the end of the table, sparing Jacquot just the leanest of acknowledgements as he passed by, Naomi West asked if anyone had seen the Canaletto exhibition which had toured two years earlier. There were enthusiastic nods and disappointed shakes of the head.

As for Gilles and Claudine, there was no sign.

At Jacquot's table, one of the waiters pulled back his chair. *'Petit déjeuner, monsieur, ou le buffet?'*

'A coffee first, and then, well, maybe I'll help myself.'

'D'accord, monsieur.'

While he waited for his coffee, Jacquot glanced around the room. Apart from the painters ranged around their club table, there were three other guests having breakfast – the Dutchman van der Haage, stirring his coffee into a whirlpool, then tapping the spoon against the cup; Ginoux, in the far corner, spectacles hung round his neck, looking neatly dapper as he buttered some bread; and Bressans, leafing idly through a magazine, attention firmly fixed on the page, determined not to catch Jacquot's eye.

Jacquot's coffee arrived and as the waiter set out the cafetière and a bowl-sized cup, Ginoux pushed away from his table and got to his feet. Shooting his cuffs, he hurried importantly from the room as though there was urgent business to attend to and too little time to get it all done.

Bressans was next, dusting croissant crumbs from his chinos and polo shirt – a green one this time – as he got to his feet. If it hadn't been for the storm, Jacquot was sure that he would have taken the terrace exit and the long way round to Reception, rather than exchange any kind of greeting with Jacquot this early in the morning. As it was, Bressans kept two tables between them as he made for the door of the Salle du Matin, delivering only the curtest of nods as he passed by.

And then, with only van der Haage and the painters left, Gilles Gavan and Claudine arrived.

From his table in the corner of the room, Jacquot watched her glance around and then see him, tip her head, smile, while

Gavan settled with the group, exclaiming at the weather, asking how everyone had slept in his fractured, enthusiastic English, and assuring them that he had something of a surprise for them to make up for the dreadful weather.

'The Master?' asked Joanne.

Gavan shook his head. 'Tomorrow, hopefully. It has still to be confirmed. In the meantime, if you have finished your breakfasts, let us meet back here in, say, ten minutes?'

As the group chattered away, Jacquot got up from his chair and crossed to the buffet table laid out against the terrace window. He hoped that Claudine would notice, and come and join him.

But it was not to be. He was helping himself to scrambled eggs, the rain battering against the window, swirling in angry whirlwinds across the terrace, when Claude Bouvet, his face drained of colour, pushed through the swing doors leading to the kitchen.

He caught sight of Jacquot and came right over: 'You had better come quick, monsieur.'

65

The kitchen was quiet, the usual heat and hurry reduced to a leisurely buffet service, just two young sous-chefs wiping down surfaces and clearing up their stations, the scent of freshly baked bread and a *plongeur* scouring out saucepans.

Following Bouvet past the central range, Jacquot knew what was going to happen.

Someone had found Mademoiselle Ladouze.

Jacquot's missing person was about to become a homicide.

At the back of the kitchen, Bouvet pushed through a pair of heavy-duty plastic doors and led Jacquot down a long curving corridor lined with latched metal doors – storerooms for dry goods, cool rooms and freezer units – a light switch and temperature gauge set beside each one. At the end of the corridor a commis-chef stood nervously at the top of a flight of stairs. He looked about nineteen or twenty with spots on his chin and a tangle of greasy blond curls tucked under a commis' toque.

'It's down here,' directed Bouvet, and he bustled down the stone steps with Jacquot and the commis following behind. At the bottom of the stairs he turned left along another corridor that opened finally into a vaulted cellar-room. There was a musty smell here, of damp stone and mouldering decay, the room lit by a single bare bulb cradled in a wire guard screwed to the wall, the only sound a close growling of thunder and a spatter of rain on a single latched window.

Jacquot looked around. The place was crowded with junk, a graveyard of old bed-springs, empty bottle racks, and out-of-date or broken kitchen equipment kept there presumably to cannibalise, one entire corner crowded with straw-bottomed demijohns. But, so far as he could see, there were no apparent signs of recent violence.

Against the furthest wall was a line of old fridges, freezers and washing machines.

'It's there,' said Bouvet, pointing to the line of fridges.

On one of them, a freezer cabinet, a tiny green light glowed.

Leaving Bouvet and the commis-chef standing just inside the door – Bouvet taking a series of deep breaths and muttering with each exhalation: '*Catastrophe, catastrophe, c'est une catastrophe!*' – Jacquot approached the unit. A straining electric whine came from the back of it.

'You found it?' he asked, without looking round at the commis.

'Yes, boss. 'Bout five minutes ago.'

'And what were you doing here?' Jacquot continued, squatting down on his heels and inspecting the front of the unit. It had once been white but time and hard duty had dulled the colour, its side panels, where it had once stood beside other units, smeared with a collar of hardened yellow grease, and its front scored with scratches and dents. Even the green light had a wan flicker and the dial beneath it, set at 'Max', was haloed with dirt.

'I asked what you were doing here,' said Jacquot again, when no reply was forthcoming.

'Havin' a smoke,' admitted the commis.

'What's your name?' asked Jacquot, turning to look at the lad.

'Bastien. Bastien Délignes.'

'Long way to come for a smoke, Bastien,' said Jacquot, turning back to the freezer. 'What's wrong with the corridor? Or the stairs?'

'Maître Cancale,' explained Bastien. 'He's got his office at the top of the stairs, and a nose on him like a truffle hound when it comes to smokes. Smell a pack in your pocket, he can.'

Bouvet broke in, as though a change of subject might somehow help alleviate his problems. 'Maître Cancale insists all our chefs are non-smokers. Off and on duty,' he explained. 'He, like me, agrees that smoking ruins the taste buds. Not good in a chef,' he said, turning a chill, admonishing look on Bastien. 'But then,' Bouvet shrugged, 'they all do . . . smoke, I mean. If I didn't turn a blind eye, I wouldn't have a working kitchen. Maître Cancale, however, is a little more . . . *rigoureux*.'

Jacquot nodded, smiled to himself, wondering how he'd get on with a man like that. If Cancale didn't like his brigade smoking, how did he feel about his diners? He and Madame Hublé would make a fine pair.

'You come down here a lot, Bastien?'

'You know, when I can. Outside, if it's not raining.'

'Last time?'

'I was on dinner service, last night. Maybe ten-ish.'

'And the light wasn't showing?'

Bastien shook his head. 'Not that I can remember, otherwise I'd've taken a look then, wouldn't I?'

Leaning forward, Jacquot felt under the unit – nothing but cold stone and cobwebs. 'But this morning, you noticed it?' he asked, wiping the webs off his fingers, rolling them into a ball and flicking it on to the floor.

'That's right. That's why I opened it up. There's nothing should be in here. Like, it's all rubbish, you know?'

'Anyone else know about this? The other chefs?' Jacquot thought of the two sous-chefs he'd seen in the kitchen. Neither looked as if they'd been told that a body had been found in a freezer, but you never knew.

'No, monsieur,' Bastien assured him. '*Personne.*'

Bouvet nodded. 'I happened to be in the kitchen; there was a problem with some of the left-over supplies,' he explained. 'Bastien came straight up to me, asked if I could go with him. I had no idea . . .'

'Good,' said Jacquot. 'Let's keep it that way. Not a word, *c'est compris?*'

Pulling a handkerchief from his pocket, Jacquot got to his feet, eased his fingers round the lid handle and slowly exerted the pressure needed – not too fast.

'It's an old blast freezer,' said Bouvet. 'Had it about three years but we needed a bigger one. There wasn't room in the kitchen for the both of them, so I had it moved here.'

'How long ago?' asked Jacquot, feeling resistance.

'End of the season, last year,' replied Bouvet.

With a rubbery sucking sound the plastic lips of the seal parted, the resistance eased and the lid creaked open. An icy breath of air wafted across Jacquot's face and a thin fog of condensation rolled upwards.

Beneath it, illuminated by a hinge light that had turned on automatically as the lid lifted, hunched and curled in a head-between-knees position was a human body.

Rounded back, shoulders and the back of a head. The hair was dark and the material stretched across the shoulders was thin enough to show the line of the vertebrae and ribbing. There was also a frosty pink stain around the edge of a tear on the right shoulder. Jacquot knew it was blood, probably leached by the rain. He knew, too, that when the body was properly recovered from the freezer and defrosted there would be more blood on the front, the position of the cut indicating a slice to the carotid artery.

Jacquot nodded to himself, pursed his lips and slipped a hand to his ponytail. He pulled the coil of hair through thumb and forefinger. Once. Twice. Three times.

It was just as he'd expected, exactly what he'd been waiting for since Bouvet instructed him to lift the bedcovers in Mademoiselle Ladouze's room.

There was only one problem.

The body in the blast freezer did not belong to Mademoiselle Ladouze.

66

I t was the gold stud in the right ear lobe.

Jacquot had seen it before.

Which ruled out Mademoiselle Ladouze.

And Jacquot knew when and where he'd last seen it.

Not eighteen hours earlier. In Monastère's swimming pool.

Carefully, Jacquot moved his fingers across the shoulders, pressed the tips against the body. Icy-cold and rock-hard – no movement save a slight crackling between clothing and skin and no remaining give to the flesh. Next he slid a hand past the exposed ear stud, and into a gap between the side of the head and the tops of the thighs. His fingers tingled from the cold but there was no difficulty identifying what he felt.

'It's a body, isn't it?' asked Bouvet, now wringing his hands.

Jacquot nodded.

'Mademoiselle Ladouze?'

'No,' replied Jacquot, noting the question. Had Bouvet been expecting someone else?

'Tell me, how cold do these things go?' asked Jacquot. 'The maximum temperature?'

Bouvet frowned. '–50, I think. If we need things frozen quickly – say, soft fruits, compotes, coulis . . .'

'So how long would it take to freeze something as large as a body?'

'Maximum setting? Maybe a couple of hours. Three hours. But this is an old machine. It's been worked, you know? With this machine it could take longer.'

'Is there a defrost on this?'

Bouvet shook his head. 'Only on the lowest setting. If it's on Max, whatever is in there is going to the main freezer.'

Jacquot nodded and closed the lid, then leaned across and switched off the power from the mains. The green light flickered out and the motor coughed, wheezed and shut down.

'I suggest we keep the lid closed for now.'

Crossing to the window, Jacquot unlatched it and pushed it open. A fresh steely smell of rain burst into the damp, musty room.

Jacquot peered out. A narrow line of steps led past it.

'Where do the steps lead?'

'From the back of the kitchen down to a small herb garden,' replied Bouvet.

'If it hadn't been for the storm, that's where I'd have gone for my smoke,' volunteered Bastien. 'There's a small landing halfway down.' He glanced at Bouvet, shrugged apologetically.

Jacquot closed the window and looked at the floor beneath it. Some of the flagstones were missing, the layer beneath made up of packed dry earth.

Behind him Bouvet gave a little cough. '*Excusez-moi, mais* . . . If it's not Mademoiselle Ladouze, then who exactly is it?'

'His name is Monsieur Erdâg Kónar. The gentleman with the American girlfriend. I saw him—'

But Jacquot got no further, interrupted by a long, high-pitched scream that echoed down from the top of the stairs.

67

Jacquot reached the top of the stairs first, easily, taking two steps at a time, with Bastien not far behind him and a panting Bouvet bringing up the rear. Up ahead, Jacquot could see the group of painters crowding the corridor, Claudine, Madame Becque and Gilles Gavan with their backs to him. They were all looking at something on the ground. A body.

'Please,' said Jacquot, easing between Gavan and Madame Becque. 'Please, if you would let me through.'

He looked where everyone else was looking.

Outside one of the storeroom doors, on the stone-flagged floor of the corridor, lay the crumpled form of Grace Tilley. Her companion, Marcie Hughes, was kneeling beside her, fanning her face with a palette board, an arm supporting her shoulders. As Jacquot watched, Grace's eyes flickered open, her features pinched with shock, skin as white as alabaster.

'Oh my,' she managed. 'Oh dear.'

'Take it easy, take it easy, honey,' Marcie reassured her. 'You had a fall.'

Grace looked up at the faces around her, one after another. 'A fall, yes,' she said, reaching up to calm Marcie's furious fanning.

'Did you hurt yourself? Did you bang your head?' asked Marcie, putting aside the palette and reaching for Grace's hand.

'No, sweetie, I'm fine. I'm fine. It's just . . . My legs went to water. Just gave way a moment there.' And then she seemed to remember something, her eyes opening wide. 'Oh my, oh my. There's a . . . Did you see it? Did you see them? It was just . . .'

'Are you able to stand, madame?' asked Jacquot, kneeling down beside her.

'Oh yes, oh yes, I'm fine, thank you.' She looked at Jacquot, gave him an uncertain smile, recognised him. '*Oui. Merci. Très bien, je pense.*' Then, gripping Marcie's upper arm, and with Marcie and Jacquot helping her, she pushed herself into a sitting position. 'I really should get off the floor . . .'

Between them, Marcie and Jacquot hoisted Grace to her feet and Marcie set about brushing her down.

'I'm fine. I really am, Marcie.'

Jacquot took his hand from her arm and Grace wavered slightly, but then recovered.

'Some water,' she said. 'I think I'd like to have a glass of water.' She looked at everyone, then saw Bouvet hovering beside Jacquot. 'And I think someone should call the police,' she added in a quavering voice.

'It's all in hand, madame. Please, do not worry yourself,' said Jacquot. And then, turning to the others, 'What's happened here?' he asked. He caught Claudine's eye. In the corridor lights her face was as pale as Grace's, the same blank look of shock in her eyes, as though she'd seen a ghost.

'It's in there,' replied the sous-chef Jacquot had seen wiping down work surfaces in the kitchen a little earlier. 'In the store-room, there,' he said, nodding to a closed steel door with a hefty fridge handle set into it.

Stepping past Madame Tilley, Jacquot reached for the latch and eased the door open.

68

G iven the angle, the door opening towards the back stairs
  he had just raced up, Jacquot realised that, given their
current positions only the sous-chef – who'd obviously been
leading the group to the storeroom – Gavan, Claudine, Madame
Becque and, of course, Grace Tilley, would have seen what
Jacquot could now see.

He heard a whistled intake of breath from behind him –
Bastien – and a low groan from Bouvet. They'd seen it too.

Checking that there was a handle on the inside, and holding
up a finger to the others, indicating that they should give him
a few minutes, Jacquot stepped into the cold room and closed
the door behind him.

In the course of his career, Jacquot had seen many dead
bodies, in any number of hideous circumstances, and often in
equally hideous conditions. But there was something deeply
unsettling about the still, sterile scene that greeted him inside

that storeroom, as though somehow the whole arrangement of the bodies had been deliberately staged – set up – for maximum effect.

Lying on the polished concrete floor was a pig carcass, its stiffened limbs pointing up into the air, its stretched skin smoothly pale in the neon-light flickering above Jacquot's head, the opened cage of its ribs red and shadowy.

But where that pig carcass had presumably once hung there was now a body, a woman's body, the point of an S-shaped steel hook glinting from beneath an armpit.

As Jacquot knew only too well, a hanged body – suicide or murder – had a kind of reassuring straightness to it, arms and legs pointing downwards, an insistent gravity giving the body a certain elegant – if morbid – symmetry of line. Save, of course, for the stretched neck and bloated face looking either up, down or to one side, depending on the position of the knot.

The body in the Monastère's storeroom was different. Hung by the left armpit from a butcher's hook, the woman appeared oddly and grossly out of kilter, the left elbow pointing away from the body and left forearm hanging loose. On her right side, however, the fingertips of her right hand reached nearly to her knee and her right foot appeared to be a good few centimetres lower than the left foot, both shod in cream espadrilles, both pointing to the cold stone floor where a puddle of pinking water had formed beneath the body. This disconcerting imbalance – as though the body was somehow shrugging in mid-air – was heightened by the slant of the blue cummerbund and the hem on the white cotton dress she wore.

Jacquot stepped forward, reached for the left index finger and bent it. There was no resistance, the joints moving easily.

He didn't need anyone from Forensics to tell him that Mademoiselle Ladouze had been dead a great deal longer than the body downstairs in the blast freezer.

For Mademoiselle Ladouze, it surely was.

He had never met her, never seen a photo. But it could only be Bressans' companion from Marseilles – the same kind of dress Jacquot had seen in the video footage, the kind of dress that Roland Bressans and Auguste Vilotte had said she'd been wearing the last time they saw her. The espadrilles, too.

Slowly, taking in everything, Jacquot walked around the body, noting the slanting pitch of the dried wound – a blade of some description, left to right, opening up the front of her bodice, slicing across her breastbone, then pushing between the ribs and into her heart; the corresponding, and darkened, Rorschach-like patterning of bloodstains on the front, sides and back of the white dress; and, beneath his feet, a thin crunching of sand – he had a good idea where that came from. Leaning under the fall of her hair he looked up at her. She still had a surprised look on her face, lips a shade of reddish blue that turned her teeth yellowy, cheeks grey, eyes dilated, staring into an unseen distance.

Turning from the body, Jacquot went to the storeroom door, opened it and looked out into the corridor. Five pairs of eyes – Bouvet, Gilles, Claudine, Bastien and the sous-chef – locked on to his, Claudine managing the smallest of smiles. As for the others – Naomi West, Hilaire Becque, Joanne Nicholls, Philip Gould and Marcie – they had left the corridor, and taken Grace Tilley with them.

'Mademoiselle,' he said, looking at Claudine, 'maybe you could check on Madame Tilley. And please stay around; I will need to speak to you in a little while.'

'Of course,' said Claudine, looking relieved, and she set off towards the kitchen.

'The rest of you, maybe you could come in here,' he said, opening the door for them.

69

Jacquot could just as easily have spoken to them outside in the corridor but he was keen to see how they'd behave with a body hanging from a hook.

He stood aside as, one by one, they stepped through into the storeroom, crowding into a corner away from the body. Jacquot stayed where he was and watched their reactions – Bouvet searching for something in his pockets, the two young chefs casting their eyes on to the stone floor and Gavan looking at the body with a kind of curious intensity, as though he'd never seen anything quite like it.

It was just as Jacquot had expected.

'I'm assuming,' he began, addressing Bouvet, 'that this is Mademoiselle Ladouze?'

'Yes it is,' replied Bouvet, tugging a handkerchief from a pocket and wiping his mouth.

'You're quite certain?'

'Absolutely, Chief Inspector. *C'est sans doute*,' replied Bouvet.

At the mention of his rank, Gavan and the two chefs shot Jacquot a startled look.

'So who saw her first?' asked Jacquot.

'Me,' replied the sous-chef. 'That would be me.'

Jacquot turned to him. He was a wiry little fellow, no taller than Jacquot's shoulder, and Jacquot was pretty sure he'd never have had the strength nor the height to hoist Ghislaine Ladouze up on to the hook. Whoever had done that would have been taller and had some muscle on them. Unless it was the two chefs working together. Between them they could probably have managed it.

'And you are?' asked Jacquot.

'Luc Grégoire,' he stuttered. 'Second *pâtissier* and breakfast chef.'

'So what exactly happened, Luc?'

'Well, see, a little bit after you came through the kitchen with Monsieur Bouvet, Monsieur Gavan here, arrived with the painting group, asked if it was OK for them to come through.'

'You were expecting them?'

Luc nodded.

'You'd been told about this? About their visit?'

'This morning, monsieur. Maître Cancale left a note – told us what he'd done and how I should push up the room temperature a few degrees before the painters arrived and check everything was OK. He told me to do it the moment I read the note, but . . . well, I just forgot, I suppose.'

'It was to be a still life,' Bouvet interrupted. 'Alexandre set it up yesterday with Gilles. It was the storm, you understand. Monsieur Gavan needed something . . . something for his group to paint . . . indoors.'

'Soon as I opened the door I saw her,' Luc continued, as though Bouvet hadn't spoken, nodding at the body without looking at it. 'I closed it sharpish . . . but not sharp enough. That's when the lady saw what was inside . . . And fainted, you know? Nothing I could do about it. It wasn't my fault.'

Jacquot kept a straight face. The lad was worried about a guest fainting, when another guest was hanging from a hook; dead, murdered.

'So Monsieur Cancale was here last night?' asked Jacquot, turning to Bouvet. 'Here in the kitchen?'

'That's right, Chief Inspector. I saw him myself, carrying the carcass in here, getting it up on to the hook. I asked if I could help, but he managed it himself.'

'You were here too? Last night?'

'Every night, after service,' said Bouvet. 'I just do a walk through, you know. Check everything's as it should be. Grease traps, gas rings, filters, fridges. That sort of thing. Old habits . . .'

Jacquot thought about this, and then asked, 'What's usually kept in here?'

'Vegetables, Chief Inspector. In boxes and sacks. Alexandre had already cleared them out by the time I saw him.'

Jacquot turned back to Luc. 'So what happened when the group came into the kitchen?'

'Like I said, I knew what it was all about, didn't I? We weren't that busy so I said, come on through, follow me. I brought them down here and just opened up the door. Saw the body and closed it quick as I could.'

At that moment, the same storeroom door was pulled open and another voice cut into the proceedings.

'Well, well, well,' said the voice. 'Some still life.'

70

The new arrival was dressed in neatly creased jeans, a white T-shirt and a pair of scuffed trainers. His hair had either just been washed or was greasy, black strands flopping over his forehead.

'Ah, Maître,' said Bouvet, turning his back on the body to make the introductions. 'Chief Inspector, this is Alexandre Cancale; Alexandre, this is Chief Inspector Jacquot.'

Jacquot nodded a greeting, taking the man in. Cancale had the bruised, beefy look of a front-row forward, with powerful shoulders stretching the cotton T-shirt across a broad chest. He had small black eyes set under black tufted eyebrows, his cheeks and chins were heavily stubbled, and a moustache and goatee beard had gathered round his mouth like a gin-trap. Just the kind of man, Jacquot decided, to lay a hot blade across a junior's arm. In a temper he suspected that Cancale would be a formidable opponent, a sense that personal control was not an attribute the Master-Chef was overly familiar with.

'You got here fast,' said Cancale lightly, as though he was used to seeing corpses hanging from hooks, and not in the least surprised to find such a thing in one of his storerooms.

'Monsieur Jacquot is staying with us,' explained Bouvet. 'We had a missing person. He came to investigate.'

'Well, by the look of it, you've found her,' said Cancale, stepping forward as though intending to inspect the body more closely, as though it was nothing more than a joint of meat.

Jacquot reached for his arm. 'Monsieur, if you wouldn't mind.'

Cancale stopped, held up his hands. 'OK, OK, I understand.'

'Tell me, monsieur,' began Jacquot, 'do you know the victim?'

Cancale shrugged. 'If she dined in Le Réfectoire, I would have stopped at her table, had a few words. That sort of thing.'

'And did you? Did you meet her?'

Cancale bent down for a better look at the face. 'She certainly looks familiar. Maybe . . .'

'Were you on duty last night, monsieur?'

'Not the whole night. I came down towards the end of service. Around ten. There's a new lunch menu this week. There were things to arrange.'

'And after that?'

'I went to my office . . . paperwork.'

'And then?'

'Then I remembered the rain. And the painters. Monsieur Gavan, here, asked me if I could set something up for them . . . a still life maybe. He wanted to do something in the kitchen, but I knew we'd be too busy in there, and too cramped, to have room for half-a-dozen painters. So I suggested one of the cold rooms. We agreed on the pig . . .' Cancale nodded at the carcass on the floor. 'It looked good.'

'And you put it up yourself?'

'I was going to get one of the boys to do it, but I forgot. By the time I'd finished in the office everyone had gone.'

'And what time was that, monsieur?'

'Around midnight, wasn't it, Claude?'

'That's right.'

'And you left together?'

'No, I left Alexandre to finish off,' said Bouvet.

'Me, I was done here in another ten minutes,' added Cancale. 'Maximum.'

'And you live where, monsieur?'

'An apartment, other side of the kitchen. And I've got a place down in St-Mas.'

'And that's where you went, the apartment, after preparing the . . . still life?'

Cancale nodded.

'And did you hear anything when you were there?'

Cancale tapped his trainer on the floor. 'These stone floors, Monsieur Chief Inspector, you wouldn't hear an elephant.'

'A door slamming? A door like this one?'

'Nothing. Not a sound.'

Jacquot took this in, seemed to think for a moment, then turned to the two chefs. 'Bastien, Luc, you can get back to your duties now. If I need anything more from you, I'll come and find you. Also, I would appreciate it if you kept this quiet for now, *compris*?'

Bastien and Luc assured Jacquot that not a single word would pass their lips, and they hurried away to the kitchen.

When they had gone, Jacquot turned to Gilles Gavan. 'I

would be grateful, too, monsieur, if you and your group limit your activities to the hotel. I will need to speak to them – and to you and your assistant – individually. Given the storm, I don't imagine that should be too much of a problem?'

'No problem at all, Chief Inspector. *Pas de tout*. Of course, of course. Anything I can do to help.' And with a nod to Bouvet and Cancale, Gilles Gavan scurried gratefully after the two chefs, tugging the arms of his jumper over his shoulders.

When he'd gone, Jacquot turned to Bouvet and Cancale.

'Messieurs, if you please . . .' He gestured to the body.

'You want to get her down?' asked Bouvet anxiously.

'Shouldn't we leave her where she is?' asked Cancale. 'Scene of crime and all that?'

'This is not a crime-scene, monsieur. This is not where she died. Also, it would seem . . . decent, to make her more comfortable. So . . . Monsieur Bouvet, if you would take the legs . . . and you and I, Monsieur . . .'

In less than a minute, the hook still clamped into her armpit, Ghislaine Ladouze's body was hoisted off the rail and lowered to the floor. While Bouvet pushed away the pig carcass with his foot, Cancale found an apron on a peg and laid it over the top half of the body.

As soon as it was done, Jacquot opened the door and ushered them out into the corridor.

'How low can we set the temperature?' he asked, securing the door.

'A little above freezing,' said Bouvet. 'Would you like me to adjust the setting?'

'*S'il vous plaît*. As low as it will go. And now, messieurs, tell me,' Jacquot continued, 'what's the access like here?'

'You mean the kitchen? The storerooms?' asked Bouvet.

Jacquot nodded.

'Well, we do not lock the kitchen itself, monsieur. There is no need. Just the wine store, the spirits cupboard. Otherwise . . .'

'So someone could easily get in here at night?'

'If they wanted to, Chief Inspector, but there is nothing to steal. And we always have at least two members of staff on duty at night. For Room Service orders, you understand. They would certainly hear or see something.'

'They stay in the kitchen all night?'

Bouvet shook his head. 'There is a small staffroom off the kitchen. A TV, sofa beds, bathroom . . . They need to be on hand if any orders come through – at any time of night.'

'What about the steps outside? The ones leading to the herb garden. Could someone come in that way? Is there a path?'

Cancale gave a grunt. 'There's a path all right, but you'd need to be a mountain goat to manage it,' he said. 'It runs around the walls but I wouldn't like to try it, not with the cactus waiting for me. And lugging a body? I don't think so . . .'

Jacquot considered this, then turned to Bouvet.

'So, Monsieur Bouvet. I'm afraid now that everything changes. Our "missing person" has turned into what appears to be two murders, the crimes committed in your hotel . . .'

'Two murders?' exclaimed Cancale. 'You mean, she's not the only one?'

'Downstairs, in a freezer . . .' whispered Bouvet. 'Another guest . . .'

'. . . Which means, monsieur, there is nothing I can now do to keep this under wraps. There is a process, I'm sure you understand, and I would appreciate your full cooperation. I will, of course, make sure that everything is kept as discreet as possible, but guests and staff will have to be interviewed, statements taken. After all, it is more than likely that one of them is a murderer.'

Bouvet paled and Cancale guffawed. 'Now here's a way to start the week,' he said with a leery grin.

'So what exactly will you need?' asked Bouvet. 'I mean, what happens now?'

'To start with, Forensics will have to be brought in. They'll send a team up, half a dozen men, probably later this morning . . .'

'You'll be lucky,' came a voice from behind them.

The three men turned.

It was Champeau, soaked to the skin and grinning from ear to ear. *'Il pleut comme les vaches pissent.* You should see it. Like Niagara. And taken half the road with it.'

71

Twenty minutes later, the wind grown too savage to countenance umbrellas, Jacquot, Bouvet and Champeau, raincoats pulled over their heads, hurried across the bridge to the Luissac road.

'Told you,' shouted Champeau, dancing around them with a gleeful little laugh as they took in the damage. 'The road's blocked for sure.'

The lad wasn't wrong, Jacquot decided. The storm chute that he'd passed the previous day, almost concealed by a bank of ferns, was now a raging torrent cascading down over the road. And doing so with such extraordinary force that it had swept away three of the barrier posts at its outer edge along with a good-sized section of road. It looked as though someone had taken a ragged scoop out of it, the thin cover of tarmac not yet carried away split and sagging precariously, littered with small rocks and stones that the waters had brought down and spewed out. Even a few steps clear of the water, Jacquot could feel the power of it through the soles of his shoes.

As far as he could see the only way to make it past the cascade was by getting behind the waterfall where a narrow tunnel curved away between the pummelling water and the hillside. The road surface here, what remained of it, still looked reasonably stable and, clinging to the undergrowth on the bank to stop being snatched away by the water, someone plucky, or mad enough, might just make it through. Jacquot shook his head. If anyone was going to give it a try, it certainly wasn't going to be him.

'Do you know how long it's been like this?' he asked, turning to Champeau.

'Last night. Late.'

'You know that, or it's just a guess?'

'I came for a walk.'

'What time? Do you remember?'

Champeau pulled off his hood and turned his face to the rain. It was as if he hadn't heard Jacquot's question. And then:

'Two o'clock. Maybe a little after.'

'You usually do that? Go for a walk in the rain?'

'I like it,' replied Champeau, giving Jacquot an exaggerated wink.

Jacquot looked at the boy . . . the man . . . ? It was impossible to tell how old he was. He had the body of a man, albeit a little rickety, but the open, friendly face of a child, a simple, beguiling innocence about him as though everything was some kind of joke, something to be considered and then laughed at. Not ridiculed . . . laughed at.

'It's the Bassin Vert,' shouted Bouvet, as they hurried back to the Monastère, the rain splattering against their raincoats, the wind tugging at their clothes and buffeting them into an unsteady trot. 'An old cistern. Must have flooded and broken its bank.'

Jacquot leaned into Bouvet and asked: 'Don't you have a heliport here, monsieur?'

'Well, not exactly a heliport,' replied Bouvet. 'But we have had helicopters land on the tennis court before. If they're not too big, you understand, and if we have enough warning to get the net and the fencing down. But in conditions like this, monsieur, I don't think anyone would try it.'

Back at the hotel, Jacquot returned the macintosh that the front desk had lent him for his trip across the bridge and paid another call on the Réfectoire kitchen.

Just as the storm made non-resident bookings unlikely, so the same storm – in the form of the cascade – meant that the kitchen was dramatically short-staffed for the lunch service. With more than an hour to go before the dining room opened, there was already a sense of urgency. Cancale had pulled on his chef's jacket, and a baseball hat turned back to front, and was putting Luc and Bastien through their paces. Even the *plongeur* had been dragged away from his steaming sinks and drummed into duty at the slicing boards, cutting his way through a basket load of shiny green peppers. On the central range where the three chefs worked, pot lids clattered, gas rings flamed and heated oil and butter spat and hissed at whatever was put into them, almost drowning out a humming sound-track of vents and filters.

As Jacquot pushed through the swing-hinged service doors, Bastien and Luc glanced up at him, but Cancale paid no attention, elegantly filleting a silvery mound of sea bass. His knife worked like a hairdresser's scissors, flashing around the fish as though hardly touching the flesh, yet suddenly two more *filets* were added to the pile, and another head-and-tailed skeleton scooped off the board into the bin beside him.

Coming round the service station, Jacquot headed for Bastien – the smoker.

'Do you have a list of room service orders?' he asked. 'For last night?'

Bastien reached behind him, levered off a wedge of paper from a hook above his station, flicked through it and handed three sheets to Jacquot.

'*C'est tout*,' he said and turned back to his work.

Jacquot thanked him, then read through the slips: Room 1 – Ginoux – 2.45 a.m.; a hot chocolate, blinis, salmon and crème fraîche. Room 7 – 11.30 p.m. Was that Monsieur Gould or Madame West, Jacquot wondered? The beef sandwich and mustard that had been ordered suggested Gould. And then, finally, Room 4 – 9.30 p.m.; Mademoiselle Branigan and the late Erdâg Kónar. The order, he noted, was for Tequila, champagne, an Eggs Benedict and lamb.

'Who delivers the orders, after the waiting staff have gone home?' asked Jacquot, putting down the three room service orders.

'Last night? After service, it was me,' replied Bastien, shuffling a handful of shiitake mushrooms in a pan of bubbling butter. 'The earlier one? Didier probably.'

'Did you see anything, or anyone, on your way up or back?'

'*Rien. Personne.*'

'And Monsieur Ginoux? When he opened the door, was he dressed, or in pyjamas?'

Bastien paused, let the skillet of mushrooms rest over the flame. Then shook them again with a clatter. Finally he said, 'A bathrobe. Bare feet. At first, I thought . . . you know . . . ?'

Jacquot smiled. 'Thanks,' he said, and left the kitchen.

72

M eredith Branigan was swaddled in a Grand Monastère robe, with a hand towel wrapped turban-style round her head, when she opened the door to Jacquot.

She looked radiant, he thought, a warm pink glow on her cheeks, eyes bright and sparkling, the honey-tanned skin of her temples and forehead stretched smooth by the tight grip of her turban. With her hair bound up in the towel, her neck was bare, long and curved, wisps of spun-gold hair dancing across the skin. And then, rising up at him in waves from the soft white folds of her gown, he smelt her, a sweet flowery scent given power by the heat of her bath and kept warm by her body.

'Mademoiselle Branigan, *bonjour*,' he said with a small bow.

For a second she seemed not to recognise him, as though she'd been expecting someone else. Then she placed him.

'Well, hi. I mean . . .'

He could see immediately that she was flustered, as though trying to work out how best to deal with a man she'd flirted with the day before and who, it seemed, had now decided to come calling. A hand sprang to her throat and reached for the collar of the gown to close it.

'I am sorry to trouble you, mademoiselle. I wonder if I might have a word?'

'Why . . . why yes, I guess. Sure.' And, still a little uncertain, she stood aside, indicating that Jacquot should come in, then closed the door after him.

'Do you mind if I get myself dressed first. A couple of minutes?'

'Of course, mademoiselle. Please. There is no hurry.'

While Meredith Branigan was dressing in the bedroom, Jacquot strolled around the salon. It was as cleanly and leanly furnished as the other guest salons he'd seen. On the coffee-table was a room service tray for one, a silver cloche concealing the smeared remains of scrambled eggs, and a napkined nest of bread and croissants. Jacquot touched the coffee pot. Still warm.

In her bedroom, Meredith dressed hurriedly, leaned down to check her appearance in the mirror, and wondered what this visit was all about. She hoped that Erdâg wouldn't suddenly make an appearance. He'd been difficult enough the day before when he'd found her chatting with this man in the pool. Finding him in their salon would probably send him into a real spin. He was terribly possessive, which she rather liked – a glance, a smile from a waiter was enough to make his cheeks flare and his black eyes narrow. As she brushed through her hair, Meredith decided she'd rather like it if he did return. Wherever he was.

Out in the salon, Jacquot had made himself comfortable in one of the armchairs by the fireplace. He stood when Meredith returned – knotted white shirt, bare midriff, Capri pants – and waited till she sat before doing so himself.

'So . . . Mr . . . ?'

'Jacquot. Daniel Jacquot.'

'Right, that's right,' she said, tucking her legs under her. 'I remember. So, how exactly can I help you?'

'Two questions,' said Jacquot. 'First, do either you or Monsieur Kónar know Mademoiselle Ghislaine Ladouze?'

'You mean the looker? The one with the old guy? I know who you mean, sure. And Erdâg, too. He doesn't think I notice but, whenever she's around, he can't keep his eyes off her. But we don't, like know her, or speak to her. A "hi" maybe. But that's it.'

'*Très bien*,' said Jacquot. 'Thank you. And the second question . . . I was wondering, mademoiselle, if you happen to know where your friend Monsieur Kónar is?'

Meredith frowned, gave it some thought. 'You're not telling me he's with *her*?'

Jacquot smiled, held up his hands. 'No, no, no, mademoiselle. I assure you . . .'

'Then it beats me, Mr Jacquot. Out filming somewhere, I guess. That's all he ever seems to do.'

'And when was the last time you saw him?'

'Well he was here last night, all right, but when I woke this morning he'd gone.'

'So last night was the last time you saw him. Can you recall exactly the time?'

'Around eleven, I guess. We'd just had dinner, room service, you know, and we're in bed, watching this movie . . .' Meredith paused, started picking at strands of her hair, running her fingers through it as if searching for knots, tilting her head, as though she wanted Jacquot to have time to imagine the scene. 'Just the greatest movie. *Kramer vs Kramer*. You ever see it? Meryl Streep and Dustin Hoffman. Incredible. I met her one time, you know? Just a wonderful . . . inspirational actress. And so *sweeeet*. Just so lovely. The most caring, gentle, sincere, warm, genuine human being . . .'

'*Vraiment*,' said Jacquot, with an accommodating smile.

The smile caught Meredith's eye, the way the lips pushed two tiny wrinkles into his cheeks, like two tiny brackets set either side of his mouth.

'. . . And that little boy of hers? Making the French toast? You remember that? I wept. I truly did.'

Jacquot leaned forward in his seat, clasped his hands, trying to follow whatever it was she was saying. 'So, mademoiselle, while you were watching this movie, at about eleven o'clock last night, your companion, Monsieur Kónar, left you in bed . . .'

Meredith put up her hands to stop him right there. 'Hey, don't ask *me*,' she exclaimed. 'One minute I'm there in the courtroom watching Meryl trying to get her son back, pleading, you know, so frail, so strong, so determined, and the next, there's a blast of thunder out there' – she motioned to the windows – 'and it's morning. I mean . . . hey, how do you like that? And this is supposed to be the south of France, right? Where the sun shines and all. I mean . . .'

'So you fell asleep watching the movie?'

'And I guess he must have turned it off . . .'

Jacquot nodded. 'So do you think Monsieur Kónar went to sleep as well, or did he get up early this morning before you woke?'

She shrugged. 'Like I said . . .'

'Monsieur Kónar is an early riser?'

'Not necessarily,' she replied, a coy smile hovering around her lips. Bringing her legs out from under her, she reached forward to the bread basket to break off a piece of croissant. 'Hey, you want some coffee? I should have asked.'

Jacquot shook his head. '*Non, merci*. Thank you. So you don't know if he left the room last night, or maybe early this morning?'

'No . . . I guess . . . I don't know.'

A loud shudder of thunder sounded outside the room, a deep, volcanic rumbling that rattled the shutters. Meredith Branigan shivered and pulled down the knot of her shirt as though this might afford some extra warmth or protection from the elements.

'*Excusez-moi*, but you said something about filming?'

'That's right. You didn't know? About Erdâg? Like he's maybe one of the great film-makers. Like, like, like . . . really famous. He won a prize down in Cannes the other day. Real big news. And he's here making this film and all, so of course he never goes anywhere without his camera.'

'He is making a film about Monastère?'

'Not the hotel, silly,' she laughed. 'The painter guy. The one who lives here?'

'Auguste Vilotte?'

'Hey, don't ask me,' she said, holding up her hands. 'All I know is that Erdâg's going nearly mad trying to get in to see this guy. Three days it takes for a first meeting and then it's like "I gotta see him again, I gotta see him again." Then the rest of the time he's, like, shooting everything. The countryside, the hotel, the waiters . . . you name it.'

'You have known him a long time, mademoiselle?'

Meredith Branigan gave him a look, her eyes narrowing. 'Hey now, you sure are asking a lot of questions, Monsieur Jacquot.'

'*En effet*, mademoiselle, it is actually . . . how do you say . . . ? Chief Inspector. I am a policeman.'

'A policeman? I thought you were a guest. A journalist. Writing the place up. That's what you said.' And then, putting it all together, she added, 'Has something happened? To Erdâg?'

'Before I go any further, might I just ask one or two more questions – just a formality, you understand?'

'I guess . . . Sure. Go ahead.'

'I ask again. You have known him a long time?'

She shrugged, picked at a crumb on her trouser leg. 'Like, maybe, a couple of weeks?'

'And the two of you arrived here?'

'Tuesday. In time for dinner.'

'From where?'

'Down Cannes. For the Festival, you know. We drove up. Bit of R&R . . .' Meredith flushed. 'Just a rest, you know?'

'And you are leaving?'

'It was supposed to be last Saturday, but now it's tomorrow.'

'And the reason you've extended your stay?'

'It's Erdâg's idea. He wants to see this guy again. The painter. Another meeting.' And then she frowned. 'But what are all these questions?'

Jacquot took a breath, kept his eyes on her. 'It is with great regret, mademoiselle, that I must tell you that your companion, Monsieur Erdâg Kónar, has been found dead.'

There was a moment's breathless silence as Meredith took this in. And then she tipped back her head and laughed. 'No, no, no. You're kidding me. Come on, it's a set-up, right?' She cast around the room as though looking for a hidden camera. 'You can't be *serious* . . .'

'There is no kidding, mademoiselle.' Jacquot spread his hands. 'I am very sorry.'

The laugh, the smile, vanished. 'Like how? How did he get killed? He fall or something? He crash the car? He got struck by lightning? What?' Her voice rose with each question, growing more tremulous, more uncertain, her eyes latching on to Jacquot's as though waiting for a punch line.

'I believe someone has killed him, mademoiselle. He has been murdered.'

'Murdered? Here at Grand Monastère? No, that's not possible. He was here, just last night. This morning . . . It can't be . . . It just can't be . . .'

Jacquot said nothing.

'Please, this can't be happening.'

And then, suddenly, Jacquot noticed that the dazed, shocked look that had settled across her features was replaced by another, more urgent expression. Her hands sprang to her cheeks.

'My God! Oh my *God*! The Studio. I gotta call the Studio. I gotta call BeeJay.' She jumped out of the chair, brushed past Jacquot in a swirl of scent and cool cotton and hurried to the phone, picked it up, put it down. 'Goddammit, where's his number. I . . . I . . .'

Jacquot got to his feet, followed her across the room as she searched for her bag, found her address book, then scrabbled through its pages for a phone number.

And the next moment the book was tumbling to the floor and Meredith Branigan was in his arms, sobbing, her face pressed against his shirt, pressed so close that he could feel

the heat of her breath with every word. 'It's just not true . . .
It can't be . . . I can't . . . I can't . . . I don't . . .'

Jacquot led her to the sofa, made her comfortable and went
back to pick up the address book.

'Tell me the name you want to call,' he said gently.

The sobs quietened. She wiped at her eyes. 'BeeJay. It's an
LA number. Under . . . W. Wilson. BJ Wilson. He's my agent.'

Jacquot found the name and numbers, reached for the phone
and dialled. He handed the phone to Meredith. 'It's the home
number. The time difference . . .'

Meredith took the phone, gave him a grateful look.

'While I am here,' said Jacquot, 'would you mind if I had
a look through Monsieur Kónar's things?'

'Sure, of course. He's got a case in the bedroom. A few
things here and . . . Yeah! Hi! That you, BeeJay? It's Merry.
Yeah, I know, I'm sorry. Yeah, yeah, yeah, it's important . . .
real important.' She cupped the receiver in her hands, lowered
her voice. 'Look, BeeJay, you gotta help me . . . There's a
problem over here.'

73

While Meredith explained everything to her agent in Los Angeles – more concerned, Jacquot suspected, about her own involvement and the possible repercussions than any further thoughts for Kónar – Jacquot made his way round the salon.

At the writing desk, he slid open the single drawer and pulled out a document case. Inside were two passports. He flipped open the first – American – Meredith's. Then the second. Italian. Kónar's. He flicked through the pages – in the last twelve months a smudge of visa stamps for the US, Russia, Croatia, the Lebanon. He turned to the personal details. Date of birth: 12/8/50. Forty-six. From what Jacquot remembered, Kónar looked younger than his age. Place of birth: Rovinj, Croatia. Current address: 37d Via dei Coronari, Rome.

Jacquot put the passports back in the drawer and, seeing nothing more in the salon, moved through to the bedroom. It had a faintly musky scent overlaid with the sweet sweaty lingerings of sleep. The bed was unmade but had clearly been slept in by two people – unless, of course, Mademoiselle Branigan had made it look that way. It didn't strike Jacquot as likely, but still . . . Or was the crumpled quilt and pillow on one side of the bed simply the result of Kónar stretched out beside Mademoiselle Branigan as they watched television? Before she fell asleep. Before he left her . . .

In the salon, Jacquot could hear Meredith trying to explain why she'd just disappeared like that from Cannes. But she'd left a note, she protested. She was clearly getting a telling off.

Behind the blue-glass screen separating bedroom from bathroom – a tub of smooth-hollowed pink Sarragon marble sat in the middle of the room and large enough to accommodate at least two people – Jacquot went through the various toiletries. Most of the shelves above the sinks – matching Sarragon marble – were taken up with Meredith's kit, but a small area was clearly Kónar's. Laid out neatly on a linen cloth were a razor and foam, toothbrush and Italian toothpaste, a bottle of eau de cologne and a hairbrush.

Back in the bedroom, Jacquot went to the armoire on the left of the bed – Meredith's – filled with enough clothes to dress an army of catwalk models for any occasion. He went round the bed and opened the doors of the other armoire. Inside, neatly folded on four shelves, were three pairs of blue jeans, a pair of pressed black trousers, T-shirts, sweats and shirts. Below the shelves were three pairs of espadrilles and a pair of black elastic-sided boots. And a black zipper bag.

Jacquot pulled out the bag and opened it up. A tangle of wires and adaptors, a box of video batteries, a recharger, a TV/Video converter and half a dozen cassette cases. Three of the cassettes were still sealed in their plastic wraps, two had sticky labels fixed to them – 'Vilotte' and 'Monastère' – and the last case was empty. So far as Jacquot could see, there was no camera in the case. Keeping the two tapes and the converter, he placed the black zip-up bag back in the armoire.

With a final, cursory look around – a biography of Vilotte on the bedside table with indecipherable pencil scribbles in the margins, copies of *Screen International* 'Festival Edition' on the floor beside the bed and, in a bedside drawer, a laminated evening performance pass for Cannes' Palais des Festivals, an opened carton of Lucky Strikes, along with a bunch of keys – Jacquot left the bedroom.

Out in the salon, Meredith had finished her call and was pacing up and down in front of the fireplace, arms clasped across her chest as though she was cold.

Jacquot held up the tapes. 'I would like to borrow these, if you wouldn't mind? They belong to Monsieur Kónar.'

Meredith stopped pacing, looked at the tapes and then shrugged. 'Sure, help yourself.'

Outside a violent flurry of wind raced across the closed shutters with a frightening rat-a-tat-a-tat and she started.

'I wonder,' continued Jacquot, 'can you recall how many cameras Monsieur Kónar possessed?'

Meredith gave it some thought. 'Just the one. That's all I ever saw. A Webcam.'

And then, taking Jacquot by surprise, she said, 'Can I see him?' Her voice was low and soft, almost imploring, like a mother for a last sight of her son, her face crumpling with sorrow, tears welling in her eyes but bravely held back.

Yet for all its simple power, it seemed to Jacquot that there was something hollow about her request. The way she phrased it, the way she held her body, the accompanying play of emotion across her face . . . It was as though she was playing a part, reading from a script. Or maybe, giving her the benefit of the doubt, it was just simple curiosity, an opportunity to see what a dead body looked like, up close and personal, something she could add to her repertoire of life experiences. Whatever it was, it didn't quite ring true. She may have been shocked by her lover's death, but she wasn't in mourning. Pretty on the outside, thought Jacquot, but there was something chill as ice inside. And not too far inside either. It was clear that Meredith Branigan had a career to think of, before anything else.

Gently Jacquot shook his head. 'Not right now. It wouldn't be a good idea. Later, maybe . . .' When he's defrosted, thought Jacquot. 'But you've been very helpful, mademoiselle . . .'

'Meredith, remember?'

'Meredith. So, is there anything I can do, anything I can get for you? Perhaps I should ask Madame Bouvet . . . ?'

'No, no. I'm fine. Fine. Please don't worry on my account.' And with that she walked over to him, held him by the shoulders and reached up to kiss him on the cheek. 'And thanks. Thanks for . . . well, being so understanding.' She tried a brave smile. It almost worked.

As he closed the salon door behind him, Jacquot decided he didn't have much time for Mademoiselle Meredith Branigan.

74

It was only a few steps along the loggia from Mademoiselle Branigan's room to Roland Bressans' door, a cool draught of air thrown out by the rain hammering down into the cloister. Jacquot knocked and waited a few moments until the door was pulled open. Since breakfast in the Salle du Matin, Bressans had changed his green sports shirt for a blue one. Jacquot wondered how many he had tucked away in his suitcase – by the look of it, one for every colour in the rainbow. Some peacock.

Just like the last time Jacquot had visited, Bressans was on the phone. He nodded him in as though Jacquot were a waiter delivering room service, closed the door behind him and brought the call to a swift end, as though he didn't want Jacquot, or anyone else, to know what he'd been talking about. He replaced the receiver and turned to Jacquot.

'Chief Inspector, I really must insist. I have tried to be as helpful as possible, but I can't remain here another moment.

I'm sure you understand. I have meetings, a very tight schedule, there are people I need to see . . .'

'Well, I'm afraid you won't be going anywhere at the moment, monsieur. Thanks to the storm the road to Luissac is impassable.' As if to underline this, a crackling snap of thunder exploded outside and seconds later, a shiver of lightning flashed down.

'Impassable? What are you saying?' He glanced at the cassette tapes in Jacquot's hands.

'Exactly that, monsieur. A portion of the road has been washed away. Until the storm passes and the rain stops there is nothing we can do, nowhere we can go.' Without invitation, Jacquot settled himself in an armchair, stretched out his legs and crossed his ankles. 'But, to keep us occupied, there is still the question of Mademoiselle Ladouze.'

'And? And? What am I supposed to do about that? She's gone off in a huff, probably. Gone back to Marseilles. Or Vilotte's hidden her away somewhere. Who knows?'

'And she leaves all her clothes? Her purse? Her case? The keys to her apartment? No note. No message.' Jacquot shook his head, tut-tutted. 'I don't think so, monsieur. And, as of breakfast this morning, I know so.'

'You *know* so? You've found her? You know what's happened?'

'I may not know yet what happened, but I certainly know where she is.'

'And? And? *Merde alors*, man, spit it out.'

'At this very moment, monsieur, your companion Mademoiselle Ghislaine Ladouze is in one of the kitchen storerooms. She was found earlier this morning. Someone has killed her.'

Like Meredith Branigan, Jacquot knew that, apart from the immediate shock of this news, what was going through

Bressans' head had more to do with himself than the death of his companion. How his presence at Monastère, his 'friendship' with the victim, could be held against him, used by the press. Embarrass him. Maybe even scupper his political ambitions.

Damage limitation, that was what Monsieur Bressans was thinking about as he sat himself down in an armchair, shaking his head in disbelief.

'Well, I can assure you I have nothing to do with that,' he began.

Another thunderclap blasted against the walls of Monastère and Bressans flinched.

'Be that as it may, monsieur, she was your companion here. And you were one of the last people to see her alive.'

'Not me, Chief Inspector. Not me. It is Vilotte you should be talking to. He was the last one to see her alive, not me. You know that. I haven't seen her since she went to him the night she disappeared. Friday night. Since then, nothing. He's the man you should be talking to.'

'And in due course that is exactly what I will do, monsieur. But in the meantime, what with the road being closed, I'm sure you won't mind staying with us just a little longer, to help where you can with my inquiries.'

Bressans waved a hand as if words had failed him.

'And with that in mind,' continued Jacquot, 'perhaps you'd be so kind as to tell me where you were and what you were doing, say, between eleven and one this morning?'

Bressans frowned, as though he couldn't understand what Jacquot was asking.

'Eleven and one? Why, here. In my room. I had dinner in Le Réfectoire around nine and was back here by eleven.

I watched some TV and then went to bed. But why do you ask?'

'I was hoping you might be able to throw some light on another matter that has arisen since we last spoke.'

Bressans' jaw clenched tight. 'What now, for God's sake? What now?'

'It concerns another guest at the hotel. Monsieur Erdâg Kónar. The next room to Mademoiselle Ladouze, as it happens.'

'Kónar, you say? The Arab fellow?'

'Croatian, but he lives in Rome.'

Bressans nodded. 'I know him, of course. Recognise him, I mean. Always hovering about with that camera of his. But we've never spoken. *Bonjour*, *bonsoir*, passing in the corridor, the lobby. But that's it. Except . . .' Bressans paused, as a thought struck him. 'Except, now you come to mention it, he's always looking at Ghislaine. You know what I mean? Can't take his eyes off her. Even in front of his lady friend. Or is she his wife? But why do you ask? Is he involved with Ghislaine's disappearance? Is he the one who killed her?'

'To be honest, I hadn't yet considered that possibility, monsieur. And, certainly, it is a suggestion worth some consideration. Given the time frame he could certainly have murdered Mademoiselle Ladouze. Just like anyone else here at Monastère could have murdered her, be they a guest or a member of staff. But no, what I am trying to establish is who killed him.'

There was silence for a moment, a long enough stretch for the rain to be heard, the wind slapping vicious squalls of it against the salon windows. And then, 'Christ, man. You've got *two* bodies? There's been another murder? I don't believe this, I just don't believe it . . .' And then, 'Has anyone alerted the press? Do they know what's going on here?'

'Not yet,' replied Jacquot, getting to his feet and crossing to the door. 'But when the storm breaks, my guess is it won't be long . . .' Jacquot turned to Bressans, held back a smile. 'Monsieur, thank you for your time.'

75

It was a morning for phone calls. Back in his room, Jacquot made himself comfortable in one of the salon's armchairs, reached for the phone and called Cavaillon headquarters. At least the storm hadn't brought down the telephone lines.

When he finally got through to Rochet he didn't waste any time. Their missing person was now a homicide, he told his boss. And there was another body to boot.

There was a pause down the line. And then, 'Is Monsieur Bressans still with you?' asked Rochet quietly.

It was, Jacquot noted, the first time that Rochet had actually mentioned Bressans by name.

'Yes, he is. In the next room, and not at all happy. I have told him he must stay in order to help with our inquiries. Thanks to the storm he doesn't have a lot of choice.'

'Is there any possibility he might be involved? With one or both of these deaths?'

For a moment Jacquot wondered if Rochet was trying to think up some pretext to have Monsieur Bressans spirited out of the place, and out of trouble. To mollify his superiors. But he dismissed the thought. The Rochet he knew would go so far, but no further.

'Right now, he's as much a suspect as anyone here at Monastère,' continued Jacquot. 'His companion, Ghislaine Ladouze, is dead, and so is the man in the next room. Also, apart from his continual protestations of innocence, he has been unable to furnish any alibi other than being in bed, alone, asleep.'

Down the line, Jacquot heard a soft sigh from Rochet. There was little doubt his station chief would be making another phone call as soon as he finished this one, and equally clear that he didn't relish the prospect.

But Jacquot had been right – so far, but no further.

'In your hands, then, Daniel,' said his boss quietly. 'One can only do so much, *n'est-ce pas?*'

After speaking to Rochet, Jacquot had the switchboard put him through to Jean Brunet.

'The road from Luissac's pretty much impassable,' Jacquot told his assistant after bringing him up to speed on developments at Monastère. 'But there's a landing spot at the hotel. Maybe we could . . .'

'A chopper? Not until these winds drop, Chief. And what with the low cloud and rain, visibility's not up to much either. I'll put the call through, but you can reckon on a few hours yet before anyone will be able to get to you. Is there anything more I can do at this end?'

'Tell them, the quicker they can get here the better, but for now I need everything you can get on the latest victim, Erdâg

Kónar. More checking, I'm afraid, and see if you can get the Italian authorities to go through his home. Via dei Coronari. 37d. Rome. Oh, and if you've got time, there's another name you could check. Céleste Maroc. Possibly local. Died about thirty years ago. Would have been in her twenties or thirties.'

When he'd finished briefing Brunet, Jacquot put down the phone and looked around Ghislaine Ladouze's salon. The last time he had been here, on his way down to breakfast, just two hours earlier, it had been a missing person he'd been called in to investigate – just his intuition to suggest it might be anything more.

Now it was confirmed.

What's more, not one body but two. Two victims. With nothing, as yet, to link them beyond being guests at Monastère, and their discovery in various parts of Monastère's kitchens – neither of which was the actual murder scene. In Ghislaine Ladouze's case, that was the bedroom next door. As for Monsieur Kónar, they had still to find it.

And thanks to the storm still raging beyond the shutters, there was no way Fournier and the forensic boys would be able to provide any assistance, nor any of his team from Cavaillon.

For now, Jacquot was on his own.

Getting up from his chair, Jacquot went to the TV and slid the first of the two cassettes into the video player, the one marked 'Vilotte', then returned to his seat.

From the first frame – crossing the second courtyard with what looked like Madame Champeau walking ahead of him towards the tower – it was clear that this was a record of Erdâg Kónar's first – and so far as Jacquot knew – only visit to the Master.

It made for riotous viewing, Jacquot decided when the film came to an end. No wonder Erdâg had wanted to hold on at Monastère for a second outing with the great man. As far as Jacquot could see, Auguste Vilotte had spent most of the time swearing and cursing at his visitor, rampaging after him, while Monsieur Kónar made every effort to keep out of his clutches.

But there was a certain pathos to it as well, the mad rantings of an old man stumbling towards the end of a great career. Jacquot had no doubt that, with judicious cutting, Kónar would have been able to turn those twenty or so minutes into something altogether more moving and remarkable.

Removing 'Vilotte' and inserting 'Monastère', Jacquot returned to his seat and pressed 'play'. After five minutes of hand-held shots of the hotel – the cloister, the loggia, the courtyard – he fast-forwarded the tape, managing to identify most of the locations where Erdâg Kónàr had chosen to film without slowing the tape down.

As the images flashed across the screen it was clear that – unlike the first tape of Vilotte and Madame Champeau – there were no people in this second tape, no guests or staff in any of the shots.

Which was why Jacquot paused the tape when he saw that Kónar had filmed a car coming across the bridge. He pushed the 'play' button and the film returned to normal speed, a black Citroën drawing to a halt in the Monastère's cobbled parking lot. Jacquot recognised the car immediately. He'd seen it first in Cavaillon, outside Tabac Rafine. Just moments before he first saw Monsieur Ginoux ordering those cigars.

As if to help with the identification, Kónar, clearly filming from the battlements, zoomed in on the roof of the car just as the driver's door opened. A man climbed out, closed the door, then started walking to the Monastère's gate. Dutronc.

And then he stopped, turned, looked up at the battlements – and the TV screen blazed into static.

76

As the tape ended, Jacquot's phone began to ring. He switched off the TV and picked up the receiver.

It was Claude Peluze in Marseilles.

'Type "O" confirmed,' his old partner from Marseilles growled. 'Got it from her own doctor. Found his number in her address book.'

'You got into her apartment already?' asked Jacquot, moving to the sofa.

'I'm known for charming concierges. It's one of my specialities. Didn't you know that?'

Jacquot said he didn't, but wondered how Peluze would manage with the widow Foraque.

'And? What's it like?'

'The business. Very, very nice. Two-bedroom apartment about a block from the Opéra. Fourth floor. Great kitchen, great bathroom, fucking *huge* salon. Good stretch of balcony.

Reasonable view. Seventeen-thou a month and not a franc less.'

'You sound pretty sure.'

'I ought to be. I'm looking at her bank records as we speak. Stack of them, in a file. She was a neat and tidy girl, your Ghislaine.' Peluze cleared his throat. 'Says here: Standing order. Seventeen-thousand francs, the seventh of every month. Payable to Agence Gouvron . . . one of the big rental outfits. You know it.'

Jacquot did. Solid, respectable. He wondered what they'd say if they knew they had a high-class hooker as one of their tenants. Maybe they did know, maybe they had lots of them.

'And?'

'Like the concierge told me – Mademoiselle Ladouze has been here about two years, and never any trouble. No visitors to speak of, so we can assume she plays away. As well as bank, phone and credit card statements we've also got her phone book, photo albums – pretty much anything you need.'

'Parents?'

'Looks like mother only. Local number.'

'Then someone's going to have to pay her a visit,' said Jacquot.

'She's turned up, then?'

'I'm afraid so.'

There was a moment's silence. Both men knew it was the worst thing a cop had to do. Break bad news to a parent. And both knew, too, that it never got any easier.

It was Jacquot who spoke first. 'Tell me,' he said, moving on, 'did you find out from your lady friend downstairs when she last saw Ladouze?'

'Am I hearing right?' replied Peluze, equally happy to move on. 'Is that some country *flic* asking whether a Marseillais homicide detective knows how to do his job?'

'Did you or didn't you, you sack of—'

'Wednesday morning. Around ten, eleven. Said she was going to be away for a few days in the country. Got picked up in a blue Beamer, but Madame couldn't see the driver. Said the windows were blacked out.'

Jacquot knew the car. It was parked next to his at Monastère.

'Thanks, Claude. I owe you.'

'I know,' Peluze replied.

'Just one more thing. Do me a favour, will you? A Legion name. Dutronc. Emile Dutronc. Belgian passport. Lives in Paris. That's all I've got.'

'*Laisse-toi faire*. I'll call you,' said Peluze, and the line went dead.

77

Putting down the phone, Jacquot lifted his feet on to the sofa, slipped his hands behind his head and crossed his ankles. Not the way, perhaps, to begin a murder investigation, not quite the way to proceed when you have a woman's body lying beside a pig carcass and another body jammed into a blast freezer.

But somehow Jacquot felt no pressing sense of urgency. With no forensic team to examine the bodies and point out possible leads, and no police back-up from Cavaillon save the telephone, there wasn't very much he could do except watch and wait.

And ask questions. On his own. Lying there on the sofa, the wind and rain rampaging outside his windows, flashes of lightning shivering through the slats of the shutters and thunder growling around the heavens like a burglar on noisy floorboards. Trying to patch it all together.

Starting with the basics. Always a good place to begin.

Two bodies. Two homicides.

And the first question to ask?

Were the two murders connected in any way?

Jacquot gave it some thought.

Well, both may have taken place at different times and in different places – Ladouze, late Friday night or early Saturday morning in the bedroom next door; Kónar, sometime within the last twelve hours, in a place yet to be identified since the murder certainly hadn't happened in the storeroom – but there was no shortage of other significant connections.

Both victims had been guests at Grand Monastère; both had died from stab wounds although, with Kónar doubled up in the blast freezer, Jacquot would have to wait to confirm this; both bodies had been found within the Monastère's kitchen area; and both victims had arrived at Monastère within a day of each other.

And for the same reason.

To visit the Master – Ladouze to seduce paintings out of the old man for Bressans' museum in Marseilles; and Kónar to make a film about him.

So, yes, in a number of significant ways the murders were connected. But if there were connections, what was the link – or links – between Ladouze and Kónar, a call-girl from Marseilles and a Balkan film-maker? And why would anyone want to kill them?

Which brought him to the next question.

One killer? Or two?

At this early stage Jacquot favoured just the one. Two killers operating in the same place, within forty-eight hours of each other? And using the same weapon? *Pouff!* The odds were not good.

Next question: Was the killer a man or a woman?

A safer bet, that, Jacquot decided. Even a strong-limbed, determined woman would have had difficulty carrying Kónar to that basement room and stowing him away in that freezer. And surely only a man could have hoisted Ladouze on to that hook?

Or chosen to lift her on to the hook.

Why would a woman have even bothered?

But maybe there *were* two killers . . .

Say, two women at work . . . ?

Or a man and a woman . . . ?

Tiens, tiens, thought Jacquot. The basics, the basics. One step at a time . . . And then he paused.

A butcher's hook and a freezer cabinet.

Now that was interesting . . .

One body almost on display, almost certain to be discovered quickly. The second body, hidden away. If it hadn't been for Bastien taking that smoke, Kónar could have spent days in that blast freezer without being discovered.

Was there a reason for this? Was there some explanation? Was this a possible pointer to two separate killers?

Interesting . . . certainly interesting. But for the time being, Jacquot decided, it was something he'd keep on the back burner.

Moving on . . . moving on . . .

. . . To another important question: Given one killer, was he still on the loose? Still prowling around Grand Monastère?

It seemed a good bet to Jacquot. No one had checked out since Ladouze went missing on Friday night, and it would have been a tight squeeze for someone to confront and kill Kónar after Meredith last saw him at about 11 p.m., haul him to a basement cellar, load him into a freezer, tidy his tracks and get away before the road to Luissac became impassable.

Possible, maybe . . . But not, in Jacquot's opinion, very likely.

So, a killer on the loose in Monastère it had to be. A man.

Jacquot got up from the sofa, found a pack of cigarettes, a light, an ashtray and stretched himself out on the sofa once more, the ashtray balanced on his stomach, the curl of smoke soon rising straight and true while the wind whistled outside his windows.

But was the killer on the staff roster or guest list, he wondered?

Given that the road to and from the staff annexe in Luissac was impassable – it would have been dangerous enough trying to get across in daylight; at night it would have been madness – then the number of suspects among Monastère's staff was limited.

Jacquot counted off the names on his fingers. Ten in all. Most of whom could surely be dismissed.

Did either Bastien or Luc or the *plongeur* look like they could kill? No.

Did the two waiters who had served him breakfast in the Salle du Matin that morning look like they could kill? No. Or the other sous-chef? No again.

Did Champeau fit the bill? Well, he certainly looked strong enough to heave the body around. But a killer? Unlikely.

Or Didier, the concierge?

Or Bouvet, the owner?

Not *really*, decided Jacquot.

But then again . . . Who could say?

Who'd put money on them not being involved in some way? Jacquot hadn't spent twenty years working for Marseilles' *Judiciaire* without learning, sometimes to his cost, about the outsiders, the long shots, the unlikely ones. The ones who looked like they wouldn't harm a fly; the ones who welcomed you into their homes; the ones who couldn't do enough for you; the ones who were alibied up to their elbows. Murder, Jacquot had discovered, was never less than a very surprising business.

All he was prepared to say with any degree of certainty was that, out of his ten staffers, the only convincing candidate was the last on his list – Cancale. The man who'd lost his temper three years earlier at La Ferme Bertrand in Besançon and branded a junior with a red-hot knife blade.

But why would he want to kill Ladouze and Kónar? And then hide them in his own kitchen?

And what about the guests? Who among the Monastère's six male guests was a contender? A potential killer?

Jacquot went through their names: Bressans, Ginoux, Gavan, Gould, van der Haage and Dutronc.

Which of them would he put money on?

Well, Bressans for sure. He was fit enough, as well as cruel, scheming, selfish, greedy . . .

Ginoux? The man didn't look like he could kill a bug, but he had a driver who was built like a barn door. An ex-Legionnaire who unquestionably did know how to kill and may, in some foreign theatre of war, have done just that. Trouble was, Dutronc was staying down in Luissac . . . Except . . . if anyone could make it through that cascade . . .

Then there was Gavan, Gilles Gavan. The gallery owner from Aix. Slender, but fit, too. He could easily have managed Ladouze and the hook. But dealing with Kónar and getting him into the freezer? That might have proved a tad more demanding. Still, Jacquot knew enough gay killers not to discount the man quite yet.

And what about Gould? Overweight, turquoise hat-bands, the only man on a painting course made up almost entirely of women. Jacquot shook his head. Nothing pointed in that direction. Not yet anyway.

The same went for Lens van der Haage. Jacquot simply couldn't see it as a possibility.

So – Bressans? Possibly Ginoux or Dutronc? Or Gavan? Or, at a very long stretch, maybe Gould or van der Haage?

But there was one other name that stood out.

Neither guest nor staff.

Vilotte. The Master himself. Auguste Vilotte. Over in the watchtower.

Where did Vilotte figure in all this, Jacquot wondered? What odds on Vilotte as the killer?

As far as it could be established, Vilotte had been the last to see Ghislaine Ladouze alive – just as, Jacquot reminded himself, Meredith had been the last to see Kónar alive. And then there was the film Jacquot had watched of Vilotte chasing after Kónar and threatening him with all manner of violence. In other circumstances, Vilotte would have been hauled in for questioning with some enthusiasm.

Except . . .

Did the old fellow have the strength? The strength to murder two fit and able young people and then move their bodies? Ladouze from her bedroom to the kitchen storeroom, via the second courtyard where, Jacquot suspected, she'd initially been buried. And then Kónar, from wherever he was killed to the basement freezer?

Jacquot didn't believe it was possible. He recalled how Vilotte had heaved him backwards in that rugby clinch the first time they'd met, and there'd been power there, for certain. But surely never enough to hoist Ladouze on to a meat hook, or struggle to the death with a man like Kónar?

Unless, of course, he'd had help?

Which brought Jacquot back to two killers . . .

He sighed. That was always the problem. Start with the basics and before you knew it you were going round in circles.

Jacquot stubbed out his cigarette and wished it had been a joint. A joint would have helped.

Sliding the ashtray on to the table, he clasped his hands across his stomach, recrossed his ankles and stared at the ceiling. So many questions and, right now, so few answers.

What was it van der Haage had said to him, after their tour of the hotel, that first afternoon as they walked back to the lobby? About the renovations. How he had known what to do 'because the stones spoke to me'. These stones, he'd told Jacquot, were the 'fabric of history', and it would have been foolhardy of him to ignore the whispers of the centuries.

Jacquot wished those same walls would speak to him now. Tell him what they had seen three nights earlier. Here, in this room, where Ghislaine Ladouze had died, at the foot of her bed, cut down more than likely by the missing fruit knife. With someone standing over her, watching her shock, her pain, and the light fade from her eyes as the lifeblood pulsed from her body and soaked into the bedcover, quilt and mattress.

Jacquot was wondering whether the killer had it in mind to strike again – and who might be a possible target – when there was a soft knocking at his door.

78

'You said you wanted to speak to me?' said Claudine Eddé when Jacquot opened the door. Her face was still pale with shock, but she managed a brief, uncertain smile. 'I thought . . . possibly there was something I could do?'

'Please, come in. Come in,' said Jacquot, opening the door wider and standing aside. 'It's good to see you. I'm sorry you had to . . .'

Claudine held up her hands as she stepped past him.

'What could you do? You weren't even there . . .'

Jacquot closed the door, followed her into the salon and gestured to the sofa. 'So, tell me. How is Madame Tilley?' he asked, taking an armchair.

'We took her through to the Salle du Matin and someone got her a cognac. It seemed to do the trick. But Marcie insisted she have a rest. Which is where she is now. Although, according to Marcie, Grace is not as delicate as she may appear.'

'Well that's good, that's good,' said Jacquot. 'And it was a most disturbing scene.'

'Disturbing? I should say . . .' Claudine glanced round the salon. 'Was this her room?' she asked.

'Yes, it was.'

'It's much grander than the ones downstairs,' she said, taking in the carved mantle and the frescoed panels. And then, unexpectedly, 'Is this where she was murdered?'

Jacquot paused. 'What makes you think that?' he asked.

'I'm sorry, perhaps I shouldn't . . .'

'No, no. Please, go ahead. You said you wanted to help. Another person's observations . . .'

'Well. It was just . . . there was . . . from what I could see, of the body, there was that terrible stab wound but no blood. So she couldn't have died there.'

'You are correct. Her body was left in the storeroom, but she did not die there. *En effet*, she was murdered next door, in the bedroom.'

Claudine clasped her arms around her and shivered.

'Can I get you a drink? Anything?'

'Isn't it too early?' she asked, pulling at the bracelet watch on her wrist, glancing at the time.

'It wasn't too early for Madame Tilley,' Jacquot reminded her. 'And you saw exactly what she saw.'

'Then I will. Thank you.'

Jacquot went to the armoire. 'Another cognac? Or something stronger?'

Claudine smiled. 'A cognac will do fine, thank you.'

Jacquot poured two and brought them over to the sofa.

'So what now?' asked Claudine, warming the brandy in her

cupped hands and taking a sip. 'Now that your missing person has been found.'

'I will try to find out who killed her. And find out, too, who put another body in a freezer cabinet.'

The extra information, about Kónar, was deliberately offered. Claudine wasn't a guest, hadn't been in the hotel when Ladouze went missing and had been sitting with Jacquot at the piano when Kónar had probably been killed. But Jacquot was a policeman and he knew it was important to test such assumptions.

And Claudine responded just as he had expected. Just as he'd hoped. Her eyes sprang open and cognac spilled over her wrist.

'There's another body?'

'*Je regrette* . . .'

'Another guest?'

Jacquot nodded.

'*Mon dieu* . . . The world . . . It has gone crazy.' Claudine tipped back what remained of her cognac, wiped her lips with her cuff, and held out her empty glass. 'This time, I don't care what time it is!' she said.

Jacquot took the glass, went to the armoire and refilled it. Outside a sustained clap of thunder cracked beyond the windows like the trunks of mighty trees snapping apart.

'So who would you say it was?' he asked, handing Claudine her drink. 'Which guest?'

She looked into her glass and swirled the liqueur around. 'The Italian,' she said at last. 'The man with the camera.' Not a question. A statement of fact.

'*En effet*, Croatian, but, yes, living in Rome.' Jacquot smiled, and then, 'You sound very sure?'

'I am.'

'And why is that?'

'Because he is the only guest I haven't seen this morning. Everyone else was in the lobby or the Salle du Matin having breakfast. But then . . . wait a minute . . . *un moment* . . . Nor did I see his companion. The American.'

Jacquot nodded. 'That's right, you didn't. Mademoiselle Branigan was not at breakfast. And nor was she in the lobby.'

'Is it her, then? Is she the—'

'No,' replied Jacquot. 'You had the right person to begin with. The man with the camera. Monsieur Erdâg Kónar.'

'So what are you going to do now?' Claudine asked, leaning back against the sofa, cradling the glass in her lap, her eyes searching his.

Apart from kiss you? thought Jacquot.

But he made no move. With a body lying on a storeroom floor, another crammed into a blast freezer and a killer somewhere close by, such behaviour would hardly have been appropriate. But that hadn't stopped Jacquot thinking about it from the moment this woman stepped into his room. Just having her there, so close, within reach . . . those lips, her eyes, the warm soapy scent of her . . . Right then it was the one thing that Jacquot wanted to do more than anything else in the world. Kiss her. Hold her. What he had wanted to do the night before, playing those smoky tunes for her in the bar, then walking with her through the cloisters to her room. That particular moment when she paused at her door, turned . . . That's when he should have done it. He should have kissed her then. Held her and kissed her.

Because last night he'd been investigating a missing person. Now it was a double murder.

Timing, timing. So many things came down to timing. Including, he thought ruefully, murder.

'I asked what you were going to do next?' said Claudine, a small frown creasing her brow. 'If there's anything I can do to help?'

Jacquot snapped to.

'At this moment, I would be very grateful for any help . . .'

'So? What would you like me to do?'

'Well, you can do what the best kind of policeman does in a situation like this. Keep your eyes and your ears open. Watch and listen. Then, later, it would be good if we could speak again?' Jacquot filled these last words with as much meaning as he could muster.

But Claudine appeared not to notice.

'*Mais, oui. Bien sûr.* And you?'

'Me? I must find the man who did this, before, maybe, he strikes again.'

Claudine suddenly looked alarmed. 'You think there will be another murder?'

'I certainly hope not, but I cannot be certain.'

'So when will your colleagues arrive? When does it all start happening?'

'If you are talking about the investigation, it has already begun. Me, and you, sitting here. As for any colleagues, well, it may be some time before they are able to join us.'

'Why is that?'

'Because a large portion of the road to Luissac has been swept away, and there is considerable flooding below St-Mas. Also, until this storm passes, it will be impossible to fly in by helicopter. For the time being, we are cut off. We are on our own.'

'So what's your next move?'

Jacquot pushed away from his armchair and reached for his jacket. 'There is someone I have to see.'

Later, when Jacquot remembered Claudine's visit, he realised that she had never once used his christian name. And he had never used hers.

79

Jacquot found Madame Champeau in her glass-walled office overlooking the laundry hall. He'd been directed there by Madame Bouvet – her face a picture of grim disbelief, her fingers working her wedding ring violently enough to bring forth a genie. But it wasn't Madame Champeau whom Jacquot had come to see.

Set beneath the Monastère's lobby and lunch terrace, the laundry was an old room and a large one – more than twenty metres between retaining walls and at least five metres from the crown of its cobwebbed vaulting to the worn, shiny-smooth flagstones that covered its floor. For more than five hundred years this room had served the same purpose in the daily life of Monastère, generations of postulant monks stoking the fires that boiled the water that was used to wash the monastery's dirty linen – vestments, altar cloths, habits, bedding.

The first thing that Jacquot saw as he pushed through the

plastic-strip door and stepped into Madame Champeau's domain was a rank of vaulted alcoves burrowed into the far wall, alcoves where great copper boiling vats had once stood on stone hearths, vats now planted with palms and ferns and cacti and set around the Monastère's lobby and bar. These same steaming vats had been placed beneath stone flues which, at the end of the seventeenth century, the then-abbot, Hubert of Valence, had ingeniously rerouted to run beneath the stone flags of the chapel, making matins more amenable than they might normally be expected to be during the long and chilly winter months.

Though Jacquot didn't know it, Monday was usually Madame Champeau's busiest day. Laundry from an under-staffed weekend to be sorted and washed, dried, ironed and aired; housekeeping crews despatched to public rooms and guest suites – their wicker baskets filled with fresh linen, their cleaning trolleys loaded with mops, cloths, buckets, polishes, disinfectants and replacement L'Occitane toiletries, desk stationery, and supplies for the mini-bars.

But that Monday morning the row of washing machines that had replaced the copper bowls sat silently in an open-windowed row when normally they'd be humming. Spin driers stood empty, wicker baskets were neatly stacked and the cleaning trolleys were tidily parked to the left of the door.

And that, Jacquot knew, was how it would stay until the storm passed and the road became passable, until Madame Champeau's domestic staff from Luissac and St-Mas were able to get through to Monastère. Until then, guests would have to make do with the sheets and the towels they already had. And if their rooms were a mess, well, then, they'd just have to be patient, or tidy them up themselves.

Taking it all in, Jacquot spotted the wall of louvre-panelled airing-cupboards that Madame Bouvet had told him about and, rising above them, the flight of stone steps that led to the housekeeper's office, conveniently placed, Madame Bouvet had said, between the laundry hall and Madame Champeau's living quarters. Picking his way between the ironing tables, airing racks and sewing machines, Jacquot headed for the stairs. He was certain to find her there, Madame Bouvet had assured him, and sure enough, as he reached the top of the stairs, he spotted her through the glass-panelled wall, working on some linen.

With none of her brigade able to reach Monastère and time to herself, Madame Champeau was unpicking the embroidered 'GMdE' from the corner of a sheet, turning it in the light from a desk lamp. Behind her chair, but adding hardly any natural light, was a waist-high oriel window that looked east along the rain-drenched slopes of the Grand Lubéron, a rolling tide of charcoal clouds smudging all perspective. Pick-pick-pick went the needle, the scarlet threads of embroidery teased away from the Monastère's finest Frette linen.

Jacquot paused on the landing, in the shadows beyond the pool of light in which she worked. He was close enough to see the glint of the needle as it worked away at the embroidery, close enough to see the threads unravel. He knew immediately what she was doing. Years before a friend who ran a hotel in Marseilles had asked him, unofficially, to find out why he was spending so much money below stairs. It had taken only a few days to establish that his head of housekeeping was 'selling on' – one sheet a month, or a pair of pillow-cases, or a quilt cover, or a set of hand towels (all easily accounted for as 'wastage' – torn, stained or stolen by guests). A couple of tedious hours removing giveaway embroidery, and a few hundred francs in the hand.

Jacquot also knew it was unlikely to stop there. As well as purloined linen there were 'adjusted' supplier invoices which allowed for the 'sale' of unwanted cleaning supplies, guest toiletries, sewing kits, stationery and such like – usually to smaller hotels whose management was happy to pay a fraction of the usual price. It was a scam, not particularly profitable but still reasonably rewarding. A little bit here, a little bit there. Over time it all added up. And few people, bar Jacquot's friend, ever noticed.

What astonished Jacquot was how many of these people considered such profits legitimate perks – as though it was a part of the remuneration for a job well done, as though they were somehow entitled to it. It appeared that Madame Champeau was no different, even if she already had a very lucrative income stream in the shape of introduction fees for the Master.

As she pulled out the last thread of the 'M', Jacquot ran through some figures. In the last few days she had taken a thousand francs from him and probably the same amount from Bressans, Kónar, West and Ginoux, not to mention whatever figure she'd negotiated with Gilles Gavan for the painting groups' audience with the Master. Maybe eight thousand francs? Not a bad haul. Indeed, such a profitable sideline that he wondered why she would bother with the sheets. But he knew the answer. It was human nature, pure and simple. A wad of notes in the hand, pushed into an apron pocket, was as seductive a drug as a shot of the harder stuff. And impossible to stop once you'd started.

But Jacquot wasn't there to catch out a petty thief. He was

there to find a murderer. And it was time to get on with the job.

Stepping out of the shadows, he reached her door and rat-a-tat-tatted on the glass panel, making the pane rattle in its loose wooden frame.

The sound made the housekeeper start, so absorbed had she been in her work on the sheet, and as Jacquot pushed open the door he saw the tip of the needle jab into the top of her thumb. In an instant a tiny blot of blood burst from the skin and dripped on to the half-erased Monastère monogram.

'Monsieur, can I help you?' asked Madame Champeau, bundling the bloodstained sheet beneath her desk, barely able to contain her irritation at the disturbance, and its consequences. As they both knew, it would take some work to remove that tiny red smear from the corner of the sheet.

'*Bonjour, madame*. I hope I didn't disturb you, but Régine Bouvet said I would find you here.'

'And? What is it you want?' she asked, squeezing her thumb tip until a second bubble of blood rose from the wound, then putting it into her mouth and sucking hard enough to hollow her cheeks.

'I would like to see the Master. Auguste Vilotte.'

Taking the thumb from her mouth, she said, 'The morning is never a good time with the Master. That is when he is at work. But . . . maybe I could arrange something for Wednesday or Thursday?'

'Now would be better,' replied Jacquot. 'If you wouldn't mind.' He placed his hands on the back of the chair in front of her desk and leaned forward.

'I'm afraid, monsieur . . .'

'Actually, it's Chief Inspector. Now, if you'd be so kind . . .'

Jacquot watched the face harden, the neck flush, the spine straighten.

'*Comme vous voulez* . . . Chief Inspector.'

Madame Champeau rose from her desk and, still sucking the end of her thumb, opened a drawer and pulled out a ring of keys. 'If you'd care to follow me.'

'I assume you've heard about the murders?' Jacquot asked as she led him down the stairs to the laundry hall.

'Sometimes Le Grand Monastère is not so *grand*,' she replied testily. 'Sometimes it can be a small place, too, monsieur. So, yes, of course I have heard.'

'May I ask who from?'

'From my son, Philippe. And from my nephew.'

'Your nephew?'

'He works in the kitchen. An apprentice. Today he washes dishes, tomorrow he will be a great chef. It is the way, is it not?'

'Let us hope so,' said Jacquot, pushing aside the plastic doorstrips for her to pass through. A minute later, at the top of another flight of stairs, she did the same for him, holding open the service door beneath the lobby staircase.

'So when did you last see either Monsieur Kónar or Mademoiselle Ladouze?' he began, as they crossed the lobby, heading for the cloisters.

'Monsieur Kónar, yesterday afternoon. He'd been swimming. The lady in Room 3? What did you say her name was?'

'Ladouze. Ghislaine Ladouze.'

'Mademoiselle Ladouze I haven't seen since Friday evening. Until this morning, I thought she had checked out. I mean, you *are* in her room. You should know.'

'And where was that, when you last saw Mademoiselle

Ladouze?' asked Jacquot, their footsteps ringing out on the flagstones of the cloister, the lawn littered with palm-fronds, the wind whipping this way and that, the rain pelting down and spouting from the gargoyled guttering.

'Where we are going now,' replied Madame Champeau. 'Le Maître had requested a meeting. I simply escorted her to his door. Just as I am doing now with you.'

'And who else has visited the Master since Mademoiselle Ladouze?'

Madame Champeau didn't need to think. 'The Master's art dealer, Monsieur Ginoux from Paris; the painter, Madame West; Monsieur Bouvet and the architect Monsieur van der Haage.'

'And that is all?'

'That is all, monsieur.'

'And could anyone visit without your knowing?'

'It's possible, but if the Master wanted to be alone he could easily lock his door and not answer.'

Madame Champeau pushed through the door marked *Privé* and led the way into the second courtyard, keeping to the covered walkway to the left where the new rooms were. Outside in the open, rain smacked on to the sandy mounds and splashed into the puddles that had formed.

Reaching the door to the watchtower, she knocked once and pushed it open.

'Le Maître has had a busy few days, so please don't tire him,' she said. Without waiting for an answer, she turned on her heel and went back the way they had come.

80

'You again.'

Vilotte worked the palette knife from his bent fingers, dropped it on to the brush ledge of the easel and turned towards Jacquot, sandalled feet apart, knuckled hands on hips, bearded chin pushed out like a cannibal contemplating dinner. The canvas he'd been working on the last time Jacquot had visited had progressed quite considerably, those few early charcoal strokes now grown to a dark oblong of grey shadowed with smeared, slanting squares of pine-bark brown knifed on to its surface. On to this brooding ground, Vilotte had added four vertical stripes of red and blue. And a couple of cross sweeps in green. Already there was a sense of a figure turning away, running. It was still difficult to say.

'So what is it this time?' asked Vilotte.

Beyond the easel, Jacquot could see himself refracted a hundred times in the cracked mirror. Was this how

Vilotte saw the world, he wondered – fractured, splintered, broken?

'It's good of you to see me,' Jacquot began, the smell of linseed and white spirit as strong as ever.

Vilotte shot him a contemptuous look. '*Mes fesses!* You didn't give me any choice. You just walked in without a word. I'm sorry, but I'm not ready to receive visitors. Morning's a good time for me. The light's good – usually,' he added, nodding to the window, the rain sheeting down, the dark, sailing clouds split open by forks of lightning, a crack of thunder ricocheting across the valley.

'A new work?' asked Jacquot, moving towards the easel, disregarding the frosty, dismissive tone. The distraction seemed to work.

'A new work but an old subject,' replied Vilotte. 'And a new approach. Rejection. Loss. Letting something you hold dear slip through your fingers, because . . .' Vilotte's eyes narrowed. He knew he'd been steered. 'But I don't like talking about new work. It taints it, you know? Showing, talking, discussing – they take away the power.' Reaching past Jacquot, he caught hold of the nearest sheet hanging from the ceiling and gave it a tug.

Jacquot looked up. The sheets, he could now see, were hitched to a curtain rail screwed into the beams and, as Vilotte pulled the one nearest to him to hide the painting from sight, all the other drapes followed, shifting around the room like carriages pulled by a train.

'So,' he continued, arranging the folds to conceal the painting, 'what can I do for you this time, Monsieur *Flic*?'

Satisfied that the painting was properly covered, hidden from sight, Vilotte went to his chair and eased himself into it. As far as Jacquot could see there was no wine bottle to hand, or plastic cups, and no box of cigars.

'I'm here about Mademoiselle Ghislaine Ladouze.'

'The woman who disappeared?'

'That's right,' said Jacquot. 'Yesterday you told me she was here Friday night. Rather a late visit, wasn't it?'

Vilotte adjusted the folds of his nightshirt, plucked at the bunch of material in his lap, wiped his hands on his chest. It was as if he didn't want to answer the question, thinking that if he remained silent for long enough, it would go away, the fact that it hadn't been answered somehow forgotten.

Jacquot recognised the diversion. It was always the old who tried it. Old men, old women. Sometimes they were the hardest to interview. And all the time, you never quite knew if they had something to hide or not.

'A late visit?' he said at last, when he realised that the question was not going to disappear, would have to be answered. 'Is that what you said?'

'That's correct.'

'Late if you go to bed with the birds, maybe. But, my age . . . day or night makes little difference. And time is so short . . . so short. A day. A month. A year . . . So many things to do.' A great sigh fell from his ruby lips.

'And you said she stayed how long?'

Vilotte shook his head, pulled at his beard. 'An hour? The whole night? Who can say? She was here, and then she was gone. Old one minute, young the next. It was . . . tantalising.'

'And what was the purpose of her visit?'

'I wanted to talk. About the old times. And so did she. She was . . .' Vilotte screwed his eyes tight, as though wincing from pain, then opened them wide.

'She was . . . ?'

'She knew so much. Our friends, the places we went. Knew

the stories, too.' Vilotte paused once more, turned to the broken mirror and gazed at it as though watching the scenes from some distant screenplay unreel in front of him. Then he looked back at Jacquot, narrowed his eyes. 'But in the end, you know, I began to see through it. Knew what she was after. Just like she'd been when I first knew her. Wafting around the room, always touching her little titties, stroking her *clicli* . . . Always looking out for the main chance, looking for something . . . money, personal things . . . squirrelling them away. I didn't like that, you know. Never have.'

'And what exactly do you imagine she was after?' asked Jacquot, knowing the answer full well.

'What everyone is after when it comes to the Master. A memento. A signature. Some little trinket. But she wanted more.'

'What "more" exactly?'

Vilotte turned, gave Jacquot a look. 'There, you're doing the same as her. Trying to trick me.'

'Monsieur, I assure you . . .'

Vilotte's voice rose a fraction – petulant now. 'I told you. I told you before, stop "assuring" me the whole damn time. I've got a brain. I've got eyes. I can see. I know . . . You people, you just . . . If you had seen what I have seen . . .'

He was starting to ramble now, Jacquot was certain, twisting and turning in his barber's chair as though the chair had him trapped, held him, his hands clasped to its padded peppermint-green arms.

Jacquot waited, hoping he hadn't lost his moment, then began again, taking a different tack.

'I'd also like to know about another guest. Monsieur Kónar? I believe he visited you?'

Vilotte shook his head as though to clear the previous images and gradually ceased his twisting, slowed the chair, released the arm rests, quietened. When he spoke, his words were softer, but no less pitched.

'The Balkan? Looked like Pablo? Yes, he was here. Bastard wanted to make a film about me. The last of the Masters, he said. Something like that. Told him to piss off, I did. Fuck off. I wasn't interested.'

'And how did he take it? Your refusal to cooperate?'

'It was like he didn't hear what I was saying,' replied Vilotte, sharing with Jacquot a complicit, would-you-credit-it look. 'And there he was, filming the whole time. Bold as a back-street hooker. Camera up to his face. And mine. Inches away, you know? Never asked if it was OK. Just pulled out the blessed thing and started filming. Asking questions, moving around enough to make me dizzy. Even went upstairs, would you believe? Didn't pay a shred of attention when I said "Enough, get out." ' Vilotte caught his breath, then levelled his eyes on Jacquot. 'My work is private. When it is with me, it is mine and no one else's,' he said, gesturing with a bent finger at the hidden painting. 'Afterwards, then they can scrabble for it. Then it's in their world and I don't care any more. But here, in my studio, in my home . . . that's different. That man . . . Baff! A foreigner. He had no respect.'

'His body was found this morning.'

'He's dead too?'

Jacquot smiled. 'Who said the girl was dead?'

Vilotte sucked in the beard around his lips. 'Obvious, isn't it? It's why you're here, asking questions about her? She's got to be dead. Stands to reason. But it wasn't me, I'll tell you that. Me? Pah! I'm an old man. Can't hardly hold a brush any more.'

'So when did you last see him? The Balkan?'

Vilotte gave it some thought. 'Yesterday? Thereabouts.'

'Can you remember what time?'

'Evening.'

'Before or after midnight?'

'Before?' Vilotte shrugged.

Jacquot took this in. If, as now appeared likely, Kónar had left Meredith to visit the Master around eleven on Sunday night, then Vilotte had probably been the last to see him alive. Two murder victims, and in both cases Vilotte had been the last to see them alive.

'This was his second visit?'

'Second, that's right. With the camera again. I told Madame after the first time that I didn't want to see the *con* again, but he must have bribed her. They all do. Pay her money for the privilege. And she's got an eye for the silver, that one. Franc's her favourite name. But he didn't stay so long the second time.'

'How come?'

Vilotte chuckled. 'Took a knife to him, didn't I? Threatened him. Said I'd cut out his heart, slice off his *couilles*, mash them into a *boudin*. Being a dago, he might not have known what I was talking about, but he got the message. 'Course, it didn't stop him filming. Never stopped. But he was backing out the door all the time. Didn't know if I was joking or not.'

'And were you?'

'Maybe if I'd had a few more drinks inside me I . . . might have cut him a little, you know. A gift from the Master. Something for him to show his friends, eh?' Vilotte chuckled and swiped at the air with an imaginary knife. *'Touché!'*

'Do you want to know how they died?'

'Pouff! Quelle différence? Ils sont morts.'

401

'Do you mind if I look around?'

'Help yourself.'

'No knives.'

Vilotte let out a gargle of a laugh that descended into coughs. 'No knives. No knives. You're OK. I trust you.' And he stretched out his legs, rested them on the trunk by the barber's chair, carefully crossing his ankles as though he had no intention of going anywhere. 'Go ahead. Don't be shy. Look wherever you want. Me, I've nothing to hide.'

81

There were two floors above the studio, reached by a rickety wood staircase that followed the curve of the wall. There was no banister and Jacquot let his fingers trail against the stone, the wood beneath his feet creaking ominously as he climbed.

As his head came level with the first floor, Jacquot saw immediately that the space had been given over to a bedroom, a magnificent scroll-ended *bateau-lit* adrift and unmade in the centre of another circular room, a room noticeably smaller than the studio below. Beside the bed, doubling as a bedside table, was an old bakelite radio with a semi-circular dial, its flex snaking across the floor to an electric point. Beside the radio was a scatter of magazines, an unopened bottle of the Pétrus they'd drunk on Jacquot's last visit, a corkscrew, a clean coffee mug and a stack of what appeared to be books or ledgers, a rusting hurricane lamp balanced on top of them.

Removing the lamp, Jacquot picked up the top one and opened it. An album. Photos left loose between the pages fell to the floor, a cascade of images, most of them black and white, some colour. Jacquot knelt down and picked them up, turning them over where they had fallen face-down, looking at them.

He might not have been an expert, but he'd seen these faces before, recognised them, as anyone would. Famous faces. Here, talking to a matador, Picasso; here, a Neptune-like Dali standing up to his waist in water, pulling at the ends of his moustache, a large *pain couronne* balanced on his head; and here a man in a wheelchair, clipped white beard and round spectacles. Jacquot guessed it was Matisse because he recognised the cut-out figures on the table in front of him.

And the places: a bullring; a country house terrace with canvasses set out to dry; a cluttered studio; a lunch party under a sunshade; and what looked very like the line of cypresses on the road leading to Monastère, though no building could be seen. Jacquot tucked the photos away, put the album back and slid out another.

In this one every picture was in place, neatly bracketed, captions written in tiny white lettering on the black boards. There was a sheet of tissue between each page, not a single sheet bent or torn or folded over. Whoever turned these pages, turned them carefully, reverentially. And on every page, every picture – four to a page, two to a page, six to a page – the same person. And every caption the same name. *'Céleste à Cimiez'*; *'Céleste, Auberge des Templiers, Collioure'*; *'Céleste au jardin Vauvenargues'*; *'Raoul et Céleste, Promenade des Anglais, Nice'*.

Céleste. The same woman on the cassette back in his room. Here on a beach, at a table, in a deckchair; here in culottes, in gypsy dress, peeping out from behind a fan, a bandanna tied in her hair; laughing, looking stern, asleep in the shade.

So young. So fresh. So beguiling.

Céleste Maroc. Ghislaine Ladouze. There was no mistaking the likeness.

Putting the album back, replacing the lamp, Jacquot looked around the room. Compared with the chaos below, the space here was surprisingly tidy: a few threadbare rugs on the bare wooden floor, a pile of clothes on a chair and, beneath the stairs leading to the next level, a tapestried six-panel screen that concealed a bathtub, washbasin and mirrored medicine cabinet. All around the room, the curving stone walls were bare of decoration – not a picture, not a photo – nothing save a line of canvases propped against the wall, their stretchered backs to the room.

'You'll find four canvases up there,' he heard Vilotte shout up from below, as though the old man knew exactly what Jacquot was thinking, what he wanted to do. 'Take a look, by all means. But you can't have them. They're sold. You couldn't afford them anyway,' he added with a throaty cackle.

The canvases stood side by side. Four of them, as Vilotte had said. Jacquot went over to them, tipped the first one back and peered down at it. Through the daubs and smears of oil, in shards of pale blues and greys and muddy purples, was a giant upside-down face.

A bearded face – Vilotte himself?

It was difficult to be certain. Jacquot looked at the other three. All the same subject but different angles, different colours. A face, essentially. Self-portraits. Even at this odd angle, looking down at them, on the slant, they were extraordinary works. Jacquot was no expert, but these were stunning. And

Vilotte was right. He'd never be able to afford them. He wondered how much they'd been sold for? And who to? The dealer Ginoux? According to Bouvet, he came down from Paris every year, paid a visit. Sometimes he left with a wrapped canvas. Sometimes he didn't.

Carefully letting the last painting settle back into place, Jacquot crossed to the washstand, bath and mirrored cabinet set beneath the stairs. No razor, no hairbrush on the stained porcelain sink, but a finely tined comb wedged with a matting of grey hair, a toothbrush, a flannel, and a grimy nugget of L'Occitane soap.

Jacquot opened the mirrored door of the cabinet. Three shelves. Nothing but proprietory-brand medicines – tablets for indigestion, for headaches, for colds and flu, a wrinkled tube of ointment for eczema. And, Jacquot noted, a roll of plasters, blue, probably appropriated by Madame Champeau from the first-aid kit in Monastère's kitchen. Beside the roll of plasters, standing side by side, were three brown medicine bottles, a few pills in each.

He picked up each of the bottles, read the labels: Décotafam, Priletothamine, Mestastirepmocal. Prescription drugs. A doctor's name and surgery address in Cavaillon were stamped on the labels. Cours Bournissac of all places, just the street where Jacquot lived.

Jotting down the names in his notebook, Jacquot closed the cabinet and climbed the final flight of stairs. Like the floors below, the room was circular, its ceiling latticed with beams, and its main, north-facing window commanding what Jacquot could see would be a stunning view of the Calavon Valley and Monts de Vaucluse were it not for the low ceiling of scudding black cloud and blustering sheets of rain.

Jacquot wondered what van der Haage must have thought when he stood here first, saw the space, the potential. The Dutchman must be itching to get his hands on all this. What a fabulous suite it would make.

Turning away from the window, Jacquot surveyed the room, bare of any decoration save a metre-wide square of pink plaster smoothed on to the stone wall. Facing this plastered square was a paint-smeared bentwood rocking chair set beside a stack of metal film canisters. And beside that, balanced on a bar-room stool, an ancient film projector. An electric flex, knotted and coiled, snaked across the floor to a point.

Jacquot picked up one of the canisters, shook it. There was the sound of something tumbling around inside. He twisted open the lid – a dusty spread of ash, cigar stubs and the stale, cold smell of tobacco. He fixed the lid back on and opened another. A reel of film. He slipped it out and pulled a length of the celluloid free, held it up to the window. Tiny, brown snapshots the size of a thumbnail, a girl sitting on a wall, a bandanna in her hair. Metre after metre of the same shot, any movement in the pose too minuscule to make out.

Now Jacquot knew where the film in his video had come from.

82

Down in the studio Vilotte seemed to be dozing. His hands dangled from the arm rests, his head was tipped back and a soft rumbling rose into his open mouth. Coming off the bottom stair, Jacquot realised how easy it would have been for Bressans to steal the film, smuggle it out. Waiting for the old man to fall asleep, like now, then searching through the rooms upstairs until he found what he wanted.

But Vilotte was not asleep.

'You find anything, Monsieur *Flic*? Any bodies? Any blood? A murder weapon? You coming back to arrest me?' He popped open his milky blue eyes and, pushing his feet against the trunk, he spun the barber's chair around.

'Nothing, monsieur. Nothing at all. Did you think that I might?'

But Vilotte wasn't listening. He was looking past Jacquot at the easel, as though the sheet that covered it wasn't there.

Hefting himself out of the chair, he tossed the sheet aside, the rollers that secured it rattling in the track above their heads.

'Open the trunk,' he told Jacquot. 'Top row. Give me the third tube from the left.'

Vilotte didn't turn, transfixed by the canvas in front of him, just punched out a gnarled left hand.

Jacquot did as he was told. Lifting the lid he saw rows of silvery, labelled paint tubes, sections for brushes, blackened bags of charcoal and tumbled sticks of pastel and chalk.

So the trunk was a paintbox. He'd been wondering.

Finding the tube that Vilotte had requested, Jacquot passed it to him.

Without a word of thanks, Vilotte twisted off the cap and squeezed a thin snake of yellow on to his palette. Half screwing back the top, he placed the tube on the easel ledge, picked up the palette and began to work the yellow with a snatch of blue, mashing the two colours together with the edge of his palette knife, cutting and slicing at the giving puddles of oil until he was happy with the mix. Taking a wedge of it on the end of his knife, he leaned forward and scoured another green vertical stripe down the right-hand side of the canvas, executed with a focused intensity, a series of rough, plastering daubs that billowed and stretched the canvas and looked, Jacquot thought, like an arm held out.

'So tell me about Bressans,' said Jacquot, closing the lid of the paint trunk and sitting on it.

'Bressans? The pimp from Marseilles? A taker.'

'Pimp?'

'He may be rich, he may have a gallery, he may pretend to know something about art, Monsieur *Flic* . . . But he's still a promenade pimp. Same as all the others. Out on the make.

Something for nothing and I pick up the bill. Like I said, dropping round for one last fuck . . .'

'How many times has he visited?'

Vilotte was mixing a darker green. Unable to get his thumb through the palette hole – or maybe he knew he could never get it out once he'd got it in – he clasped the board to his belly.

'Twice maybe. Three times. Who knows?'

'This year?'

Vilotte nodded, leaned back to the canvas.

'And what exactly was it that he wanted?'

Vilotte reached for the hanging cloth and pulled it towards him. Wiping the blade of his palette knife in a fold, he let it fall back and started working a slice of the green with a smear of red.

'I asked—'

'I know what you asked. Wait, please.' Vilotte leaned forward and jammed the brown on to the canvas, working the clod of oil in a long arc around the green slash. Standing back, he looked at it. 'Good,' he said softly. 'Good.' And then, glancing around at Jacquot, 'Like I said, something for nothing.'

'More precisely?'

'*Jésu Christi!* Don't you have a brain? Paintings. He wanted paintings. Said he'd take whatever I chose to give him. What I have here – my things – even this palette.' The old man waved it in Jacquot's direction and a crust of dried oil broke away from its edge and fell to the floor. 'To celebrate my work, he said, my contribution. Hah! As if . . .'

'Surely, that would be—'

Vilotte swung round. 'And you know what else? He wants it all for nothing. For nothing. He has just the place, he tells me. On the waterfront in Marseilles. An old Customs House. He's bought the property already, he says. Is going to give it to the city – filled with my things. Says I'm the greatest of the great, that I must have a suitable memorial, and he can give it to me.'

'Sounds like a generous offer,' said Jacquot.

'Generous? Generous? He may give the work to the town, he may give the museum, too. But think, think what's left, man,' said Vilotte, brandishing his paint-scabbed palette knife.

Jacquot tried to do so, then remembered what his old friend Salette had said. 'A political appointment? A seat on the board?'

'Yes, yes. That, too, for certain. But there's something else.'

Jacquot struggled to think what it might be. Was there something he was missing? Something he hadn't realised about Bressans, what he was up to? He shook his head.

'Repro rights,' snarled Vilotte. 'For the catalogue, he said. Said he could get it printed himself. Family business. But it's not just the catalogue that rogue's thinking. *Mais non. Pas de tout*. Think postcards, Monsieur *Flic*. Millions of 'em. Three francs each. Buy a handful. He must have thought I'd lost my marbles.'

Vilotte turned back to the canvas, shaking his head at Bressans' gall.

Well, well, well, thought Jacquot. And then, 'Tell me, monsieur. How do you sell your pictures?'

'Paintings. They're paintings.'

'*Bien sûr*. Paintings, I mean.'

There was a silence, another wad of brown was scraped off the palette board and smeared on to the canvas, each daub accompanied now by a grunt. It struck Jacquot that he was watching a master at work. One day this would be a moment to remember and treasure. Watching the great man paint.

'I have an agent. A dealer,' said Vilotte at last, standing a pace back from the canvas and tipping his head to one side. 'He comes down here, sees what I've done, takes it away.'

'He has a gallery?'

'An address book, Monsieur *Flic*. An address book. Much better. No rent on an address book.'

'He sells the paintings in advance?'

'These are Vilottes. Of course. Or he knows who wants one,' replied Vilotte, stepping further back from the canvas, then leaning forward to peer at it. It was as if something had caught his eye, something that shouldn't have been there. He moved to the side, looked again. Stepped back, leaned forward. Peered at the canvas as though he was inspecting the weave, not the paint.

And then something happened that took Jacquot completely by surprise, something he couldn't possibly have anticipated.

It began with a low moaning that grew into words. 'No, no, no. You're wrong,' spat Vilotte. 'All wrong. It's not you . . . It's not . . . You're . . .'

Words which at first Jacquot assumed were spoken to him.

It didn't take him more than an instant to realise his mistake.

'Bitch, bitch, bitch,' screamed Vilotte, spittle flying at the painting, and he flung the palette from his hand, sent it clattering on to the floor. 'You piece of . . . You . . .' and he swung his arm upwards and brought the palette knife slashing through the air and into the canvas.

The blow was delivered with such venom that Vilotte's fist followed the blade through the ripped canvas, the sleeve of his dishdash pushed up his arm. The easel rocked, teetered, then regained its balance, but the painting slipped from its mooring and swung to the floor, hanging from Vilotte's wrist like an oversized bracelet. Pulling his arm free, Vilotte tossed the canvas to the floor and flung the knife after it.

For a moment he just stood there, panting lightly, gazing at the torn canvas and then he began to laugh.

'You see? You see how it is? So quick. And so soon. Sometimes, it's weeks before this happens. Hours of work. Days of work. And suddenly you realise you've taken a wrong turn. Then it's over. You must start again. All over again.'

He stumbled to the barber's chair, dropped himself into it with a gasp and looked up at Jacquot.

'I'm finished,' said Vilotte, squeezing a thumb and forefinger into the corners of his eyes. 'It's enough. I need to rest. Come tomorrow. We'll talk again then. After the painters have been.'

'Can I get you something?' asked Jacquot, getting to his feet, still stunned by Vilotte's outburst.

The old man shook his head, wincing as he did so.

'I'm fine. I'm fine. Just leave me. Tomorrow. Come tomorrow.'

83

It was late and most of the guests were finishing their desserts or sipping their coffees when Jacquot pushed through the Réfectoire's glass doors, hoping he hadn't missed lunch. Conversation was muted, but seemed to drop to an even lower register as he crossed the flagstoned chamber, every eye glancing in his direction. A policeman, not a journalist. The murders. Word had clearly spread that two bodies, not just one, had now been found.

As far as Jacquot could see the only guests missing were van der Haage, Bressans and Branigan – either they had finished their lunch already or they had ordered room service. He nodded to Gilles Gavan at the club table, returned Claudine's uncertain smile but otherwise made no eye contact with any of the other diners, walking directly to the table he'd been given on Saturday evening.

A waiter appeared with a short menu card, the same lad

who'd served Jacquot's breakfast coffee in the Salle du Matin. Jacquot took it, glanced at it, ordered, then held the lad back, whispered something to him.

Five minutes later, after his wine had been presented and poured and his vichyssoise served, he saw the waiter stop as instructed at Monsieur Ginoux's table. Wiping his mouth with his napkin, Vilotte's dealer pushed back from his table and walked over.

'Monsieur. I believe you would like a word?'

Jacquot got to his feet, reached out and shook Ginoux's hand. It was small and soft; a woman's hand, the perfectly manicured nails polished to a lacquered shine. Ginoux was about half his size, but he looked fit and sharp, probably quick on his feet, like a scrum-half with the ball in his hands. A slippery eel, Jacquot guessed, with the acceleration, from a standing start, of a scalded cat.

'If you wouldn't mind, monsieur?' Jacquot gestured to the chair opposite and Ginoux took a seat.

As they made themselves comfortable, the hum of conversation around them increased a notch but Jacquot had a feeling they were still being watched by every table. Was Monsieur a suspect? Was Monsieur in league with the police? With ears straining around them, Jacquot smiled, lifted his spoon and asked if Ginoux minded if he continued with his soup.

'But of course, please. I had the same myself. A fine soup, but a little sharp, a certain . . . bitterness.'

Jacquot tasted the soup, tried to detect the bitterness that Ginoux had noticed, but could taste only the chill cream thickened with potatoes and flecked with chives.

'A little too much green from the leeks, I suspect,' continued Ginoux. 'It's an easy mistake to make. A couple more slices of the knife where the white stalk starts to green. Every chef does it. It's as though they need colour to cook, I always think. But there you are.' Ginoux smiled and settled back in his chair.

'You have a keener sense of taste than I, monsieur.' Jacquot took another sip. 'For me it seems . . . just about perfect.'

Ginoux smiled again but kept his lips together, gave Jacquot a well-there-you-are look.

'So. Chief Inspector . . . Not a journalist after all?'

'How did you know I was a journalist?' Jacquot finished his soup with a fleeting sense of regret. Bitterness or not, it had been superb. He could easily have eaten another bowl of it and, as the waiter removed the plate, he had to hold himself back from making the request.

'My driver overheard one of the guests,' replied Ginoux.

'Ah,' said Jacquot. 'The large gentleman with the rather severe haircut.'

This time Ginoux's lips parted in a chuckle. His teeth were white and sharp and the gums a glistening candy pink. A dental hygienist would have had trouble finding anything to do in that mouth, thought Jacquot.

'Too long in the military, I'm afraid. Old habits. But he is a superb driver . . . and remarkably efficient. So, monsieur, what is it that I can do to help with your investigation?'

Before Jacquot could answer two waiters appeared at the table, one serving his *rognons de veau* from a silver, scalloped chafing dish, the second bearing a wedge of golden *dauphinoise* and a small frisée salad.

'Some wine, monsieur?' asked Jacquot, as a creamy *jus* was spooned on to the *rognons*. 'It's a Lubéron. Château La Verrerie, '88.'

'It sounds . . . perfect,' said Ginoux, with an expression that suggested he rarely dropped below *troisième crus* but was prepared to make the sacrifice on this occasion.

A second wine glass was brought to the table, the wine poured.

'*À vot' santé, monsieur,*' said Ginoux. 'And to your investigation.'

They chinked glasses and sipped their wine, Ginoux rolling it over his tongue, biting at it with his teeth, before swallowing with a cheek-puckered wince.

'A most regrettable state of affairs,' continued Ginoux, putting down his glass then checking the collar on his suede blouson and patting down his hair. 'It's at times like this that one despairs of the human condition, *n'est-ce pas*? Murder, bloodshed. The animal instinct taking control. Terrible, terrible.'

'You are quite right, monsieur,' replied Jacquot. 'Terrible. So I hope you won't mind if I ask you some questions?' He cut through the first of the kidneys, a feather of blood seeping into the cream sauce.

'Not at all,' said Ginoux. 'Please, ask whatever you wish.'

'According to hotel records, you are a regular visitor to the Grand Monastère?'

'Hotel records or Monsieur Bouvet?' asked Ginoux. 'No, no, I'm only joking. Yes, the hotel records are correct. I come down at least once a year. And have done so for . . . ooohh, maybe fifteen years. It's like home from home.'

'And home is . . . ?' asked Jacquot lightly, turning to the *dauphinoise* and scooping up a mouthful. It was hotter than he'd expected. He reached for his wine, hoping that Ginoux hadn't noticed, but aware that he probably had.

'Paris. Allée des Fauves, a couple of blocks from the Place des Vosges.'

'And the reason for your visits?'

'The Master. Auguste Vilotte. I am his friend and his agent. I arrange commissions on his behalf, prepare occasional exhibitions and work on his *catalogue raisonnée*. So, archivist too. He really is a quite exceptional painter. Have you seen his work?'

'As a matter of fact, his most recent work.'

'Really,' said Ginoux, looking interested for the first time since he'd sat at Jacquot's table. 'The self-portraits?'

'It didn't look like a self-portrait to me,' replied Jacquot, breaking up the cake of *dauphinoise* with his fork to cool it before scooping up another mouthful.

'Really,' said Ginoux again, eyes narrowing, but not prepared to give anything away, to admit that something was going on to which he was not privy.

'It's hard to be certain but it reminded me of someone running away,' continued Jacquot.

'Aaaahh yes,' said Ginoux, as though he knew exactly the painting that Jacquot was referring to, though Jacquot suspected he did not. 'A recurrent theme. Particularly the early work.'

'He commands high prices, I should imagine,' observed Jacquot, slicing through a kidney and spearing one half with his fork.

Ginoux spread out his hands. 'High for some, maybe. For others, for true collectors, a pin-prick of financial inconvenience compared to the pleasure of knowing that a Vilotte will be replacing the Bonnard above the fireplace, or the Picasso in the library, or the Matisse in the hall.' Ginoux closed his eyes, waved his hand, as though enraptured at the very thought.

Jacquot swallowed his mouthful of kidney and reached for his wine, pausing a moment to savour the taste in his mouth. In his opinion, the Verrerie '88 was a perfect match for the *rognons*, and he'd have chosen it above any Bordeaux. As Patric at La Tilleul had said . . . when in the Lubéron . . . And he was right. Whether Ginoux knew it or not.

'As you now know, monsieur,' said Jacquot, mopping the last of the kidneys through the bloodied cream sauce. 'We have two bodies. Two guests. The first was a Mademoiselle Ladouze. Might I ask if you knew her, or met her, or whether you might have spoken to her, seen her around the hotel?'

'No to the first three, but yes to the last. She was . . . quite remarkable.'

'In what way, particularly?' asked Jacquot, already knowing the answer, but intrigued to see how Ginoux would field the question.

A waiter appeared, removed Jacquot's plates.

'*Un dessert pour monsieur? Ou du fromage?*'

'A *chêvre*, please. And some honey.'

After the waiter had gone, Jacquot reached for the bottle and offered to fill Ginoux's glass.

Ginoux shook his head, held up his hand – enough, thank you.

'You were saying, monsieur . . . ? About Mademoiselle Ladouze.'

'Where to start? Everything in its place, of course . . .' – Ginoux smiled – 'but with a . . . with an energy that electrified the air around her. She drew the eye, like a fine painting. Was she a model?'

'A call-girl, monsieur.'

'Ah,' replied Ginoux, as though stumbling upon an unpalatable truth. 'I see.'

'And her companion? Do you know him?'

'I know *of* him, monsieur. But the gentleman does not know me. Nor shall he.'

'And how do you know of him?'

'By repute, monsieur. He is . . . a businessman.' The word was loaded with disdain. 'There is hardly any more to say on the matter. But if you were to press me, I would say he was a shameless self-promoter. I can't imagine there is anything he wouldn't consider if it served in any way to increase his creature comforts or the size of his bank account. Thoroughly unscrupulous.' If Ginoux had asked for a finger bowl, washed and dried his hands, Jacquot wouldn't have been the least surprised.

Jacquot nodded. 'Do you know what he is doing here, at Monastère?'

'He is opening a museum, I believe. Doubtless he is here to scrounge something off the Master. If he is, he will be sorely disappointed.'

Jacquot took this in, nodded. 'Tell me, can you remember the last time you saw Mademoiselle Ladouze?'

'I remember exactly. Friday evening, after an early dinner. On the stairs from the cloister garden to the top corridor. I was going up to my room, she was coming down from hers.'

'Did you know that she was going to visit Vilotte?'

Ginoux frowned. 'No. I did not.'

'Does it surprise you?'

Ginoux shook his head. 'As I said, she was very . . . striking. And the Master has always admired a pretty face.'

'Did you speak to her, when you passed her?'

'Only to wish her *bonsoir*.'

'And can you remember what she was wearing?'

'A scarf tied in her hair, a blue cummerbund, and one of those layered, frilly white skirts. Like a gypsy might wear. They were very popular a few years back.'

'You have a good eye, monsieur. And a good memory.'

'Thank you,' said Ginoux, acknowledging the praise with a modest tip of the head. 'It is my job after all.'

'And Monsieur Kónar? What of him, monsieur?'

Ginoux pursed his lips, shook his head. 'No, monsieur. I do not know him. I have seen him in the restaurant, around the hotel, you know. Always playing with that little camera of his. Is he a photographer, something in the movies?'

'Why do you ask that, monsieur, about the movies? He could just have been an enthusiastic amateur, like many tourists who come to the Lubéron? Something to show the neighbours when he returns home.'

'Because he was staying here with that American actress. I forget her name but she was in all the papers a few days back. The week before last. The festival in Cannes. I assumed that since he was with her, he was probably in the same business.'

'And when was the last time you remember seeing Monsieur Kónar?'

Ginoux steepled his fingers and gave it some thought. 'Again, that is easy. Yesterday evening. Just before it began to rain. He was coming down from the battlements.'

'And how did he seem to you?'

'In a hurry. He seemed . . . *un peu distrait*.'

'Did you speak to him?'

'Just a nod, you understand. One guest to another. Maybe "*bonsoir*". I cannot really recall.'

A waiter approached and served Jacquot his *chèvre*, a thin white disc which Jacquot proceeded to anoint with honey.

'I've never seen honey poured on *chèvre*,' remarked Ginoux.

Then you haven't lived, thought Jacquot. 'It's a favourite

down here in the south. I'm surprised you haven't seen it before.'

'I must try it sometime.'

'Please, have some of this. Let me get you a knife, a plate.'

'No, no, no, no, monsieur,' pleaded Ginoux, holding up his hands as if in horror at the very thought. 'Really. I couldn't. *Pas une autre chose . . .*'

Jacquot shrugged, lifted a wedge and popped it into his mouth. 'And tell me, monsieur. What of your companion? Your driver? A Legionnaire, if his tattoo is anything to go by.'

Ginoux looked surprised. 'You are an observant man, monsieur.'

'Like you, it's part of the job.'

Ginoux smiled, nodded. 'Of course, of course. And you are exactly right. He is a Legionnaire. Or was. His name, as you probably already know, is Emile René Dutronc. From Ghent originally, but now resident in Paris. He has worked for me nearly ten years, and takes very good care of me. Also, in my line of work it is a good idea to have someone close by who knows how to look after himself. And me.'

'How so, monsieur?'

'The art world – at my level – is a precarious place. And ruthless. It is necessary to protect oneself. For instance, I will be returning to Paris in the next few days with four of Vilotte's canvases. The self-portraits. It will be a valuable cargo. A great deal of money is involved. And there are many people in my profession who would dearly love to get their hands on Vilotte's work.'

Jacquot had no doubt that Ginoux would have included Roland Bressans amongst that number.

'Believe me, Chief Inspector,' continued Ginoux, fixing his

eyes on Jacquot's *chêvre* as he drizzled another spoonful of honey over it, 'there have been certain . . . moments, in the last ten years, when I have been very grateful for his . . . let us say, for his company.'

Jacquot took a bite of the cheese, savoured it. Sweet and fresh. The man didn't know what he was missing. And then, 'I will need to speak to him, of course, ask much the same questions as I have put to you.'

'Of course, monsieur. That is not a problem. I am sure he will be happy to help with your inquiry, though I should tell you that he is not the most forthcoming of conversationalists.' Ginoux spread his hands. 'So, monsieur, is there anything else I can help you with?'

'Just one or two questions. Your whereabouts after seeing Mademoiselle Ladouze in the cloister?'

'I went straight to my room. There was a documentary on Delacroix I wanted to see. Canal Plus.'

'And last night, I believe you ordered room service?'

Ginoux raised an eyebrow, smiled. 'I did indeed. Around 2.30, I think. I'd been working on some figures, hadn't realised how late it was.'

Jacquot took this in. 'Tell me, monsieur, how did you find the Master? When you were with him?'

Ginoux sighed. 'Not good, I'm afraid. Each time I come down, I fear the worst. He seems . . . less focused. He drinks a lot, I know. But it is more than that. The years are catching up with him. He is old, his mind is not what it once was.'

'But he can still paint.'

'He has his days . . . but his hands . . . I'm sure you have seen his hands.'

As if to underline this, Ginoux laid his own hands on the

table, lacquered fingernails shining in the light. 'So, Chief Inspector, how long do you suppose we will be held up here. For your investigation?'

Jacquot shrugged. 'A day or two at the most. As soon as I've collected statements from staff and guests and the weather changes to allow in our Forensic team. Is there some reason you might wish to leave earlier?'

'None at all, monsieur. How could I complain at having to spend a few more days at Le Grand Monastère? So, if there is anything further I can help you with, you know where to find me.'

Ginoux stood up from the table. It was clear he felt he had spent enough time being offered inferior wine and watching good food being abused.

Jacquot reached for his napkin and also stood. The two men shook hands and Paul Ginoux, with a small bow, excused himself.

Finishing his cheese, Jacquot called for the waiter and ordered some coffee. And a small calva. While he waited for them, he went over his conversation with Ginoux.

Everything tallied. Everything seemed above board. It appeared that Ginoux had nothing to hide, was happy to help. He may have had a motive – killing Ladouze to scupper Bressans' plans – but only if he'd known about those plans. And if he had known what was going on, if Vilotte had told him, then Bressans himself would have been the more logical target.

But then Jacquot couldn't quite see Ginoux hoisting Ladouze's body on to a hook – or even wanting to. Or, indeed, having too much success in a scuffle with Kónar.

Of course, there was always Dutronc to do it for him . . .

As soon as he could, he would have to have a little talk with the reticent Legionnaire.

The coffee arrived, the calva too. He sipped the coffee, swirled the calva. And as he did so, two further observations occurred to him.

Ghislaine Ladouze had no longer been wearing a headscarf when they found her.

And Monsieur Ginoux had no trace of a cut, scratch or graze on any of his immaculately manicured fingers.

84

'**M**ay I join you?'
Jacquot looked up with a start. It was Claudine. He jumped to his feet, offered her Ginoux's chair, which she took.

'I have just a few minutes. Gilles wanted me to help with this afternoon's session. Try to raise everyone's spirits.'

Jacquot glanced at the painters' club table. It was deserted, the waiters already clearing it. He hadn't noticed the group leaving. Through the Réfectoire's curtained glass doors he could see them working at their easels in the lobby.

'I am sure you will have no trouble doing that, mademoiselle.'

She smiled. 'Claudine, please.'

'*Très bien* . . . Claudine.'

'I'm afraid I have been a terrible policeman,' she continued. 'I have nothing to report. Everyone is terribly upset. I cannot imagine any of the group having anything to do with this . . . this . . .'

'My feelings exactly,' replied Jacquot, shaking his head. 'But please do keep watching and listening, you never know . . .'

Once again, Jacquot felt a strong desire just to lean across the table and kiss her. He hoped it didn't show.

And then, 'By the way, there is something you could help me with,' he began, trying to keep his mind focused. He should never have ordered the calva. And then there was that brandy earlier.

'Of course. Anything.'

'Delacroix. The painter. You have heard of him?'

She gave him a pained look. 'If I hadn't heard of Delacroix, Daniel, I would be a very poor artist and an even worse art historian.'

Jacquot savoured the sound of his name on her lips.

'Ferdinand-Victor-Eugène,' she continued. 'Born in Charenton-St-Maurice, 1798. Died in Paris, 1863. A fabulous colourist. Really very special. My favourite work is *Massacre at Chios*. There was a wonderful documentary the other night – I was glued to it. But what about him? What do you need to know?'

Jacquot waved her question away. She had told him all he wanted to know. 'Nothing, nothing important. I just . . . Anyway, tell me about your painters. What have you and Monsieur Gavan lined up for this afternoon?'

'The lobby – staircase, vaulting, pillars, cloisters. And chalks and pastels only. Basic tools, but the hardest to master. Joanne, the English lady, says she saw a patch of blue in the sky, but Gilles doesn't want to risk it.'

'And Madame Tilley?'

'She's there, too. Marcie tried to put her off, but she would have none of it.'

'So, a full house?'

'*Exactement*. Which reminds me,' she said, glancing at her watch. 'I mustn't be away too long.'

The two of them got up from the table and headed for the lobby.

'By the way,' she said, turning back to him. 'Did you notice anything when you came in for lunch?'

'Notice what?'

'The smell. In the lobby. Not music this time, but incense.' She pushed open the door and took a deep breath. 'Can you smell it? So far, it's just Gilles and I who've noticed it.'

Jacquot let the Réfectoire's door close behind him and stood beside her. He'd smelt nothing crossing the lobby on his way to lunch, but now the place seemed suffused with a thick, musky scent. The hairs on the back of his neck bristled.

And there, in the background, soft, distant . . .

'And voices . . .' he said. '*Écoute*. Like a kind of . . . chanting. Plainsong. Do you hear it?'

She smiled, brushed her hand against his sleeve, leaned towards him as though sharing a confidence. 'Gilles couldn't hear the voices.'

85

The *Anglaise* had been right, thought Jacquot. As he waited for van der Haage to answer his knock, he looked up at the sky through the cloister arches and spotted a patch of blue inching across the battlements. It was still some way away, but the storm was definitely passing, the rain less predatory than it had been when he and Madame Champeau had visited the Master.

Behind him, he heard the door open and turned.

'Ah, Monsieur van der Haage. I wonder if I might have a word?'

On the few occasions Jacquot had seen him, Lens van der Haage had been wearing a creased cotton jacket, thin needlecord trousers and an open-necked shirt. Now he was dressed in baggy blue jeans and a floppy white T-shirt that only emphasised his reedy frame, his eyes wide behind round tortoiseshell glasses.

'Monsieur Jacquot. Chief Inspector. Yes, please, come in.'

He pushed his glasses up on to the ridge of his bony forehead and ushered Jacquot in. 'Dreadful, dreadful. The whole thing. Claude and Régine are mortified.'

'They are not the only ones, monsieur,' replied Jacquot lightly.

Van der Haage didn't quite know how to take this remark. He gave an uncomfortable chuckle, said, 'Of course, yes, of course,' and closed the door.

Van der Haage's room was scrupulously tidy though no one from Housekeeping would have called by to make it so. The bed was perfectly made, the top of the writing desk almost geometrically arranged, and the towels which Jacquot could see in the bathroom were neatly folded, piled into a pyramid – largest at the bottom, smallest on top.

The only thing out of place was on open suitcase.

'You are leaving Monastère?' asked Jacquot, taking the chair by the desk while van der Haage perched on a corner of the bed.

'As soon as the road permits. And, of course, your investigation.'

'Is there not work to be done on the watchtower? I was under the impression that Monsieur Vilotte had agreed to move.'

'He did agree, and then he changed his mind. It seems I will have to wait a little longer to complete my work here.'

'I'm sorry to hear that, monsieur.'

'It is the way these things sometimes happen,' van der Haage replied wearily. 'So. How can I help, monsieur?

Not wishing to waste any time, Jacquot got straight to the point, asking much the same questions he'd put to Paul Ginoux. Did van der Haage know either Mademoiselle Ladouze or Monsieur Erdâg Kónar? When had he last seen them? The answers were predictable.

No, van der Haage knew neither guest, had spoken to neither of them and couldn't really remember when he had last seen them.

'I spend a lot of my time here, in my room, working. Or with Claude and Régine,' he explained. 'Otherwise . . .'

'I quite understand, monsieur.' And then, 'I notice you have injured your hand?'

Van der Haage glanced at the thin strip of plaster covering a knuckle on his right hand. 'Oh it is nothing. A graze . . .'

Jacquot got to his feet. 'Well, thank you for your time. It is greatly appreciated.'

'Anything I can do, Chief Inspector.'

86

Jacquot had probably spent no more than ten minutes with van der Haage, but when he stepped into the cloister he noticed immediately that the rain had stopped, and there was just the sound of water drip-dripping from the loggia roof on to the flagstone border of the lawn. The wind had dropped away, too, just a stiff breeze riffling through the palm fronds, and the thunder had moved south by the sound of it, grumbling irritably on the other side of the Lubéron highlands, bearing down on Aix and Marseilles. In the square of sky above him, canoe-shaped clouds raced across a thin blue sea.

Glancing at his watch, Jacquot decided that now was the moment to have a word with Maître Cancale, before the dinner service started and he was too busy to talk. Crossing the Monastère's inner courtyard, he hurried up the front steps and pushed through into the lobby where the painters were working on their scale and perspective jollied along by Gilles and

432

Claudine. The scent of incense was no longer detectable and any distant chanting was now replaced by the soft, irregular scruffing sound of chalk on paper and the bleating of a telephone behind the reception desk.

Jacquot was passing behind Naomi West, who'd selected the main staircase for her pastel study, when the concierge Didier beckoned him over. 'Monsieur, a call for you.'

Jacquot took the phone. It was Claude in Marseilles.

'After all the help I give you, and what do you do? Just send us the worst fucking rain we've ever seen. *Merci beaucoup!*'

'A bath will do you good, *mon vieux*. Take off your clothes, run into the street and enjoy.'

There was a 'pouff' down the line from Peluze. 'You've been too long in the country, *mon ami*. It's rotting your brain – the little you've got. But down to business,' he continued. 'Dutronc. Emile René. As you said – Belgian, like me. But not as warm or as friendly. A *Sergeant-chef* in the Second Regiment. Two Rep, we call it. And by all accounts, one of the real bastards. Initial training in Calvi where he signed up in 1962, aged twenty. No info before that – but then, in the Legion, that's no surprise. And as far as I can see, there's no police record either here or in Belgium. I put in a request with Interpol, but that will take a few days to come through. You know what they're like . . .

'Anyway, this Dutronc knocks up an exemplary record right from the start. Did the lot – and volunteered for it too. Mountain, desert, jungle and sea. Seems there's nothing he can't do.

'First posting in '63. Algeria. Stayed there, on and off, till the Legion got out in '67. Got out, mind. Not "withdrew". The Legion doesn't have a word for that – in any language! Anyway, Dutronc gets his third stripe and first serious mention in '76.

Djibouti, the school bus kidnap? Stormed a terrorist position across open ground in daylight. Single-handed. After that he transferred to the GCP – *Groupe Commando des Parachutistes* – and shows up in pretty much every action undertaken by the Legion: Chad, Lebanon, Zaire, you name it . . . Jesus Christ!'

Even Jacquot could hear the explosion. 'What was that?'

'Just the biggest goddamn thunderclap you ever heard,' replied Peluze. 'And right outside my fucking window, by the sound of it . . . Jesus Anyway, where was I? OK, OK, I got it. Dutronc. By '84, records are slim, which in the Legion means he's doing covert action. Last reference is January '86. Action on the Slovene-Croatian border. An extraction – some local warlord flexing his muscles – but everything went tits up. The word is the rebels knew the team were coming and organised a surprise party for them. Eight of the boys went in – usual configuration, two groups of four – but only your friend, Dutronc, got out. According to his debrief report, they were held in some farmhouse near Crjadj – that's a small market town close to the Slovene border. They were held there a week, beaten up, played around with. And then, *pour encourager les autres*, they were taken out each morning into the yard, the whole group, and one of them was shot. Slowly. Ankles first, knees, elbows, then a bullet in the head. In front of everyone. At the end of the week, Dutronc was the last one left, but somehow managed to make a run for it before his early morning call. He headed north towards the Italian border and they chased him the whole way. It took eight days but they cornered him in Trieste. He took three bullets and they left him for dead. Job well done. But somehow he survived, even made it back to the regimental base at St-Christol. Six months later, he takes retirement – full honours, full pension. And that's the last the Legion heard of him. Just a bank account in Paris where the pension's paid in.'

'And that's it?'

'*C'est tout*. Nothing after '86.'

'Thanks, Claude. I owe you.'

'That's what you keep saying, and I'm still waiting.'

'Book a table. I'm there.'

'Yeah, yeah,' growled Peluze. 'Heard it all before.' And then, quietly, 'A word of advice, old friend. This Dutronc character, he may be out of the Legion a few years but make no mistake, he'll still be some tough son-of-a-bitch.'

'I'll bear that in mind.'

'If you come across him, remember to be polite.'

87

Beyond the service counter with its line of warming lights, five chefs were working their stations, prepping the last of the vegetables, the fish and meats and sauces, the *pâtissier*, Luc, glazing his confections with a finely tipped brush. Now that the rain had eased, some of the staff had finally managed to make it up from Luissac.

Jacquot spotted Cancale immediately. He was standing at a carving board in the centre of the room, a smooth wedge of blood-red calf's liver flattened out under the palm of his hand, the blade of his knife slicing downwards and sideways into the meat.

'Thanks for the *rognons* at lunch. And the cutlets yesterday afternoon,' said Jacquot, watching a thin slice of liver curl away from the blade to crumple on the board. 'They were remarkable.'

'Salt,' said Cancale, glancing up from his cutting board, then settling his gaze back on the liver for another slice, the blade parting its glass-smooth surface, the pressure of his hand opening the flesh like a bloody grin. 'You always got to watch the salt. Remember what the animal eats. It stays in the meat. All that coastal grazing. Forget that and you've fucked it. Kidneys is different but it still comes down to the salt. A twist of the grinder a second before you take them out.' He waved his knife at the chefs around him. 'I tell 'em the whole time. Watch the salt.'

'I see you've cut your finger,' said Jacquot, nodding at Cancale's knife hand.

Cancale frowned, then lifted his right hand, inspected the plaster around the top of his middle finger. 'Occupational hazard,' he grunted, wiping the blade of his knife with a damp cloth – two swipes, one each side, handle to tip; holding the knife up to inspect the steel; then laying it down.

'Don't chefs normally wear blue plasters?'

'That's the theory,' grunted Cancale. 'But when the blood's pumping out, you don't bother too much about colour.'

'You do it here, in the kitchen, or at home?'

Cancale went to the sinks and ran tap-water over his bloodied hands. 'This one?' he asked. 'I don't recall. Plain plaster? It must have been at home. Even the best chefs, *hein*?'

Jacquot nodded. 'Any idea when?'

'Monsieur . . . I do it so often, I lose count. This? Couple of days maybe.' Without a thought he stripped the plaster from his finger and inspected the wound, sniffed it melodramatically. 'Two days – Saturday.' He rolled up the dressing and tossed it into a bin. 'So, monsieur, apart from your interest in my health, what is it I can do for you?'

And so Jacquot began – the same old questions.

'I just wanted to confirm that you did not know either of the guests – Mademoiselle Ladouze and Monsieur Kónar? That you had not seen or met them before?'

'Apart from my rounds in the dining room – meeting, greeting, shaking hands . . . Yup, that's it.'

'And the last time you saw them?'

Cancale leaned down, pulled a skillet from a shelf and clattered it on to one of the rings, his every movement measured, sure, seamless. It was, thought Jacquot, like watching the Master mix paint. A clove of garlic rubbed brusquely over the surface, a drop of olive oil and a smear of butter brought to a bubble, a sprinkle of pepper, followed by a single sage leaf. Cancale watched the leaf until it began to twist then flung in the two slices of liver.

'Like I said,' Cancale continued, raising his voice over the hiss and spitting, 'I get to speak to a lot of people. The guests. At their tables. But me, I'm standing, they're sitting; there's candlelight. You don't see so good, you know what I'm saying? As to when I last saw them . . .' He shrugged. 'The lady? To be honest I can't really say. The other one. The man? That would have been . . . after lunch Sunday. Down by the pool. You were there too, weren't you? Back when you were a journalist.'

Cancale shuffled the skillet over the fire and then, with a dexterous flip, the livers rose from the pan, turned in mid-air and hissed back on to the hot iron. It was expertly, almost unconsciously done. Not just one slice, but the two, at the same time. Jacquot wondered at it.

'And Friday night, early Saturday morning you were here? At the Monastère?'

'And Sunday night, too. In my apartment. Like I told you earlier,' Cancale replied, reaching thumb and forefinger into a bowl of sea salt and tossing the crystals on to the meat. Another shuffle, another toss and he was shovelling the weeping livers on to a plate. He took up a fork, cut off a corner and offered it to Jacquot. '*Voilà* . . .'

Jacquot took the fork and popped the liver into his mouth. It was sweet as honey, soft as mousse, singed with a scent of sage.

'Once again, remarkable, monsieur. Quite remarkable.'

'Timing,' said Cancale, taking back his fork and setting to work on the liver. 'It's all down to the timing. And salt.'

And then he turned, lifted his head, nose twitching.

'I can smell smoke,' he said.

Jacquot looked around to see if Bastien had stolen out for a cigarette. He hadn't. He was spooning stock into a copper-bottomed *saucier* with a rapt concentration.

'Can you smell it?' asked Cancale. 'It seems to be coming from . . .'

88

Philip Gould picked up the dice and cast them with a flourish on to the backgammon board. Across the table Marcie Hughes held her breath. The first die landed on a six, but the second spun and spun. The two players watched it weave across the board before it tapped against a counter and came to a halt. Another six.

'YES! Yes-yes-yes-yes-YES!' said Philip, pouncing on the last pair of counters outside his home board and slamming them down where one of Marcie's counters was about to break out and make a run for it.

The two of them were sitting in Philip's room, one game in, best of three, his door and all the windows flung wide open to let in the cool scent of rain-drenched stone and grass. The first to finish their sketching in the lobby, they'd decided on a game before getting ready for dinner.

'My throw, I think,' said Philip, admiring the bar he'd built up – every point, one to six, covered.

Marcie grimaced. 'Of all the low-down, lucky—'

'Skill, dearest one. And native cunning.'

But skill and native cunning were in short supply. Philip threw just the once, moving two of his counters before Marcie was back in the game, coming in on a six and leaping the bar with a five. His next throw was low and hers was high. Two minutes later Marcie was back in the game and sprinting for the tape. A double four and she had three counters left on the two-point, Philip just the two counters, on the five- and three-points.

He rattled the dice in his cup, then spilled them on to the board. No spin to stretch the agony. Just a one and three. He moved his counters, looked up and smiled at Marcie.

'A double would be useful,' he teased; it was the only throw that could win her the game.

So she threw it. Double one. Not enough. A single counter left.

Philip squeaked with delight. 'Oh dear,' he said, lifting his dice cup and shaking it like a cocktail mixer. 'Oh dear, dear, dear . . .'

'A double would be useful,' taunted Marcie.

'Or anything over a three,' he added and tossed the dice on to the board. Two and a one. There was a moment's stunned silence.

'And the girl from Tappahannock wins the game!' cried Marcie with delight and slapped her hands on her knees.

'Jesus H . . .' said Gould. And then, a frown settling across his features, he looked towards the door. 'Do you smell something burning?'

89

Claude Bouvet recognised the smell immediately. He was coming back across the Monastère's bridge and was feeling pleased with himself. Five minutes earlier he had stood on one side of the rent in the Luissac road and old Marol, the garage owner from St-Mas, had stood on the other. They had met up to assess the damage and consider how best to proceed. Both agreed that the cascade tumbling down the hillside was already greatly reduced in both force and volume and Marol confirmed that, if the rain kept off, he would be up first thing in the morning to see what he could do. He had a couple of sheets of steel panelling back in the workshop that should do the job, he told Bouvet, which they could lay across sleepers and secure with sandbags. It wouldn't be perfect, he'd warned Bouvet, but it would be enough to provide access to and from Monastère. The alternative, as Bouvet well knew, was waiting for the roads department to turn up, and, given the flooding and damage on more important routes than this one, it could be weeks before anyone got round to Monastère.

So Bouvet was feeling relieved as he set off back to Monastère – one problem sorted – and was breathing in that particular Provençal scent that he loved so much, the scent of passing rain, when another, more sinuous, scary note added itself to the brew.

It was two years since he'd last smelt it – a flash fire in the hills above St Raphaël – but he recognised it immediately. The only problem was there was no way it could be a forest fire. It was too early in the year and they'd just endured almost twenty-four hours of torrential and unremitting rain.

And then, seconds after identifying the smell and realising that it couldn't be a forest fire, Claude Bouvet saw the smoke.

Rising from the western corner of Monastère.

From this angle he couldn't see the watchtower, but he knew that was where the smoke was coming from.

With a suddenly pounding heart he broke into a run.

90

It was Champeau who raised the alarm. He'd been searching for a button in the second courtyard. It was the bottom button on his uniform waistcoat and the moment he realised it was gone, shortly after staff lunch, he could think of nothing else. He was certain it had been there when he dressed that morning, so sometime between then and his lunch-break it must have worked loose, dropped off. His mother would throw a fit if she noticed. And not much evaded her eagle eye.

Like all things in Champeau's world, the search for this missing button had been carried out with his usual mix of method and obsession. After turning over his bedroom, he'd moved to his mother's salon, their bathroom, and the small galley kitchen, crawling round on his hands and knees – peering under beds, kitchen units, any place where the small silver button could have rolled.

When he'd finished with the apartment, he'd set off in the

last of the rain for the Luissac road, where he'd gone that morning with Monsieur Bouvet and the *flic*, eyes raking the ground. Nothing.

Back at Monastère, he checked behind the reception desk, through the Salle du Matin, the kitchen, the cloisters, the loggia and the battlements before remembering the second court-yard. He'd been there right after lunch, helping Monsieur Og, as he called the Master, with some moving that needed doing. Maybe it had fallen off there.

Taking advantage of the last light and retracing his footsteps across the yard – easy to see in the rain-soaked sandy surface – he became aware of a strange smell in the air and a distant sound of crackling. He looked around, tried to locate the source, tried to identify the particular scent. He knew it was familiar. Rich, sweet and oily. Old wood. Paint. Spirits. Which made him turn towards the watchtower.

At first he could see nothing wrong, the stone no longer a pale gold in the setting sun but dark now and thrown into dusky shadow. And then . . . just a curl through the shuttered window on the first floor, a wisp of smoke. It seemed to have a life of its own, coiling around itself as it slid between the shutter slats, thickening as it rose into the air.

The thing that struck Champeau was that it somehow didn't fit with the tower. It was alien, something he'd never seen before. What could Master Og be doing? What strange spells was he casting now, what odd behaviour in the old man was manifesting itself in this ribbon of grey smoke even now seeping through the topmost shutters? Then he heard sounds again, louder this time: a crackle of wood and the sudden explosive smashing of a window. The first-floor shutters were flung open but instead of the Master, all Champeau could see was a twisting column of orange flame and black smoke spouting through the blasted window.

Fire . . . Fire . . . Fire . . .

The word came to him slowly, its significance somehow lost on him. For a moment he thought of La Fête de la Saint-Jean and he remembered how, years before, Monsieur Og had dared him to leap through the flames when there were still enough people living in Luissac to celebrate Midsummer's Eve with a traditional bonfire.

But that was years ago, and this was now. And there were still ages to go before Midsummer's Eve.

Which meant . . .

Fire!

Now the word hit home.

A fire. The tower was on fire.

For a moment Champeau wasn't sure what to do. He knew he had to do something, but he couldn't quite think, or remember, what it was.

And then . . . Of course. Fire drill. You raised the alarm.

He tried to shout 'fire' but the word somehow didn't make it into his mouth. He gave a little cough, even putting his hand in front of his mouth as Madame Régine and his mother had taught him. And now there was phlegm in his mouth, a really good piece with the kind of solid lungy texture that he knew, should he choose to try, he could probably spit as far as the colonnades. Maybe even to the roof. Maybe even over the roof.

And he was by himself, after all . . .

But a sudden roar distracted him. He looked back at the tower. Another window had burst open on the top floor and a second spout of flame crackled into the air, sparks now beginning to shower into the darkening sky . . . like flickering orange stars.

And then the word came back to him. Fire. It was a fire. It was dangerous. People could die. And then . . .

Old Master Og lived in the tower . . . Was Old Master Og in the tower?

Without a thought in his head beyond saving Master Og from the flames, Champeau spun on his heel and ran for the main courtyard. He needed help, he needed to tell someone. Monsieur Claude, or Madame Régine. Or Didier. Or someone. A fire. They had to do something. They had to put it out.

'Fire,' he called out, swallowing the gob of phlegm which for some reason he'd kept in his mouth.

'Fire! Fire! Fire! Fire!' he shouted.

And then, as he raced through the door into the cloister, he took a breath and screamed the word into the evening sky.

'FIRE! FIRE!'

91

Naomi West had just reached her room, was taking off her jacket and wondering whether she should run a bath or not, when she heard the boy Champeau calling out in the cloister.

It could have been no one else, she thought, the kind of grunting way he spoke. A hunchback. It would never happen back home, someone so clearly disadvantaged, in a job where people could see him. And in a hotel of all places . . . The French . . . They really were far behind the rest of the civilised world. By which, of course, Naomi West meant the United States of America.

She decided to leave the bath for a moment. There was a certain demented urgency about the boy's voice which demanded attention, so she opened her door and stepped out, almost bowled over by Philip and Marcie who were running down the corridor.

'There's a fire,' shouted Marcie. 'I can smell it. Has anyone seen Gracie?'

'Where d'ya think it is?' babbled Philip anxiously.

'The next courtyard,' said Naomi giddily, as they spun past her. 'There, look. It's smoke. It must be the tower.'

Ginoux's blood turned to ice. He had just put down the phone after confirming with his lawyer in Paris that the funds he'd requested had been duly wired through to the Master's account in Cavaillon when he heard someone shouting 'Fire' in the cloister below.

Some sixth sense told him that this was no practice drill and that it really was a fire.

The same sixth sense told him where the fire was.

Jacquot followed Cancale out of the kitchen, through the service doors and into the main dining room.

'Can you smell it now?' asked Cancale again. 'I tell you, there's a fire somewhere.'

Jacquot was certain that the spirits of Monastère were playing their tricks again and that Cancale had fallen for it. But then he, too, caught a whiff of something – something hot, acrid and cindery.

It did, indeed, seem like there was a fire somewhere.

And then, as they passed into the lobby, they heard what sounded very like the word *FEU!* out in the courtyard. And Champeau came bursting through the front door, hair wild, arms flailing, screaming the word over and over. '*FEU! FEU! FEU! FEU!*'

'*Merde*,' said Cancale. 'There really is a fire!'

And the two of them began to run.

Sitting at the bar, sharing *un coup* with Madame Bouvet, Lens van der Haage heard Champeau a split second after Madame

Bouvet. They both looked at each other, put down their drinks and hurried to the lobby where Champeau was now spinning like an out-of-balance top.

'*FEU! FEU! FEU! FEU!*' he cried, as Cancale and Jacquot raced past him.

In the corridor beyond the kitchen, close to the top of the stairs, Madame Champeau had stooped to retrieve a silver button from a gap between the flagstones. The button was wedged between the stones as though it had been trodden in, so deeply embedded that it was easy to miss. But Madame Champeau had an eye for such things. Yet despite her best efforts, the button would not be budged. It would take a screwdriver to lever it up, she'd decided, which was when she heard what sounded like her son's voice.

Hilaire Becque was standing in her underwear by an open window when she heard the hullaballoo outside. Reaching for a pair of jeans, tugging a cashmere polo-neck over her head, she opened her door and looked out. It seemed everyone was running to the door marked *Privé*, pouring through it like bathwater down a plug. Closing the door behind her, she headed in the same direction.

Roland Bressans followed everyone else, joining the crowd in the second courtyard, everyone brought up short by the scale of the conflagration, huddled together against the wall furthest from the blaze, the heat already too great to venture any closer.

It looked to Bressans like the funnel of a mighty ship spouting flame instead of smoke, a roaring, crackling tube of fire shooting upwards, a frenzied scatter of sparks dancing attendance. Now that the skies had cleared, you'd have been able to see it for miles. Why even now, the inhabitants of Roussillon and St Pantalèon and Gordes would probably be able to see the column of smoke rising into the sky, imagining maybe some eccentric and extravagant bonfire party to celebrate the passing of the storm.

But this, Bressans knew, was no bonfire party. This was no celebration.

This was the end of his dreams.

Damn the man, he thought. Damn him and damn him and damn him a thousand times over.

Only the architect, Lens van der Haage, seemed unconcerned.

'A natural funnel,' he observed, with quiet satisfaction. 'Like a chimney. And with the windows on the ground floor, a perfect flue.'

He tried to estimate the progress of the fire, stoked by the hanging sheets and the oily rags and the newspapers and the paints and the spirits that the Master left lying around. By now the studio floor would certainly have collapsed, and with the windows blown out and a wave of mouldy air sucked up from the basement to feed the blaze it wouldn't be long before the cross beams and stone-dry floorboards in the studio ceiling did the same, a river of fire racing ahead up the staircases, waves of it flooding through the old man's bedroom and up again into the projection room. Soon, any minute now, van der Haage estimated, the weight of the old man's bed would bring down the floor, further fuelling the flames until, finally, the top-most beams would tumble, timber on blazing timber, into the pyre below.

'Could it spread?' asked Régine beside him, suddenly

alarmed, concern for the recently completed renovations either side of the tower showing on her face.

'I don't believe so,' replied van der Haage and he raised his eyes to admire the gorgeous plume of flame roaring up into the darkening sky. According to the records it had survived one fire four hundred years ago. He had no doubt it would survive another.

Sure, there would be damage to the stonework but, so far as he could see, there was no way the fire could spread to the rooms either side of the tower, the conflagration confined within those thick, rounded walls. And right now there was nothing they could do anyway. Nothing a fire brigade could do to bring it under control. Even if the *pompiers* could get to them. By the time they arrived it would have burnt itself out. This blaze would be over sooner than any of them expected.

It couldn't have been planned more perfectly, he mused.

Apart from occasional glances at the fire, Jacquot kept his attention fixed on the crowd of onlookers – moving amongst them, watching their expressions: Paul Ginoux, pale with shock; Bressans, in a blue silk scarf, chewing the insides of his cheeks; Madame Champeau, shaking her head; Cancale, scratching his stubble in wonder; Claude Bouvet, open-mouthed, hardly breathing; Régine whispering to van der Haage whose round spectacles looked like fiery portholes; Meredith Branigan silently oh-my-gawding, oh-my-gawding; Philip Gould, arms round the shoulders of Marcie Hughes and Grace Tilley, pulling them into him; the *Anglaise*, Joanne, holding up her hand to keep off the heat; both Gilles and Claudine shivering with horror; and there, near the back of the crowd, Hilaire Becque, tears streaming down her cheeks.

As he stepped past Naomi West she reached for his arm and, shouting over the roar of the flaming pyre, asked: 'Is he in there? Is he in there?'

Breathlessly, Champeau pushed through the crowd until there was no one between him and the tower. He watched the flames, then turned, chuckling at the enormity of it all, to see the same fire flickering over the faces in front of him.

And then the thought struck him again, and he turned back to the tower, now exploding in a frantic shower of sparks that spiralled up into the sky.

Master Og. Where was Master Og? Surely, he couldn't be . . .

And then it all made sense. His wide, witless features creased with concern and in that instant he knew the old man was gone, heavenwards with the sparks.

92

As van der Haage had known it would, the fire burnt itself out surprisingly quickly. When he, Bouvet and Jacquot returned at midnight, after the rest of the company had gone to their rooms, as subdued a group of guests as Monastère had ever had, there was just a thin wisp of smoke rising into the moonlight, a ticking heat humming off the walls, and a shifting glow of orange light through the blackened windows.

With van der Haage leading the way they checked the newly renovated rooms on both sides of the tower. The walls here, van der Haage told them, were at least a metre thick, and the only indication that a fire had raged not three feet away was a cracked mirror on one wall, a few patches of blistered paint and a warm touch to the stone.

'There are no connecting or supporting beams to carry the fire,' explained van der Haage, as they trudged across the yard and back the way they had come. 'No way for it to burn through.

If, however, the fire had started in one of the suites, then we might not have been so fortunate.'

'Fortunate is not a word I'd use,' said Jacquot. 'A man died in that tower.'

'An old man,' retorted van der Haage, a hard edge to his voice. 'A man who very probably started the fire himself. We all know it, yes? The way he lived in there, it was bound to happen sooner or later.'

Jacquot gave the Dutchman a brief, chill look but made no reply. He knew as well as any of them how careless the Master had been – all those paint tins filled with spirit and jammed with brushes and palette knives, all those newspapers and magazines spread like a carpet across the floor, the stamped-out cigarette ends, cigar stubs and tossed matches. And that forest of sheets – hanging from the beams like stalactites, crusted with dried paint. Jacquot might not have liked the cool, considered tone, but van der Haage was right – the place was a blaze waiting to happen.

Trying to prove that it had been started deliberately, as Jacquot believed, and not accidentally, would be no easy case to argue.

Part Five

93

Jacquot came awake to a growing, percussive clattering. It had started as a distant drumbeat in some soon-to-be-forgotten dream, but while the dream faded the drumbeat somehow survived, pushing its way into his consciousness, drawing closer, passing overhead outside his window, rattling the shutters.

Thunder?

He tried to concentrate.

No, not thunder. The storm had surely passed.

And then he had it – the rotor blades of a helicopter beating through the still, morning air.

Jacquot leapt from the bed. He knew what was happening. He considered a shower and a shave, but dismissed it. Hopping on one leg and then the other, he pulled on trousers and hurriedly buttoned a shirt. There was no time to lose.

Jogging through the gateway of Grand Monastère, he turned to the left, his shadow reaching out in front of him. He felt good. The storm was past, the wind had died and the sun was already warm, casting the hollows of the Grand Lubéron into misty pools of shadow.

The chopper had circled and was coming in to land by the time he made it to the tennis court, a ledge of flat land cut into a slope of garrigue-covered cliff a few hundred metres beyond Grand Monastère. If a guest played too vigorously here, lobbed the ball too high, there was no ball-boy in the world who could ever retrieve it.

Coming to a halt at the side of the court Jacquot pulled his jacket together and watched the great machine settle. As he stood there, watching it come to a rest, it seemed that the rushing, blurring blades brought out the sharp wet cindery smell from the fire the night before, but a moment later it was snatched away.

With a shortening whine, as the skids connected with the ground, bouncing a little, the blades of the chopper slowed to a whoosh-whoosh-whoosh, slicing through the early morning air. Almost immediately a slide door was pulled open and a half-dozen bootee'ed figures alighted. All were dressed in white Nyrex suits. All were hooded and each man carried a silvered metal case. Only two of the figures were identifiable. Fournier, in his whites, but with the hood not up – the bald head immediately recognisable. The other figure, stooping apprehensively, far lower than any of the others, was his assistant from Cavaillon, Jean Brunet.

Seeing the familiar figures headed in his direction gave Jacquot a warm, coursing pleasure and he realised for the first time that, for the last three days, he had been on his own. As well as pleasure there was also a sense that the horrors of the last twenty-four hours could now be shared and, hopefully, brought to an end. A mystery solved. Somehow he was certain of it.

'Morning, boss,' said Brunet with a grin, trying to capture his whipping tie. 'Thought you might like some company.'

'Chief Inspector, *bonjour*,' said Fournier, coming up behind Brunet, his team depositing their bags outside the sweep of the blades before heading back to the chopper for the rest of their gear. 'Glad we could get to you. The flooding in the valley is not so bad now and most of the approach roads to St-Mas are open, but rather than take any chances, we borrowed the bird, stopping in Cavaillon to pick up your friend. So what do you have for us this time?' he said, his team gathering around them.

'Two bodies. Probably a third, but I don't expect there's much to find of the last.' In an instant, Jacquot remembered the previous night's flames reaching into the sky attended by a constellation of twisting sparks, the smell of old wood and white spirit leaching the night air, the warm burn on the cheeks, even at a distance.

They started walking toward Grand Monastère, gravel crunching underfoot, the group pausing to look back as the rotors picked up speed again and, with a clattering roar, the chopper lifted off and swung away down into the valley.

'There was a fire,' continued Jacquot. 'A bad one. There can't be much left. As for the other two, we've got a man and a woman. Caucasian. The woman died first. The man maybe forty-eight hours later. A single knife wound. I believe both bodies were moved post-mortem, and one, the woman, looks to have been partially buried.'

By now they were pushing through into the lobby, a number of guests coming down to breakfast, standing back to watch the forensic team follow Jacquot through the Salle du Matin and into the kitchen. In the corridor beyond, Jacquot led the way to the storeroom.

'I had the temperature turned as low as it would go, a few degrees above freezing,' said Jacquot as he pulled on the latch and swung the door open. 'She was hanging from a butcher's hook. The rail there.'

Fournier put down his case, its metal sides grating against the stone flags, and stepped into the room.

'You took her down from the hook?' asked Fournier with a tsk-tsk.

'It seemed the decent thing to do,' said Jacquot with a shrug.

'Decency, Chief Inspector, is not a science. You should know that. So the site has been compromised?'

'Correct. But, like I said, this is not the murder scene.'

'Nevertheless,' said Fournier, kneeling down and lifting the apron that covered the top half of Ghislaine Ladouze's body. The knees were slightly lifted and the skirt tucked between the thighs. From the knees down the skin was a soft, powdery grey like the branches of a dead tree.

'Pretty woman,' said Brunet stepping forward, looking over Fournier's shoulder.

'That's what they all tell me,' said Jacquot. 'But I only saw her like this.'

Fournier snapped on a pair of gloves and ran a finger down the length of the wound. He nodded. 'Like you say, probably a knife. Serrated edge.'

Jacquot noted the word 'probably'. Typical Fournier. Never a man to leave anything to chance. You never knew, in forensics . . .

'There's also sand between the fingers, in the hair, and on the floor, too. Which suggests, as you said, that she might have been buried somewhere.'

'I think I know where,' offered Jacquot. 'I'll show you later, if you like?'

'All in good time,' said Fournier and, pushing back on his heels, he rose effortlessly on to this feet, the Nyrex suit swishing.

Jacquot wondered how many times a day he repeated that particular movement.

Outside in the passageway, Fournier's boys were already at work, popping up the clasps of their cases, pulling on gloves, adjusting their masks. Just another day's work. One of them had already unpacked his camera and was shooting off frames of the corridor, the flashlight batting off the metal doors.

'And the other body?' asked Fournier.

'Downstairs. Another storeroom. I'll take you there,' said Jacquot, and he set off with Brunet, Fournier and a couple of his team following.

At the bottom of the stairs, he pointed to the right. 'Laundry Hall's down there, the body's this way.'

When they reached the storeroom, Jacquot switched on the light and pointed to the freezer. 'I turned off the power but kept the lid down,' he said. 'The body was frozen when I found it, but it's unlikely he'd been dead more than eight or nine hours. And I'm guessing a knife wound.'

Standing beside him, Brunet looked around the room, taking in the flaking stonework, vaulted ceilings and drapes of dusty cobwebs too high to be easily reached with a brush. Jacquot knew what his assistant was thinking. It was a room that suited its purpose, a place where the redundant, obsolete and broken were stored until they could be taken away.

Not unlike the body that one of the machines concealed within it.

'A single killer, do you think?' asked Brunet.

'I certainly hope so,' replied Jacquot, watching Fournier put down his case, kneel beside it and open it with a double click. He straightened the inside hinge arms and pulled out a mask, strapped it over his face. Getting to his feet, he went to the freezer and lifted the lid, pushing it as high as it would go, until the hinges screeched.

After peering down at the body for a few moments, he turned to Jacquot.

'I'll start in here, if that's all right?' he said, not expecting any argument, his mask puckering as he spoke. 'The chopper's coming back at four, so we don't have long. Soon as I can, I'll run you through what we find. Just surface stuff, for now – anything we pick up that may be useful – but no written reports until I get the bodies back to Avignon.'

'That would be good,' replied Jacquot. He'd worked with Fournier on three separate occasions – a car wreck in a gully near Brieuc, a tramp in a cellar in Maubec and the body of a teacher in a Cavaillon wine depot. The forensics man had a sharp eye, knew how sometimes the little things made all the difference, gave the poor inspecting cop something to chew on. Jacquot loved those little details.

Fournier turned to his colleagues. One was rigging up a couple of high-wattage lamps, the other pushing the plug into an electric point by the door. The room was suddenly thrown into a blast of aching-white light and lancing shadow, the still air filled with motes of dust they'd stirred up from the wreckage around them, dust the single caged bulb would never have revealed.

'Let's get some pictures first, Christophe,' said Fournier, getting down to business. 'The hall stairs and then in here.'

Fournier glanced at Jacquot and Brunet as though they were now surplus to requirements, would only get in the way.

Jacquot knew the look. 'If you need me, tell someone at the desk and they'll come and get me.'

Fournier nodded. 'Leave it to me.'

Jacquot nodded and he and Brunet headed back to the stairs.

'It's good to see you,' said Jacquot as they reached the top.

'You too, boss,' replied Brunet. 'Trust it hasn't been too harsh here at the Monastère?' Brunet's eyes glittered.

'Another life,' smiled Jacquot. 'But no. No complaints. Tell me, how are things going with the Italians?'

'Slow. As expected. Rochet's going to see if he can speed things up.'

'Good. And Maroc?'

'Just as you said. Local girl. Born Apt. Died in a car crash late sixties.'

'Record?'

'Not a thing.'

94

A blue umbrella sky. It was the first thing that came into Claudine's mind as she pushed open the shutters and leaned across the window sill, taking in the view of the valley below her and the distant slopes of the Monts de Vaucluse. Sinatra's 'blue umbrella sky', shot with splintered streaks of white cloud.

Gilles had woken an hour earlier. She'd heard him shower, come back into the bedroom, dress and then, quietly, leave the room. And all the time, as she lay there in their bed, pretending to sleep, she'd thought of the policeman, Jacquot, trying to remember the last time she'd woken up in her bed and thought about a man.

A long time, she decided, watching the swallows dart through the air. Eighteen months since she'd found her husband in bed with her best friend and in all that time no one had come close. They'd tried, of course – a friend of her husband's (the nerve), a graduate student on the summer course she'd taught at the College of Fine Art in Aix, the picture framer in Cavaillon six months single after a bitter divorce – but they'd got nowhere, coming up hard against the thick, cold shell she'd cased around her heart.

The thing was, after eighteen months, she wasn't used to it – this change in her mood – wasn't certain how to respond, whether she should allow herself to respond. But that was ridiculous, she chided herself. She should open up, let herself go. And it wasn't as if she didn't know him. She'd met him before, in Marseilles, so she was hardly throwing herself at him. And he was so . . . comforting. That was the word. So big and . . . and gentle. Unlike all the others who'd tried their luck, she felt no threat from him – in any way – just a kind of vulnerability that he brought out in her. She wanted, she realised, more than anything, for him to wrap those arms of his around her . . . And she had a feeling he wanted to do exactly the same thing.

She mustn't let it slip, she was saying to herself, she mustn't close down, when, leaning there at the window, she heard it. A distant hammering that, as it drew closer, seemed to throb through the air like a giant pulse.

At first she looked up into the sky, trying to find the source of the noise – a helicopter, it was a helicopter – but then her eye was drawn to a black shape the size of a beetle chasing its shadow across the valley beneath her, no more than fifty metres above the lavender fields of Calavon and heading in their direction. As she watched, it suddenly reared up and, seconds later, battered overhead, close enough for her to see the metal panels riveted to its belly, a vicious, roaring downdraught spilling across her upturned face.

Downstairs in the Salle du Matin, Gilles was sitting with

the painters – all but Madame Becque and Naomi West, both of whom, Gracie informed her, had decided to take their breakfasts in their rooms. 'Poor Hilaire sounded quite shattered,' confided Gracie. 'But you ask me, that Naomi is just playing it for all it's worth.'

Marcie leaned over the table, a buttered croissant in her hand and a crumb of it in the corner of her mouth.

'The cavalry's arrived. You hear it? According to Didier, it's to be fingerprints and statements most of the morning . . .'

'But the good news is,' added Gilles, finishing his coffee and reaching for the pot, 'that the road to Luissac should be open by lunchtime. So, as soon as the gendarmerie have finished with us, and since, I regret to say, there is now no opportunity to meet with the Master . . .' – a sad hum of murmuring shifted around the table – 'I would like to propose a last group outing. To Roussillon. It's not far and the ochre cliffs . . . well, you won't believe it. Seventeen different shades of red, the locals will tell you. And just as many yellows.' He looked around the table. 'If you're up to it, that is?'

'A great idea,' said Philip, wiping the corner of his mouth with his napkin and getting to his feet. 'Get some fresh air into us, do us all the world of good.'

Gilles turned to Grace and Marcie. 'What do you think?'

'I agree with Philip,' said Marcie, and Grace, beside her, nodded.

'Just the thing,' she said. 'Joanne? What about you?'

'What do I need to bring?' she laughed. 'Point the way.'

'So,' continued Gilles, 'why don't we meet in the lobby at midday. And if it's just the six of us, we can all fit in the van. I'll have Monsieur Cancale prepare some lunch baskets, so there's no need to worry about anything.'

'Bravo,' said Philip, patting his tummy.

As the group chattered on, Claudine went to the buffet and helped herself to fruit and yoghurt. She was on her way back to the table when the service doors to the kitchen swung open and Jacquot appeared, heading in her direction and talking to another man, presumably another policeman. Jacquot caught her eye, held up his hand to the other man and came over.

'As you've probably heard, the forensic team is here.'

'I saw them arrive,' replied Claudine, feeling uncertain about her voice. She cleared her throat.

'I can't talk now. But . . . maybe I'll get to see you later?'

She knew immediately he wasn't talking about the investigation and her heart started to thump. She could tell there was something else on his mind – even if he was busy.

'*Mais bien sûr*,' she replied. 'I'd like that.'

And then, with no hint of warning, he leaned forward, held her shoulders and kissed her. Just like that. A little clumsily maybe, on the side of the lips, but a kiss all the same . . .

A kiss. A kiss.

And his eyes were closed. His eyes were closed!

And then, before she had time to respond, to say something, he had turned and followed after his friend. And she was left standing there, a yoghurt in one hand and an apple in the other, staring after him, feeling her legs start to tremble.

'Claudine? Claudine?'

It was Gilles. She turned towards the painters' table.

'Joanne was saying that she seems to have run out of yellows. Do you have any?'

Claudine came to. 'Yes, of course. No problem,' she said, taking her seat.

Joanne smiled. 'You are kind. Thank you,' she said. And then, eyes twinkling, she leaned towards Claudine and whispered, 'He is rather dishy, isn't he?'

And Claudine felt a hot blush race up into her cheeks.

'Yes . . . Is he . . . ? Do you think so? Yes, I suppose he is. The detective, you mean?'

Joanna didn't say another word. She didn't need to.

95

U p in Jacquot's room Brunet sat in the chair by the writing desk, legs straddled around it, arms hanging loose over the back. It was how he sat in Jacquot's office back in town. Probably the way he sat at home – watching TV, eating a meal; you rarely saw Brunet take a chair in the conventional manner. Only a year in Cavaillon, but Jacquot knew his assistant's ways, the man's style. Working so closely with someone, it wasn't difficult.

He was a fine assistant, too, one of the best. Knew what you wanted before you asked, and knew how to get it – by fair means or foul; the latter, Jacquot suspected, more often than the former. For the last twenty minutes, hardly moving, he'd listened intently to Jacquot's take on the murders – time frame, background, characters. He knew the names, he knew the players, now he was finding out how they worked. The dynamics of the group, as Jacquot saw it: Bressans and Ladouze; Kónar and the actress; the Bouvets and Vilotte; the various members of the painting group; the architect, the art dealer, and the dealer's *gorille*, the Belgian Dutronc.

Jacquot was succinct and to the point, briefing Brunet but also testing out some of his arguments, putting into words his own theories. Brunet knew better than to interrupt. It was the way his boss worked. The way any good detective worked, saying it out loud, threading the beads together, matching the shapes and colours until finally you had yourself a necklace.

'So who's in the frame here? Guest, staff or outsider?' asked Brunet, when Jacquot finished.

'Not an outsider. It just doesn't work for me. Comes in, does the job and disappears? Then does it all over again two days later?' Jacquot shook his head. 'It's got to be someone closer. Possibly staff, but more likely one of the guests. I've got it down to three. Motive, means and opportunity. The only trouble is one of them wouldn't have had the strength to carry the bodies.'

'An accomplice? Two of them working together? Two killers?'

Jacquot shrugged.

'You want to tell me the three?'

'Not just yet. Do the rounds, introduce yourself, ask a few questions. Then tell me what you think. You got a print kit?'

'Never leave home without it,' replied Brunet, nodding to the shoulder bag by his chair.

'Good. It'll be a way in. Oblique, chit-chat. Catch them with their guards down.'

'What about statements?'

'Not much point. Ladouze and Kónar died at night. Probably late at night, early morning. Apart from the room service boys, and Didier and Champeau on the front desk, everyone else will have been in bed. Or tell you that's where they were. And there's no one to say they're lying – apart, of course, from Mesdames Tilley and Hughes who share a room. As for the fire, try and establish where everyone was between, say, four and seven.'

'Also, in the desk there . . .' Jacquot pointed to the drawer.

Brunet turned and slid it open. 'The envelope?'

'Get it down to Fournier,' continued Jacquot. 'I know I'll forget . . . Tell him I found it here, in the bath.'

Brunet frowned.

'This is Ladouze's old room, where she was killed. I believe the killer left it here. Also, he'll want to snoop around. Tell him I've been as careful as I can . . .'

'Right,' said Brunet. 'He'll be a lot happier knowing that.'

'And, finally, I want you to chase up a Christian Clénord. He's Vilotte's doctor in Cavaillon. Cours Bournissac. I need to find out about these drugs.' Jacquot tore out the page from his notebook where he'd written down the names and handed it to Brunet. 'What are they for? What do they do? And everything you can get on Vilotte's state of health. If the good doctor refuses to help, tell him that his patient is now sadly deceased so confidentiality can take a hike. And if that doesn't work, tell him you'll be round to his surgery in five minutes with a half-a-dozen gendarmes. That should persuade him.'

'*C'est fait,*' said Brunet.

96

Bressans opened the door, saw who it was and left Jacquot to close it behind him. He returned to his briefcase on the writing desk, sorted through some papers. He did not invite Jacquot to sit.

'I heard a helicopter,' he said, his back to Jacquot. 'Your team?'

'My team, yes.'

Bressans slapped down the lid of his briefcase, spun the combination lock, then turned to face Jacquot.

'I have been very patient, Chief Inspector. But I really cannot afford to remain here any longer.'

'I quite understand, monsieur. And you are free to go, of course.'

As Jacquot expected, this easy agreement startled Bressans. 'You have a killer?'

'Not yet, monsieur. But it will not be long.'

Bressans smiled. 'And it's not me?'

'No, monsieur, it is not.'

'Do you know who?'

Jacquot held up his hands. 'At this moment . . . I just don't think it's you.' Though I would dearly love it to be, he thought to himself.

'Maybe I should hold on,' said Bressans with a sly smile, lips glistening. 'To see the close of play.'

'As you wish, monsieur,' replied Jacquot, noting the sporting reference, wondering to himself whether Bressans had found out about his sporting past. It seemed a likely bet. He'd probably checked him out straight after that first meeting on Saturday afternoon. Another call to his uncle. Who is this man, Jacquot? How good is he? What do we know about him? Is he open to persuasion? Can he keep his mouth shut? Aaahhh, he's that Jacquot, is he? The one who scored the try? Yes, of course . . . Now I know the name . . . Something along those lines, Jacquot guessed. A man like Bressans wouldn't have wasted a moment finding out about the opposition. It's what he did, after all.

There was a moment's silence. And then Jacquot spoke: 'If you don't mind my saying, you seem surprisingly . . . relaxed at the loss of your ambitions, monsieur. All that work, that planning, the expense. All gone up in smoke.'

Bressans shrugged, as though used to these kinds of setback. 'It is a tragedy, of course. A great loss.'

Jacquot nodded, as though in agreement. 'Tell me, monsieur, before you leave us. How did you find out about Céleste?'

Bressans paused, gave Jacquot a long, calculating look.

Jacquot knew what he was thinking. Was this a trick?

'The man himself. The Master. He told me about her,'

replied Bressans, somehow sensing it was safe to answer. 'The second time I visited. February, March. He was drunk, maudlin. I shall never forget the look in his eyes, clinging to the past, hopeless for the future. If you ask me, he was losing his talent, as well as his mind. Or maybe one led to the other – whichever way round it was. But it was crystal clear to me how important she had been to him. I think Céleste was the woman who influenced him more than any other. And nearly ruined him.'

'Ruined? How do you mean, she "ruined him"?'

'Well, he was clearly in love with her. That's how it sounded. Loved her to distraction, but didn't get much in the way of return. I got the impression that she was a hard nut, that she seemed to take pleasure in criticising him, his work, the way he lived. She mocked him. Told him he couldn't paint. That he was not the artist he thought he was. It undermined him.'

'So why have Ghislaine Ladouze impersonate her? Wasn't that a risk? That he might turn on her?'

'That was not my reading of it, Chief Inspector. Not at all. Céleste left him, remember? And for nearly thirty years all he wanted was a second chance. To have her come back. So he could show her what he'd done and . . . and, maybe, finally, earn her approval. And that's how I told Ghislaine to play it. I thought if I could engineer such a rapprochement, then maybe the new Céleste could persuade him to show his works, to be proud of them, and thereby claim his stake in art history.'

'Through your patronage?'

'You have to admit, Chief Inspector, it was inspired.'

'Tell me, monsieur, how did you come by the film? How did you know such a film existed?'

'Why, he showed me, Chief Inspector. He took me to the top floor and played me all those old films. Of her. And the more I admired her, the more he showed me. That's when the idea came to me.'

'And some time after that you stole one of the films.'

Bressans waved his finger. 'Borrowed, Chief Inspector. Borrowed. I had every intention of returning it. He got drunk again. I put him to bed, then went back to the top floor. There were many films there. These tin canisters. I took just the one. The first he showed me.'

'And Ghislaine?'

Bressans sighed, shook his head. 'She could have been Céleste's twin. With a bit of work the likeness was extraordinary.'

'How long did it take you to find her?'

'Between my last visit and now. I had a photograph printed off the film, showed it to Madame de Ternay, and asked if there was anyone she knew.'

'And she did? Just like that?'

'One or two possibles, but I knew immediately that Ghislaine was the one. And I was right. When I picked her up last week, when I saw her in the gypsy dress, the way she wore her hair. It was uncanny. And it worked. She had him. Even posed for him, I think.'

'And then someone killed her.'

Bressans spread his hands. 'As you say . . .'

'So who do you suppose would do such a thing?'

'My first thought, of course, was Vilotte. That maybe she'd gone too far. Or he'd seen through her. Vilotte follows her to her room, kills her. But Vilotte was old, and sick. I have no doubt he *could* have done it – in some blind, old-man rage – but there was no way he'd have been able to move her to wherever it was you found her. A storeroom, wasn't it? No, no, no. It would have been far too much for him . . .'

'And your second thought?'

'Ah,' said Bressans, as though he'd just remembered. 'My second thought, yes. Now this, I think, you will find interesting. Of course I can't be certain, which is why I didn't bother mentioning it earlier, but I don't believe that this was the first time that Ghislaine had been here. To Monastère. Of course she said it was, but girls like her, professionals, they know the ropes. Know, for instance, that clients never like to hear that they've been somewhere before – with someone else, if you know what I mean. So they put on an act for the client. What a fabulous place. How clever you are. But she didn't fool me. There was something about the way she behaved here. With a certain . . . familiarity.'

'So you believe she had been here before? With another client?'

Bressans smiled. 'She knew where everything was, Chief Inspector. Knew where the light switches were, knew how to open the bedroom door, knew the sheets were Frette . . . that sort of thing. How else could she know, unless she'd been here before? It is, after all, the kind of place where ladies like Ghislaine are often brought.'

'You think someone recognised her?'

'It's possible.'

'Someone with a grudge?'

'Maybe, Chief Inspector. Or maybe something to hide?'

'No one I have spoken to has said they recognised her. That she was familiar. The staff. Guests.'

Bressans gave a shrug. 'Well, there you are.'

'There's something you're not telling me, monsieur.'

Bressans shook his head, smiled sadly. 'I have told you every-thing I know. Maybe more than I should. These observations – about Ghislaine having come here before? The possibility that someone recognised her? They are simply that. Observations. But perhaps you will find them useful. Perhaps, Chief Inspector, they will lead you to your killer.'

97

Jean Brunet was lugging his satchel through the doors leading to Le Réfectoire as Jacquot came down the main stairs, heading for the front desk. They met in the centre of the lobby.

'I feel a lunch coming on,' said Brunet with a grin. 'You should see them in there. Madness. But the food . . . There's a *gigot pré-salé,* poussins, three kinds of *confit,* and a *daube de lotte* that tastes like . . . well, you wouldn't believe. I've never seen anything like it. They're working some kind of magic in there. It must be illegal. Someone's got to do something about it.'

Jacquot smiled. 'So how's it going?'

'Staff done, now it's the guests.'

'Any plasters on fingers?'

Brunet frowned, gave it some thought. 'Just about all of them. I never knew Monastère was such a dangerous place.'

'Blue plasters?'

'That's right. In case it comes off in the *daube*. Easier to find.'

'So, what did you make of them?'

'Nice enough lot. Cancale looks a bit of a monster, but that Madame Champeau, down in her grotto . . .' Brunet shivered. 'Face like a hawk, hands like talons. You know what her christian name is?'

Jacquot shook his head. He hadn't thought to ask, but wasn't surprised that Brunet had.

'Félice,' said Brunet with another grin. 'Don't you think it suits her? But her boy's a good 'un. Not all there, of course, but his heart's in the right place. Been following me around since I started with the kit. Wanted to be the first to go. And now he's the expert. Telling everyone how to roll the fingertip on the pad, handing them wipes afterwards. Sweet lad.' Brunet adjusted the bag on his shoulder. 'Oh, by the way . . .'

'Yes?'

'All that food back there, I nearly forgot. Fournier said to tell you you were right. Both victims were stabbed. But with different knives. The girl, a small blade with a serrated edge. The man, larger and longer with a smooth edge.'

98

Régine Bouvet was sitting at her desk. She was speaking on the phone. *'Oui, je suis désolée, monsieur.'* When she spotted Jacquot standing at Reception she waved him through into her office. It was brightly lit – a half-dozen downlighters set around the vaulted office – and neatly arranged. Filing cabinets, fax machine, a large wall calendar, a pot of orchids on a window sill that looked out on to a corner of the inner courtyard, and two desks facing each other – Régine's far more ordered than her husband's. As she spoke, she leafed through a reservations book and held a pencil in her hand. Jacquot could see that half a dozen names had already been scribbled out.

'Oui, absolument. La route est très bien inondée, et à ce moment l'hôtel reste inaccessible. Peut-être un autre soir? Oui? Jeudi soir. Bien sûr. Voilà, monsieur! Je vous en prie ... De rien, de rien. Merci. À jeudi, monsieur.'

Régine put down the phone with a *'pouff alors'* and turned to Jacquot who had taken her husband's chair. 'Twenty bookings in Réfectoire for tonight, and another twelve for tomorrow lunch. Until the road is properly fixed, what can I do? Claude says it will be fine. Me, I'm not so sure. If there was an accident . . . ? It's simply not worth it.' She gave him a what-do-you-think look.

'Better to be safe than sorry, madame.'

'Exactement. The council say they can get a team up tomorrow, but you know councils. And we have new guests waiting. Some more Americans. Six of them. Holed up in Cavaillon until they can get through. And yesterday the fire. And, of course, we have the murders. I try not to think of it, but every time I go into the kitchen . . . well . . .' she shivered, spread her hands as though unable to find the right words. Then she gathered herself. 'So, Chief Inspector, how is everything progressing? Will your people be here long? It's a little – how shall I say – disconcerting, having them troop around in those white suits.'

'The team will be here until four, madame. And they may well have to come back during the week. As for their suits, well, you could always tell your new arrivals that they are . . . pest controllers?'

A horrified look crossed Régine's face, and then she began to chuckle. 'I am sorry, Chief Inspector, you will think me a terrible woman – and I know it must sound horrible – but when you run a hotel it's difficult to decide which is worse. Cockroaches or murder.'

Jacquot laughed too. He hadn't thought of it like that. And then: 'Tell me, madame, do you happen to know the name Maroc?'

'Maroc? Maroc? You mean the Luissac Marocs? Of course

I do. *La Famille Maroc* used to run the bakery here. Just off the main street. For a long time we were neighbours. Mother refused to live in the hotel. Said it was haunted. So we moved down there, just two doors away.'

'And the name . . . the family . . . were they . . . ?'

'Moroccan? *Non, non, monsieur*. That is just a coincidence. Sometimes names have echoes, you know. They make you think the wrong things, or mislead you. *Par example*, we have a guest who comes here each year. Monsieur Bonn. He is a *négociant*. He lives in Bordeaux. We buy much of our wine from him. But he is not German. And he has never been to Bonn. We laugh about it.'

Jacquot smiled.

'And then there's Monsieur Ginoux, of course.'

Jacquot frowned, his interest piqued. 'Ginoux?'

'You don't recognise the name.'

Jacquot shook his head. 'I know he's a guest, but . . . no. No, I don't.'

'Well, Monsieur Ginoux is an art dealer, right?'

'Yes.'

'But there is another Ginoux, *n'est-ce pas*?'

'I'm afraid, madame . . .'

'Why, van Gogh, of course. His painting *Café de la Nuit*? In Arles? *En effet*, the café that van Gogh painted was the Café de la Gare. And the *propriétaire* of Café de la Gare was . . . Monsieur Joseph Ginoux. He is in the picture itself, standing by the billiard table. The same man who, though van Gogh believed him to be his best friend, finally betrayed him. Signed the petition that saw him taken off to that asylum in St Rémy. And van Gogh never found out that it was Ginoux. Terrible.'

'You know a lot about art, madame.'

'This and that. It's my friend Gilles . . . But I'll tell you something else that is funny,' she continued, 'Monsieur Ginoux's address? In Paris?'

Jacquot tried to recall the details, the notes he had taken, the lists of guests that Claude Bouvet had given him.

And then he remembered.

Jacquot and Régine said the words together: 'Allées des Fauves.'

'*C'est ça, exacte.*' She clapped her hands. 'Matisse, Vlaminck, Derain . . . the wild beasts. An art movement, *n'est-ce pas? Les Fauves. Fauvistes. Fauvisme*. But it is all coincidence, of course. Just coincidence. Though Monsieur Ginoux did once admit to me that he bought his home in Paris as much for the address as the house itself. Not that he is a wild beast, of course. A kitten,' Régine continued. 'Always so polite, so charming, so quiet. And his room, during his stays with us, when he leaves . . . always spotless. The towels folded, the bathroom sink as if it has never been touched. The bed made even though the linen is changed daily. Most guests—'

'Coming back to the Marocs, madame. I believe there was a daughter?'

'Céleste,' said Régine without a moment's hesitation, as if she knew what Jacquot was after.

'That's the one.'

'A beauty. But *une tigresse*. Every man and boy in the district was after her. They say . . .' – Régine lowered her voice – 'they say, for a long time, that she was the Master's mistress. Auguste Vilotte. And by all accounts it was a fiery . . .' – she put a hand to her mouth – '*Je m'excuse* . . . it was a tempestuous affair.'

'And what happened to her. To the family?'

'I was young, maybe nine or ten. The old man died at his ovens, I remember that. And Madame soon after.'

'And Céleste?'

'She was much older than me. After her parents died, she moved away. To Apt, I think. An aunt. After that . . . I don't know what happened to her.'

'Did her affair with Vilotte continue after she left?'

'Who knows? As I say, it was a long time ago. I was young.'

'One final thing, madame. The watchtower. Now that the Master is dead, the property will revert to you?'

Régine shot him a look, any friendliness momentarily put on hold. 'But of course, Chief Inspector. Monsieur Vilotte only ever had his father's lease. And since there are no dependants or heirs, and only a few more years to run . . . So, the property is ours again.'

Jacquot gave it some consideration, then smiled. 'Thank you, madame, you have been most helpful.'

99

Paul Ginoux was having lunch in Le Réfectoire, at a table by the windows. With the storm now past, the glass panels had been slid open, a shifting breeze catching at the drapes, the sunshine splashed across the terrace momentarily turning to shadow as tatters of cloud scurried south as though late for an appointment.

Like Bressans, Ginoux looked remarkably relaxed for a man who had lost everything he had set his heart on. There was a calm about him. His knife and fork worked the plate and he ate his food with unhurried ease. Another day, another meal.

As Jacquot approached his table, Ginoux looked up, smiled.

'Do you mind if I join you, monsieur?' asked Jacquot.

'Not at all, Chief Inspector. Please, take a seat. A glass of wine, perhaps?' He indicated the bottle on his table, the napkin collared around its neck failing to conceal the Château's celebrated label and vintage.

'It is a great temptation – even if it's not a Lubéron – but on this occasion, I regret I must pass.'

'You need to keep a clear head,' said Ginoux with a small smile.

'*Exacte*. A clear head.'

Jacquot watched Ginoux get back to his food, astonished to see the crisp coat from his duck *confit* lifted off and deposited on the side of the plate. Not to be eaten. Discarded. Instead, Vilotte's dealer concentrated on the flaking red meat beneath. Jacquot wondered at the waste. Couldn't believe it. Was tempted to lean across and help himself to that glorious, unctuous skin. The best bit, he always thought.

'Tell me,' Jacquot began. 'You are leaving today?'

'If I can, it would be most convenient.'

'You are free to go, monsieur, of course. It's just . . .'

'Just?'

'Just a long way to drive to Paris. If you leave now, it will be late . . .'

'I will not be driving straight through. There is business I must attend to in Lyons. That is as far as I will go today. Then, tomorrow, there is a colleague in Geneva I will visit. After that, my driver will take me home.'

'So tell me, monsieur, apart from the loss of the Master, has your trip here been successful?'

'If you mean, do I have the paintings I came for, then no, it has not been a successful trip. A price had been agreed, but I had still to take possession.'

'I am sorry to hear that, monsieur.'

A waiter appeared, cleared away Ginoux's plate and cutlery, the bread basket, the butter. Another waiter appeared to brush crumbs from the cloth. By the time the last crumb had been swept away, a *plateau du fromage* had been brought to the table, a clean plate, a knife.

Ginoux thanked the waiter, turned back to Jacquot. 'Some cheese, Chief Inspector?'

Jacquot shook his head. 'Tell me, monsieur. Did you like your client?'

Ginoux chuckled. '"Like" is not the word I would use,' he replied, cutting himself a thin wedge of Camembert. 'Admire, certainly. He is . . . was a great painter. Maybe not quite of the first order, but very, very high in the pantheon. Not quite genius, but very, very close.' Ginoux examined the cheese he'd cut and put it into his mouth. 'And despite the terrible loss,' he continued, 'there are compensations. There may be no more new Vilottes, but those that remain will rise sharply in value . . .' Ginoux checked himself.

'You have Vilottes of your own?'

'Small ones only,' replied Ginoux modestly. 'From the beginning, right from the very start, I knew that Vilotte would be big. And over the years I kept back one in every six Vilottes I sold, each time choosing the smallest, the least attractive, the least saleable, and paying anonymously the lowest amount that I could get away with. Quietly, over the years, I have collected eleven canvases. As an investment.'

Jacquot smiled. A slippery eel indeed. 'And what of his own collection?' he asked. 'Vilotte's private collection?'

Ginoux's expression gave nothing away. He cut another slice of the Camembert and ate it slowly, thoughtfully.

'Without question,' said Ginoux at last, 'and with the greatest respect to the Master, that, in my opinion, could be by far the more tragic loss. I never saw what he had and, as far as I know, nor did anyone else, but, like everyone in my world, I heard the stories. At the end, you know, Picasso wouldn't have him in the house. Said he'd seen Auguste stay at a restaurant table to settle the bill but pocket anything they might have drawn, sketched, noted down. Unlike the rest of them – Picasso particularly – Vilotte didn't so much steal ideas or styles as . . . memorabilia. As if he'd known that one day all those scraps of paper he's supposed to have picked up and kept would be worth something – if things turned bad for him, perhaps.'

'Which of course they would be.'

'If it's true, which I believe it may be, then yes,' Ginoux continued, selecting another piece of cheese, his knife playing between a *chêvre* and the Camembert. He plumped for the Camembert again and spread it over a crust of bread, popped it into his mouth. 'Yes, it would likely have been a most valuable collection. He knew them all . . . Matisse, Chagall, Picasso, Dufy, Miró, Dalí – there was hardly an artist of note from the twentieth century who did not, at some stage or other, share a drink or a meal with the Master. Of course, it's hard to say what he might have collected. The quality. The completeness. But . . .' Ginoux spread his hands at what might have been.

'This supposed collection of Vilotte's,' said Jacquot lightly. 'Did you know that Monsieur Bressans was making a play for it, planning a way to secure it?'

'If it existed, monsieur. If it existed. As I said, the Master has never shown anything. Nothing of it has been seen. As for Monsieur Bressans . . .' Ginoux said the name with a condescending smile, a real dealer considering a pretender.

'But you knew what he was up to?'

Ginoux waved his knife. 'It was not difficult to guess. At first I thought he'd be after Vilottes. The self-portraits perhaps. For his . . . museum. And then it struck me that perhaps he'd been taken in by the stories he'd heard. The stories we've all heard. But the girl . . . I have to admit the girl was a brilliant touch.'

'You knew about Ghislaine Ladouze?'

'Again, I guessed. At first I thought he'd brought her as a kind of . . . incentive. And, as I told you, she was a quite charming creature to look at.'

Ginoux took the last of the Camembert and smeared it on to a piece of bread. 'But it wasn't until I passed her on the stairs on Friday evening that I realised what Monsieur Bressans was really up to. Most inventive. You had to give him credit.' Ginoux put the cheese in his mouth and chewed appreciatively. 'And the Master fell for it. No question. When I saw him the following day, he was quite beside himself. Quite irrational. Confused. It was a mean trick to play.'

'And what alerted you to this plan? Mademoiselle Ladouze?'

'It was the scarf in her hair. The gypsy dress. The moment I saw her dressed that way . . . well, I recognised her immediately. I had seen the original after all. Photos the Master had shown me. And the films, of course. At first I couldn't understand . . . This girl, what was she doing impersonating Vilotte's great love? And then I realised. There could be only one answer. Monsieur Bressans was up to no good.'

'And is that why you killed Mademosielle Ladouze? To scupper his plans? To get rid of the competition?'

Ginoux had been reaching for the *chèvre*. His knife froze above the cheese platter.

'I did not kill Mademoiselle Ladouze. That is quite ridiculous.'

Jacquot could see that Ginoux was rattled and he pushed his advantage. 'But what I can't understand is why you should also kill Erdâg Kónar?'

'Kónar?' spluttered Ginoux. 'What possible connection . . . what reason . . . why should I bother?'

Jacquot held his eye, waited a moment before replying.

'You're quite right, monsieur. An absurd suggestion. But it is one I wished to put to you . . . to see how you responded. Like your *confit*, monsieur, a policeman must sometimes remove the skin to find the meat.'

Jacquot pushed away from the table. 'Thank you for your time, monsieur. And your understanding. *Et bonne route.*'

And with that Jacquot turned and left the dining room.

100

Jacquot met Lens van der Haage and Claude Bouvet coming through from the second courtyard. Didier had told him that that was where he would find them. Both men were in shirt-sleeves, both shirts covered in sooty marks. It was clear they had been to the watchtower, trying to estimate the extent of the damage and to plan the next phase of their renovation. No time like the present. Which was exactly what Jacquot was thinking.

He made straight for them, as they stepped into the cloister and made their way across the lawn.

'I wonder, messieurs, now that I have the two of you together, whether we might have a word?'

'By all means,' replied Bouvet. 'Should we go to my office?'

'Here will do fine,' said Jacquot, directing them towards one of the benches set around the courtyard garden. 'Why don't we sit here for a moment?'

The two men made themselves comfortable and Jacquot leaned against a cloister pillar. In the middle of the garden, working his way around the stand of palms, Champeau was collecting up the fronds that had fallen during the storm. He had quite an armful already, and it looked like he intended picking them all up in one go before loading them into his wheelbarrow. He acknowledged the three men with a cheerful beam and an enthusiastic nodding.

'I thought I should let you know,' began Jacquot lightly, 'that I have made arrangements for our fire inspection team to come out and take a look at the watchtower. It is, after all, a matter of course in such circumstances. I hope you don't mind. We will also have to seal the area off from staff and guests alike until their investigation is completed.'

'Investigation?' asked Bouvet, looking suddenly anxious.

'As I said, it is usual in such circumstances.'

'Exactly what do you mean, "circumstances"?' asked van der Haage more pointedly.

Jacquot looked him in the eye. 'Why, suspicious circumstances, monsieur.'

'But I thought it was an accident,' said Bouvet. 'I mean . . . I thought it was agreed. All that flammable stuff. Like Lens said, it was a fire-trap. All you needed was the old man to leave a cigar in the ashtray, or kick over one of those ridiculous hurricane lamps of his . . .'

'I, too, thought it an accident – for exactly the same reason, monsieur. But I was mistaken. Hence the investigation.'

'How mistaken?' asked van der Haage.

'It now seems certain that the fire was started deliberately.'

Bouvet and van der Haage looked at each other.

Jacquot wondered which of them would be the first to speak. It was van der Haage.

'And how could you know that with such . . . certainty?' he asked.

Beside him, Bouvet seemed to nod his agreement, as if that was exactly the question he would have asked.

'Because, messieurs, there was someone keen to be rid of the Master, Monsieur Vilotte . . .'

There was a moment's pause, before van der Haage straightened his back and tried to look affronted. 'If you're suggesting for a moment . . .'

'Monsieur, I am a policeman. It is my job to make suggestions, and to reach conclusions. I am here to investigate not two, but three murders. And in so doing I tend not to tread lightly, or be concerned by suspects' feelings.'

Neither man blinked at his use of the word 'suspects', Jacquot noted with interest, and neither made any effort to deny the possibility of their own potential involvement. The death of Vilotte was – and they both knew it – of great benefit to both of them. It would have been ridiculous for them to try and deny it.

'Monsieur Jacquot,' began Bouvet at last. 'Chief Inspector. Of course, I understand we must be suspects. Régine and I, and Lens too, will all benefit from Monsieur Vilotte's unfortunate demise. But that does not mean we are his killers.'

'So you are confident enough to account for Monsieur van der Haage? You may be certain that neither you nor your wife has committed this crime, but can you also be so certain for your friend?'

Bouvet had begun to chuckle at the very possibility of such a suggestion, but the laugh began to lose its certainty, his eyebrows twitching together into a frown. 'Well, that's to say, of course, it's not possible to be absolutely . . .'

'If you're thinking that I am Auguste Vilotte's killer,' interrupted van der Haage, 'it is quite understandable for you to entertain such a thought. We've been waiting months, years, to start work on that watchtower of his. And with the other murders . . .'

'. . . It might have seemed like a good idea to stage one of your own, and have the police suspect the killer or killers of Mademoiselle Ladouze and Monsieur Kónar?'

'Well, yes . . . something like that, I suppose.'

'And did you? Was it you, monsieur?'

Van der Haage shook his head furiously, eyes blinking behind his spectacles. 'Not at all. Of course not.'

'Or was it actually Monsieur Bouvet here? Or his wife? Or the two of them, working together?'

'That's unthinkable. I've known them so long . . .'

'But still possible.'

'Not at all. Of course not. No. But . . . No, not Claude or Régine. Never.'

'And I agree, monsieur. Unthinkable.' Jacquot pushed away from the pillar, clapped his hands together.

The two men remained seated, looking up at their inquisitor, still not certain exactly what was going on.

Behind them came a clumphing sound as Champeau dropped the palm fronds he'd collected into the wheelbarrow.

'So, messieurs. Thank you for your time. By the way, have either of you happened to see Madame West? I believe she stayed behind rather than join the painting party. I tried her room a moment ago, but she wasn't there.'

Bouvet, ever helpful, gestured behind them, to the second courtyard. 'She's through there, Chief Inspector. Painting the watchtower.'

101

It was an astonishing painting. At first Jacquot could see no similarity between the burnt-out watchtower in the far corner of the courtyard – its walls and windows mascaraed with scorch marks – and the paper-puckered watercolour that Naomi West had managed to paint. Certainly she'd caught the blue sky and the scatter of clouds fleeing past but that seemed to be the extent of it, the crumbling stonework of the old battlements and the stark, blackened boldness of the tower rendered as a cube-like smudge of grey and terracotta. And, to Jacquot's untutored eye, completely out of proportion.

Naomi West stood away from the easel, cast a look at the watchtower then stepped forward, adding a streak of black from the topmost corners of the doorway. Coming up behind her, Jacquot gave a warning cough. He didn't want to take her by surprise

'It was irresistible,' said Madame West, without turning, as though she had known someone was standing behind her, was accustomed to an audience. 'The tower. So strong, so bold, don't you think? And now, such poignancy.'

'You are right, madame. And you have rendered it very well indeed.'

'You're most kind, Chief Inspector. But this is only a sketch, one of many.' She gestured to an open portfolio leaning against the leg of the easel, a dozen or so studies of the watchtower already stowed away. 'I shall use them when I get back to the States for an altogether more daring treatment. You will not know this, but I have started work with spray-guns. Tiny nozzles, a powerful spray. It is very effective.'

'I am sure it is, madame,' said Jacquot. 'I am sure it is.'

A silence settled between them. Swallows were back around the tower, darting towards nests that no longer existed, the feathery rush of their flight and their tiny desperate shrieks reaching across to them.

'A great loss,' said Jacquot at last. 'A great man.'

Naomi West picked up a cloth and wiped away a spot of paint from the corner of her paper. It left a reddish smear across the top of her painting, compromising what had so far been a reasonable attempt at sky and clouds. But she didn't respond.

Jacquot began again. 'It must have been a great disappointment for the others not to visit the Master. Surely the highlight of their trip, *n'est-ce pas?*'

'As you say, for the others. Myself, I am not a great fan. He's a little out of date. And, to be brutally frank, he was losing his touch. His last series of paintings – The Spirits and The Haunting – were very disappointing. Of course, there were buyers. But then buyers, certain collectors, don't always know good art from bad. The name is enough. Here, look, I have a Vilotte. That sort of thing. A cocktail party to announce its hanging. All the *fol-de-rol*. For a Vilotte! Me, I'd be looking for a Freud or a Basquiat. Those are names worth remembering, Chief Inspector. Mark my words, those are the names everyone will be talking of a decade from now. Not, I regret, Monsieur Auguste Vilotte.'

'At least you were able to meet him by yourself.'

Naomi rinsed her brush with a swift, practised shake and wiped it on her apron. She tilted her tray of colour tablets and selected a pale rose. Then she glanced around at him. It was the first time she had properly looked at him.

'Very briefly, Chief Inspector.'

'That would have been Sunday night? When we met in the cloister?'

'That's right,' she said, applying the brush to the battlements.

'And did you see anyone else while you were there?'

'No, it was just the two of us.'

'And you stayed how long, madame?'

'Maybe half an hour. It . . . it was not a successful visit.'

'How not successful?'

'I think he had been drinking. He . . . made a pass. A rather gross pass, as a matter of fact. It was shocking. Quite shocking.'

'Perhaps he misunderstood the . . . aah, nature of your visit. And it was rather late.'

'It was he who stipulated the time, not I. I should have known better, that's all.' She finished with the rose and her brush tinkled in the glass of water.

'Perhaps you should have, madame. But why would you want to see him if, as you have said, he was not what you might call your favourite artist?'

'I personally may not rate him, but others do. Also, I had some work I wanted him to see. Without the others being around.'

It wasn't difficult to imagine how Vilotte might have reacted if she had shown him the kind of work she had produced that morning.

'So, thank you for your time, madame. You have been most helpful. And good luck with your painting,' Jacquot added. Because you'll need all the luck going, he thought.

As he turned away, Brunet came panting down the passageway from the cloister. He waited for Jacquot to reach him.

'Thought you'd like to know, boss. Seems one of your painters . . .'

102

'*Viens! Viens! Entré,*' a voice called out when Jacquot knocked on the door of Room 5. He pushed it open and saw Madame Becque resting on a sofa at the foot of a large, postered bed, a patch of fresco – fragments of haloed saints – covering the wall behind it.

'Madame, please excuse me,' began Jacquot. 'I just called by to see how you were and, if you are able, perhaps I might ask you some questions?'

'*Mais bien sûr*, Chief Inspector. Please, make yourself comfortable.' She smiled at him, did not seem at all surprised that he should have called on her. As if, somehow, she'd been expecting him.

Jacquot pulled out the chair from the writing desk and brought it closer to the sofa.

'So, ask away,' she continued and, leaning over the back of the sofa, she reached for a school pencil case and a sketch pad on the bed. 'Do you mind?' she asked, settling it on her lap and unzipping the case. 'I think better when I'm working,' she continued, selecting a dark blue crayon and starting to draw, looking up to study him. 'You have a strong face, monsieur. Good lines. Tsk . . . a mistake already, and I haven't even started.'

With a grim set to her lips, she ripped the sheet from the pad, scrunched it up and threw it across the room, aiming for the waste-basket by the desk. It hit the lamp and tumbled in.

'*Voilà*,' she said, gave him another look and started sketching again. 'Unless you want me to prattle on, Chief Inspector, you had better start asking your questions. Once I'm up and running I'm hard to stop.' She gave him a quick smile and settled back to her sketch.

'To start with, let me say how sorry I am that you had to see . . .'

'*Dieu!* Such a shock, such a surprise. Whoever could have done such a thing? Hanging her up like that. It would have to have been a man, of course. No woman could have supported that weight. And, anyway, no woman would have thought to do such a thing.'

'My thoughts exactly,' replied Jacquot. 'Unless she had help.'

'There, you see.' Madame Becque looked up from her sketch, just a fleeting glance. 'That's why you're a policeman. I'd never have thought of that. Two killers, why ever not?'

'Possibly, madame. At this stage . . . Until we have more information. So tell me, did you know the deceased, Mademoiselle Ladouze?'

'Was that her name? I didn't know. And no, I didn't know her.' Madame Becque sat back and held out her sketch the better to examine it. 'Your nose, monsieur, is a problem. Noble, but no less a problem for that.' She squinted at him, took a bead and looked back at her pad. There,' she said with a quick shading. And then, '*Ooh là là*, but she was a beauty. Just the loveliest girl. But hard, too, you could see that.'

'How do you mean "hard"?'

'I mean the poor thing never had a chance to understand her loveliness. It was taken from her, turned into a currency. That's all it was to her, I suspect. A means to an end.'

'You knew what she was? What she did for a living?'

'Staying here with that man? It wasn't difficult to work it out, Chief Inspector,' she said, shooting him a knowing look over the top of her sketch pad.

There was silence for a moment save the sound of the crayon scratching against the paper.

'Tell me, madame. When was the last time you saw her?'

'Friday evening, I was on my way to dinner. I saw her across the garden, out there. I saw her go through the door into the second courtyard and that was that. The last time I saw her. Of course I didn't think then that it would be the last time.'

'And was she alone?'

'Quite alone.'

'And her companion. Monsieur Bressans? Do you know him?'

'I know of him. I recognised him. He is in the papers a lot, a shameless self-publicist, I believe. And such terrible teeth.'

'And what about Monsieur Kónar?'

'The other poor soul?'

Jacquot nodded. 'His room is just above yours.'

'Only around the hotel,' said Madame Becque. 'A rough-looking fellow but handsome, too, in a cruel sort of way. But far too short. When his friend, the American girl, had her heels on, she was a good head taller.'

'But you didn't speak? Didn't get to know them?'

She shook her head, started shading again, the crayon whispering over the paper.

'And what about the Master, Auguste Vilotte? Did you see or visit him during your stay?'

Madame shook her head. 'We were supposed to be visiting this afternoon, did you know that? I'd been so looking forward to meeting him. There,' she said, holding out the pad and giving her sketch the once over. 'A passable likeness, but not a work of art,' she continued. Then she carefully separated the sheet from the pad and offered it to Jacquot. 'For you.'

'*Merci bien, madame.* It is very fine,' he said, admiring the portrait.

She waved her hand dismissively.

'I see, madame, that you have cut your finger.'

She stopped waving her hand to examine the pink plaster on the inside of her thumb, almost hidden in the palm of her hand. 'Oh that, it's nothing. Sharpening my pencils. I use a scalpel. It's like a razor, does the job so well and so quickly. But quite lethal. I should take more care. It belonged to my husband, Henri.'

As she said the name, a breeze licked at the drapes by the window, stirred through the room.

And Jacquot knew the moment had come, sensed it immediately, indeed had been waiting for it.

The moment when everything would change. In an instant. From the next question on.

'*En effet*, Madame Becque, not quite a husband?' he said, reaching across to slide the sketch on to the writing table. He saw it shift in the draught, so he got to his feet, trapped it beneath the lamp. He sat back in his chair, crossed his legs, waited.

505

Madame Becque said nothing, simply looked down at her hands, picked at the plaster. And then, '*Alors*, you *have* been doing your homework, Chief Inspector. I suppose you had to. And you're right. We were not married.'

Lifting the rug that covered her legs, she pulled out a small bag, clicked it open and fished out a packet of cigarettes, a lighter.

'I didn't know you smoked, madame?'

'Like a chimney, Chief Inspector. My hus—' she paused, corrected herself. 'Henri hated the smell. But he was the one who died of lung cancer.' She gave a throaty laugh, more at the irony of his death than its actual fact. 'Six years ago. But I'm sure you already know that, too.' She lit a cigarette, stowed the pack and lighter back in her bag.

And then something seemed to catch in her throat and she swallowed and braced herself against crying.

'He always wanted to, you know – marry, I mean. But it was me. I . . . I wanted to keep my independence. Something silly like that. I didn't want to be married . . . all the rigmarole. But back then, hah, you had to keep up appearances, *n'est-ce pas*? *Les voisins*. The neighbours. I'm sure you understand. So no, we never married.' She took a drag of her cigarette and looked around for an ashtray. Jacquot found her one, passed it to her. 'You don't have to marry someone to love them,' she continued. 'That's what I always said to him, you know? A piece of paper, a silly little ceremony . . . Now, of course, now I wish I had married him. It would have made him so happy. But I was so stubborn. So stubborn all those years. To be together was enough, I told him. And so the years passed. But you know what? He never stopped asking. Not once.'

Madame Becque stubbed out her cigarette, not even half-smoked, and turned her face to the window. It was as if she didn't know whether she was going to laugh or cry. After a few moments, she managed a chuckle. 'He was the kindest man you can imagine. There was no one like him.'

'And how did you meet?' asked Jacquot gently.

Now Madame Becque really smiled, as though she was grateful for the diversion, and she swallowed the tears away, just as he had known she would. 'I was studying to be a pharmacist. At L'École Pharmacienne in Paris. Henri was at the Sorbonne, a medic. The two places were close, just a few blocks apart. We met at a café on the Boul' Miche. It's where we all went back then. Cheap and cheerful, you know. He spilt a *chocolat* on my dress. I thought it was an accident, but afterwards he told me it had been deliberate, a way to start talking to me. I was very cross. It had been my favourite, and most expensive outfit.'

'And after Paris, after your studies, you moved with him to Vernon?'

'That's right. We graduated the same year. He found a position at a hospital there and I got a job in the local *pharmacie*. In time, I took it over.'

'And how long was it before you discovered that your husband was . . . before you discovered what Henri was doing?'

For a long while, Madame Becque did not reply. And then she seemed to come to a decision. She sighed. 'Not at first, for sure. But gradually, I came to suspect . . . after he left the hospital and started his own practice. As I said, he was the kindest man, couldn't bear the suffering he saw. The elderly, the dying, the families . . . There was nothing he wouldn't do for his patients . . . When he realised they were lost, and in pain, simply surviving from day to day, when he saw how the families suffered for their loved ones . . .' Madame Becque shrugged. 'He made it so easy, so quick. Sometimes just the tiniest adjustments to a dosage . . . And no one ever knew.'

She reached for another cigarette, holding a hand around her lighter to keep the flame steady as she lit it, the ashtray balanced in her lap. 'You may not know this, monsieur, but there are many doctors – indeed, many nurses – who do the same. We should be grateful for them. It takes great courage to do what they are prepared to do. And they risk everything. *Le tout, n'est-ce pas?* We read about it in the newspapers, don't we? Every week there is a story. A doctor, a nurse . . . they are discovered. And it is the end for them. *Finis.* And reading those stories in the papers, we make our judgement. It cannot be this way, we say. We cannot allow it. It is wrong. The law. But I am sure that all of us think the same thing. That when it is our turn, please God, please let there be someone close at hand who will take that risk, someone, like my Henri, who will . . . relieve us, ease the pain.'

'When did you know for sure what it was that he was doing?'

'As I said, when he left the hospital and started up his practice. That's when he told me. There was one particular case . . . one of his patients . . . He asked me to help. Not being in the hospital, treating patients at home, it was not so easy for him to secure the necessary drugs. Which is when I became . . . well, I became, I suppose, a kind of accomplice. I told him I understood what he was doing. I approved. It was the right thing to do. So I started providing certain medicines.'

She rolled the cigarette between her fingers, watched the smoke coil from the tip. 'And then, suddenly, without any warning, it was Henri's turn. Out of the blue. Such a shock. I remember he sat me down at the kitchen table to tell me. Cancer. So far advanced . . . and neither of us had known.

Sometimes he'd complained of feeling tired, but that was all. And doctors? Doctors are always tired, *n'est-ce pas*? And that was it. Six months. We had six months more together.'

'You helped him?'

'I nursed him, at home, and when the time came . . .'

Madame Becque fell silent.

'And you have carried on this work? Helping . . .'

'That is correct. I know it is the right thing to do, and I know that Henri would approve. That is enough.'

'Which is why you are here in Luissac.'

She didn't exactly nod her head . . . more of a tilt downwards, as though she wished Jacquot to continue, before she made any further comment.

'You came here to "help" Auguste Vilotte. Something that his own physician, Dr Clénord of Cavaillon, was not willing to do. He did, however, give Monsieur Vilotte a telephone number, a name, someone who might be able to help. Someone he had known at medical school. Henri.'

'You are very thorough in your investigations, Chief Inspector,' she replied.

'I have an assistant, madame. He is the one who is thorough. And persuasive, too.'

'So it would seem. And you are right. One day I received a telephone call from Monsieur Vilotte. He told me he was dying and that he had heard I could help if times became hard. I told him that was correct and that when the time came he could call me. A few months later, just after Noël, he called back. So here I am.'

'He had a cancer.'

'A tumour, in the neck. It was spreading upwards. At any age it would have been inoperable.'

'Dr Clénord told my assistant that in his opinion Monsieur Vilotte had no more than six months to live. And he had told the patient so. That was a month ago. The last time Dr Clénord saw him.'

'That would be a generous assessment. Certainly no longer.'

'Was Vilotte in pain?'

'You mean *in extremis*? No, he wasn't. Not yet. But he was getting close. Maybe weeks away, soon to take to his bed. As for pain . . . you have to remember it is the exhaustion it causes, as much as the suffering. He was tired. He had had enough. And there was something else, too. As his condition worsened, he believed the tumour was starting to affect his reasoning . . . And, more important, his ability to paint. Which it probably was. Sometimes he honestly believed he was going mad. Things didn't make sense, he said. And he wanted it to end. On his conditions.'

'And the drugs he was prescribed? They didn't help?'

Madame Becque gave a short little laugh and shook her head. 'Priletothamine is a painkiller, but the dosage is never high enough to do the job properly. What else? Mestastirepmocal? An inhibitor, something to slow the spread of the disease. A very high dosage but about as useful as a wall of sand when the tide is coming in. And there are side-effects, too – loss of appetite for one – which is why he was prescribed Décotafam. And dizziness, too. Like being drunk.'

The breeze returned, shivered through the room and snatched away the smoke from her cigarette. She smiled again. 'Chief Inspector, whether you agree with what went on here or not, the truth is that Monsieur Vilotte wanted to die on his own terms. And I came here to help him do it. To . . . assist.'

'And yesterday was the day he chose to do it?'

'Correct. I went to see him in the afternoon while the others were drawing in the lobby. I told them I was tired, that I wanted to rest.'

'How exactly . . . ?'

'He had everything planned to the minutest detail. I helped him up to the top room. I sat him in his rocking chair. I uncorked his wine and I started up his projector. He told me which film. How to work the machine. And then I mixed the . . . solution. Twelve grammes of Sodium Pentobarbital in water. All I did was hand it to him. I did not make him drink, that was his decision . . . And he swallowed it without a thought. Without delay.'

Madame Becque fell silent. She took a breath, stubbed out her cigarette.

'And that was it. I left him, watching his film – an hour to run, and forty minutes to live. He would have gone to sleep, drinking the finest wine, smoking a good cigar, watching scenes from his life. What better way to go?'

'And what about the fire? Were you involved in the fire?'

Madame Becque nodded. 'Of course I was. He'd planned that, too. Said a fire would get rid of any evidence of my involvement – which was true enough. And anyway, he wanted to take everything with him.' She mimicked his voice, deep and gruff. ' "Let the vultures go hungry," he said.'

Despite himself, Jacquot smiled. He could hear the old man saying it.

'Did he light the fire himself?'

Madame Becque shook her head. 'Down in his studio, there was a candle in a jar of white spirit. He'd timed it – how long before the candle flame ignited the spirit. One centimetre. One hour. He knew then he'd be gone. All I had to do was light the candle as I left. Which I did.'

Jacquot sighed, got to his feet. 'I suppose that if I arrest you, take you in for questioning, that you will deny everything that you have said to me this afternoon?'

'You would be correct in that assumption, Chief Inspector.'

'And beyond Dr Clénord giving the Master your husband's telephone number . . . it would appear I have no other evidence to call on, nothing to suggest a crime has been committed?'

'I believe you are correct again.' She said it with no pride, no satisfaction. A simple statement.

She had done this before, Jacquot knew. And she would probably do it again. She would know how to protect herself.

Enfin, there was nothing he could do.

'There is one other thing I should tell you,' said Madame Becque. 'Earlier, you asked if I knew Mademoiselle Ladouze. I told you I did not. Which is true. But I do know what happened to her.'

'Auguste Vilotte killed her.'

A flicker of surprise crossed Madame Becque's face. 'You knew that?'

'I guessed. It makes sense.'

'Again, you are correct. But I don't know why. He wouldn't tell me. All he said as I led him up the stairs was that he was going to hell and would try to make the best of it. I told him he was surely going to heaven. Which is when he told me what he'd done.'

'He thought she was someone else . . .' said Jacquot.

'Maybe, I can't say.'

'Did he say where he killed her? How he killed her?'

'In her room, he said. He followed her to her room, stabbed her . . .'

'. . . with a fruit knife,' said Jacquot.

She looked at him, nodded.

'And then he left her there,' continued Jacquot.

'That's what he told me, yes. As for your other body, Monsieur Kónar, I cannot help you. But if it was Monsieur Vilotte who killed him I know that he would have told me. When you help people at that very special moment in their lives, they tell you things. There is no reason not to. So I am afraid, Chief Inspector, it seems you still have a killer to catch.'

Jacquot went to the desk, lifted the lamp. 'Thank you for the sketch,' he said, looking at his smiling face. 'And you do yourself an injustice, madame. You really have caught me.'

103

Leaving Madame Becque's sketch in his room, Jacquot headed for the Monastère's gate and the road to Luissac. For the first time that day, as he started across the bridge, he allowed himself to think of Claudine. And the kiss.

He hadn't planned it. It had just happened. When he came out of the kitchen with Brunet and saw her standing at the buffet table, tall and slim, looping a fall of hair behind her ear, then turning and smiling at him, all he knew was that he had to go over and say something. But at no time in that space of seconds had he considered the possibility that he might kiss her. Other times, yes – after playing low and smoky piano for her; when she came to his room the morning they found the bodies; when she joined him at his table after lunch – but not there, not then, not at the buffet table in the Salle du Matin. Thinking back on it, he guessed he must have done it because he hadn't really known what to say to her, or that what he had said – something about seeing her later – just hadn't seemed to hit the right note.

And a kiss did? A rather clumsy kiss on the side of her mouth . . . Neither one thing nor the other . . .

Maybe, maybe, he thought.

Of course he wished now that he'd waited a moment after letting her go, after his lips left hers, to gauge her reaction. See her response. But he hadn't. He'd just spun on his heel and left her there. Hadn't even looked back.

And now he was paying the price. Not knowing. Not knowing. Did she, or didn't she? Would she, or wouldn't she? If he'd waited just a second longer, she'd have let him know what she thought about it. Good or bad. One way or the other. But then, however it turned out, at least he'd done something. At least he'd let her know the way he felt. He just hoped she felt the same.

Coming off the bridge and rounding the bend Jacquot came to the damaged section of road. In just a few hours without rain, the hillside cascade that had caused all the damage had been reduced to a trickle, and where before there'd been a yawning gap in the road, three metal sheets had now been set across it, supported on lengths of sleepers and sandbagged into position. It wasn't the tidiest piece of roadwork that Jacquot had ever seen, but it looked strong and stable enough to bear the weight of a car. If Claude Bouvet got his way, those new arrivals currently stuck in Cavaillon would be having dinner in Le Réfectoire tonight.

Walking across the sheets, peering over the edge – only because he hated heights and always felt compelled to test his nerve – Jacquot reached the other side of the gap and took a deep, deep breath. With a headful of glorious scents – wet dust, oozing resin and, from somewhere hidden, the sinuous

licks of wild allium – he walked on down to Luissac, butter-
flies flexing their wings on rain-shiny leaves, lizards scuttling
out of reach before turning to fix him with a blinkless stare,
the sound of every step he took drowned out by the insistent,
frenzied buzzing of unseen cicadas. Somehow they always
sounded much louder after rain. It wasn't until he reached the
first houses that the soundtrack softened, their calls lessened.

Walking down Luissac's main street Jacquot looked around.
Somewhere a dog barked, a cock crowed, but otherwise the
village was deserted. Up ahead, the road opened into an empty
square, three peeling plane trees each side of it, some benches,
a war memorial with a toppled plastic wreath, overlooked on
four sides by shuttered windows.

As he crossed the *place*, Jacquot knew with every step that it
was time to stop thinking about kisses and a certain lady and how
nice it was to be out and about on a sunny day after rain. There
was work to be done. Some questions to be asked. And as he
turned past the church, Jacquot spotted the man he'd come to
see – barefoot, a pair of black shorts and a white T-shirt.

The legionnaire, Dutronc, was hard at work, wiping down
the sloping black hood of Ginoux's Citroën. The car stood in
a circle of wet road, a hose lay coiled by the front wheel, and
beads of water glistened like sweat on its polished black body.
As Jacquot approached, Dutronc stood up from the hood and
squeezed out his chamois cloth, wringing it into a tight rope-
like cord, snapping it out with a flick of his wrist.

'Monsieur, *bonjour*,' said Jacquot.

Dutronc turned to look at him, grunted something and leaned
back down to work on the bumpers.

'A moment if you please,' continued Jacquot, remembering
what Peluze had said to him about being polite.

Dutronc continued working the cloth across the chrome. Finally, he stood up and turned to Jacquot.

'Monsieur?'

'You are Emile Dutronc?' asked Jacquot, taking in the shoulders, the crop of black stubble on head and cheeks, the fat lips, the tiny eyes. If he ran a hundred metres in less than ten seconds, he'd have made a frighteningly effective winger, thought Jacquot. But he looked too stocky for speed, Jacquot decided. A centre maybe. Or something brutal in the scrum.

'I am.'

'My name is Daniel Jacquot, Chief Inspector Jacquot of the Cavaillon Regional Crime Squad. You may be aware that there has been some trouble at the Monastère . . .'

'Trouble? Is that what you call it?'

Jacquot shrugged, conceded the point. 'Two murders, you're right. So you heard?'

'The road may have been blocked, monsieur, but the telephones still work.'

'Would you mind if I ask you some questions?' Peluze's influence again.

'Would you mind if I work while you ask them? I need to finish.'

'You are leaving today?'

'I'm picking up the boss in an hour, driving him to Lyons.'

'Then I had better be quick. Did you know the guest Mademoiselle Ghislaine Ladouze? She was two rooms down from Monsieur Ginoux.'

'*Non*, Monsieur, I did not know her,' replied Dutronc, the chamois squeaking over the Citroën's headlamps. 'But I recognised her type.'

'Her type?'

Dutronc stood up, squeezed out the chamois and gave Jacquot a look.

'You seem like a man who knows the world, monsieur. I am sure there is no need to explain.' Dutronc went round to the boot, lifted the lid and packed the chamois away in a plastic bag. Leaving the boot open he went to the hose, disconnected it from the tap and came back to the car. Looping it a half-dozen times round a muscly forearm, he dropped the hose in after the chamois and closed the boot.

'You mean, she was a working girl?'

'If that's what you want to call her. That's how she seemed to me. Prettier than most, I grant you,' said Dutronc. 'But . . . yes. A working girl.'

'And what about Monsieur Kónar? Did you know him?'

Dutronc pulled a set of keys from his pocket and locked the Citroën. Then he left the car and walked to an open doorway as though he had not heard the question.

'I asked . . .' began Jacquot.

'I heard you,' said Dutronc over his shoulder, and he disappeared through the door.

Jacquot looked around. There was not a soul to be seen. A dog came round the corner, stopped to sniff at a wheel, then trotted on. A wise animal, thought Jacquot, as he followed warily after Dutronc. Stepping though the door he was in time to see Dutronc's bare legs at the top of a flight of stairs before they turned to the left and disappeared.

'Monsieur, I would be grateful . . .'

'Come on up,' Dutronc called down. 'It's cooler here than the street.'

For a moment Jacquot hesitated, then he started up the

stairs, senses straining. At the top was a long corridor. There were four doors on each side. The last door, overlooking what must have been the back of the house, was open.

'I'm in here,' came Dutronc's voice. Then Jacquot heard the sound of a shower.

Jacquot made his way down the corridor and stepped into the room. It was large, stone-floored, the ceiling beamed, the walls lime-washed. Three windows had been flung open on to the garden below. There was a suitcase on the bed, the shorts and T-shirt Dutronc had been wearing lying beside it.

In the next room the shower was turned off and a moment later, a towel wrapped round his waist, Dutronc came back into the room. He cut an impressive figure. Somewhere in his fifties, Dutronc was a wall of muscle, his body covered in a pelt of dark hair.

'Take a seat,' he said, nodding to a pair of chairs by the windows.

Jacquot did as he was told, made himself comfortable, felt a soft breeze from the garden.

'You don't mind if I dress?'

Jacquot shook his head. 'Sure. Go ahead.'

Dutronc went to a chest of drawers and pulled out a shirt, socks, underpants, a pair of trousers. He tossed them on to the bed then pushed the drawer closed. He pulled off the towel, rubbed it over his head and face, and his chest seemed to double in size with the movement. He hung the towel on the handle of the bathroom door and reached for his underpants, stepped into them, snapped the band round his waist. 'You were asking about Monsieur Kónar? If that is his name. Whether I knew him?'

'That's right. And did you?'

'Yes,' he replied. 'I knew him.'

'As a guest, you mean? You saw him around the hotel?'

Dutronc shook his head. 'More than that. Much more.'

'How "more" exactly?' asked Jacquot, feeling a prickle of excitement.

Dutronc looked straight into Jacquot's eyes. 'Ten years ago, in Trieste, Monsieur Kónar shot me. Three times. Here, here and here.' He lifted a fist and pointed a stubby finger at three shiny spots of skin in the matt of chest hair. They looked like tiny pink nipples. 'If it hadn't been for Monsieur Ginoux, I would have died.'

There was silence in the room. A bee floated in through one of the windows, buzzed around briefly, then departed the way it had come.

'You recognised him straightaway?' asked Jacquot, not altogether certain how to proceed.

'It's ten years, monsieur. People change. It wasn't until I saw the camera . . . Then I knew.' He reached for his shirt, shook out the folds and undid the buttons.

'And Monsieur Kónar? Did he recognise you?'

'Not at first,' Dutronc replied, pulling on the shirt, redoing the buttons, one by one, from the bottom up. 'But at the end, he knew who I was.'

'At the end?'

Dutronc took a deep, controlled breath. When he spoke, he spoke quietly, matter-of-factly. 'At the end, monsieur. When I killed him.'

'You killed him?'

'With a knife.' Dutronc moved to the bedside table, opened the drawer and pulled out a sheathed hunting knife. 'This knife.' He held it up for Jacquot to see and then tossed it on to the bed.

'Where? When?'

'In the Monastère's cloister. Beneath the palm trees. Very quietly. On Sunday night. A good place to die. More than he deserved. We lay together in the grass while you spoke to that lady. If you had flashed that torch on to the cloister lawn, you would have seen us.' As he spoke Dutronc picked up his trousers from the bed, pulled them on, tucked in his shirt and zipped them up.

'So you're confessing to his murder?'

'Confessing, *oui*. To murder, *non*.'

Dutronc sat on the bed and it seemed to collapse under his weight. The suitcase and knife slid towards him but he pushed them back. He reached for his socks and, one by one, tugged them on. When he'd finished, he sat back, hands on his knees, and looked at Jacquot. 'What I did with that knife, monsieur, I did for seven friends. A kind of justice. A debt finally settled.'

Jacquot remembered what Peluze had told him.

'This was 1986? In Yugoslavia?'

Dutronc smiled. 'You know your dates, monsieur. Croatia. A place called Crjadj.'

'And what happened in Crjadj?'

Dutronc gave a grunt, shook his head. 'Every morning for seven days, Monsieur Kónar and his chums shot a friend of mine. They took it in turns. One guy for the ankles. One guy for the knees. One for the elbows. And one for the head. Seven shots each morning before breakfast and for one of us it was over. But they took their time. Maybe fifteen, twenty minutes to do the job. And the rest of us had to watch.'

Dutronc looked away from Jacquot and gazed out of the windows, remembering. 'The first morning Kónar started with the ankles of Sonni Meckler, our radio man. And each morning he worked his way up. Knees next – Pieter Gelling, *Adjudant-chef*. Then elbows – Moussef, *caporal*. And on the fourth morning he put a gun in the mouth of my very good friend, *sergeant-chef* Bru Haldde, and blew his brains out. Then, the next morning, back to the ankles – *Legionnaire première classe* Gregor Adulaski; the next morning, knees – *caporal-chef* Monti Smit; then elbows – *caporal* Pedro Gonzalo. And that last morning, it would have been me lying on the ground there, with Kónar pushing the barrel of his gun between my teeth.'

'But you escaped?'

'I escaped, monsieur. You are right. But they followed me. All the way in to Italy. To Trieste, where Monsieur Kónar got a second chance and took it.'

Dutronc's shoulders sagged, his head dropped and he stared at the floor between his stockinged feet.

'But it wasn't just the gun he was handy with. When he wasn't shooting, do you know what Monsieur Kónar was doing? He was filming it all. Up close. He liked to have blood hit the lens. It made him very happy. That's when I recognised him. When I saw that camera of his.'

'I understand why you're telling me this,' said Jacquot at last, filling the silence, 'but you must know it makes no difference . . . It doesn't alter what . . .'

'I am telling you all this,' said Dutronc, his head lifting, his eyes latching on to Jacquot, 'not to escape your justice, monsieur, but because . . . you should know that I am not ashamed of what I have done. I did what I had to do. And I would do it again, right now. Without a thought. It is as simple as that. For my friends. And neither am I frightened at the price I will have to pay. In fact, my only anxiety, now that I have told you all this, is that Monsieur Ginoux, who saved my life in Trieste, will have to drive himself home. And he is a very bad driver.'

For a moment, Jacquot thought his eyes were deceiving him. He closed them, looked again. A bead of sweat was sliding down Dutronc's cheek. Sweat; it had to be. But it wasn't sweat. It was a tear.

'So what then?' asked Jacquot. 'After you killed him in the cloister?'

'I hid him,' said Dutronc, wiping an arm across his face.

'In the basement storeroom?'

Dutronc nodded.

'Why there?'

'It was out of the way. I couldn't leave him in the cloister.'

'How did you get the body through Reception?'

For a moment Dutronc said nothing. And then, 'The boy. Champeau. He was on duty. The old guy was asleep.'

'Champeau?'

'I made a deal with him. I won't tell on you, if you don't tell on me. He liked that. It was like a game.'

'Tell on him?'

'I saw him bury the girl after the old boy killed her. I saw him carry her through to the cold-room, hang her from the hook. He showed me where he'd stowed her Saturday night. In the freezer. It seemed as good a place as any.'

'You saw Vilotte kill Mademoiselle Ladouze?'

'I saw him go to her room. And I saw him come out. But the boy had nothing to do with it. He worshipped the old man, would have done anything for him. Shifting the body like that, hiding it . . .'

Jacquot took it in, worked it through. He reached into a

pocket, pulled out his cigarettes and lit one. The smoke curled through the window and he watched it coil away.

'So, monsieur,' said Dutronc. 'What do we do now? What are you waiting for?'

For a moment, Jacquot wasn't sure.

What was he waiting for?

He smoked the cigarette in silence, sitting there in the chair by the window, a line of sunshine slanting across the floor. On the bed, Dutronc sighed once and hung his head, clasped his hands as though in prayer.

When he said the words, Jacquot knew it was impulse – *un coup de tête*.

Like the kiss.

But as soon as he said them he knew he was right.

'I was wondering, monsieur, whether you'll be taking the autoroute to Lyons. Or the old N7. The autoroute is faster, of course, but I think you'll find that the N7 is the prettier road.'

104

In the end it was the blue plaster that made Jacquot's moment of madness possible. Otherwise, it could all have gone horribly wrong.

It was late afternoon. The breeze had dropped and the sky was a rich, thickening blue. Jacquot was standing with Brunet and Fournier at the edge of the Monastère's tennis court, waiting while the forensic team loaded the body bags into the helicopter and stowed their gear.

Fournier was giving Jacquot a brief rundown on his findings. 'When I got the body out of the freezer, there was grass in his hand and mud on his clothes,' said Fournier. 'I'd say he was killed in the cloister. It's the only lawn I've seen.'

'Makes sense,' said Jacquot.

'There was sand too, at the bottom of the cabinet. And a blue scarf. You ask me, the girl was put there as well, before she got hung on the hook.'

'Sounds like a single killer, then.'

'That's how it looks,' replied Fournier. 'Oh, I nearly forgot . . . that plaster your man gave me? There's not just blood on it, there's a flake of skin, too. Eczema. You can still smell the ointment on the gauze – Eczetramol, if I'm not mistaken. A common brand, but reasonably effective.'

The word took a moment to sink in.

Eczema. Eczema. Eczema.

And then: the medicine cabinet. Vilotte.

The rest came easy. He'd have a word with Madame Becque. She owed him a favour, surely? Time to call it in.

'Seems to me,' continued Fournier, 'whoever has eczema here could well be your man. Where did you say you found it, again?'

'In the storeroom,' replied Jacquot lightly. 'Under the blast freezer. Must have fallen off when the killer loaded a body in.'

'Well, there you have it.'

Beside him, Brunet frowned but said nothing.

Ten minutes later, the helicopter lifted off the tennis court and banked away towards the Calavon Valley.

In a companionable silence, Brunet and Jacquot walked back to the hotel.

Outside the Monastère's gates stood a long black limousine, its uniformed driver standing by an open boot.

As they drew closer, Champeau came hurrying through the gate, two hefty cases in his hands, and a third under his arm.

'You're a strong lad,' said Brunet, and Champeau, dropping the cases into the limo's boot as though they were no heavier than a bunch of bananas, struck a pose, a grin from ear to ear, flexing his biceps like a circus strongman.

Jacquot recognised the luggage and as he turned to the gate, its owner appeared, stepping out of the shadows into the sunlight, swinging a small vanity case. She was dressed in white Capri pants, red stilettos and a blood-red blouse.

When she saw Jacquot, she pulled off her sunglasses. 'Oh hi. It's you.'

'Mademoiselle. You are leaving us?'

A look of panic clouded her face. 'Well, sure. If it's OK? I mean . . . You don't need me any more, do you?'

'No, mademoiselle, I don't need you any more.'

'Well, hey, that's a relief. I thought there for a moment . . .' Her driver closed the boot and opened a door for her.

'You are going home?'

'Uh-huh. New York. LA. Studio jet.'

'Then I wish you *bonne chance et bonne route*, mademoiselle.'

'Well thank you so much,' she said settling herself and the vanity case in the back seat. The driver closed the door and a moment later the window buzzed down. The sunglasses were back on. '*Merci beaucoup*. And *au'voir* to you.'

'*À la prochaine*,' replied Jacquot.

105

It had been a great day for the painters in the fields below Roussillon. And then it had all gone horribly wrong.

Claudine had asked Gilles to stop off at her place on their way back to Monastère. She said she needed something pretty – and clean – for the painting group's last dinner together. So he dropped her off and waited while she dashed in and found something suitable.

A long, low-cut blue frock. A hairbrush. Toothbrush. Some make-up.

And a razor for her legs.

And twenty minutes later it happened, speeding back to Monastère. Grace had just leaned forward to give Philip a piece of her chocolate bar when there was a loud 'pop', a flailing of rubber against tarmac and the van lurched to the right.

Regaining control, Gilles slowed his speed and nursed the van to the side of the road.

Philip and Gilles, with help from Claudine, had managed with some difficulty to change the shredded tyre and replace it with the spare. But the spare was as good as flat and they had to find a garage before attempting the road up to Luissac and the bridge to Grand Monastère.

For this reason they arrived back at the hotel far later than they had anticipated and, after being assured by Lenoir that La Réfectoire would remain open, they raced off to change for dinner, eager to find out what had been happening in their absence and to catch up on all the news. The forensics, the police, the statements, the fingerprints . . .

Claudine, too, was anxious to find out what was happening and before going with Gilles to the room they were sharing, she excused herself and went upstairs to Jacquot's suite. She knocked on the door. Twice. But there was no answer.

Downstairs, she made for the reception desk where Didier was on the phone.

'*Oui, monsieur, enfin nous sommes ouvert, c'est vrai. Un plaisir, monsieur, À demain. Oui.*' Replacing the phone in its cradle he looked up enquiringly at Claudine.

'*Oui, madame?*'

When Didier heard what she wanted, he put on a desolated look . . . '*Je regrette*, madame, the police are no longer here. They left by helicopter some hours ago.'

'And the Chief Inspector?' asked Claudine hopefully.

'No,' replied Didier. 'Chief Inspector Jacquot did not go with the helicopter.'

Claudine's spirits rose.

'I believe he left by car. With his colleague.'

Claudine's spirits fell.

'He waited around, I know, had a drink, but eventually he left. He did, though, leave this message for you.'

Didier looked beneath the counter and brought out an envelope.

So why didn't you say that in the first place, thought Claudine and her spirits rose once more. She took the envelope and turned away, walking into the centre of the lobby, slitting it open with her thumbnail, fumbling for the note inside.

But there was no note. Just a card.

A business card.

She took it out. His name, the address and phone number of Cavaillon Regional Crime.

Nothing more.

And then . . .

She turned the card over. Just two lines:

> *Let there be oysters,*
> *Under the sea . . .*

Despite her disappointment, she smiled, felt an unaccountable swell and shiver of excitement.

Oh, there'll be oysters, OK, she thought, slipping the card into her pocket. And the rest . . .

And as she headed for Gilles' room, to quickly shower and change for the painting group's farewell dinner, she began to hum a little tune she knew . . .

> *Chili con carne,*
> *Sparkling champagne . . .*

106

Alone in his room Champeau knelt before the brass-bound trunk that Master Og had asked him to carry from the watchtower's *grande salle* the previous afternoon. Reaching into his pocket he found the small metal key that Master Og had given him and fitted it into the lock. Turning it to the right, he felt resistance, so he turned it to the left and the mechanism slotted into place. Leaving the key where it was he placed his hands on either side of the lid and lifted it open. Up and up went the lid, a rusty screeching of hinges, until two bands of webbing snapped tight at either side and held it just a few inches past the perpendicular.

Champeau took his hands away and the lid swayed for a moment, then it steadied. Peering inside, what surprised him was that the trunk should be so full. Full to the brim. And yet so light on his shoulders as he carried it across the cloisters, through the lobby and down to his room.

But it was difficult to make out what was in there, the lid casting the contents into shadow. So Champeau pushed the trunk round until his bedside lamp properly illuminated its interior.

Crumpled, silvered tubes of paint with colourful square labels, a collection of small paintbrushes, a brown paper bag filled with nuggets of charcoal, a spill of crayons, chalks, each item kept tidily in its own partitioned section, each section no more than a few centimetres deep. It was a fitted tray. He looked for the loops and found them, teased his blunt finger-tips into them and heaved the tray upwards. Swinging it out, he laid it on the floor, then looked back inside the trunk.

And he knew at once why it had been so light. Nothing but paper and cardboard tubes and ribboned books. Just a glance and it looked liked this was where Master Og kept his paints, tray stacked upon tray, the trunk filled with supplies, each tray easily removed to get at whatever it was he wanted. Just a giant paintbox. But there was only the one tray, just the one level. Not so much a false bottom as a false top, Champeau decided, reaching for one of the pieces of paper and holding it to the light.

Blank. But through the paper, on the other side, he could see some markings. He turned the paper and looked again. A picture. A child's pencil sketch, by the look of it. A single thick pencil line that looked like the outline of a country, or an island perhaps – a map of some kind. It made no sense so he turned it upside down and the outline arranged itself into . . . a bird. That's what it looked like now. Like a pigeon or a dove. But such an odd shape. Such a bird, Champeau knew, would never fly. It looked lumpen, broken, misshapen, its head – for that was certainly the head – turned back, while the wings . . .

Champeau put it to one side, let it float to the floor, and picked up a handful of the papers beneath. More drawings in a similar, child-like style – birds, flowers, horses and what looked like bulls. He had to squint to see them, to make out what they were. But they all looked the same . . . All misshapen . . . Crooked. Crippled. And each piece of paper dated, each one signed with a scrawled name that he couldn't make out bar the first and last letter – a large 'P' and a small 'o'. Why, he wondered, would anyone bother to put their name to such silly pictures?

He reached in for another handful. More animals, more birds. And ladies now. Naked ladies. Bodies sprawled back, legs in the air. Big fat thighs. Knees drawn up to chests. And there for all to see, ladies' secret black shadowy places cut sharply with a line that made Champeau flush. Grotesque. But . . .

Putting them to one side, he reached in and levered out one of the books, its two stiff covers secured with ribbon. Loosening the ties he opened it up. Here were larger, thicker pieces of paper – stiff as starched linen. A bowl of fruit on every one. Different fruit, different bowls, different colours. And a different signature on each. He mouthed the names slowly. De-rain; Du-fy; Vla-min-ck; Se-gon-zac; Va-la-don; Lau-ren-cin; H-Ma-tisse.

He closed the book, reached in for another. Boats this time – sailing out at sea, splashed by waves, tipping over, beached. But just three names – Mar-quet; Cam-o-in; Sig-nac. He put it aside, pulled out another book, and another, and another – racehorses, gardens with palm trees, factories with smoking chimneys. And more women. Women, women, women! Laughing, crying, sitting at mirrors, taking baths, towelling dry. Naked again, plump and pink.

Bored with the books, Champeau turned to the cardboard tubes, pulling away the tape that held the round plastic lids in place. In each was a roll of canvas which he fingered out, opened up, studied. Such strange shapes – triangles and squares close up but, as he discovered, if he drew back his head, changed the focus of his eyes, they turned into people, buildings, fields, forests.

On and on he went, digging deeper into the trunk, opening, looking, then casting aside until the floor around him was littered with papers and canvases and empty cardboard rolls.

And then he discovered there *was* a false bottom. Another layer at the bottom of the trunk. With two loops at each side to pull it up and out. Juggling the tray upwards between the flushed sides of the trunk, it finally came loose with a faint 'phut' of pressurised air.

He laid the tray aside and looked inside once more, at the very bottom of the trunk. His arm snaked in and he felt around in the shadows. He pulled out a cheap penny whistle and put it to his lips. It had a metal taste which he didn't like and the sound he made had no tune to it, a flat tinny note. He dropped it to the floor and reached in again, bringing out a pair of silver clippers inlaid with mother-of-pearl; then a set of linen napkins tied with ribbon and embroidered with the letters HM; then a tangle of metal that looked, Champeau decided after close examination, like a charging bull; then a striped cotton sailor's shirt stained on the front with what appeared to be a splash of old red wine – he held it up against his chest. It looked like a reasonable fit, and he liked the stripes, so he tossed it over the trunk and into the wicker basket where he put his dirty clothes. His mother would get that stain out in no time.

And then, suddenly, the trunk was empty save one last thing, a single book, a journal of some kind, right at the very bottom. He pulled it out, admired the marbled covers and flicked through the pages – palm trees again, and camels, and strange buildings with round domes, and men in long shirts like the ones the Master wore. Page after page. But every image recognisable, painted in the most gorgeous colours. It was a nice book, he thought to himself. A nice cover and nice pictures, so he took it across to his bookshelf and pushed it in with his Tintins and Asterix albums. Hergé and Uderzo and Delacroix side by side.

Then, turning back to the mess on the floor, Champeau had a flash of inspiration. It was his mother's birthday in a week. If he worked hard he could turn all this into a lovely big scrapbook for her.

All his own work.

And he'd start with that bird, he decided, the bird that would never fly, something small to get his eye in. Colour it in with Master Og's crayons. And then the bulls and the flowers and the horses.

He sat down by the trunk and found the picture of the bird, then reached for Master Og's paint tray, with the chalks and charcoals, paints and pastels. He selected a bold lime-green crayon to start with and carefully, tongue between his lips, minding not to go over the pencil lines, he filled in the body of the bird. Green wings first, then a gold breast and a head of sunset pink. He wondered about a blue sky background, maybe some trees and a field below it, but decided he'd done enough. He held it out in front of him. There, that was much better, he thought. You had to know when to stop.

Putting the bird aside he reached for another sheet – a bull this time, twisting down to charge. A small square for the head, a rectangle for the body and pins for legs and horns. He decided on a black bull with glaring red eyes and a lolling pink tongue – like the one he'd seen that time in Arles – and he reached for the colours he needed.

This was fun, he thought, as he worked away. And he had a week to do it. And there was so much stuff here he could use.

A pair of scissors. Some glue . . .

It would be her best birthday present ever.

Patrick O'Brien
April 1st, 1915 – August 29th, 2006

Now you can buy any of these other bestselling
Headline books from your bookshop
or direct from the publisher.

FREE P&P AND UK DELIVERY
(Overseas and Ireland £3.50 per book)

The Cat Who Had 60 Whiskers	Lillian Jackson Braun	£6.99
Stripped	Brian Freeman	£6.99
Red River	Lalita Tademy	£7.99
Dead and Buried	Quintin Jardine	£6.99
Smoked	Patrick Quinlan	£6.99
Copper Kiss	Tom Neale	£6.99
The Death Ship of Dartmouth	Michael Jecks	£6.99
Green Eye	Vena Cork	£6.99
A Passion for Killing	Barbara Nadel	£7.99
Guardians of the Key	Clio Gray	£6.99

TO ORDER SIMPLY CALL THIS NUMBER

01235 400 414

or visit our website: www.madaboutbooks.com

Prices and availability subject to change without notice.